LADY SLINGS THE BOOZE

SPIDER ROBINSON

ACE BOOKS, NEW YORK

The quote that appears on page 1 is from the *Rockford Files* episode "Chicken Little Is a Little Chicken," by Stephen J. Cannell, TM & © 1975 Universal City Studios, Inc.; reprinted by permission of Universal Studios and the author. All rights reserved.

This Ace Book contains the complete text of the original hardcover edition.

LADY SLINGS THE BOOZE

An Ace Book / published by arrangement with the author

PRINTING HISTORY
Ace hardcover edition/November 1992
Ace paperback edition/December 1993

All rights reserved.
Copyright © 1992 by Spider Robinson.
Cover art by Richard Hescox.
This book may not be reproduced in whole or in part, by mimeograph or any other means, without permission.
For information address: The Berkley Publishing Group, 200 Madison Avenue, New York, NY 10016.

ISBN: 0-441-46929-9

ACE®
Ace Books are published by The Berkley Publishing Group, 200 Madison Avenue, New York, NY 10016.
ACE and the "A" design are trademarks belonging to Charter Communications, Inc.

PRINTED IN THE UNITED STATES OF AMERICA

10 9 8 7

This book is dedicated, with respect and gratitude, to

David S. Alberts, D. M. Bennett, James Buckley
Larry Flynt, Ralph Ginzburg, Maurice Girodias
Alvin Goldstein, Bob Guccione, William Hamling
Hugh Hefner, E. H. Heywood, Jack Kahane
Ed Lange, Charles Mackey, Marvin Miller
Edward Mishkin, Lew Rosen, Barney Rosset
Samuel Roth, Harold Rubin
Henry Steinborn, George Von Rosen

and all the courageous others who served or risked prison time for the right of all Americans to possess and enjoy pornography (literally: "writings of harlots"—such as this story) and other erotica.

· Acknowledgments ·

This book contains *homage* to (or, as Woody Allen says, "outright theft from") Donald Westlake, John D. MacDonald, Leslie Charteris, Stephen J. Cannell, Roy M. Huggins, Juanita Bartlett, Raymond Chandler, Robert Parker, Marco Vassi, and John Cleve. In addition to them, and to all those heroes cited in this book's dedication, the author wishes to thank:

—G. P. Putnam's, the first major mainstream American publisher to print a work deemed obscene by many (Vladimir Nabokov's LOLITA in 1958);

—Philip José Farmer, Robert A. Heinlein, and Theodore Sturgeon, who created the first sf characters with genitalia and a disposition to use them;

—Kristine Kathryn Rusch and Dean Wesley Smith, the only magazine editors in contemporary sf who were willing to serialize any of the Lady Sally McGee stories;

—Susan Allison and Peter Heck of Ace Science Fiction (corporate descendant of the above-mentioned G. P. Putnam's), who published those stories in book form;

—my agent Eleanor Wood, who got Susan and Peter to pay more than they wanted for the privilege;

—David Myers, who turned me on to Nikola Tesla, with Margaret Cheney's remarkable biography TESLA: MAN OUT OF TIME (Laurel, 1981), and the Jugoslavian film *Nikola Tesla* (with Orson Welles as J. P. Morgan!);

—Mary Mason and Mike Doellman, who provided other invaluable research data pertinent to this book;

—Amos Garrett, Harry Connick, Jr., Holly Cole, "Spider" John Koerner, Ray Charles, Paul McCartney, Dexter Gordon, and the entire catalog of Holger Petersen's Stony Plain Records and Tapes, which music kept me sane and productive during this book's creation;

—Richard "Lord" Buckley, for having stomped upon this sweet, swingin' sphere;

—and of course, my wife Jeanne and daughter Terri, *sine qua nihil* . . .

This book would not have been possible (or near as much fun) without all these people, and their ilk.

A harlot with sincerity and a square egg:
they both do not exist.

—Japanese proverb

Writing is not necessarily something
to be ashamed of.
But do it in private,
and wash your hands afterward.

—WOODROW W. SMITH

LADY SLINGS THE BOOZE

1. The Dick...

> "This game's *over*, man! You gotta move your Boss or Rocky's gonna lay a subpoenie on him; then his Torpedo is gonna smoke your Old Lady, and all your Heavies'll be doin' time—except for maybe your Mouthpiece, but Rocky's Sheriff got him put in the corner—you got nothin' left but Punks and Junkies: you're *through*, Jimmy."
>
> —ANGEL MARTIN to Jim Rockford, commenting on a chess game, in the *Rockford Files* episode "Chicken Little Is a Little Chicken," by Stephen J. Cannell

IT was noon before they finished scraping Uncle Louie off the dining room table.

So I missed the big Math final at ten, and with all the fuss afterward, everybody feeling sort of sorry for me—and a little grossed out by what had happened to my uncle—Mr. Cathcart never got around to making me make it up, so I ended up passing Math that semester. And it was that very night, after I thought over everything I'd seen and heard of the cops who responded that morning, that I made the decision to become a private detective instead of a cop when I grew up. I'd been trying to make up my mind since I was six. So it was a memorable day. Add all the pluses and minuses and take an average, you'd have to say it was a pretty good day all in all. Kind of rough on Uncle Louie, of course. And it ruined that table. But it turned me away from a life of crime.

Well, serious crime.

Anyway, the point I started out to make is: can you imagine what I felt like when I came downstairs and saw Uncle Louie like that? Tremendously scared and nauseous and excited all at the same time? Heart banging and buzzing in my ears and dry mouth and shaky knees? Knowing there was really nothing to be afraid of any more, but still scared to death, feeling more like a thirteen-year-old than usual? But at the same time almost happy at getting to see something like that, knowing that now I'd have a real, gruesome, Mike Hammer kind of story to tell all the guys, already planning how to tell it?

Well, that's just how I felt that night twenty years later, walking up the long curving driveway to that damned mansion.

This was exactly the kind of opportunity I'd been praying for—and I was so scared I was nauseous, or possibly the other way around. Feeling like more of a thirteen-year-old than usual. That particular mix of feelings made me think of Uncle Louie for the first time in years, and I heard going through my head the same words I'd said to myself that morning when I'd found him. *God, please don't let me do anything to fuck this up. This time.* I just managed to stop myself short of promising to make a novena again—which I hadn't even followed through on the last time. I kept walking toward the mansion, concentrating on looking bored.

Just as I was approaching the door, I pressed my left arm against me, intending to take a little comfort from the solid presence of my gun. But there's something about those trench coats they never seem to mention in the books or movies. There's a lot of extra material under the armpits that doesn't really need to be there, all bunched up. I've tried a dozen different brands, and they're all like that. So squeezing the gun was a mistake. And doing it right by the door was bad, because of the black-and-white sitting by the door. Never wake up cops by dropping a .45 on the pavement next to them. Especially not there.

So there was some conversation, and they let me live, and I returned the favor. Reluctantly: the skinny one had a laugh exactly like a mule braying—*hee! . . . hee! . . . hee!*—and the fat one . . . Well, anyway, by the time I entered the mansion I was flustered on top of everything else.

So if you want to know what the place looks like inside, you'll have to look it up someplace. I kept telling myself to look around and memorize it for my memoirs some day, but I kept forgetting. I had a lot on my mind. There were a lot of big rooms, I remember, and a lot of stairs, and a hell of a lot of carpet everywhere, so thick it was like walking on a furry sponge mattress. I wanted to take off my shoes. I promised myself I would on the way out.

The butler was black as Lenny Bruce's humor and so old I wanted to ask him how the boat ride had been. He didn't offer to take my trench coat or fedora. He moved like that Lincoln robot Disney had at the World's Fair if there'd been a brownout. He went up stairs one at a time instead of one after the other. He stopped outside a big door with an elaborate frame and turned to me. "You are armed, sir," he said gravely. It wasn't quite a question.

"Isn't everybody?"

He held out his hand. I shrugged . . . and squeezed my left arm against me. The gun sank an inch into the carpet with a *plop*.

He waited, without changing expression.

I sighed, and dropped the sap and the brass knuckles on the carpet beside the gun. "Fluoroscope in the foyer?" I asked. "Or just a metal detector? Professional interest."

He waited patiently, hand still outstretched.

I shrugged again, and added the switchblade to the pile on the floor.

"We *are* running late, sir," he said sadly.

I stood on one foot, took the little .22 holdout from the ankle holster, and placed it on his upturned palm. It usually gets by: no metal parts. "The only other weapon I have on me," I said, "is attached. But I promise not to touch it."

He didn't even frown at the crudity. He looked at the pistol, dropped it on the carpet with the rest of the swag, and swept it all delicately to one side with one foot. It left a trail in the carpet.

"While I'm here," I qualified.

He ignored that too. "Thank you, sir. This way, please. He's expecting you."

He opened the door, announced me, stepped aside so I could enter, and left, closing the big door soundlessly behind him.

WELL, you know what he looks like. He looked like that.

"You're doing okay," I told him.

He frowned at me. He'd had his mouth open to speak and I'd derailed him. "Excuse me?"

"Sorry. I just thought you might ask me how you—never mind. What can I do for you?" I was being overeager. The whole trick to being a smartass detective is to let them give you the straight lines, and then come back with the snappy zingers.

He stared at me impassively for a while. Then when he did start to speak again he paused for a moment with his mouth open to see if I was going to interrupt again. I waited for my straight line. I thought about a cigarette, but there was no point: there were ashtrays visible.

"Are you sure you're not French?" is what he finally said.

Maybe Bogie could have come up with a clever response to that. The best I could do was to say, "Excuse me?" just the way he had.

"Like in those panther flicks?" he amplified.

I blinked. "Excuse me?" I said again, and I'd like to see Travis McGee do better.

"Not related to that Inspector Clazoo or whatever it is?"

I understood now. It was my destiny to spend the rest of my life saying "Excuse me?" to an old bald Jew with a face like a dissipated elf. All right, so be it. "Excuse me?"

He shook his head. "I guess not. But I could have sworn he was a relative of yours. You're just like him, Quigley."

"In what way?" It wasn't much, but at least it wasn't "Excuse me?"

"Two ways. You're a moron. And you're unbelievably lucky."

At last I got it. He was referring to that Inspector Clouseau guy in the Pink Panther movies, who keeps blundering his way into success.

Things were looking up, in the sense that he had finally uttered a comprehensible sentence. But it certainly wasn't a very promising start to the conversation. I mean, I had expected a certain difficulty in establishing mutual respect. PIs get used to the fact that most people—and nearly all their clients—privately consider them one or two steps above athlete's foot in the food chain. But having someone start out by telling me that I was a moron was sort of a new low in customer relations.

And besides, he had it exactly backwards. I'm a genius, with incredibly *bad* luck.

"You know," I said, "I just figured out how come you manage to get elected. It's been puzzling me."

"Flattering my constituents, you mean?"

"No. Being able to say a sentence like that. It's your voice. You sound *exactly* like Elmer Fudd after speech therapy finally conquered the lisp. People want you to succeed. They feel you've got it coming, after overcoming forty years of being humiliated by a bunny."

You don't ever want to play poker with him. He did nothing at all for ten seconds. But it wasn't like turning to stone. It was more like he was still listening to me say something, concerning which he had formed no opinion so far. When he did speak, it was as though someone had rolled the tape backwards three lines of dialogue and restarted it.

"Let me give you an example of what I mean," he said reasonably. "You believe all the crap you read in detective books. That makes you medium dumb as citizens go—but for a licensed private investigator in the City of New York, that makes you compare unfavorably with a newborn gerbil. You're not only big enough and tough enough to wrestle a gorilla, you're stupid enough to try. You actually think you can come in here and smartmouth me like a TV private eye, and all I can do about it is hope I catch you red-handed in a felony sometime before the last commercial. Somewhere in your head you *know* I can wipe myself with your license anytime I want, but still you come in here and get fresh with me. That's the moron part I spoke of." He was speaking calmly, illustrating his points with small gestures, sure he could make a reasonable man like me understand. "As to the lucky part . . . well, that should be self-evident. You've lived this long. But as a more immediate example, there is a chance, practically a good chance, that you could end up walking away from this with your freedom, your license *and* your health. Who could believe such a thing? I know: but there it is." He spread his hands expressively.

I decided I had established myself as a smartass. A really tough guy deals with intimidation by ignoring it, right? "How?"

"By doing exactly what all the TV private eyes do. By pulling off a miracle, to deadline, by incredible dumb luck—and with *absolute* discretion. If you don't, I'm going to cancel the Joe Quigley Show in mid-season."

And there it was. Exactly the opportunity I'd spent my life getting ready for. A shot.

I could hardly believe it. Ever since I was a kid I'd been waiting to have some big shot threaten me with total ruin if I didn't solve a big hush-hush case fast. I wanted to kiss him. You've never seen anybody look so nonchalant.

"How much discretion are we talking about?" I asked, studying a fingernail.

"You were never here. I don't know anybody who'd know anyone you know. We've never walked on the same real estate, even at different times. Any information you receive from me, or that you turn up as a result of your investigation, is to be between you and me and the principals involved. You will divulge nothing to anyone else. That includes grand juries, city, state or federal, judicial or legislative inquiry, and your confessor if any. And one other thing: you will treat La . . . uh, the principal here . . . with the utmost respect at all times. If she reports to me that you knocked ashes on her carpet—hear me, now—I will make you *wish you were on Rikers Island*. Do you believe I can do that?"

Oof. A little hard to imagine. I'd even rather be in New Jersey. But I knew the answer was: "Yes."

"Good. Do we have a meeting of the minds?"

I was in hog heaven—but I was also a professional. I turned my fingernail another way and inspected it again to see how it looked from that angle. "Not quite. I haven't told you my rates."

"I burn to know."

"Two hundred a day plus expenses."

He flashed his famous grin for the first time. "*Rockford Files*. James Garner. At least you follow good trash."

He had me cold. "The best," I agreed. "Just like with him, it's not negotiable." I tried for Garner's I'm-not-budging expression. "And I also get medical expenses for job-related injuries. After all, we're using smaller dollars these days."

"I seem to remember Rockford almost never gets paid."

I shrugged. "Is it a deal or not?"

To my surprise, he hesitated. "It's not that I'd have the slightest difficulty making it drop off the books," he mused. "Partly I'm curious to see what you'd do if I said no, you gotta work for free on this one. And mostly it goes against my grain to pay an overgrown adolescent who's built like a linebacker two hundred dollars a day to hang out in Lady Sally's House."

I had to work to control my face.

Lady Sally McGee's House? Not maybe the most famous, but surely the most legendary whorehouse in the greater New York area? I'd heard of it for years, but always very quiet, and third-hand at least. They said you had to know Somebody, real well, to get invited there. Until today, I hadn't known anybody who knew anybody who knew Somebody. I opened my mouth to say I could manage to pay *him* two hundred dollars, and absorb my own expenses—

"Oh screw it, it's a deal," he said.

"What's the situation?"

He pursed his lips, and shook his head. "I need backup on my judgment. You go see the Lady, and if she decides to fill you in, then nobody can blame me. If she doesn't, you get one day's pay and a hearty handclasp—for something that never happened."

"Can you give me a hint? What sort of beef are we talking? Do I bring a fingerprint kit, or a bazooka? Or a dozen condoms?"

He steepled his fingertips. "I would say you should bring along all of that garbage you dumped on my carpet outside. And if you know where you could borrow a brain for a while, bring that by all means. But mostly bring your luck, Quigley. And . . ." He sighed. " . . . your best judgment, such as it is."

"What does that mean?"

He frowned. "I don't know if I can make you understand. I want you to be absolutely candid with me in this matter . . . up to a point."

"I'm not following you."

"You are *not* going to get cute with this, like a TV detective. You will share with me fully any *relevant* information you learn. But it is possible—" He paused, and twisted his face up so badly that I wanted to offer him some Metamucil. "—that in the course of your investigation you will turn up information I do not have a need to know. And the hell of it is, by and large you're the one who'll have to decide when that is. I can only say: don't screw up."

I didn't have the slightest idea what the hell he was talking about. But he looked so uncomfortable that I got the idea he must have just done something noble. And maybe given me some kind of backhanded compliment at the same time. "I'll do my best," I said simply.

"Exactly what I'm afraid of. Any more questions?"

"Yeah. Why me?"

"Because every once in a while you're so dumb, you're a genius. That Favila case, for example. Most people can only see the obvious if it makes sense. You proved you can see the obvious even when it's stupid. That may turn out to be what's called for here."

I was a little stung. The Favila case had been one of my professional high points to date, had come *this* close to being a triumph. "I see," I said stiffly. "You need me, so you treat me like shit."

"I only do that for two reasons," he said. "First, of course, because you are shit . . . and second because you look like that moron on the tube, what's-his-name."

"Hey," I said, stung again, "that's not my fault."

"I know. No one would look like him that could help it. Forget it. You know where Sally's is?"

"I don't need to. The cabbie will know."

"True. Use the north entrance—and for God's sake don't use my name at the door if there's anyone else in earshot. Report to me, verbally, here, when you've cracked it. Not before. If there's anything you need, at all, the Lady will provide. And nothing goes in writing."

"Can I go now?"

"Not yet. Look at me, Quigley. I know I've succeeded in hiring you. I think I've even succeeded in engaging your attention. But before I let you leave here, I want to be sure I've succeeded in scaring the living shit out of you. I want you to throw away whatever smart-aleck closing line you've got prepared, and just say these words: say, 'I'm going to be a good boy, sir,' and then get the hell out of here. Will you do that for me, Joe?"

I wanted this job more than I wanted a nymphomaniac secretary with legs up to here, but there are some kinds of shit a man just can't eat. "Screw yourself, sir," I said. Besides, I'd been polishing an exit line since I'd first gotten the call, and it was going to be a beaut.

He smiled faintly. "You think the worst I could do is have you ruined, disgraced, raped and beaten to death. It's much worse than that." The smile broadened into that oddly telegenic grin again. "If your performance in this assignment is not satisfactory, *I will put your real first name out on the street.*"

—and on the other hand, certain other kinds of shit are quite palatable with a little necessity sprinkled on them. I could always save my exit line for the *next* time a major VIP wanted to hire me. "I'm going to be a good boy, sir."

"I know you are, 'Joe.' " The grin vanished. "I'm counting on it."

I left, and found my own way out.

I collected my hardware from the butler on the way out the main door. He wouldn't give it to me until I put my shoes back on. I stepped out into the cool muggy night, stuck a Lucky in my mouth, and heard imaginary music swell in the background.

On my way past the black-and-white I decided I had to do something, make some kind of move, a scene-closer to redeem my pride and get us to the commercial. I leaned into the passenger's window and stared the fat cop in the eye. "Your mother wears combat boots," I stated, and blew smoke in his face.

He looked me over, thought about where I had just come from and how confident I seemed now. "And shoulder pads," he agreed finally. "Why? You want to meet her?"

"*Hee . . . hee . . . hee!*" said the skinny one.

I gave up and walked away. At the foot of the driveway I turned around and looked at the mansion. What do you say when you haven't got a good way to end a scene? Say good night, Gracie.

"Good night, Gracie," I said, and hailed a cab.

MENTIONING the Favila case had been a low blow, I thought as the hack headed over the bridge into Brooklyn. Except for that one little flaw at the end, it had been a classic of sheer mystery-solving. Who could have guessed a man could spend his entire life in New York City, and end up . . . well, at least partly unsophisticated?

With my luck, you'll remember the case. It started when a janitor found a corpsicle floating in a rooftop swimming pool next to Central Park one August morning. A stiff, but I mean *stiff*. Frozen solid, just beginning to defrost around the edges from being in the pool. In August. He was in a funny half-crouch position, with his hands up in front of his face and the fingers spread, as if he'd been examining a crystal ball underwater when he froze. No ID at all, wearing frozen jeans and shards of a frozen tee shirt, nothing else on or with him at all. The janitor swore he'd had to unlock the door to enter the area, the lock hadn't been tampered with, and the only other access to that roof was by helicopter. Fingerprints and dental charts went through all the computers without a match, and he didn't fit any Missing Persons reports. The local cryogenics outfit took some hard questioning, but they were able to prove they had no corpsicles missing. Every meat locker within a ten-block radius got combed, but nothing turned up.

A friend of mine, a gold shield named Murphy, caught the case. It just about drove him nuts. One day I happened to be standing with him on the roof of the building in question. I was there because I'd been following him around for over an hour, trying to borrow money from him. All he wanted to talk about was the Frozen Stiff.

"It just doesn't make any goddam sense, Joe," he said. He turned around in a slow circle, looking at the city laid out around us. "Where is the nearest place to this spot where you could freeze a guy solid as a leg of lamb without anybody noticing?"

Without thinking, I pointed straight up.

"Right," he said, snorting. "I'm about ready to believe it *was* some outer space monster. He was planning to drink the pool for the chlorine and wanted to chill it properly first. Hell, it doesn't even matter where it was done. *Wherever* they froze the son of a bitch, how did they get him all the way *here* without being seen— and *why?*"

I started to get very excited. "Murph—"

"Why take all that risk?" Murphy went on, talking more than half to himself. "You got a corpsicle, bust him up with a hammer and leave him in the shower. *This* is like something out of a fuckin' comic book. You know the weirdest part of all? The Coroner says he was *suffocated*—without a mark on him, for Christ's—"

"Murph, listen, this is important to both of us," I said. "Can you let me hold a twenty for a couple of days?"

"Things are hot just now," he said absently. "This Knapp Commission crap, I practically been living on my salary for months. I tell you, it's gotta be some kind of radicals. The guy looks like he could be some kind of spic—Central America, maybe, some kind of weird CIA shit—"

I tried one more time for the twenty, but he pretended not to hear me. So screw him. I left him there on the roof, went straight to my office, borrowed a fistful of plane schedules from the porno distributor down the hall, and called a press conference.

It was great, at first. Everybody looked bored and dubious when they first saw the office, then sat up straight when I outlined my deductions. I had them spellbound, and when I was done they actually applauded. I was on all the news that night, and the next morning's editions all gave prominent coverage to my confident prediction that the victim would turn out to be a poor peasant from Belize, tragically killed by his own ignorance and his hunger to live in America.

It seemed so simple. My kneejerk wisecrack answers to Murphy's questions had suddenly made a twisted kind of sense. *Where's the nearest place to freeze a man solid?* A mile or two away—straight up. *How do you get him to a rooftop without being seen?* Easy. A skyhook.

Freeze him in the stratosphere, and then let him fall . . .

Looked at from that angle, it was obvious. A starving peasant, let's call him Juan Valdez, burns to live in *El Norte*, whatever it costs him in discomfort. He sneaks out onto an airport tarmac, and worms his way up into the wheelwell of a big brute on a nonstop run to New York, gambling that when those huge wheels come up, there will still be room for him in there. He expects to arrive cramped and sore and half dead with hunger and fatigue, but so what? Sure enough, the wheel fails to crush him after takeoff. He begins to rejoice. He knows even less about the stratosphere than he does about America.

By the time the stewardesses are thawing out frozen dinners for the paying customers inside, Valdez is a frozen dinner himself, his suffocated corpse clinging to the huge tire like an ice sculpture of a monkey.

The plane is circling over Manhattan when it lowers its wheels and drops Valdez, a cryonic bomb. By the kind of cosmic luck that recently caused a woman in Ohio to be hit by a meteorite *for the second time*, he makes a perfect landing in an empty pool.

If he hadn't landed in water, maybe somebody might have figured out the huge treadmarks on his face and clothes. But then, if he hadn't landed in water, nobody would have found anything but a couple of buckets' worth of crushed ice, I guess.

The major airline schedules showed that only one big direct flight from anywhere in Central or South America would have been over Manhattan that night, a 707 from Belize. *Voilà*: Quigley Solves Mystery. The story was a natural for the media sobsuckers, and it got a lot of play.

But not as much as the follow-up got.

Well, how was I to know? Try this experiment yourself—I've tried it dozens of times in bars, and as long as they don't know the Favila story it always works. Walk up to any person in New York, any race, color or creed, and ask him to show you where Hispanics come from. I'll bet you a hundred dollars he points south.

I don't know, maybe nothing newsworthy ever happens there, or maybe there's some big secret conspiracy of silence, but unless the conversation is about conquistadores, you just don't ever hear anybody talk about Spain.

So when it turned out that Hidalgo Favila was a half-mad freebase addict from Barcelona who had crawled up into that wheelwell because everybody said the best coke got transshipped to America, I looked pretty stupid. And mentioning that was the only way the media wolves could sneak out of looking stupid themselves. Get it right, you're a star. Get it half-right, you're a gas giant. I took a lot of ribbing, and business went down so sharply that I thought seriously about slipping off the straight and narrow and becoming a cop.

The only thing that saved me is that reputation doesn't really mean as much as it used to once. There is so *much* yammer-yammer on the air and in print these days that nobody could keep up with it, much less remember it. I mean, look at Richard Nixon. There's always somebody who didn't get the word. Before long, business was right back up to putrid again.

But to make a long story short, every time somebody reminds me of the Favila case, it drives me crazy. I keep replaying the memory in my mind, right up to the moment when I say " . . . from Belize . . ." to the reporters, and then trying to make my memory-mouth add, " . . . or possibly from Spain." It never works, and it takes at least ten minutes to derail my mind once I start doing it.

And it drives me just as crazy when somebody points out my resemblance to that jerk on TV. *I* never asked him to steal my face . . .

So I was only a few blocks from Lady Sally's House when I finally managed to get my mind back on the job at hand.

I knew the general location of the place, but the actual neighborhood surprised me a little. It was a kind of a dumpy, run-down warehouse-y area . . . but it didn't have the hardcore funky sleaze to it that you'd expect around a really first-class whorehouse. No bombed-out abandoned buildings, or burned-out cars, or roving packs of bull fruits looking for gay-bashers to chain-whip, or dull-eyed junkies nodding around a trash can fire. It looked like the kind of neighborhood you could walk with the safety catch on.

The hack jockey pulled up in front of an enormous mausoleum that filled an entire block. Seven stone steps led to a huge front door with an elaborately carved marble frame and a stained-glass transom. On either side of it were a pair of red globe lights, a classical touch I admired. There were tall windows on either side of the door, but their heavy curtains were drawn and very little light from inside escaped.

"Here you are, cap," the cabbie said.

I consulted the mental map everybody creates the moment they get in a cab. "I want the north entrance," I said.

He turned around to look me over. "You'll never carry it off," he decided. "You can't wear the clothes."

"Huh?" I said. I hate it when I say that. Even "Excuse me?" is better.

"That's the VIP entrance. You're the wrong type."

They're all out-of-work actors these days. "Just take me to the north entrance, okay, pal?"

"Everybody's got the right to audition," he agreed, and drove me around the block.

It was a lot darker around the back. As I was paying the jockey I asked him if I'd have any trouble getting another cab around there at night. "Maybe if you were on fire," he said, "or carrying a machine gun." I got out and he drove away.

The north wall of that building at ground level was a featureless expanse of interleaved stone blocks, with a single entrance right in the middle of the block. The door was recessed back in a sheltered, roofed doorway whose walls projected out a few feet onto the sidewalk. There was a single low-wattage light (*not* red) above the door. I looked closer and saw the sliding peephole in the door. I turned around and looked across the street, and saw another featureless wall, this one of brick. I realized that no one could photograph you standing at this door without being seen. At worst they could snap you ducking into the doorway recess, which a man might do to get out of the rain or light a cigarette out of the wind. This was the VIP entrance, all right.

I reached for the doorknob. There wasn't any. There wasn't any place to put a secret key I didn't have. There was no electronic lock keypad to try and crack the combo for. No buzzer or intercom panel. No room between door and frame to slip in a credit card, or even a scalpel blade. Even Jim Rockford would have had trouble with that door. Maybe the Seventh Armored would have too.

I lifted a fist to knock, and the door swung open noiselessly.

Most of being cool is training your face never to look surprised. The rest of it is, when you *are* surprised, walk forward at once. I entered, and the door shut behind me. It was street-dark inside, and I interpreted the shadowy figure before me as a naked courtesan.

A dimmer switch was turned up slowly, and I found myself staring at a smiling grandmother in a silk robe. Possibly a great grandmother, and certainly a good one. Seventy-five if she was a day, the kind of sweet-featured chipper old lady you see in the After of laxative commercials. I liked her on sight. Not just her face, either, I realized with surprise. It wasn't a granny-type robe, and she wore it damned well . . .

I controlled my face and walked forward again, sticking out my hand. "It's a pleasure to meet you, Your Ladyship," I said. And I was going to add, "My name's Joe Quigley," and kiss her hand, but she spoiled it by taking my hand in both of hers and bursting into very girlish laughter.

"Bless your heart, grandson," she said. "Flattery like that will get you a hell of a lot."

I started to say, "Excuse me?" but decided I had done enough of that tonight. "Ma'am?"

"Let's start over, dear. I'm Ruth."

"Oh. I need to see Lady Sally McGee."

"Who doesn't? Pardon me, dear, but are you a member?"

"Not yet." She started to look sad, so I tried, "Uh . . . I was sent by the most hated man in New York."

It worked. "Of course. We've been expecting you." She took my trench coat off me and made it disappear. I never noticed her take my hat, but a while later I didn't have it. "This way."

Do you know how strange it feels to follow a senior citizen—and realize you're watching her butt? She was some granny. I found myself thinking maybe I'd buy her a drink on the way out.

Go ahead, laugh. You've never met her.

We went through another door—just as tough as the outside door; I don't know how she got it to open for her—and down a long hall. The carpet was expensive, but didn't overdo it like the other one. The lighting was so indirect I couldn't spot the source. The air smelled funny. Kind of nice. Halfway down the hall, corridors branched off to left and right. I glanced to either side as we passed and saw two doors—with knobs—in each wing, numbered D-1 through D-4. They were set far apart from each other: big rooms. Next to each door was a tiny peanut bulb, and two of them glowed like rubies. Except for them, the place felt like a pricey hotel in midtown Manhattan. There was even a room service tray outside one of the doors. As I passed, a hand and bare arm came out of that door at low level and deposited a teacup on the tray; I heard someone speaking in what sounded like Russian.

At the end of the hall was an elevator—which *did* have an electronic lock keypad. Ruth tapped out a code, and the doors slid apart. I failed to catch the code: she had fast hands for an old woman.

"Her Ladyship will receive you in—" Ruth began, then pressed a finger to what I had taken for a hearing aid. "—the Boys' Bedroom, thank you, Mary. I have to stay here, Mr. Quigley, but you'll find it: the second door on the left," she finished. She held the doors for me.

I hadn't told her my name. "Thank you, Ruth."

"You're welcome. Has anybody ever told you you look a little bit like—"

"Yeah."

"Oh. Sorry. Enjoy your stay."

There certainly was that possibility. I got in. The building was four stories tall, but there were only two buttons in that elevator. I pushed the top one, the doors slid shut, and I rose.

On the way up I tried to remember a quote I heard in a bar once, something about wondering what the guys who make the wine drink, and how good it is. I mean, a guy who can screw eight million people every day, the place where he goes to get screwed himself must be something pretty special, you know?

This *definitely* beat staking out midtown fleabags with a Polaroid during lunch hour . . .

2. The Jane...

THE elevator opened again, and right away I had to do the control-the-face-and-walk-forward bit again. There was a little naked guy in the hall.

Well, for a second, anyway. And practically naked. Leather bondage straps crisscrossed his upper body, and he wore a little thing like the front half of a loin cloth, and felt slippers. His face made me think of Jiminy Cricket. He was about fifty and maybe five-five. He was carrying a big pile of clean white sheets and pillowcases in his arms. A good investigator can see that much in a split second.

Which is all I got. The instant he saw me he let out a squeak like a mortified mouse and vanished.

I was out of the elevator a half second later and looked both ways, but he was gone. His shadow was just making the turn to the right, hurrying to catch up. Maybe Tinkerbell could sew it back on for him.

I gave my head a little shake to settle my brains, and went to the second door on the right.

I saw the little ruby light lit up beside it, but I went in anyway. Then I controlled my face, walked forward . . . stopped, said, "I beg your pardon, Your Eminence. Carry on," and walked backward, until I was in the hallway again. The door shut itself, and I wiped sweat from my forehead.

Damn, Ruth had said second on the *left* . . .

I gave my head a large shake to jumpstart it, and retraced my steps to the elevator. I counted two doors to the left, three times, went there, counted again, and knocked this time.

"Come in, Mr. Quigley," said a feminine voice with whiskey throat and a high-class British accent.

I took a deep breath and went in.

And fought my face and walked forward—

Look, it was *not* a perfect replica of my room in my parents' house back when I was a teenager. No better than eighty percent accurate. I used to pin up the Playmate of the Month at the foot of the bed, for example, not on the ceiling. And the bedspread was different, and now I think of it the window was on the wrong wall. But it was close enough to make me want to gape. It even had the bunk beds, and the Brooklyn Dodgers pennant . . .

The room had two occupants.

The first one I took in was the woman against the far wall. Did you ever see that bodybuilder Jayne Mansfield married? If you put both of them in some kind of mad scientist machine and combined them, you'd get what I saw standing at parade rest. She was almost as big as me. She was oiled, like a recoilless rifle. She wore sweatpants, and a tank top muscle-shirt, to which she was totally entitled, and gold bands around each bicep, and black tennis shoes with steel toes. Her haircut made her look like Joan of Arc after a long course of every hormone supplement there is. She had bodyguard's eyes. No: Secret Service eyes. They can kill anybody they want. I kept my hands very still at my sides.

This was, you will understand, sort of the backwards of what I was expecting. Maybe Mike Hammer himself could have managed to maintain an erection in that woman's bedroom. But even he wouldn't have tried to do anything with it. Not without a direct order. I watched her for a full five seconds, until I was fairly sure she had no immediate plans to collapse my ribcage for any reason, then showed her my back teeth for a moment and turned to her companion, seated at the desk on the right.

Considerable improvement . . .

Did you ever see that movie *A Pocketful of Miracles*? Where Dave the Dude drops a bundle turning broken-down old Apple Annie into a Countess for a day, so she won't disappoint this daughter that's been in Europe for the last twenty years? Well, the way Bette Davis looked when they got done making her over— not the Before, the After—that's what this woman looked like. If she walked into the White House the same time as a bunch of tourists, the staff would cut her out of the pack and take her right up to the Oval Office without even asking her name. Buckingham Palace, same deal. Before I could stop myself I pulled my tie up, loosened it again, buttoned the collar button (for the first time since I'd owned the shirt), pulled the tie tight again, and buttoned my double-breasted. She couldn't have seen the wrinkled bit of tie that now hung below the knot in the back, but I was painfully aware of it. I could feel dirt under my fingernails, and behind my ears. I could feel my ten o'clock shadow growing.

And I could feel something else growing too, in my pants—even though she wasn't showing much more skin than any other Countess would have. I mean, she had *impact.*

She had hair so red I decided no one would dye it that color, in upswept waves. Her gown was greener than the stack of money it must have cost, and left one shoulder bare. Impressive cleavage. I guessed her at fifty or so, but like Ruth downstairs in terrific shape, right down to the skin on the backs of her hands. In the right light, you'd have bought thirty-five, no trouble. Even the *wrong* light wouldn't have put you off, either. She had something she wasn't ever going to lose. No detectible makeup. Wedding band on one hand, a diamond the size of a salted whole peanut on the other. Emerald necklace and earrings. Twinkling eyes. One eyebrow raised slightly, apparently permanently. She'd seen it all, and enjoyed most of it.

I wanted to bow. But I didn't want to look even a little bit like I might be reaching for my armpit, not with that Amazon watching. I kept my hands at my sides, clicked my heels and bowed like Eric von Stroheim. "A pleasure to meet you, Your Ladyship," I said.

This time I had the right one. "So I'm told," she agreed throatily, "and I won't argue. Welcome to my House, Mr. Quigley."

She sounded . . . well, not drunk: nobody with a British accent that classy ever sounds drunk. Not even really what you'd call high. Elevated, maybe. One sip past a happy glow. Merry . . . "It's certainly a very impressive place, ma'am."

"Yes, it is. You must see it later."

What had I just been doing? Never mind. "I'd like that. Uh . . . I frightened a little naked guy with an armful of linen out in the hall; I hope he wasn't an important customer or something."

Lady Sally McGee's eyes twinkled. "My fault. I had Mistress Cynthia instruct Robin not to let you run across him until you were acclimatized—so naturally he tried to earn a spanking. Don't worry about it. And don't mention it to Cynthia, when you meet her: that'll teach him! Let me introduce Priscilla. She is the bouncer here."

Ah. "Ah." Not one of the whores. "Not one of the working girls."

"Of course she's a working girl; you don't think she bounces people for free, do you? But no, she is not presently one of my artists."

They called them "artists" here, huh?

Heroic actions aren't always something you can see. Right then I did a heroic thing nobody else knew about. I kept myself from saying, "I may not know much about art, but I know what I like." It took some doing, but hey, I'm a professional.

"Hi, Priscilla," I said as politely as I knew how. "I'm Joe Quigley."

"Hi, Joe," she said, in a friendly enough way. She didn't offer to shake hands, but I didn't mind that a lot.

"Would you care for a drink, Mr. Quigley?" Lady Sally asked. On the messy desk, sitting on a Math textbook—the very one I'd never read, by God!—were two glasses with stems and a bottle. The kind of wine with a cork, and nothing on it in English anywhere.

I'd have preferred even cheap bourbon. But I can't turn down a free drink; I've got my license to think of. "Tenderly, ma'am."

She smiled for the first time. "Then I'll entrust you with one." She poured, doing that little twist thing after each one, and handed me a glass. I did another Von Stroheim as I took it, and touched my glass to hers. Our eyes met, and I lost track of where I was for a moment . . .

Toast, toast, toast . . . nothing trite, nothing corny, nothing crude. There went most of my repertoire. I remembered one I'd heard a wise old barkeeper say once, and used it: "To all the ones who weren't as lucky."

Her eyes widened slightly, and then got a faraway look. "Yes," she said in that husky Tallulah Bankhead voice, "I will drink to that."

So we did.

It wasn't wine at all. It was some kind of berry juice, a kind I didn't know, and it was very tasty for something nonalcoholic. Delicious, actually. I finished it thirstily, and set the glass down again. I thought about a cigarette, and decided against it.

"Well," I said, "you know why I'm here, Your Ladyship. And that makes one of us. I can't say I'm in any hurry at all to get down to business, but I do like to know what I'm goofing off on. Do you want to . . . excuse me—" I broke off and held up one finger, because just then the berry juice began to hit me. I closed my eyes momentarily, locked my knees and went inside, gauged the impact—about like an ounce of fine brandy, it felt like—made the necessary adjustments, and opened my eyes again. "—to tell me about the job, or shall I just hang around the place until I de-douche it? De*duce* it. Up to you, but the meter's running." There; I had it under control.

She looked impressed. I realized she had sandbagged me . . . and I had passed the test. "You're quite right, Mr. Quigley. Your time is valuable. Do sit down and we'll get right to it."

I pulled up a chair and sat backwards on it. "Call me Joe."

"Certainly, Joe. And I'm Sally."

"Yes, Your Ladyship."

"About the job, then, Joe . . ."

And then silence descended for maybe ten seconds.

Finally she frowned and finished her own berry juice. "What I want you to do, in essence, is to find the Little Man Who Wasn't There. *Without* letting any of my clients or artists *know* that he isn't." She blinked and glanced down at her glass. "I'm sorry, that's not very clear—"

It was more or less what I'd been expecting to hear. "Sounds straightforward to me," I said. "Can you give me any leads on *exactly* where he ishn't? Isn't?"

She blinked again, and then rallied. "Well, I can give you some specifics on where he hasn't been *so far*. But of course there's no way of knowing where he won't appear next. More elixir?"

"You'd need three words to say anything sweeter," I said, and accepted another few fingers. "Okay, I'm in. What's my cover?"

"Well," she said apologetically, "I'm afraid you'll simply have to pass as a new artist. If you think you're up to it . . ."

"NOW wait just a damn minute!" I said.

She looked surprised. "Do you have a problem with that? From what . . . our mutual friend said, I'm afraid I took the liberty of assuming you'd—"

"In the first place, what the hell do you mean by that crack about, ' . . . if I'm *up* to it . . . '?"

"Ah, I see. Pardon me, I misspoke myself. I meant to say, ' . . . up *for* it . . . ' I'm always getting my propositions mixed—damn it, there I go again: I meant *prepositions*. Blame it on the elixir. Reminds me of the time I came before a judge who was fond of . . . uh . . . English studies, and managed to end my sentence with a proposition. Be that as it may, Joe—"

"And in the second place—" I tried to interrupt.

"—the job pays fairly well," she went on. "Over and above your regular two hundred a day and expenses, of course."

"What the hell do you think I am?" I demanded.

She looked confused. "In the words of the ancient jape, I thought we had settled that, and were dickering over the price."

"Listen here, Your Ladyship: I'm a *private* dick, you understand the distinction? Find yourself another boy!"

"One of my specialties, as the bishop confided to the actress. Come now, Joe—be honest with me: have you really never once fantasized about turning pro some day? Developing the talent God gave you? Never felt that by all rights they ought to have to pay you for it? I warn you that if you say no, I shall be forced to assume some tragic accident has cost you certain standard male equipment—"

"Jesus, Lady—"

"—your ego, I mean. You haven't ever thought about it?"

I made the instant subconscious decision to be candid. Maybe I didn't care if I offended her any more, or maybe I just didn't want to lie to her. "Sure I have," I said. "That's why I don't want any part of it. In the first place I'd hate the impersonality, the commercialism, and in the second place I'd hate the constant pressure to get it up, and speaking of that you know just as well as I do what kind of women have to pay for it, and as for crabs and clap and so on I already took that class, thank you, and most of all if I *was* to start charging for it, at fair market value, there wouldn't be a woman in Brooklyn who could afford it!"

I broke off, even though I had a few more points to make— because she was staring at me, apparently dumbfounded.

After a few seconds of silence, she managed to find some words. "Joe, are you familiar with the phenomenon Samuel Delany calls 'rupture'?"

"Hey, I never get *that* carried away."

"There it goes again. Rupture occurs when you think you are in the middle of a conversation with someone . . . and suddenly discover that you've merely been making noises at each other, that there is a previously unsuspected chasm between you beside which the Marianas Trench is a pothole. We have come to a point of rupture, Joe. You don't know what I mean, and I'm not sure I understand what you said. I think we must be using different maps."

"Oh yeah?"

"Either that, or you're a real jackass."

I did what PIs always do when insulted: shrugged, and went for a wisecrack. "Not much point in being a fake jackass, is there?"

"Ask the man who sent you here."

That reminded me that The Man would be upset with me if I blew this commission—and he *had* succeeded in scaring the shit out of me. "*Touché*. Okay, let's rewind to where we went wrong and start over. What were you really asking me to do, when I thought you wanted me to 'Rent-A-'Rection'?"

She shook her head. "It won't help, I tell you. We've got different maps. The street I'm pointing to doesn't exist on yours."

"Okay. How do I get one of *your* maps?"

"You'll just have to draw your own, I'm afraid."

I sighed. "Look, Lady, I'm not *trying* be to difficult. But how the hell am I supposed to do that?"

Priscilla spoke up. "Map-making isn't hard. Just tricky."

"I'm listening," I said politely.

"Four stages. The obvious three are: look around you carefully, record what you see, and integrate it. It's the very first part that'll trip you up, and it's the most important of all."

"It's the whole thing," Lady Sally corrected. "The other three happen automatically; you couldn't stop 'em if you tried—once you do the first thing."

Damn it, the PI isn't supposed to be the straight man. "Which is?"

"Throw out all the old maps you already have in the glove compartment," Priscilla said.

Lady Sally nodded. "Forget all the reports of earlier explorers. You can't discover America if you keep shying away from the edge of the world. And if you do find it, you'll waste years asking to be taken to Kublai Khan."

I brought my glass to my lips . . . looked at it, and set it down. I reached for my deck of Luckies . . . realized a teenager's bedroom wouldn't have any ashtrays, and put it away. "Look," I said finally, "the dialogue is getting so clever here I'm starting to lose it. Let me see if I can put it in English, okay? What I think I'm hearing is: you got some kind of sneak thief in the joint; you want me to nail him; naturally you want it done discreet; so you want me to pose as a prostitute while I run him down; you don't believe I know what that involves here; so you want me to keep an open mind and scope the place before I make up my mind. Is that close?"

"Reasonably close," Lady Sally agreed. "We can fine-tune it as we go along. If we do."

"So what's the plan? You give me a Grand Tour of the place, visiting-fireman-style, and along about dawn I come back and give you my answer? No hard feelings if I take a pass?"

"Something like that."

I thought about it. I'd been to a few Houses before . . . but never anyplace near as classy as this. And all I'd ever gotten to see of them was a crummy parlor—in one case, more of a bus station waiting room—and a hallway and a crib. It came to me that, given a choice, I'd almost rather tour a whorehouse than use one. Especially this one.

And there was no reason the two had to be incompatible. As Clint Eastwood once said, "It do present mind-boggling possibilities, don't it?" There were a lot worse ways to earn two hundred bucks . . .

"I'd be a fool to refuse," I said.

"YOU certainly would," Lady Sally agreed. "I don't give many tours of my House—and this will be the first one I've given for free. Well, let's say, 'on spec.' All right, let's get this show on the road if we're going. Mary!"

I looked around. Still just the three of us.

"Yes, Lady," said a cheerful voice that seemed to come from the middle of the room.

"Is Tim busy just now?"

There was a five-second pause. "Not any more. His eleven o'clock just left."

"Ask him to come see me here, would you, dear?"

"Sure thing. It'll be a few minutes."

"Naturally. Thank you, love."

"You're welcome, Lady!" Whoever she was, she was jolly.

"Tim will show you around," Lady Sally told me. "Just tell him you're thinking about hiring on, and duck every question you can."

I frowned. "I still don't know if that's the way to go. Look, I'm pretty good with my mouth. When I was born I passed myself off as a doctor; if I could have reached the doorknob I'd have got away clean. I could fake being a hooker to a civilian, no sweat. But I don't think I can fool another hooker for very long. Especially if you're right, and I don't really know much about it. There's nothing I hate more than trying not to look surprised."

She shook her head. "Listen to me, Joe: in the first place, I would venture to guess that less than a quarter of the men who seek to enter my employ have ever worked professionally before. And those who *have* are nearly always as ignorant as you are of how things are done here. Tim won't be surprised if you look a little . . . well, confused."

"If you say so," I agreed dubiously.

"And you'll find that people don't ask a lot of personal questions without encouragement."

"All right. Before he gets here, why don't you tell me a little bit more about the specific problem you want me to deal with?"

"No."

"How am I supposed to know what to keep my eyes out for?"

"Joe," she said patiently, "if you report to me at dawn that you are not prepared to go undercover as one of my artists, you are not ever going to know any more than you already do about my problem. If we proceed, you'll be briefed. Just soak up the place."

That made sense. "Fair enough."

"I'll see you at sunrise. Most people find Tim fairly non-threatening. If you—"

The invisible Mary interrupted. (This place certainly seemed to have its share of people that weren't there.) "Pris—"

"Yes, Mary?"

"Developing situation at the Bower; Class Three."

I was a little surprised. It didn't make Priscilla look happier; just more alert. "On my way!"

"Kate will meet you," Mary said, but Priscilla was already gone. She moved like a panther chasing a cheetah, and nothing she did including closing the door behind her made the slightest sound. I felt almost sorry for the ass or asses who were making trouble in the Bower, whatever that was. (Bower-y bums?)

Lady Sally watched her go expressionlessly. "As I was saying—" she began, but the door opened again and a tall slender guy came in.

"I *love* it when she does that!" he said, eyes shining. "Like a cat on ice skates. She cornered in third gear, and I swear she wouldn't have left a trail on rice paper."

He was in his late twenties, medium length black hair, green eyes, six two or three, a hundred and sixty pounds tops, very fit. He had a pleasant, youthful face. If you were his agent you'd have pitched him as the Hero's Best Friend, or the Eager Rookie. He wore dark slippers, dark slacks, and a green silk shirt. It was buttoned up to one short of his throat, but the sleeves were unbuttoned. That made me look closer. They weren't bracelets. They were rope marks.

Most people found him non-threatening . . .

"Excuse me," he said to me. "I could just watch Priscilla run like that for hours."

"Pleasure to meet a fellow sports fan," I told him.

He turned to Lady Sally. "You called, Your Ladyship?"

"Tim, this is . . . I'm sorry, what is your name?"

"Taggart," I said. "Ken."

"Hi, Ken. Pleased to meet you too." We shook hands. Nice grip.

"Mr. Taggart might be joining the staff, Tim," Lady Sally said. "I'd like you to take him on an inspection tour. Would you mind?"

"I'd be happy to. My dance card is clear for the rest of the night."

"Any problems just now?" she asked obliquely.

He grinned. "Naw. I've got her right where I want her: I'm eating out of the palm of her hand."

"How are things generally, dear?"

"With me? Couldn't be better," he said, with obvious sincerity. "Why do you ask?"

She smiled back at him. "You know perfectly well why."

"Yes, I do," he said, and made a little bow. Not a Von Stroheim, a Japanese monk kind. "I love you too."

"Very satisfactorily. Now be off with you, children; Mother wants to brood. Tim, you go ahead, and Ken will catch right up with you, all right?"

"I'll be right with you," I agreed.

"Sure," he said, and left.

When the door had shut behind him I turned to Lady Sally. "You first," I said.

"I'd like you to leave *all* your weapons here on the desk, please," she said, with just enough emphasis that I knew she'd received a full report. "I don't like people walking around my House armed. There's a gun check at the front door; they'll be waiting there for you with your overcoat when you leave."

I shrugged. "How about if I keep the blackjack? I might meet the Little Man Who Wasn't There."

She frowned slightly. "True. All right."

I put both guns, the knucks and the switchblade on the desk.

"Now you," she said.

"You don't happen to have somebody . . . well, more like my kind of guy available to show me around? A little more . . . I don't know . . ."

"Butch?" she suggested.

"The guy's got rope burns on his wrists, for Christ's sake. I just don't think I could be very simpatico with a guy like that."

The twinkle went out of her eye. I have to say I was sorry to see it go. "Mr. Quigley," she said, all the tiddliness gone from her voice, "I begin to wonder if this is a waste of time. Yes, I have artists on staff who are 'more your kind of guy'—and they would teach you very little. The most important lesson you have to learn about my House you will get through your head right now, or get the hell out: within these walls, you will be tolerant of anything you find strange. I don't insist on sophistication, but I won't accept rudeness. Think what you like about Tim's tastes—or those of anyone here, artist or client—but if you don't show perfect respect to each one of them, at all times, I'll have Priscilla kiss you goodbye. That will be all for now."

I stopped at the door and turned back. This was where a wise-crack was supposed to go. "Uh . . ." I said.

She looked up—and softened when she saw my face. "I beg your pardon, Joe. Look here: I probably have two dozen artists on staff whose sexual tastes and proclivities closely overlap your own. But not one of them suffers from the delusion that theirs is the Only Right Way To Be. That syndrome is the single most common sexual psychosis of this era, and it is my belief that it is virtually always the victim's fault. But I could be wrong."

"I don't know about that," I said. I felt lousy.

"You are not a bad man, Joe Quigley. For your place and time. Plop you down in the Renaissance just as you are now, you might be the Bertrand Russell of your day. Will you keep one thing in mind for me? No one is going to ask you to do anything you find repulsive—or even uninteresting, I promise." Suddenly she smirked. "That is, they might very well *ask*—but they will take a no philosophically, and for keeps."

"I get you," I said. "Thanks. Uh . . . one last thing. Just to keep things straight. Is an 'inspection tour' the same thing as being comped?"

The twinkle was back. "Yes. But remember, you've only got 'til dawn."

"I'm a business-first kind of guy," I assured her.

"Just remember one other thing."

"Yeah?"

"*I* know your real name too."

I blinked. "Yes, Ma'am."

3. The Spot...

> Behold how good and how pleasant it is for
> brethren to dwell together in unity . . .
>
> —Psalms cxxxiii: 1

"I'LL show you some of the Function Rooms first," Tim said as we strolled down the hall.

I was startled. "You hold *conventions* here? Speeches and panel discussions?"

He chuckled. "Not that kind of function room. I mean each one has a specific function. You just left the Teenager's Bedroom, male version. The female version's pretty much the same, and it's occupied at the moment anyway. Same for the Doctor's Examining Room and the Executive's Office. But here's the Locker Room—"

I understood him now. Fantasy scenario rooms. I'd heard of such things—but I'd never expected to see any as *realistic* as the one I'd just left . . . or the one we entered now.

It even lacked a doorknob, like real locker rooms do. And when we got inside . . . well, it was funny: it smelled right, and it didn't. I mean, there were enough authentic locker room smells—soap, water, terry cloth, basketballs, talcum—to make your subconscious accept it as a real locker room . . . but it didn't have the sour sweat and old mildew smells that usually make you want to leave one as quickly as possible. The benches between the banks of lockers were a little wider than usual, and there were more mirrors than I was used to. There was a working shower room off to the left, with a non-skid floor that wasn't completely dry yet.

"Boys' or girls'?" I asked Tim. Echo of locker room tile . . .

29

"Depends on which bank of lockers you open. Each bank has a full complement of utensils, in the locker with the lock on it. As a matter of fact, you might end up spending time here, if you decide to join us: we haven't got a good Gym Teacher at the moment."

For the sake of my cover, I tried to look as if I was giving it some thought. Beneath the surface, I gave it some thought.

"If that suits you, of course," he added. "That's the very best thing about this place: no one ever has to take a gig or a client they don't want."

Now *that* was something I'd never heard of before in a whorehouse. If it was true, then maybe it *was* conceivable that I might, for a few days, experimentally, in the line of duty . . .

"But you've got the build for a gym teacher, and a macho face," Tim finished.

There's a way he could have said that and pissed me off—not that I would have showed it. But he didn't say it like that, like flirting; he said it like a casting director. I decided I had nothing against the guy.

"Maybe," I agreed. "That leads to a few fairly basic questions, though."

"Ask away, Ken. By the way, has anybody ever told you that you look a hell of a lot like—"

"Yeah," I interrupted flatly, and he had sense enough to drop it. "First of all, what's the split here for beginners?"

He looked startled. "We're starting from square one, then. Brace yourself, Ken. There is no split. We're on straight salary here."

I stared at him. "Straight salary?"

"Weekly check, withholding taken out and everything. You get a nice chunk of circus money back from the IRS every spring."

I didn't get it. "Then you don't have any incentive to hurry up and get to the next customer."

"Exactly," he said, nodding as if I'd said something intelligent. "Some of the artists who are already pros when they get here take a while to unlearn that habit. The Lady says good art shouldn't be rushed."

Like I said, there's nothing I hate as much as trying not to look surprised. But I was beginning to like this place. "What's the starting salary?"

"Oh, we all get the same. Only way to avoid squabbles." He named a sum. "Plus room and board, of course,"

Let's just say it was significantly more than a PI makes, okay?

"And tips?" I managed to say.

He looked a little sheepish. "Well . . . tipping *is* discouraged. But it's *gently* discouraged; if somebody just insists . . ." He grinned. "But bragging about it is *strongly* discouraged. Ballpark, I'd say you could take in anything from zilch to twenty-five percent of your base salary. I can tell you I never have any trouble keeping up my Christmas Club deposits during vacation."

"Vacation?"

"Mandatory. You pick when, but it has to add up to three months a year. Paid."

I gave up: this was one of those conversations where even the hero can be forgiven for looking surprised. "Paid?"

"Full salary. To discourage you from free-lancing somewhere else. The Lady says she doesn't like to see a good artist burn out."

I was beginning to wonder if I really was in the wrong line of work. If he was telling the truth about never having to take a gig you didn't want . . . Maybe, if I did a real good job on this caper, Lady Sally would consider letting me stay on staff.

Of course, that raised the disturbing question, was I talented enough? Ten minutes earlier the question would never have occurred to me. Now, I wasn't so sure. This was a class operation.

I unbuttoned my coat and loosened my tie. "This place is something else," I said, and meant it.

"You said a mou—" Tim began, and checked himself. "Excuse me. You have to watch it around here or the double-entendres get a little thick on the ground. Uh . . . 'You said a great deal.' "

I was starting to like him. So what if he was a little kinky? It was none of my business, was it? "Around here, that's a double-entendre too, seems like."

He grinned. "You won't get an argument out of me."

Idly, I opened a locker. Hanging from a hook was a middy blouse and some girls' underwear. Not Frederick's of Hollywood stuff; I mean plain white cotton like real girls wear. Gym shorts and tee shirts were folded on the top shelf. I continued giving thought to being a Gym Teacher, and closed the locker. "The Lady must whack the johns pretty good to pay that well."

Tim's grin flickered. "We don't call them johns, Ken. We don't think of them as johns—or janes. Or tricks. They're clients."

"Sorry," I said.

"I heard the Lady say once that she'd call them 'patrons and patronesses,' if the word 'patronizing' didn't have such unfortunate connotations these days. But that's the relationship. We're performance artists, and they're patrons of the art. It just happens that about eighty percent of the time, the art involves orgasm for the client. And about the same for the artist."

My understanding was that prostitutes rarely really climax themselves. Female ones, anyway; I guess it'd have to be different for guys, wouldn't it? And—"Not a hundred percent? For the clients, I mean."

"Well, a few don't *want* orgasm. A small percentage of unfortunates aren't capable. And some folks get to having such a good time downstairs, they forget."

I tried to imagine having such a good time at a whorehouse that I forgot to get laid. I was beginning to understand what Lady Sally meant about rupture. Just about everything I thought I knew about whorehouses was wrong. Well, *here*, anyway. "Downstairs?"

"In the Parlor and the Lounges."

"Tell me about them."

"Ah, you must have come in the VIP entrance. Well, there are three others, two little Lounges and a big Parlor. It's the Parlor that's the most fun."

"Why three?"

"Some people that come to a House, especially newcomers, feel a little easier if they know that all the people they're going to meet of the opposite sex are artists. And some *prefer* to associate with their own sex. So we have a Male-Only and a Female-Only Lounge, with entrances on the east and west sides, respectively. Clients are asked to use discretion in cruising other clients there . . . but it isn't prohibited. But generally, the best party is the Parlor. We'll come to it, don't worry."

I grinned. " 'Get' to it, you mean. Those double-entendres again."

He smiled back. Then suddenly one eyebrow raised. "That's up to you, Mr. Taggart. Uh . . . the Gym Teacher's office is right over there . . . and the other boys have all gone to class. And if I don't pass Gym, my Dad is gonna *kill* me . . ."

Now here's a funny thing. I was *not* interested, okay? But I didn't get mad either, and I'm not sure I can tell you why. Maybe it was that he didn't make the offer as if he already knew the answer, if that makes any sense. I didn't feel insulted by it, any more than you'd be insulted if somebody offered you a Coke when you prefer Pepsi.

So there wasn't any anger to try and keep off my face. I studied his . . . and saw that he was not going to judge me, one way or the other, whatever I decided. So I used the rest of the second or two I had before I had to make some kind of response to let myself actually imagine what such a thing might be like—

—and I guess I must have blushed—for the first time in twenty years!—because he went right on smoothly, " . . . but the night is young, and you've got a lot to see. Maybe you'd rather continue the tour right now."

"If that's okay," I said.

"Sure," he said, and held the door for me. I took one last look around the place, thought briefly about what would have happened if a pretty girl had made me the same offer. Lady Sally was no fool. I went back out into the hall.

As we went by a door its red light went out, and it opened. A client came out, smiling beatifically, and gave us a friendly nod. I carefully avoided staring, just nodded back and kept on my way. As I got about three steps past, he registered. Long brown hair like a hippie. Big full beard too. Broad shoulders and sensitive features. Work shirt, jeans and beat-up boots. A carpenter's tool belt around his hips. And he was on a crutch . . .

I turned around to take a second look at him. He was gone. I hadn't heard the door open again . . .

Naaaaaaah.

I told myself not to get punchy, and turned around again and hurried after Tim.

"NEITHER Dungeon is in use at the moment," he said, "but I wouldn't go into Mistress Cynthia's without asking first. I'll show you Master Henry's. They're pretty much identical."

The door we went through was just like the others. But the room inside was made of immense grey stone blocks, genuine ones—which meant expensive floor reinforcement. But that was the least of its unusual aspects. It wasn't the kind of room you could take in at a glance.

Oh, a glance told you it was a dungeon. It looked like any movie dungeon you ever saw, with chains dangling from the walls and ceiling here and there, and a scattering of the usual props, cages and racks and bondage crosses and suspension rigs and so on. But there were a lot of gadgets I just plain couldn't figure out at first.

One, for instance, was simply a vertical pole, with what looked like a model of a steamboat's paddle wheel at its base. I recognized the object on the top of the pole, of course, but: "What would you want one that high off the ground for?"

Tim kind of twinkled. "That's the Stairway to Hell. Once Master Henry has someone perched up there, they kind of have to rest their weight on the wheel down below. Only the wheel *turns* . . ." He turned it with a foot to demonstrate. "So you sort of have to keep climbing, until Henry's good and ready to let you down. Which, of course, is the minute you say whatever code word you and he have worked out. It's an interesting sensation, for as long as you're enjoying it . . . and it does wonders for the calves and thighs."

I was a little distracted. When he'd turned the wheel, something had glowed briefly on the floor nearby. I had never seen a light bulb quite that shape before. It drew power from the treadmill through a long slender cord—presenting the treader with an interesting dilemma. "For the female clients only, I assume?" I asked, pointing.

"No, it can be used for men too, with a couple of rubber bands. But don't worry: an Olympic sprinter couldn't get it hot enough to really burn. Quite. Nothing in this room can really hurt you, no matter how much it looks like it, not if an expert like Henry's using it."

To each his own, I kept thinking to myself. I could think of a couple of people I'd like to see on the Stairway to Hell. But Tim made it sound like a roller coaster ride—"fun, while you're enjoying it." I glanced around the room to hide my confusion. "*That* looks kind of weird here. What's that gizmo there under . . . Oh!"

At first glance it was a kid's swing set, with a single swing. I noticed the two holes in the seat—the big keyhole-shaped one in the middle and the small bolt-sized hole just behind it—at the same time that I identified the "gizmo" on the floor just beneath it as another light bulb (this one a conventional heat-lamp) on a pole, wired to a wall socket. A second after that I noticed the spring-clips high up on either chain of the swing . . .

"That's another of Henry's endurance trips," Tim explained. "Once you're seated and slotted and the lamp's heated up underneath, you pretty much *have* to keep swinging. Henry likes setups that do a lot of the work for him. And he does enjoy the challenge of a moving target."

There was something else odd about the room. I stopped looking at individual items of equipment and tried to figure out what it was. Finally it came to me: the place didn't *smell* like a dungeon. I mean, I always expected one to smell kind of moldy and dank and sweaty and funky—and this smelled kind of more like a good hotel room. And there wasn't a bloodstain to be seen anywhere. Not even a fake one. I cast a quick glance over a sort of tool rack on the wall. "Some of that stuff looks like it could really lay a hurtin' on somebody."

"Improperly used, hell yeah," Tim agreed. "Henry generally asks the clients beforehand exactly how long they want to remember the experience afterward, and I've never known him to be off by as much as an hour. Ask him to let you sit in sometime: he can teach you more about the human nervous system than anyone but Mistress Cynthia. Even Doctor Kate asks him stuff sometimes."

A voice came out of the ceiling. The same one as in the Teenager's Bedroom, the invisible Mary. "Will you be much longer, Tim?"

He questioned me with his eyes, and said, "No, we're pretty much done here, Mary."

"Thanks, Tim. Henry and Brandi are on the way with a client."

"We're out of here."

We left and continued on down that amazing hall. "You've seen enough of the Function Rooms to get the idea," Tim said. "Now I'll show you my Studio. It's pretty typical."

"You have Studios, too?"

"Well, the Function Rooms are fun . . . but that much theater can get a little, I don't know, *elaborate* as a steady diet, don't you think? I'd say half of the clients that use them are newcomers. Generally they try half a dozen, then stick with one or two for a few more nights, and then they get it out of their systems and spend most of their time in a regular Studio. Or in the Parlor, some of them."

That reminded me of something. "You never did get around to saying what all this costs the clients."

He looked embarrassed. "Do you know, I don't know? It's different for everybody, I know that much. But I couldn't even guess at an average."

I stopped walking. "Different for everybody?"

He stopped obligingly too. We were just passing the top of a spiral staircase. Party sounds drifted up from below. "The first time a client comes here, Lady Sally interviews him or her in her office. At the end of the interview she names a fee. Flat rate, just like we're on salary. You get billed at the end of the month, I understand. I don't understand what she bases the rate on, but I do know it's subject to renegotiation if your financial situation changes one way or the other."

"What if a client doesn't tell Sally he got a raise?"

"He prays she doesn't find out, I guess. It doesn't happen often. Anyway, all I can tell you for sure is that some of my clients are stockbrokers, and some are waitresses or garment workers."

I found myself wondering what she charged PIs. I would have to ask, when all this was over. Maybe it would be smart to do a good job even if it didn't get me on staff here . . .

"That's the Women-Only Lounge just downstairs, by the way," Tim said. "You'll see the Men's Lounge later, and it's the same basic layout with different decor. It's over in the other wing."

I was slowly getting it through my head that this entire block-sized four-story building was *all* Lady Sally's House. How could you possibly finance something like this, pay the wages she did, and take busboys for clients? Then I remembered who had sent me here. It didn't take too many clients of that caliber to bring up an average.

Then I forgot all about the economics of Lady Sally's Place. Three people were coming up the hallway toward us, from the direction we were headed—and all of a sudden I realized one of them was holding a gun on the other two!

I started to go for my own heater, and remembered I was not heeled. He had me cold.

I was considerably more embarrassed than I had been back in the Locker Room when Tim had made his gentle pass—and mad at myself. *This*, I told myself, *is what happens when you start letting things surprise you. The first thing you know, some guy draws down on you and you don't even see it coming.* Yeah, Sally was going to be real happy with my work. Inside of fifteen minutes I managed to find the guy . . . and get taken by him. I felt adrenalin flowing . . .

Could I depend on Tim for assistance? On balance, I didn't think so. The guy with the piece looked like a real hardcase, shaved head and shoulders like a gorilla. The couple he was herding, an old guy and his young wife, looked terrified; they were both useless or worse, I planted my feet and got a good grip on the sap and tried to identify the caliber of the gun—

—and that was what really paralyzed me.

"Hi, Tim," the guy said as they all went past us.

"Henry," Tim said, nodding, "I see you brought dinner home."

"Rare," Henry agreed, and ushered his two prisoners into the Dungeon ahead of him. The old guy went in first—and as the girl followed, she turned her head and gave me a wink! The door closed behind them.

"That was Brandi," Tim said. "You'll like her. She's great."

I took a deep breath. "People shouldn't oughta point guns," I said very quietly.

Tim was instantly apologetic. "I'm sorry, Ken, I should have realized: you're new. Anyone else here would *know* it was a water pistol."

"Pretty damned realistic one." I was angry, that special kind you get when you know your anger isn't reasonable.

"Henry keeps it full of perfume. Bad perfume. People try hard not to get shot."

I let it go. "So Brandi is an artist too?"

"Yeah, a submissive like me. That poor client is going to have to sit there helplessly and watch while Henry does terrible things to his 'wife' . . . and I guarantee he'll be astonished by how much she likes it."

"And one client can tie up—I mean, occupy two artists at once? With no time limit?"

"If that's what he or she wants. Art takes whatever it takes. I don't know: I suppose if someone consistently wanted large numbers for unreasonable periods, the Lady might raise their rate. I'm not really sure."

Now I was baffled by economics again. Screw it: Lady Sally's finances were none of my concern. "Let's see that Studio."

"Well, we're actually out of the Function area now: all the rest of these are Studios. But mine is around the bend. This way."

We turned a corner at the end of the hall, and midway along that corridor passed another spiral staircase, much bigger than the last one, and with much more riotous party sounds drifting up from below. I smelled booze faintly, and tobacco even more faintly, and not much else. There was a live piano down there, somebody playing Hoagy Carmichael. "That's the Parlor," Tim said. "We'll be going down there soon. Don't worry, you can't miss anything: it's *always* fun there."

Just around the next bend to the left, into the wing paralleling the one I'd just seen, Tim stopped and opened a door. Inside was a studio apartment with bath.

I looked around, surprised yet again. It looked like just what I said, a studio apartment—a pretty nice one. Beer fridge. Stereo. Small TV on a mahogany dresser. (None of the three seemed to have a power cord. Sally must go through a lot of batteries.) An armchair and a closet. There was even a window, with nice curtains. The only unusual item visible was the large mirror on the ceiling over the bed—and it had a cloth tapestry covering it, with a cord dangling down near the head of the bed that let you pull away the tapestry if you wanted.

I opened the top drawer of the dresser experimentally, and now it was an artist's Studio. Very impressive selection. Same brand of condoms I use. The fur glove looked interesting. I closed the drawer and flicked on the TV. They always cop your attention, but this one tried harder than most. I shut it off again. "That closed circuit from somewhere else in the House?" I asked idly. I saw no cables of any kind.

Tim looked shocked. "Jesus, no! Anybody that likes to be watched can always go down to the Bower—I'll show you later. Anyone else here has their privacy respected, at all times."

"Is that right, Mary?" I asked.

"You're goddam right," she said from the center of the room.

"Mary has to keep an ear on the place," Tim said a little defensively. "What if a crazy got past all the screens, or a client had a heart attack? The rooms are all soundproof, they *have* to be. And yes, there are tape backups in case she gets distracted for a minute. But they're erased every week, and no one hears them except her and sometimes Lady Sally. And we try not to talk about it in front of clients if we can avoid it. The only way people can really relax here, Ken, is if they have confidence that nothing they say will leave the room."

"Well, that makes sense."

"I mean it. Clients are not used here against their will. If you like to work in places where they have hidden cameras, you're in the wrong place."

I realized he was really angry. "Look, I'm sorry. I didn't mean anything. I'm glad to hear it, okay?"

He relaxed. "Okay."

"No offense, Mary?"

"No offense," she agreed.

"So this is where you live, Tim?" I said, looking around again.

Again he looked shocked. "God, no! This is where I *work*, most of the time. My *apartment* is upstairs on the third floor with everybody else's. You've worked places where you had to sleep in the same room you worked in?"

"Well, I've heard of them," I temporized. "And this room doesn't look too hard to take."

"The one upstairs isn't a lot different," he agreed. "But it's *home*. This is more like the office." He smiled. "You're right, though, it's a pretty nice office. Want to see home?"

I guess it's silly that being invited to see a prostitute's home should feel somehow more intimate than being invited in to see his Studio. Well, it does, that's all. "Maybe a little later. I'm kind of curious to check out that Parlor."

"A much better deal," Tim agreed. "I'm a rotten house-keeper."

I glanced around. "Doesn't look like it to me."

"Oh, Robin keeps all the Studios tidy. Have you met him?"

"Uh, yeah."

"Well, let's go downstairs."

"In just a second," I said, and then waited.

So did he.

I lit a smoke, pocketed the lighter, and decided to get it off my chest. I was curious . . . and when would I ever get another chance to ask somebody? "Uh, Tim—"

"Just lucky, I guess."

"—huh?"

"Weren't you going to ask how a nice boy like me ended up in a place like this?"

"Well . . . close. Uh . . . look, I got no problem with gay—or bi, or whatever. I can kind of understand gay, I guess. I just don't understand the submissive thing." He didn't look offended . . . but he didn't take me off the hook, either. "Well, I mean, you're the first guy I knew to talk to that . . . uh . . . took that kind of work. I guess I was wondering if maybe you could, you know, explain it to me. Not what *happens*, I understand that part . . . I mean, how you could let some guy *do* stuff like that to you. If you don't mind my asking."

Look, I've got an image to think about, and part of me did feel silly, being apologetic to a masochist. But I found myself wanting to like the guy. That meant I either had to understand his kink, or make believe he didn't have it. A detective shouldn't ought to do that last one. So I asked careful.

And I guess I did it right, because he didn't get pissed off. He just gave it some thought, like if I'd asked him how come they put mailboxes in front of the post office, and then took a shot. "I guess," he said, "what I like best is the sense of being in control."

"Huh?"

"Calling the shots. Running things." He misunderstood my expression. "I know, pretty immature, huh? The Lady says not to worry, I'll outgrow it when I'm ready. She says it's not bad as power complexes go. I just love being the one who runs the fuck."

Paradoxes I was prepared to accept from this place, but outright contradictions seemed a little excessive.

This time he figured out my face. "Oh. You don't know what I'm talking about, do you? Don't feel bad: it surprises everybody the first time. It *is* sort of counterintuitive. You see, Ken, no one in any sexual relationship has as much control as the bottom in a dominance and submission scene. The tops are there to concentrate on producing intense but very specific sensations in *you*; their own are their own business. You're the complete center of attention, most of the time you're passive, you don't have to make any decisions, and all you really have to do is receive surprise gifts, from a rigidly and specifically limited menu of choices. The one thing you can be *certain* of is that if you say the First Word—or make the First Grunt, if you happen to be gagged—whatever is happening to you will ease off a notch . . . and if you say the Second Word, it will stop *instantly*."

"And sadists will all actually respect that? Every time?"

"Do you have any idea how hard it is to find a good bottom? Once you do, you don't want to risk annoying them. Oh hell, of course it's different with *real* sadists, outside in the world. The ones who aren't playing, I mean. But you go to any S&M club in the world, and tell me if you've ever heard anyone as apologetic and sheepish as a top who's just been given the First Word by a new bottom. Didn't you ever see some rich person take guff from a servant?"

"I guess."

"Once about five years ago a sicko managed to slip past Lady Sally somehow. Not interested in repeat trade. This happened to Brandi, not to me. The second time he ignored the First Word, Mary called Priscilla. During working hours, she's never more than sixty seconds away from anywhere on the second floor. They said it was twenty-seven seconds from the call until Pris arrived. He was just ignoring the Second Word. Pris . . . well, let's just say she broke something. But that was *after* she hit the quick-release knots and turned Brandi loose."

"What if they hadn't been quick-release knots?"

"She'd have been upstairs sooner—before the second one was tied."

"What happened to the guy?"

"The Lady gave him a permanent invitation to the world. Had him tossed out on the sidewalk and barred for life. Nowadays I imagine he spends his nights in search of a woman with a right-angle bend."

I winced, and shifted my Lucky to the other side of my mouth as if smoke in my eye had caused the wince.

"Sort of poetic justice, really. I mean, if penetration is possible at all for him, it must require extreme cooperation."

Time to change the subject. "So anyway, what you're saying is, nothing happens to you here that you don't enjoy?"

He nodded. "That's it. It just happens that I enjoy a slightly more exotic range of sensations than most people."

"I guess right there is what I don't get. I mean, to me, pain *hurts*. And fear is scary."

"Me, too. If I stub my toe on the way into the Dungeon, I swear as loud as anybody—and I'm terrified when I walk through Times Square, say. But pain and fear are slippery things to define, Ken. So is enjoyment. Have you ever been on a roller coaster?"

"Sure."

"Did you 'enjoy' it?"

I took a drag, and didn't answer right away.

"Ever get pinched during sex, harder than you'd tolerate from a chiropractor, and like it?"

"Well—"

"Or have you ever been in danger, been under fire or something, and realized part of you was enjoying it?"

Oof. He was getting close to where I lived, now. That was half the fun of being a PI: those occasional adrenalin-charged moments on the edge, dancing with Death . . . living fully and totally, at the edge of the void. I remembered the faint sense of *disappointment* I'd felt, just for a split second, when I'd realized that it was a water pistol Henry was packing, the brief feeling of having been cheated.

"I guess," I said slowly. "I guess I just never thought of combining that with sex."

"Neither do most folks. Lady Sally has over forty artists on staff at the moment—and two of us are submissives, and two dominant."

"Wait a second—what about that Robin guy?"

"Oh, Robin's not an artist! He's a *client*. Probably the most devoted customer Lady Sally has."

"Oh."

"And I'm not exclusively submissive either . . . because there just isn't enough demand to keep me busy full-time at it. One thing you'll find out here is that pretty much nobody is anything exclusively. Even Cynthia and Henry have clients who just want to go into a Studio with them; the flavor is enough for them."

"But Cynthia and Henry never go submissive."

"Well, back when they were training, sure: you can't be a really *good* top if you've never been a bottom. But they don't take that role any more these days, no. I guess it's like me with my power hangup: one day they'll relax a little too, maybe, but in the meantime there are people that need them, and vice versa. Their business."

I nodded. "I just want to get this straight. You submit to, uh, male and female clients, both? And Brandi too?"

"Right, and Cyn and Henry switch-hit too. No pun intended. I'd say a little more than half of the male artists are bisexual at least occasionally—and about ninety percent of the women. But Lady Sally has nothing against monosexuals. She says the only real perversions are nymphomania, satyriasis and celibacy, and she even tolerates them in the House."

"Don't you artists worry a lot about AIDS? And other VD?"

"Sure. But most of what happens here is safe sex. And every client has to leave a blood sample with Doctor Kate, before their first visit and once a month thereafter—once a week if they're into risky practices. On the rare sad occasions when someone tests positive, we restrict them to safe-sex only . . . and if it's AIDS, we send them to Ruth. She's good at counselling the dying. So far we've never had an artist infected with anything worse than crabs."

I began to feel somewhat easier in my mind about this whole thing. If you'd have told me an hour before that I'd ever find myself a little sheepish about being straight . . . "Is it all right if I ask, Tim: how did you get to the place where you found you didn't mind a little pain?"

He smiled gently. "I don't think I know you well enough to tell that story, Ken. Yet. I rarely tell it voluntarily. People usually have to make me . . ."

Oh. "Oh. Well, maybe another time, then." I thought to myself that if I had my druthers, I'd ruther ask Brandi the same question. But I had to admit I was intellectually curious. A little, anyway . . .

"Right, I'm supposed to be showing you around. But I'll give you a quick, short answer for now: one day I figured out it is absolutely impossible to rape someone who refuses to withhold consent."

I was going to have to think about that one.

"All right, enough of the second floor," he went on. "Time for you to see the Parlor."

True enough. I'd been in a bordello for something approaching an hour, and with the exception of a flash-glimpse of the Cardinal's Companion (most of her obscured by his robes), all the women I'd seen so far had been fully dressed. Surely things would be different at an orgy. "Sounds good to me. Uh . . . is there any easy way I can tell the, uh, clients from the artists?"

He looked surprised, and gave it some thought. "I don't see how. But it won't matter. If you see someone you want, just ask politely if they'd like to go upstairs with you. Since no money changes hands, it doesn't make much difference if you guess wrong."

I still had a little capacity for surprise left. "The Lady doesn't mind if a couple of artists goof off together?"

"Ken, as far as I can tell, Lady Sally doesn't mind anything human beings can do that doesn't involve former food or former people. If two artists started spending a *lot* of time together *during working hours*, she might talk to them long enough to make sure they realize they're falling in love; maybe suggest they consider working a double act. But an isolated incident or two she'd chalk off to employee morale, as long as there weren't customers being ignored. She's easy to work for—if you be straight with her."

"I'm beginning to get that through my head," I agreed. I stubbed out my cigarette. "Okay, on to the Parlor."

As we went back outside, I saw two people in the hall. The one I saw first, facing me, was why the preacher danced.

She was blonde, five-six, maybe one-forty. She was wearing slippers. A real blonde, or a thorough fake. Now *this* was more like what I'd been expecting when I started. I controlled my face and walked forward . . .

Within a few steps I had registered her companion: an American Indian, with long straight hair in an embroidered headband, and a profile like you used to see on nickels. He was replacing one of the little red peanut bulbs next to a door. As I approached, the blonde handed him the new bulb. It was an interesting thing to watch.

"Greetings, Many Hands," Tim said, and the Indian nodded gravely. "Hi, Arethusa. I want you guys to meet Ken Taggart. He might be coming to work here."

The Indian nodded again . . . and Arethusa came into my arms and kissed me.

I don't know how long it lasted. I remember thinking that she wasn't completely naked after all: in addition to the slippers, she was wearing a mild, pleasant perfume. I remember thinking that her double-breasted suit beat mine all to hell. And there was a time when I wasn't thinking anything at all.

She stepped back finally and smiled. "You're certainly equipped for it," she said positively. "Welcome aboard, Ken: I hope you decide to stay. Time we had some fresh . . . uh . . . blood around here."

"Thanks," I said. "You make it attractive." She dimpled nicely.

"We're just on our way to the Parlor," Tim explained.

"Well, if that doesn't do it, nothing will," she agreed. "Maybe I'll see you later, Ken."

"It wouldn't surprise me," I said. Tim collected a kiss of his own, shorter than mine but just as intense, then turned her loose and led the way onward. She didn't move aside as I brushed past.

We turned the corner and headed for the big spiral staircase. "What did you say her name was?" I whispered to Tim. "I didn't catch it."

"Arethusa," he said, and spelled it for me. "It may be the loveliest name I've ever heard for a blonde artist. It was the name of a nymph in classical antiquity. Now it means an orchid, *Arethusa Bulbosa*—which you have to admit is a pretty accurate description—and the books say that orchid is characterized by a 'solitary rose-purple flower fringed with yellow.' Is that great or what?"

I had to grin. "You're right. That's the best—" The penny dropped, and I stopped in my tracks at the top of the staircase. "Hey!"

"What?" Tim asked innocently.

I sighed. "All right. God damn it. I get it. What's the Indian's *real* name?"

Many Hands make light work. Right . . .

I guess it was sort of the equivalent of the berry juice thing, but the employees' version. And again I had passed. He grinned wickedly, and slapped me on the back. "You'll do just fine here, Ken. Just wanted to see if you were paying attention. Believe it or not, his real name is He Wears Funny Hats. 'Hats' for short."

"People make puns around here, huh?" I guess even Paradise has to have flaws.

"If you're thinking of working here, it's only fair to warn you," he admitted. "The Lady has a sign downstairs saying, 'No phanerogams in the Parlor, please,' for instance."

"That one I don't get. *What* kind of gams?"

"No, no. It's another scientific term. Means, 'one with visible reproductive organs.' And if you ever want to tickle the Lady, tell her she's 'spathic.' It's a geologist's term for rocks; it means, 'having good cleavage.' As you can see, working here isn't *always* easy."

"Well, you picked a good time to tell me. That was nice perfume Arethusa had on." I don't know, the segue made sense to me.

"*That* perfume," he said, grinning archly, "she *always* has on."

"Seriously, I just realized: I've smelled perfume a few times so far . . . and it just came to me, it's always the same one."

"Oh sure," he said. "We all vote on the house perfume once a week. You have to: you wouldn't believe the cacophony of smells you'd get out here in the hallway otherwise."

I was slowly getting it through my head that there were subtleties to this artist business that I had never considered. I thought all you needed was an adequate supply of clean sheets.

"Let's go downstairs," I said.

4. Run, Dick, Run...

Medio de fonte leporum
Surgit amari liquid quod in ipsis floribus angat.

—LUCRETIUS, *translated by Byron as*

Still from the fount of Joy's delicious springs
Some bitter o'er the flowers its bubbling venom
  flings.

THAT gag about "phanerogams" had warned me not to expect skin in the Parlor. So there was nothing at all about it that disappointed me.

Think of the very best party you were ever at. Now imagine one fifty percent better. You would leave that party early to come to the Parlor.

If you were ever lucky enough to have the opportunity.

Maybe it wasn't really Hoagy Carmichael himself playing "Huggin' and A-Chalkin' " on the piano in the corner. It could have been an old guy who looked just like him. Have you met a lot of guys who look just like Hoagy Carmichael, though? If he'd sung something instead of just playing while others sang, I could have told for sure, but he never did. The knot of people around the piano didn't seem to treat him like a celebrity. They just sang along, joyfully.

On that night in history, perhaps I should add, Mr. Carmichael had been dead for three years. According to public record, anyway . . .

All right, I guess I should describe the room first. It was merely impressive, mostly.

To start with, that big iron spiral staircase was so magnificent I wouldn't be surprised if Bette Davis dropped by once in a while just to descend it. The Parlor it led down to was enormous, one of the biggest rooms I ever saw in New York. I don't know the words for the kind of paneling and carpet and the decor and that, but it looked like the kind of place where Senators would gather for a quiet one after a hard day. Class all the way. It had a high ceiling and a terrific ventilation system. There were *two* bars, along the north wall, separated by three doorways, labeled, "Private," "Bower," and "Staff." Each bar looked well stocked and was doing brisk business. I did see the phanerogam sign Tim had mentioned, on the south wall. There were pictures on the walls here and there, but there wasn't one of them you couldn't have given your maiden aunt for a present. All around the acres of hardwood floor were rugs and little islands of comfortable upholstered furniture arranged to allow small conversational groups to form. There was a big crackling fireplace in the west wall, big enough to turn an ox on a spit, burning logs the size of depth charges. In either corner of the south wall were a pair of washrooms, marked with the symbols for male and female, and in the center of that wall was a door that must have led to a reception area and coat check just inside the south entrance. The only thing you could call really surprising about the physical layout was a subtle one: for the life of me I could not locate the source of the bright lighting.

That was the place. The party that was taking place in it started out surprising and got more so.

At first I took in groups. About ten by the piano, half a dozen by the fireplace, another dozen or so at the bars, maybe another couple of dozen scattered here and there around the room. I did not see anyone who didn't look happy. It seemed to be an unusually international crowd: I saw members of just about every human race, color or nationality, and heard snatches of conversation in several languages, although English predominated. Nothing too surprising yet; but as I began to resolve individuals out of the crowd, my eyes got bigger and my jaw started to get heavier and heavier. I guess you could say the surprises built to damn near a climax. Here is what I saw, pretty much in the order I saw it in:

—three U.S. Marines in full uniform minus swords or sidearms, standing at ease and listening with respectful attention to a bag lady. She was leaning on a supermarket cart and pointing to something inside it that seemed to please her a lot.

—a priest chatting with a statuesque Chinese girl in a slit-thigh gown with startling decoll . . . decko . . . half her tits were showing; as I noticed them (the priest and the brunette, I mean), she said something that cracked him up. They seemed to be playing chess, but they were using cookies of assorted shapes as markers, and seemed to have eaten all the captured pieces.

—a big guy with three days' growth of beard, dressed like a biker, arm-wrestling at one of the bars with a stockbroker type in grey cashmere; each had a uniformed cop cheering him on, and the stockbroker was winning. I noticed his watch: it looked like the big old vest pocket stem-winder kind, but strapped to his wrist somehow.

—an Arab, with one of those headdresses and everything, arm in arm with a Hasidic Jew, both laughing like hell and doing an absurd dance for a female midget dressed from neck to toes in black leather.

—a small group surrounding a man and a woman, sitting as far as they could get from the fireplace and piano. As I watched, the man took a deep drag on a cigar, paused, and blew smoke carefully. The smoke took on the shape of Alice in Wonderland. Authentic, just like in the cartoon, only pale grey. She shimmered there in the air—the terrific ventilation system didn't seem to be working in that part of the room—seemed to put something in her mouth, and then gradually she shrank. People clapped softly, and the guy inclined his head modestly. The girl sitting next to him took a drag on her own cigar, and blew a Cheshire cat. As it rose up past Alice, it lifted one leg and broadened its smile. It faded until only the smile was left, and then that dissipated too. There was louder applause, particularly from a group of Japanese onlookers, and the guy saluted her; being topped didn't seem to bother him.

—some old white-haired guy and his redheaded wife in full formal evening wear, *ice-skating* around the Parlor in each other's arms. Very well, too. Well, she was terrific; he did okay but his spine was just a little too stiff. He looked like a retired admiral. I couldn't get a good look at their skates, but they didn't leave any tracks in the polished floor; there must have been little recessed wheels or ball bearings along the bottom of those blades or something. People wandered through their dance without disturbing it. As they came by me I saw the old boy was grinning wolfishly, tears leaking from his tired old eyes. I thought I heard him saying something about "the Sprite that the Ice Gods choose," but neither of them was drinking anything.

—over there among the crowd at the piano, watching the Old Perfesser's hands—

Arethusa!

I hadn't even stepped off the last tread of the spiral staircase yet. I had left her behind me no more than twenty seconds ago, and she had not passed me. Even that stairway was not so wide that I would have missed a naked blonde going past.

And she was no longer naked. She wore . . . well, I don't know how to describe women's dresses, and it was complicated. It looked like the two people with the cigars blew it and then spray-painted it purple. If they didn't, it must have taken her more than twenty seconds to put it on. I wished I'd seen that. I wondered how long it took to take it off. Also she was now wearing earrings, and what looked like real pearls, and high heels and stockings. And her hair was styled a little differently, back off her forehead.

She looked up and caught me staring at her, smiled warmly, and left the group by the piano to come meet me. I stepped down off that last step. By the time she reached me I had my face under control, and was annoyed with myself for being so startled. Obviously this was Arethusa's twin sister. That gave rise to the speculations you would expect it to. I was just about to introduce myself, with an opening line guaranteed to charm the drawers off a lady judge in open court, when she came into my arms and said, "See? I told you I'd see you later, Ken." She settled herself against me. "Still thinking of me, I see—how flattering! You're gonna *like* working here, I can tell."

Fortunately she kissed me then, so I didn't have to worry about my face.

It was as involving a kiss as the last one had been. The dress didn't get in the way at all. The longer it went on, the more time I had to think.

The kiss itself was one of the things I thought about. She remembered what I had liked the last time, and started with that. I was forced to abandon the trial hypothesis that the invisible Mary had somehow passed a message about me down to Arethusa's twin in the Parlor. Even if you assumed Mary had some way to speak privately to someone at arm's length from a honky-tonk piano and half a dozen lustily singing people, there simply hadn't been *time* to convey information of this level of complexity.

Ergo, this was Arethusa in my arms.

Just like with the Favila case, I refused to reject my conclusion merely because it was preposterous. Arethusa had the ability to teleport through solid floors, materializing clothes around her as she went that would have taken a normal woman an hour to put on. Okay. Fine. Interesting, sure . . . but in all honesty, not really as interesting as her ability at kissing . . .

An indeterminate time later she let go of my lips and tilted her head back. "I do like a man who gives number one hugs," she said contentedly.

"As opposed to, like, a number two?" I asked, wondering vaguely if I was being insulted; and if so, if I minded.

"No, the other kind of hug is a letter A," she explained, "where you're touching right up at the top, but the further down you go, the farther apart you get, like an A. It's like shaking fingertips. Well, what do you think of the Parlor?"

I was going to say something about not having had a chance to really take it all in yet, but just then the Universe cleared its throat, gently reminding me that it existed. "Excuse me, Tim," I said. "Uh—why don't you grab a beer or something and I'll come get you when I'm ready to move on, okay?"

"As soon as I get *my* kiss," he said, not at all submissively, and I stepped back. As before, their kiss was short but dense, compressed. She pinched his butt as she let him go, and he tousled her hair. "Take your time, Ken," he told me.

"What time does the place close?" I asked.

"Sometime later this year, I understand," he said, and headed off to the west bar. I thought he was kidding.

"You look like you could use a quick one yourself," Arethusa said.

I tried for a gag myself. "Maybe after I've had a drink."

"If you like," she said agreeably, and I realized she hadn't meant what I'd thought she meant.

How much did I want that drink?

As I hesitated, torn between my duty to explore Lady Sally's House and my desire to explore Lady Sally's House, I felt a tug at my pants, just below my right knee. Assuming it was the lady midget in leather, I turned and bent to tell her that I didn't dance, but it wasn't her. It was a fairly large German shepherd. He blinked up at me and released my pant leg.

"Egsguze me, ffella," he said politely, "bud you're blocking ze sstairvay."

"I'M terribly sorry," I said, and stepped out of the way.

Well, I had just accepted a teleporting blonde, hadn't I? In a House like this, a talking dog was more or less to be expected. Odd I hadn't run into him sooner. I do remember thinking, *well,*

I'll be a son of a—but I had the sense not to say it.

"No broblem," he said. "Hi, Are'dusa."

"Hi, Ralph," she said, and bent to scratch behind his ears. He accepted it with enormous gravity. Well, I would have too. "This is Ken. He might be working here."

"Bleazed to meet you," he said, and gave me his paw. "You'll lige it here, Ken. Zere issn't a real bitch on ze whole sstaff. I perzonally guarantee it. If zere vass, I might haff been ze first sson in hisstory to giff my paw to my Maw." He . . . well, barked with laughter.

I shook his paw but made no reply. I couldn't think of one.

"Dit I dell you, Are'dusa," he went on, "zat I've come up viss a way to get rich?"

"Another one?" she asked.

"*Jawohl*. I'm goink to zell a line uff dogvood made ffrom ssmall birdss."

"And you'll call it—"

" 'Wren Din-Din,' " he said, and scampered up the staircase before she could kick him.

I stood right where I was, and when I could speak, I said, "I'm not so sure I want to work here any more."

Ice began to form at the corners of Arethusa's eyes. "Oh, yeah?" she said with a dangerous purr in her voice. "You don't think dogs can be people? Not even talking ones?"

"You don't get me," I said, trying, for my pride as a tough guy, not to blurt. I didn't want her mad at me. "Where I come from, anyone who says 'Excuse me' is a human being. What I mean is, people who make puns like that shouldn't be tolerated in a respectable whorehouse. 'Many Hands,' okay, that was clever— but that one was just *disgusting*."

She relaxed. "Well, I can't argue there. Sorry if I took you wrong, Ken. Ralph's a kind of a bigot-detector, and once in a while he turns one up even here. No offense."

"None taken. Uh . . . Lady Sally told me to be 'tolerant of anything you find strange.' I'm working on it."

"Gee," she said thoughtfully. "I can't remember the last time I thought something was strange—around here, I mean. That's strange . . ."

I found that I had reached a decision about which to have first, a drink or Arethusa. Definitely the drink first. Possibly a flock of them. "As I was drinking—" I said, and steered us to the east bar.

As we were being served Irish coffees—which they called "God's Blessings" there for some reason—by one of the only really good-looking transvestites I ever saw, Priscilla came out of the door marked "Bower." She did it so discreetly somehow that not many people noticed, even though she had a fat soaking-wet cop over her shoulder in a fireman's carry and his uniform cap clutched in one hand.

But it did rearrange things slightly where Arethusa and I were. The bartender calmly grabbed a mop and went to take care of the trail of water Pris was leaving behind her . . . and the two uniforms I'd seen kibitz the arm-wrestling earlier both said "Oh shit" in the same weary tone at the same instant, and moved off to follow Pris.

I put my hand on the sap and started to go after them, but Arethusa restrained me. "It's all right," she assured me.

Sure enough, when the two cops caught up with Pris near the exit, I saw them apologize to her. (I can read lips, did I mention? Gun went off next to my ear once, and for a month I thought I'd *have* to.) I even saw Pris turn her head and say to the woman cop, "Not your fault." And the cop hurried to get the door for her. The other cop ran ahead through the reception room and got the outer door too. The woman cop let go of her door as soon as she could to keep the draft out of the joint, but I had time to see Pris somehow sling the fat cop down off her shoulder and *loft* him underhand toward the sidewalk outside. She was a good six feet from the door at the time; it was uncertain whether the cop was going to clear the steps outside or not when my view was cut off by the closing inner door.

I glanced around. Except for the bartender and the two buttons, nobody seemed to have paid the slightest attention. These people were enjoying themselves too much to lose their concentration for a little thing like a uniformed buzzer getting eighty-sixed by an Amazon. The two smoke artists were delighting their Japanese fans with a battle between Godzilia and Rodan; flashbulbs went off like popcorn.

"None of those cops were wearing gunbelts or sticks," I said to Arethusa.

"It wouldn't have made any difference if they had," she said. "But no, the only kind of heat that anybody ever carries in here is nonmetallic and non-deadly." She grinned, beautifully. "Usually."

"And it's of very high caliber," I said, and she pinched me.

"We will stop right there," she said firmly. "There are enough sexual puns on weapons to waste a week—and if we get started, people might decide we 'shouldn't be tolerated in a respectable whorehouse.' "

Pris came back in, talking soothingly to the two disgraced cops, and all three stepped around the transvestite bartender with his mop. I turned back to the bar and took a big gulp of my cooling Irish coffee. Irish coffee sort of forces you to drink fast. It's not much good cold. Well, not as good. Arethusa took a big sip of her own, and licked whipped cream off her upper lip. It looked like something to do. So I did.

Sure enough, it was good.

When you got that close to her eyes, you could see they weren't really blue. Closer to purple. And little lavender flecks at about four o'clock in the left pupil. Her right, I mean. She blinked slower than anybody I ever saw.

For probably the first time since the ninth grade, it came to me that my breath might not be kissing sweet, and I pulled back away from her upper lip. With some difficulty.

When she spoke, I was terribly afraid she was going to ask me if I knew how much I looked like the guy on the TV news. But she didn't. "So tell me, Ken," she said, so softly I could hardly hear her amid the party noise, "have you worked before?"

"Well, not strictly speaking, not exactly, not what you'd call 'worked,' no. Certainly not in any place like this." I looked around at it. The woman with the cigar was just blowing a killer whale; as I watched, it waved its tail lazily and spouted smoke from its blowhole. Her companion blew a flock of dolphins to swim playfully around it. Whoever that guy at the piano was, he knew a real good arrangement for "Stardust." "And if you want to hear a manly confession, I'm really starting to sweat whether I'm going to make the cut or not."

She started to smile, and switched it to something more sympathetic. "Oh, Ken, don't worry! I remember when I first saw this place. By the time I'd finished the tour, I thought they were going to make me build a ship in a bottle with my tongue for an audition. Really, to work here there's only one thing you have to know."

"Just *one*?" I said dubiously.

"Well, yeah. But I admit it's a little tough to really learn how."

"Okay, I'm ready."

"Pay attention," she said.

I waited to be sure that was it, and said, "That's it?"

"That's it. Pay attention. You're being paid money; pay back attention. Real, close attention. Everything else happens naturally."

"Paying attention I'm good at," I said.

"I believe you are."

I finished my Irish coffee and reached a decision. "Arethusa? Look, I've seen the Discreet section, the whole second floor, and this place, and I'll pass on the stag and doe Lounges for now. How much have I got left to see?"

She closed one eye and poked the tip of her tongue out of one corner of her mouth, an expression which sounds silly and was utterly charming on her. "Let's see. There's the cafeteria downstairs; it's mostly just for staff, and exceptionally nice customers on good behavior—"

"I've seen a cafeteria," I said.

"And there's the Bower, of course. That's pretty striking."

"What's it like?"

"Well, there are four rules in the Bower. Take no for an answer; if there's a beef, you both leave *at once*; no information acquired in the Bower ever leaves; and don't pee in the pool. Other than that, pretty much anything goes. You'll like it: it's real pretty in there. Everything's *soft*. And warm."

"Well . . ."

"Are you shy, Ken? In groups, I mean? Don't worry if you are—a lot of people who work here feel like that. The Bower's not mandatory or anything. The Lady says the only thing mandatory around here is, 'Be kind.' And the Bower's not like a writer's workshop: it's okay to just watch."

"Later, I think. I've seen a lot already tonight."

"Well, all that's left are the apartments on the third floor—"

"Would you show me yours?"

She smiled, and finished her Irish coffee. For some crazy reason the smile reminded me of the drawing of a crossbow. "If you'll show me yours."

She led the way up the spiral staircase.

Have you ever watched a good-looking woman, dressed in cobwebs by Buckminster Fuller, walk up a spiral staircase ahead of you? Do I have to tell you she had my full attention? Stairs seemed to slide by under my feet as if I were standing on one of those wheelchair elevator platforms. Surreptitiously, I used a breath spray. We levitated to the second floor—no, I levitated, she was climbing—and she led me through a door into a regular stairwell. By the time we drifted up to the top of that, I seemed to have her in my arms like a bride to be carried across a threshold. As we stepped out into another hallway I kissed her, and somehow she steered me with the kiss in the direction of her room. It seemed like a short walk before she kissed: *this one*, and let go of me with one hand to open the door for us. I pushed it closed behind us with my back, and I swear it was the instant it clicked shut, louder than I expected, that the five extraordinary things happened.

To me four of them seemed to occur simultaneously, but I'll take them in reverse order of urgency:

First, then, a sudden powerful draft made my hair flutter.

At the same time, the door *squirmed* under my back.

As that happened, I felt a ghostly tug at my pants pocket, as if a really good pickpocket had touched my blackjack and wallet, shifted them just enough to identify them, and decided not to take either, all in a split second.

And before I could really register any of this, somebody whacked me across the head with a two-by-four.

From *behind* . . .

I'm a PI: I grasped at once that I had been hit over the back of the head. I knew just what to do. I dropped Arethusa—telling myself she almost had to land on a soft part; she'd roll out of the way before I toppled over onto her—and waited for the flood tide of blackness to rise up and crash over me, to drag me down deeper and ever deeper into the bottomless whirlpool that sucks all the woes of the world down its whirling vortex into a place of endless peace and dark . . .

NO such luck. That was the fifth extraordinary thing.

I know, in the books and movies the PI always loses consciousness when somebody whacks his skull. There are places on the skull where even a gentle rap will reliably drop a man—but the back of the skullbone is not one of them. Try it yourself. Borrow a blackjack from your mother and sap a random sample of ten guys, as hard as you like. I'll bet you fifty bucks not more than four of them go down.

Of course, I'll also bet that at least one of *them* will be dead within twenty-four hours, from subdural something or other. It means you start bleeding inside your head. Your skull doesn't get any bigger just because there's more stuff in it now, and pretty soon there's no room for brains.

If it had been up to me, I'd have lost consciousness. My goddam head *hurt*. But like I said, no such luck.

So that meant I had to catch the son of a bitch and express my irritation. Tabling for the present the matter of how he had sapped me through a solid wooden door, I spun on my heels and yanked it open—managing to miss Arethusa with it—and sprang into the corridor, slamming the door behind me for her protection.

Nothing to my right but closed doors, all the way down to a stairwell that was not hissing slowly closed. So I turned left and sprinted flat out. It hurt like crazy to run, my brain pulsed like a big grey heart, but I was willing to accept that inconvenience in exchange for the pleasure of getting my hands on the guy that had caused it. I thundered along, cornered to the right, and kept running.

The door we'd come up through was not hissing closed either, so he hadn't used it. I ran on past, making real good time now, and cornered again. Another long hallway of closed doors. I began to lose momentum, and before long I slowed to a halt, frustrated and baffled. Somehow I was certain he had not ducked into any of the apartments—Mary would hear him if he did, maybe that's how I figured—so that meant he was gone. How, I wasn't sure, any more than I knew how he had hit me through a closed door.

But my first-order hypothesis was that he was a teleport, just like Arethusa. So maybe she could help me figure it out. I turned to retrace my steps back to her apartment in the other wing—

—and as I rounded the first corner into the connecting corridor again, the stairwell she and I had used opened, and Arethusa came out, naked as an egg and looking annoyed as hell. "What is your major malfunction?" she snapped at me. "Get back in there and pick me up."

"Give me a minute, okay?" I said, or tried to, but it came out, "Guinea a midget, oh ho?" I tried to smile an apology, and felt my lips fall off.

And *then* I lost consciousness.

A flood tide of blackness rose up and crashed over me, dragging me down deeper and ever deeper into the bottomless whirlpool that sucks all the woes of the world down its whirling vortex into a place of endless peace and dark . . .

5. See the Spot Jump...

So isn't it a pity, when we common people chat-
ter of those mysteries to which I have referred,
That we use for such a delicate and complicated
matter
Such a very short and ordinary word?

—ANONYMOUS

COOL wetness occurred, somewhere downtown of my nose.

I remembered something you could do with wetness, and tried it. It worked: the wetness went from where it was to someplace else, just as expected. I was proud of myself.

Swallowing. That was what it was called.

I recognized the wetness. I had known some of it before, back when I lived on Earth—

That reminded me of my former life as a human being, and I opened my eyes. Major mistake. The moment I did, twin spears of light were thrust through the sockets and into my skull. They rooted around amid the weeds and mangrove roots at the back, located the football of pain I had been ignoring, and dragged it between them up to the forefront of my attention. I tried to scream, and mewed like a dreaming kitten.

"Easy, now," a familiar voice said. "Have another sip; you'll feel better."

The wetness came again, and I took another swallow.

"Painapple gripefruit," I said weakly, and forced my eyes to focus. Arethusa was looking at me with pity and compassion on her lovely face. In a universe of awfulness, it was something to hang on to. Even though I was seeing double.

"What did you say?" another voice asked urgently.

"The juice," I said. "It's fineapple greatpoop."

59

That didn't sound just right, so I tried again. "Grainapple pipefruit." Still not right. "Dammit, I mean 'poonapple grapefright.' You know damn well what I mean."

A warm hand took my pulse. From the angle of approach it was not Arethusa's, so I turned my head to identify the owner, and my head fell off and bounced. I squeaked in embarrassment.

When it stabilized, it seemed to be back on my shoulders again, and its right eyelid was being peeled way open, apparently by the same hand that had taken my pulse. I focused again—have to do everything twice around here—and saw a beautiful redhead. She wore a blue silk kimono loosely tied at the waist, a white lace teddy underneath it, and a stethoscope. "Tell me the name of the juice one more time," she said.

"Pry . . . pie nah pull grapefruit," I said, and smiled. I could tell I was rallying fast: the double vision was gone now. "See? I can ray it sight if I twos chew," I said confidently. Then I frowned.

So did she.

"What's the matter with him, Kate?" Arethusa asked.

"He's spooning in Speakerisms," the redhead said. "I think that means he's got a concussion. We ought to get him to a hospital."

"No!" I screamed, so loud they actually heard me. "No hospital."

"Why not?" Lady Sally's voice asked reasonably. Crowded in here.

"I've been in hospitals," I said. "They take away your pants. Then they hurt you and starve you and expose you to disease. Then they bill you for it. A lot."

"You're not wrong," the Lady agreed. "And you're not spooking in Speanerisms any more, either."

"Your Ladyship," Kate the redhead insisted, "he really ought to be—"

"What can a hospital give him that we can't, Doctor?" Lady Sally interrupted.

So Kate was an MD, huh? Well, it figured there'd be one on staff. I'd just never realized the doc might double as an artist.

"Well, constant monitoring, for one thing—"

"That's no problem," Arethusa said positively. I turned to look at her, and realized I was still seeing double—but only when I looked at Arethusa. Maybe I really was in trouble . . .

"Look, Arie, the Lady has a business to run—"

"But Kate—I *always have spare time*. As you know."

Strange as it may sound, that made a weird kind of sense. Because the Arethusa on the left said everything up to "spare time," and the one on the right added the "As you know."

SHE wasn't a teleport! Nothing so exotic as that atall. Just a pair of garden-variety telepathic twins. How silly of me to have thought she was remarkable.

And since she was both . . . that is, since both twins were named Arethusa, that meant they thought of herself as one person. If you follow. I was willing to bet they only took a single salary from Lady Sally; I mean, how could they have separate bank accounts? Arethusa—as any telepathic set of twins naturally would—thought of herself as a single person who happened to have two bodies available. So from her point of view she could spend all her time taking care of me, and still earn her paycheck.

I don't think I can take much credit for being able to believe stuff this weird without boggling. I'd sort of been prepared. After a talking dog, or an invisible man with an impossible two-by-four, what's a bicorporal harlot? No big deal. Maybe being hit on the head even helped.

WHILE I worked all this out, the argument finished without me: Kate said a hospital had equipment for sudden emergencies standing by, and Lady Sally said Kate knew damn well the crash cart always takes at least five minutes to arrive, and Pris could have me in Kate's OR in under two, or the nearest Emergency Room in five flat. So finally Doctor Kate settled for inflicting all the indignities she had handy on me, lasers through the pupils, blood-pressure cuff, blood samples, injections of this and that, you know the kind of stuff they do. Give her credit, the end of that stethoscope was warm. First time that ever happened. And even a doctor's routine loses a little bit of the sting if the doctor is a beautiful redhead dressed in a lace teddy and a silk kimono. Somebody ought to tell the AMA about that. All in all I'd have to say Kate was as nice about everything as a doctor can be and still annoy you enough to make you get well.

I know you probably won't believe it, but the words "bedside manner" never once went through my head. That night, anyway. Maybe the place was refining my wisecrack-generator a little. Most people, I think, left Lady Sally's House a little more sophisticated, with a little more class, than when they went in.

When Kate was done, and reluctantly pronounced me worth keeping, Lady Sally thanked her and sent her back to her other work. She asked Arethusa if they would step outside for a few minutes, and they did, apologizing to me first for snapping at me out in the hall. I told them to forget it.

When the door closed behind them, the Lady sat by my bedside and took my hand. Hers was warm and soft and strong. I noticed for the first time that I was in a bunk bed—that I was in the Teenager's Bedroom where I had first met her. No wonder I felt so relaxed. "Joe, I'm very sorry," Lady Sally said. "What happened to you was my fault."

"Hey," I said, "I knew the job was dangerous when I took it," and I made a sound like a chicken. It's a classical reference; let it go if you don't know it. Sally got it, fortunately. "Besides," I added, "you can't hurt an Irishman by hitting him on the head. That was your Little Man Who Wasn't There, wasn't it?"

"Yes, from what Arethusa says I'm afraid it must have been. I intended to brief you more fully at dawn, but I needed to be sure you could cope with this place first."

"Hey, Lady, I'm not sure John Carter the Warlord of Barsoom could cope with this place. The guy you want me to catch is a little more than a garden-variety sneak thief, isn't he? I should have known the . . . the man that sent me wouldn't get all this upset about a . . . a lousy stickyfinger. I guess a guy that can hit you through a closed door would qualify. But you know what really puzzles me?"

"What's that, Joe?"

"Well, look, you're, no offense but you're a madam. You run the greatest bordello I ever saw or heard of. So how come I can't bring myself to say f—" I couldn't bring myself to say it. "—in front of you?" I finished lamely.

Her smile was a beautiful thing to see. "Because you know that word has only one meaning for me, and you're not strong enough to use it in a sentence to me yet. Don't worry: when the time comes, it will roll trippingly off your tongue. And so, shortly thereafter, will I. Now, are you feeling strong enough to continue your briefing, since we seem to have begun it?"

"You mean that's all you have to do to pass your audition for this joint? Drink the berry juice, spot the pun, get socked on the skull, and you're in? I can be one of your artists now?"

"Not necessarily, no. But I am confident now that you can pass for one, for a few days at least, with help. And I feel I owe you the chance to follow through on this case, seeing that you've taken fire on my behalf already."

"What makes you so confident now?" I asked, genuinely curious. The more I'd seen of this place, the less sure I'd felt that I could live up to its eccentric standards.

"Two things: Arethusa gave you a good report . . . and you treated my good friend Ralph Von Wau Wau with kindness at the staircase. Ralph's larynx and mouth were surgically modified in his infancy by a mad behaviorist, who hoped he could train Ralph to parrot human speech. To his dismay, his subject turned out to be a mutant, with human intelligence. They had a long talk one day. Ralph's life has been a rather lonely one since. How many are willing to converse with a German shepherd? 'Anyone who says "Excuse me" is a human being,' you said. Precisely the attitude I try to cultivate in my artists."

Huh. I could see how it would come in handy around here. "Arethusa didn't get much of a chance to do research."

Lady Sally chuckled. "My dear boy, she held you in her arms and looked you in the eye and kissed you. She now probably knows more about your sex life than you do."

Huh! And I passed . . .

Well, I had been paying close attention.

My attitudes toward hookers and their customers—excuse me, artists and their clients—had evolved a great deal in the last few hours. I had started out just a little brighter than the average Joe. That is, I had been prepared to be polite to any whore who was polite to me . . . but deep down inside, I had believed that there was something somehow wrong about paying another person to pretend to care about you. Don't ask me how, but I'd learned better. I understood now that if you don't believe it's moral to pay someone to pretend to care about you, you have no business flying first-class. Or going to a bar, or a hairdresser, or a psychiatrist. Or a private eye . . .

"Do you want that briefing now, or after you've had some rest?" Lady Sally asked.

You're on duty, Quigley! I took inventory, the way I had when her berry juice had started to come on, and computed that I had about ten minutes of good attention in me, before I'd start speening in Spookerisms again. "As they say in Hollywood, why don't you give me a synopsis of the treatment?"

"Quite. Well, the first incident took place four nights ago. That would have been a Wednesday night, a little before eight. One of my artists, Sherry, was about to go on duty. She had just placed some items which she knew her first client would appreciate in the Studio she uses regularly. In the middle of changing into her working clothes, she decided to do some limbering-up exercises in the nude. As she was executing jumping jacks, something happened.

"Several things all at once, actually. She reported that she experienced sudden extreme dizziness, felt warm all over, heard a sort of high distant shriek in her ears, and experienced a sudden sharp burning sensation in her breasts and vagina. The combination caused her to cry out and fall to the carpet. Priscilla arrived quickly, and took her to Kate's examining room, which fortunately was not yet in other use. Kate diagnosed rape.

"Sherry maintained this was impossible, but Kate insisted the symptoms were unmistakable. Bruising on Sherry's arms, legs and breasts. Chafing consistent with unlubricated penetration. And a subsequent discharge which Kate positively identified as semen. The only problem being that Sherry was quite positive she'd been alone and that whatever happened had literally been over in an instant. She stated further that she had not been intimate with any male, artist or client, for over sixteen hours.

"One other small detail: examination of that Studio disclosed that its bed did appear to have been worked in."

I located my jacket hanging by the bedside and got out my Luckies. "This Sherry is a stable, reliable witness in your opinion," I suggested, lighting up.

Lady Sally placed an ashtray nearby. "I have known her to experience extraordinary and stressful events, and observe them accurately. I believed her account then, and believe it now."

The cigarette made my head throb worse. I took another puff. "Go on."

"We mutually agreed that while we were not superstitious, others in the House are: we agreed not to publicize the incident. The next evening about midnight . . ." Lady Sally broke off. "This one will require some explanation. One of my artists, Ellen, is tattooed rather unusually. She . . . collects autographs, of celebrities, done on various portions of her skin with a fountain pen . . . and then has them made permanent by a tattooist later. She bills herself as the Living Autograph Book. I imagine the psychological significance of the pen must be fairly obvious. You can please her a great deal by asking her—politely, of course—to show you where John Lennon signed. Although for my money it was Ringo who was the most creative of the four . . . at any rate, people's fascination with celebrities is so great, Ellen's unique adornments are a perennial draw. Perhaps you're familiar with the phenomenon of the groupie-groupie?

"That Sunday night, Ellen was performing for a client, an old friend, when suddenly they both experienced extreme vertigo, felt a breeze, and heard a sort of chalk-on-a-blackboard sound. They both said their first thought was of earthquake. They are both absolutely certain that when it happened, Ellen climaxed, and the client did *not*. They offer as proof the fact that he did, extravaginally, about thirty seconds later. But Ellen subsequently experienced the same inexplicable discharge Sherry had. And the *client* found some odd new bruises on him here and there.

"They puzzled together over these two things, and after a while the client shrugged and said, 'Maybe *he* did it,' and pointed to an autograph. This puzzled Ellen, as he appeared to be pointing at Rock Hudson's autograph—but when she followed his finger she saw that she had somehow acquired a new signature. It read, 'The Phantom.' It was in ink, and still fresh enough to smear.

"The whole thing was so inexplicable, they both decided the scotch in the bar was getting better, and Ellen didn't report it to me. But Mary heard, and did."

It's always annoying when the theory you've been developing stubs its toe on new facts. Reluctantly I abandoned my nice, simple teleport theory. Now that I thought about it, even if you could teleport a blunt instrument through a closed door, part of that instrument would have to be *in the door* as the leading edge was striking my skull. It came to me all of a sudden that a PI should try to avoid cases where teleportation is too simple an answer. "You folks couldn't just turn up a corpse in a locked room or something easy like that? Transfixed by a mysterious dagger of Oriental design?"

She came near to smiling. "Fortunately, none of the odd occurrences have been that drastic—until tonight, that is. The attack on you constituted a kind of escalation."

"How flattering. Do go on."

"Well, another kind of escalation happened on Friday evening: there were two incidents, virtually simultaneous and related in theme. An artist and a client were artistically involved in one of the Function Rooms about ten o'clock, and all of sudden they had swapped costumes somehow. As they differed greatly in weight, physique and gender, the effect was striking, and ludicrous in the extreme. They reported no other symptoms, no dizziness or squeaking sounds or bruising or inexplicable ejaculations, and were merely much puzzled rather than upset. At about the same time, two couples in the Bower—do you know about the Bower?"

"In theory," I said. "Go on."

"Two couples there, all clients, suddenly found that they had swapped partners, in midstream as it were. Again they were not terribly upset—it turned out that three of them had just been thinking about proposing just such an exchange and the fourth would have enthusiastically agreed—but they were all somewhat unnerved. Though not enough to prevent them finishing what they'd started. Two of them spoke of dizziness, and discovered bruises which might have been quite natural given the circumstances, but none mentioned any squeaking sounds. It chanced that there were no other witnesses present, and so again it was mutually decided that I must be selling some very potent liquor out in the bar."

"Any unexplainable 'discharges' that time?" I asked.

"Indeterminate. The floor of the Bower not only feels like sponge, it's highly absorbent and stainproof. Any such evidence would have disappeared almost on contact."

"That brings us to last night."

"Again there was a kind of escalation, in both quantity and quality. *Three* strange incidents, at two different times, and all with a certain aspect of nastiness to them. Not that all of the incidents haven't been nasty enough, but last night—" She frowned. "Well, judge for yourself. At about eleven, Mistress Cynthia was performing with a client in her Dungeon, and all at once they swapped places. They are of such different builds that considerable adjusting of straps had to have been done—apparently instantly. Cynthia bore three vivid welts in painful locations. She became so enraged that she broke free—which I would have warranteed impossible—and began chasing the client around the Dungeon, under the impression that he had somehow drugged her and effected the switch himself . . . though how he was supposed to have freed himself I cannot imagine. Priscilla had to come and rescue the poor man. He and Cynthia were both bruised, but that may have been perfectly natural.

"At roughly the same time, Juicy Lucy and a client blinked and found themselves outside in the street together. As if that weren't frightening enough, a taxiful of sailors on leave was just passing—and both ladies were naked. They reentered the House at high speed, and there was some unpleasantness when the sailors attempted to come in after them. Fortunately my receptionists are well trained, and managed not to hurt any of the sailors enough to require medical attention. I questioned both ladies afterward about dizziness, odd noises, any other strange phenomena, but they were so highly traumatized they remembered nothing. As both are female, I did not inquire about discharges. They *were* both bruised across the shoulder blades and the backs of their thighs."

"I see what you mean," I said. "This guy's sense of humor gets nastier and nastier."

"You haven't heard the third event yet. At about one-thirty that morning, the . . . the client who sent you to me was in a studio down in the Discreet Wing. He was just leaving the bathroom. Mark that: he had just finished examining himself with some care in the mirror, naked."

I shuddered. "No one ever said he didn't have guts."

She frowned. "Joe, I know it is necessary for you to be disrespectful of him, and I understand that. But I must ask you to remember that worse men than he have held his job—and that he is an old and dear friend of mine."

"Sorry. Continue."

"As he approached his artist of the evening, he heard what he could only describe as a 'chipmunk noise'—and suddenly she burst out laughing." I started to speak . . . and she glared so ferociously I stifled myself. Then suddenly her expression softened. "Damn it . . . I don't want you giving yourself a hernia, so you *may* laugh during this next part. But one wisecrack and I'll smite you on the mazzard. Looking down," she went on grimly, "the client discovered that he had been redecorated."

I began to grin. In spite of herself, and without losing her thunderous frown, she joined me. Nonetheless her voice was flat, clinical. "Most of his pubic hair had been shaved off. A rude slogan had been written across his abdomen, apparently with Ellen's pen."

I was giggling by now. "What did it say?" I asked, trying to keep my voice as sober as hers and failing.

She sighed. "Do you really need to know?"

"It might be a clue to the psychology of the individual," I wheedled.

She pursed her lips. "Let's just say it involved a crude pun on his last name." I was laughing outright now. "His testicles had been painted bright green—" My head began to hurt from laughing. "—and his penis as well—" My sides began to ache. "And a small bell, of the sort one finds affixed to the collars of cats—" At this point Sally lost it too, giggled helplessly as she finished, "was dangling from the end of it," and we howled together for a short while.

But shortly she got control of herself, and kept it. "As you can see, even a friend cannot help laughing. That is precisely why he is so upset—and rightly so. Such things should not happen in my House."

Her voice held such controlled anger that I managed to sober up myself. "Let me get something straight. Obviously *he* hasn't broadcast what happened to him—and I assume his artist can keep her mouth shut or she wouldn't be performing in the Discreet Wing. I bet Cynthia and her client haven't told anybody what happened either. But what do the staff and clients think happened to the two ladies you mentioned?"

She nodded grimly. "That one has been causing talk. The most popular theory is that they were engaged in something exotic involving a window ledge and slipped, and are both properly too embarrassed to admit it. That story may hold for a little while. But if this sort of shit goes on, it won't be too long before I'll have a panic that empties my place. That's why you were hired."

It was the first time I'd ever heard her use a word you can't say on television. I got the point: she was *pissed*. And it was clear that she had every right to be. If your whole business is getting people relaxed, the last thing you want around the House is gremlins. "Have any other weird things happened *tonight*?" I asked. "Compared to a talking dog or telepathic twins, I mean? Assaults like the others?"

She hesitated. "Aren't you getting tired by now, Joe? You should rest—"

Now *I* was pissed. Very pissed. "Arethusa felt a burning sensation," I stated.

She sighed again and nodded. "In mid-air," she agreed, "as she was falling to the floor. In a split second. And down the hall, a man of the cloth discovered that . . . never mind; there was another incident and the details are not important."

"No, they're not," I said. My head still hurt, I was still exhausted and weak. But I was all business. "All right, first of all, you keep records of who goes in and out of this place?"

"Computerized," she agreed.

"I'll need printouts. *Including* Discreet Wing clients. Second, I hear there are tape recorders hooked up to Mary's bugs: do you still have tapes for all the days in question?"

"Yes. You'll have to go upstairs to the Snoop Room to hear them, when you're well enough. Removing them from the room erases them."

"First thing tomorrow. With luck I should have this son of a bitch in a bag by tomorrow night."

I had at last succeeded in favorably impressing her. Her eyebrows went up, and she beamed involuntarily. "You really think you can catch the bastard?"

"With some planning, cooperation, coordination, and luck, yeah, we've got a good shot," I said. "At the very least I think I can guarantee he won't trouble you any more. Unless I'm completely mistaken, and what we're dealing with here is a poltergeist."

"I do not believe in either poltergeists or the straightforward ghosts presented in the film inexplicably titled *Poltergeist*," she said.

"Neither do I," I agreed. "So I think I've got it right."

"Joe, you're a marvel!" she exclaimed. "You pull this off and you're comped here for life."

It was about the most breathtaking offer anyone had ever made me, but I was so stoked I let it go by almost unnoticed. "The in-out roster probably won't do more than narrow it down a little," I said. "I imagine you get a lot of every-night regulars here."

"We do," she agreed with some pride.

"But once I have a chance to go through those tapes I think I can tell you who he is. I already know *what* he is."

"Fantastic! And what is that?"

"A guy with a time machine," I said.

6. Spot the Son of a Bitch

Love is the most subtle form of self-interest.

—HOLBROOK JACKSON, quoted in
The Portable Curmudgeon
(compiled by Jon Winokur)

TO my surprise, Lady Sally McGee frowned hugely and snorted loudly and said, even more loudly, "Preposterous!"

I was a little taken aback. I'd expected her to take a time machine more or less in stride. "Coming from you," I said, "that's rich. In a joint with a talking German shepherd and a pair of telepathic blondes, what's so preposterous about a simple time machine?"

"Out of the question," she snapped. "Dismiss it from your mind. 'Time machine,' indeed! Try something a little more plausible, for heaven's sake. Martians, say, or a teleport."

"If either of those could be stretched to fit the facts, I would," I insisted. "But they can't."

"Neither can a time machine," she said just as stubbornly. "Setting aside for the moment the fact that such a thing is absurd, it simply doesn't fit the facts known."

"Yes it does," I said. "Cripes, you didn't even need me to figure this out. Any John D. MacDonald fan would have done. Which is like saying, 'every third citizen.' Hiring a genius was totally unnecessary."

"Apparently," she said with some . . . what is that word? Sounds a little like "asparagus," and means she was trying to break my horns? Rhymes with "prosperity" . . . "asperity," that's it. "Listen to me, Joe. Just assume I have a direct pipeline to God on this one question, okay? Put time machines out of your mind and keep thinking—or you're no use to me."

Now here's a funny thing. When I know I'm right, the President of the United States couldn't get me to back down. Even Lady Sally couldn't convince me that what I *knew* was so wasn't so. But I shut my big mouth and let her change the subject. It surprised me even as it happened. I mean, I hadn't even proved to her yet why I had to be right—which is usually the very least I have to do before I'll drop out of an argument.

She had a kind of a forceful personality, I guess.

And maybe I was off my game on account of that clout on the skull. All of a sudden I decided my ten minutes were about up. "You're the boss," I said. "Uh . . . can I still have the printouts and access to the tapes when I wake up?"

"Of course," she said, "as long as you promise to do some *constructive* thinking about them."

All right, then. No point in pushing it now: tomorrow morning I'd get my hands on the proof that she needed and I didn't. Then I'd magnanimously accept her apology. "Okay. I'm going to fall out, if it's all right with you."

"Certainly. Sleep well, Joe—again I apologize for exposing you to danger without briefing you. Don't worry, I'll send Arethusa in to keep watch on you."

"That'll be a comfort," I said.

And it was.

IT wasn't that Arethusa knew a lot of fancy acrobatic tricks, or had one that could peel a banana, or any of that. She understood that I was in rocky shape. What she did, she taught me about her. And about me. I mean, when I say that she played with me, for the first time in my life I mean that the way a little kid would mean it. She *played with me*, like a kid might play with another kid that had been whacked on the head recently and needed some diversion. Well, if this was a sane culture, I mean, and kids were allowed to have sex as part of playing, like God intended. She made me think about stuff like that. I'd thought I had given up playing forever when I became a PI.

What I'm trying to say is, what happened between us wasn't at all like anybody screwing anybody, and that's a memory to kill for. She even made my head stop hurting.

"Tell me about yourself, Arethusa," I said sleepily when I could.

"I will," she promised. "But tomorrow. Sleep now."

I glanced at my watch. Four A.M. My head did feel heavy as I swung it back to her. "Well . . . okay. But I really want to know you better."

She—well, there isn't a word. I mean, "leer" is not what happens when a mature and sexually satisfied woman spots an unintentional double-entendre, but "smile" doesn't seem to cover it either. Interesting, that there is no word for a woman appreciating bawdiness. Anyway, she did that, and said, "Better than *that?*"

"Yes," I said simply. "Even better than that."

Her eyes seemed to glow in the semidarkness. "In that case, there is all the time in the world. Close your eyes."

With reluctance, I did. No problem: I could still see her clearly. "Wake me if I sly in my deep," I murmured.

"I promise." She dialed the room lights down another notch, levitated noiselessly from the bed, and made herself comfortable in a chair beside it. I heard her slip on a silk robe. A southing sooned.

I slept, and dreamed of a blonde sandwich with Quigley filling.

I came half awake at a gentle knock on the door.

I glanced at the bedside clock, thinking, *Jesus, it feels like I've only slept ten minutes, and here it is—*

Four-ten A.M. I *had* only slept ten minutes . . .

Arethusa was up out of her chair like a shot, looking pissed. Then she opened the door and got respectful.

I don't mean like J. P. Morgan was standing there and now she had to kiss ass. More like if it was Gandhi, or maybe Warren Beatty.

Which is weird, because the guy looked more like a retired pug or longshoreman or beat cop than anything else. He resembled that actor Brian Dennehy a little. He was something over fifty, big and solid and Irish as Paddy's pig, with red hair just about everywhere but on the top of his head, and a dead cigar in his teeth. He had a jaw like a bulldozer, an artistically broken nose, and very pronounced laugh lines. But he wasn't smiling now. He looked as upset as a guy that big and confident ever looks. I hoped he wasn't upset with me. He looked like one of those guys you don't want to shoot because it could annoy them.

"I'm sorry, Arethusa," he rumbled in a gravelly baritone. "I've got to talk to him, and it won't wait."

I'd have bet cash she was going to tell him indignantly that I might be seriously injured and had to get my rest and like that. But I think she decided he knew all that, and gave him the credit of assuming he wouldn't bother me anyway without a good reason. "If you say so, Mike," she said, and stepped aside to let him in. She dialed the room lights up just a bit. (I didn't see how she did it—and I remember noticing that even when the lighting brightened, it was so artfully indirect that it was hard to tell just where the bulbs were.)

I thought about pretending to be asleep, and sticking to it. But something told me the quickest way to get rid of this guy and get back to sleep was to deal with him. "I don't go on duty until tomorrow," I told him, pretending to pull the covers over my head. "Try another artist."

Serious as he was, that made the big redhead grin around his cigar. "Ah, wouldn't that be something?" he said. "Two big micks in the same bed! Yeah, they'd have to hide the women, wouldn't they?" Because he was trying to keep his voice down, you couldn't have heard him more than two rooms away. He stuck out a hand the size of a baseball mitt. "Hello, Ken. My name's Mike. I'm Sally's husband."

I already provisionally respected the guy, on Arethusa's say-so. But now my respect went up a couple of notches. For a guy like this to hold on to a woman like that, he had to be something Special. Now I *really* hoped he wasn't upset with me. In my line of work, "client's husband" is a synonym for "pain in the ass"—and he looked like he could constitute a large-size pain. I stuck my own hand out and said, "Pleased to meet you, Mike. But that 'Ken' stuff is my House name—and I don't have any secrets from Arethusa. Call me Joe."

His smile dented slightly, "I'm afraid you do . . . at least for a little while. Let's keep it 'Ken' for now, okay?"

"If you say so," I agreed. His handshake was firm but not aggressive. He'd given up that kind of childishness a long time ago.

"Arethusa, darlin'," he said, "would you do me a favor?"

"Of course, Mike."

"Go ask Sal to give you some of my special coffee, and brew up two cups drip-style? Unless you'd like some too, Ken?"

"Well . . . how long do you need me to be coherent?" I asked.

"We should be done by the time Arethusa gets back," he said.

"Then I'll pass. Unless it's *really* special." I'm a coffee freak.

"I'll have her brew you some for breakfast," he assured me. "She'll still be awake then. Thanks, darlin'. Take your time."

"I understand," she told him, and left.

When the door had closed behind her, I said, "I meant that about not keeping secrets from Arethusa. I haven't told her a damn thing yet—there hasn't been time—but she's somebody I can't lie to."

"Then just settle for keeping your mouth shut as much as possible," he advised, "at least about your case. Once it's over you can make your own decision—for now, hang on to your cover. You're just a guy who got a shot at the second greatest job in the world."

"What's the greatest?" I had to ask.

"Mine," he said. "I mean it, Joe: Sal needs this kept as quiet as possible."

"How do I know I'm authorized to discuss it with *you*?" I asked.

He shifted the cigar stub in his teeth. "Easy: you're not an asshole. Now can we get down to business before Arethusa comes back and I have to make up another errand? It just embarrasses everybody."

"Okay," I said. "Where have you been while all this crap has been going on, Mike?"

He blinked. "Fair enough." He sat heavily in the chair Arethusa had vacated. "I should have been here. I've got my own business out on the Island, night shift, but I sleep here in the House most mornings. But sometimes I get involved in things out there. The last couple of days I been showin' a guy out in Suffolk County how to use a computer system, so it was simpler to sleep out there." He looked embarrassed, a strange expression on that face. "If I'd have been here, you might not have taken that whack on the head tonight. Sal kept saying everything was fine on the phone, and I just found out different a little while ago. I'm sorry."

"No problem. It's what I'm paid for. Question is: now that you're back, am I still hired?"

I had succeeded in surprising him. "Are you kidding? In the last century I think I overruled Sally twice already. I'm lucky to be alive."

"Is that your line of work, Mike, teaching computer systems?"

He looked thoughtful. "I guess you could say that. Teaching folks about reprogramming, yeah. This guy was a little different, though: a computer is the only way he can talk to people without barking."

Some friend of Ralph's? I had to let that go: my nose was wrinkling uncontrollably. "Excuse me," I said. "I know this is changing the subject, and I know it sounds crazy, and I mean no disrespect, okay? Maybe somebody's playing a gag on you—but I'm just about certain that's not a cigar."

He looked down at it and went briefly cross-eyed. "It isn't?"

Someone had to tell him. "I'm pretty sure it's a piece of shit."

He grinned, not at all offended. "A common error." He lit a wooden match with his thumbnail and brought it toward the thing.

"What the hell are you doing?" I said, alarmed.

"Trust me: it actually smells better when it's burning."

"Jesus." I lit a Lucky for a protective smokescreen. But he was right: the smoke cut the smell, sort of.

Mike returned doggedly to business. "Okay, look: I know about the weird things that have been going on, and I know you have a theory, and I know Sal thinks it's a bow-wow, and I know why. Better than she does, maybe. What I want you to do is tell me, in your own words, what your theory is and how you got to it. Fair enough?"

"What did Sal . . . did the Lady tell you I said?" I temporized. He frowned. "Hey, do you want a discreet guy on this gig or not?"

The frown went away. "*Touché*," he said. "Okay: she says you think it's a time traveler."

Now I frowned. "Not exactly."

He waited patiently.

"But it's close enough to tell me it's okay to discuss it with you. I didn't say, 'a time traveler,' exactly. I said, 'a guy with a time machine.' They're both kind of glorified editors, but they work it different."

He looked thoughtful, and twirled his cigar meditatively. I noticed that although it was still alight, and he'd been smoking it for a while, it didn't seem to have formed any ash. "If we're dealing with an editor, we may be in real trouble here. Okay, what's the difference?"

"Well, I'm not really a big sci-fi fan, but the way I get it, a time traveler goes back and forth in time, and edits history. Like he goes back to the past and shoots his own grandfather to see what'll happen. Only I never understood why they always pick on the grandfather."

"Me either," Mike agreed, accepting the digression for its intrinsic value despite the hurry he was in. I was starting to like him.

"I mean, how can you be *positive* your grandfather has anything to do with your genes? Maybe Grandmaw put one over on him. Shoot your Mom would be my plan: you can be fairly sure *she's* a relative."

"Sound," he agreed. "So a time traveler goes back and forth in time. How is that different from a guy with a time machine?"

"Well, see, it doesn't have to be. I guess you'd use some kind of time machine to do that. But you couldn't do the kind of stuff that's been happening here with that kind. Well, maybe you could, but it wouldn't *get* you anywhere. I'm thinking of a different kind of time machine. Not a machine to go *through* time . . . a machine to *change* time."

His nostrils flared, and he put both fists on his hips. "I'll be a son of a bitch, I don't know exactly what it is you've got, Joe Quigley, but you've got it. 'Change it' how?"

I love a guy who feeds me great straight lines.

"Slow it down," I said.

HIS jaw dropped, and he lost his cigar. "*Cushlamachree*," he breathed.

Another Barnaby fan. "Mr. O'Malley!" I said in a kid's voice.

He got the reference, and ignored it. " 'Callahan,' actually. Keep talking, Joe!"

"Well, I can't really take much credit for figuring it out. I read about a scam just like it once in a book, by John D. MacDonald. The title was something about 'a girl and a watch and everything.' "

He shook his head. "Don't know it."

"You don't know every book MacDonald's written? Jeeze, are you a lucky son of a bitch. Imagine having that still ahead of you. Well, there was this guy, with this—holy shit!" I broke off and dragged hard on my cigarette.

"What's the matter?" Mike asked, still the perfect straight man.

"I just this minute figured out who the bastard is. The prankster. What he looks like, anyway: I'll know him when I see him again.

Lady Sally can probably tell us his name. But it's still going to be real tricky taking him down."

"Rewind and start over, would you, son? There was this guy in a John MacDonald book . . ."

" . . . who had this gold watch that his uncle the inventor left him in his will. And the watch was like a time machine. Every time he did something to it, twisted the stem, I think, time stopped. For everybody but him, I mean. Well, not stopped, but went *real* slow. Maybe you could think of it like suddenly he could move and think so fast that everybody else just seemed to be standing still. I don't know if it makes any difference. Whatever, he twisted the watchstem, and everything in the world froze solid but him. And then he'd go around . . . *editing* things. And when he had them how he liked, he'd twist the stem the other way, start time back up, and watch the fun. I happened to see a guy with a ridiculous-looking watch in the Parlor last night, just before I got sapped."

"*Jesus!*" Mike shouted, and then said, "Jesus!" again at slightly lower volume. The forgotten cigar butt had burned through his pants at the left thigh. He crushed it to death between thumb and forefinger and ignored the burn. The smell of burning pants and leg hair was some improvement. "Joe, you got shafted on that Favila business. You're a fucking genius."

"I know." I was really starting to like this guy.

"I see what you're driving at. It explains—"

"Just about everything I can think of," I said. "Take when I got sapped tonight, for instance. I was standing with my back against a door. I felt a draft; the door squirmed under my shoulder blades; I felt somebody touch my blackjack; and my head blew up, all at the same time. You get it? The guy just twisted his watchstem to call time-out, and opened the door. He must have had all the time in the world before I'd start to fall over backwards. He dips my sap, smacks me with it, puts it back in my pocket, and closes the door again. There's a breeze because from my point of view, the door opened and closed almost instantly." I frowned darkly. "Then, as near as I can figure, the scumbag moves to somewhere out of my line of sight and starts the tape rolling again. Or maybe he just puts it on slow-mo, until he sees a frame he likes, and freezes it there again. Like, a second or so later. I've let go of Arethusa. She starts to fall. Her legs go up in the air. Freeze frame! She happens to be conveniently lubricated, at a convenient height, in a convenient posture. Wham bam, rape you ma'am. Then he puts it back in his pants, opens the door again, squeezes past me, and leaves. Or for all I know, he hauls me out of his way and then hauls me back into place again once he's out in the hall. The cocky little—"

"Seems to me if you moved people around in that kind of time frame, you'd build up a lot of friction," Mike said.

"And in every weird incident where someone had to be physically moved, they reported feeling hot all of a sudden," I agreed. "And bruised. In the MacDonald book, it was real hard to move stuff around while it was frozen. Something about 'inertia.' I'll tell you one thing about the bastard: he's a premature ejaculator. If he wasn't, he'd have torn those girls up pretty bad." I bared my teeth. "I've got a real simple solution to his problem."

"Somehow I suspect what you've got in mind for him is just a different problem," Mike said. "Kind of on the opposite end of the same spectrum, like."

"You got a problem with that?" I asked.

"Not at all," he assured me. "It'll be a nice change for him. I'll hold your coat."

"I'm willing to leave one for you," I offered.

"Thanks, son, but these days I'm mostly vegetarian. Okay, we've got two problems to solve. No, three. How do we identify him? How do we take him? And how do we persuade Sal we're on the right track? You say you've got the first one licked already?"

"I think so. I spotted a guy down in the Parlor with a real funny-looking watch, sitting at the bar. A suit; he looked real Central Park West. Thinking back on it, he was close enough to hear me and Arethusa talking: he'd have known for sure why we were going upstairs, so he knew she'd be ready for him. For all I know, the bastard just sat there and finished his drink, gave us enough time to get upstairs, and then . . . checked the time." I shook my head, infuriated at the arrogance of the man. "Anyway, I'll bet dollars to donuts his name will be on the printout of clients who were here all four nights."

Mike pursed his lips. "That might help convince Sal."

"I can do better than that. A couple of the first people involved reported high-pitched squealing sounds. Then one of 'em yesterday heard what he called a 'chipmunk noise.' I think he meant like that record, Alvin and the Chipmunks."

Mike started. "Cripes—"

"You have Mary play back the tapes of the incidents—at really low speed—and I think you'll be able to make out the skell's voice. I think after the first couple of times, he realized what a risk he was taking by talking aloud, and quit . . . except for one last time he just couldn't help himself. I kind of know how he felt about that one: I've often wished I could get that guy to just stand there and listen until I was done talking at him. Anyway, if that doesn't convince Lady Sally, nothing will."

"That should nail it down," Mike said, nodding. "Nice thinking, Joe. All right, how do you propose we take him?"

"Well, there's really only one serious problem: we can't give him as much as a second's warning. For him, a second is as long as he wants it to be. I'd say our move is to maneuver him into a crowd scene down in the Parlor. Surround him with people that are good fighters and better actors. Then we just get Priscilla within reach of his watch arm. Put her on that arm, and three or four people on everything else, and I think we can take him. All we have to do then is decide what to do with the body."

"Sounds like it ought to work," Mike said judiciously.

"There's only one part I don't like to think about."

"What's that?" he asked obligingly.

"What's going to happen if we fuck up."

"True," Mike agreed. "He could cut every throat in the place—or worse. Well, there's one consolation."

My turn to be straight man. "What's that?"

"If we do fuck up, we'll probably never know it."

That one got to me a little. I know it's nuts, but somehow I always had it in my head that even if some guy, say, shotgunned me in the head from behind, I'd still have a split second to realize what had happened before the lights went out. I don't know why it should be worse to die *without* time for pain or regrets . . . but to me, it is. I'm not looking forward to dying—but I've spent a lifetime getting ready for it, and I don't want it stolen from me.

"Let's not fuck up," I said.

"That'd be my vote," Mike agreed.

I found that I was exhausted. I'd spilled all the logic I'd had backed up in my head since Lady Sally had left, and now there was nothing left to keep me going. I'd unwound my mainspring—if watch imagery isn't in bad taste here. Oddly enough, my head didn't hurt.

"If all goes well," I said, slurring my *l*'s slightly, "by tomorrow night the only one here with a problem will be me. No, don't say 'what's that?'—you've been good so far, Mike; I'll just tell you. My problem is gonna be, 'What the *hell* do I put in my report?' I don't think I could sell the truth to my . . ." I broke off and giggled. "S'cuse me: 'To my client,' I started to say. Suddenly the word has a new meaning." Everything was getting rubbery.

Mike grinned. "Yeah, he is a lot of people's 'client,' in Sal's terms, isn't he? I wouldn't worry about it, Joe. You just tell him, 'Lady Sally says everything is fine now,' and then turn off your ears. When he stops throwing things and turns his back on you, that means you can go now."

I smiled feebly. "Founds like sun, actually." That didn't sound right. "Ex-keys mew," I said, stifling a yawn. "I have this tenancy to spean in Spookerisms since I got whacked. It's a scéne that I'm slipy."

Mike got up from his chair, surprisingly quickly for a guy his size, and ran a hand through his thinning (hell, anorexic) red hair. "Well," he said, "when it tarts getting stuff—"

"The guff get towing," I agreed. "Nighty night. Hey, that'd be a pretty good name for a theme evening here. 'Nightie Night.' Remind me to sell Lady Tally . . ."

He paused at the door. "Joe?"

I was three quarters asleep. "Yah?"

"Travis McGee couldn't have done better."

So he *did* know MacDonald . . . and only read the McGees. Well, a lot of people make that mistake. And maybe it's just the way my life has worked out, but I don't get praised by guys like Mike Callahan a lot.

"Et your bass," I told him happily. I tried to invent a variant on winking, using *both* eyes, and found I couldn't get either lid back up again.

Ah, what the hell . . .

OF all the things that happened to me on that case, one of the parts I like best to remember is waking up the next day.

Don't get me wrong: I wouldn't want to part with any of the memories. Not even the whack across the skull, or the awful moment when I understood that my—all right, dammit, not my "girl" . . . my artist, then—when I understood that my Arethusa had been raped while I was less than six inches away, gaping like a museum diorama of primitive man.

And there isn't enough money in the world to buy the memory of Arethusa comforting me that first time.

But nice as that was, waking up the next day was maybe even a hair better. Anyway, just as good.

First I was a plant. Light lay gently on me, a bee buzzed softly, and there was something wonderful in the air.

Then I was an animal. Something simple like an amoeba or a newt. I floated in goodness; no enemies were near; dolphins chuckled somewhere; life was good.

Next a mammal of some kind. The two greatest spoors in the world crept into my nostrils and opened them wide. My heart was pumping fluid at high volume, and other organs thought the idea might be worth copying.

I evolved into a man. One of the smells in my nose was coffee—no, the quintessence of coffee—and the other one was better. A flautist good enough to play Carnegie Hall was, with incredible gentleness and delicacy, practicing arpeggio runs on my penis, like a drummer rehearsing with pads. To assist herself, she was humming the melody . . .

And finally I was Joe Quigley. I was in the prime of my years; safe in the greatest brothel on Earth; I had cracked the case of my life; the thrill of the bust was still ahead of me; and Arethusa, my Arethusa, about whom I knew almost nothing except that I needed to spend large amounts of time with her, was showing me what is at the opposite end of the Universe from an alarm clock. And if that wasn't enough, the coffee I smelled had to be Mike Callahan's "special coffee," and it had to be pretty damn special because I knew I had slept at least ten hours and Arethusa was, beyond question, wide awake . . .

I wondered idly which one of her she was.

I remembered something. Back about the time I'd reached the primate stage, I'd heard her emit sounds, and filed them for later thought. Only four syllables, but something told me even then they were very important.

Now that I had developed language skills, I played back the tape, and yes they were very important syllables indeed.

"I love you, Joe."

7. See Dick Dick Jane...

" . . . remember what I told you, kid: life is a shitstorm—and when it's raining shit, the best umbrella you can buy is art."

—Pedro Carmichael to Martin Looder,
in the film *Tune in Tomorrow*,
written by William Boyd

"KEN," I said automatically.

"Yes, Joe," she said. "Whenever anyone but Mary is listening, and for as long as you tell me." She nestled her head into the hollow of my throat and licked me. "My Ken doll. Anatomically correct. Well, somewhat exaggerated, like Barbie." She took the evidence in hand. "Men aren't built like this in real life."

"I yield to superior experience," I said. "But up until last night I thought Barbie's chest measurement was exaggerated too." She purred. "Yours are round, of course. Well, rounded. Uh . . . look, for reasons I won't go into just now, I'm pretty good at guessing what people are going to do next—"

"I'm certainly giving you enough clues," she said, and gave me one as subtle as a shotgun blast.

"Right, and I'm certainly prepared to cooperate any way I can—but my thinking was, it might be useful to have some coffee first."

"Huh. I follow your thinking."

"Yes, you do. I hate to take the time . . . but it could enhance the experience."

"I'm all for that," she agreed. Without stopping what she was doing, she made a long arm behind her and, without looking, located a brown earthenware mug sitting on a cup-warmer. She passed it to me. I took a sip.

You know how coffee never quite tastes as good as it smells? This tasted *better*. I burned my tongue, and kept sipping. Soon I was gulping.

The secondary effects took a little longer to hit, but they were just as striking, Visually it was as if the photographer had changed from Bob Guccione to Annie Leibovitz: all the Vaseline burned off the lens, and everything came into crisp (but somehow not "sharp") focus. Soundwise it was like somebody switched in Dolby C and all the hiss went away, leaving the highs intact. In terms of state of mind, a good ten years (no: a *bad* ten years) melted away. I was strong and brave, and there was hope; for once I didn't need to tell myself that maybe tomorrow would be better.

"Where does Mike *get* this stuff?" I asked.

Arethusa's answer was what lawyers call nonresponsive.

I raised no objection. She was raising a fairly substantial object herself.

God, could love of puns be venereally transmitted?

Hors d'oeuvre! Order in the courting! . . . Put the witless on the stand, in the box, and make him swear . . . Raise your rite gland . . . Do you swear to tell the hole truth . . . an' muff an' butt the truth? . . . I dew, so help me—God! . . . You're on 'er: I move for a Miss-trial . . . Erection sustained . . . We'll take a short recess . . . direct your attention to Exhibit A . . . An in-tight-ment has been laid, on my client . . . Would you care to cross eggs?— Ah'm in! . . . You're witness . . . Madam for men, does the jury have its fur dicked? . . . Bang! Bang! Bang! . . . Bailiff, ejaculate that man!

The prostitution rested . . .

(My defenses had been resting through the whole trial.)

ONCE in a while, the afterglow can be as good as the orgasm. You've been that fortunate, haven't you? This time it was better. I'd never *shared* it before. Among a thousand other feelings was a fine sweet sadness, pity for the poor man I used to be, the hundreds of thousands of hours I'd wasted. I did math in my head: more than three hundred and five thousand hours I'd lived without her. How?

Yeah, part of my head was saying, *For Chrissake, Quigley, she's a hooker!* But I'm happy to say that even then, when I was just realizing this hooker's hook was set in me, the rest of my head answered with my heart: *Yeah, and if*

I'm really lucky, she won't think of a PI as marrying down . . .

I know. I'm trying to tell you that an experienced prostitute, after five minutes' conversation and two sexual acts, not only told a client she loved him, but meant it—and you don't believe me. Subsequent events proved the point, but I won't get to them for a while. All I can tell you now is, I have trouble believing it to this day myself. At that point in my life, my only proven talents were for entertaining absurd thoughts, lying, and surviving violence. Yet Arethusa read my mind a few times and decided to love me. It forces me to conclude that even back then, I must have been a fairly decent guy.

What I'm sure of is that I never doubted her, then or ever. It took days for it to occur to me that another man in my position might have interpreted those four words as merely a professional politeness.

An indeterminate time later she rolled off me, and we smiled at each other in silence for a while. When I thought I could stand it, I finished my coffee. The warmer had kept it just right.

"That one about, 'Would you care to cross eggs?'—'Ah'm in!' was really terrible," Arethusa said.

I blinked a few times. My defenses stirred in their sleep. "You can read *my* mind too?"

She shook her head, and her blonde hair whispered on the pillow. "Only *then*," she said. "And mostly just surface stuff. But clearer than with most men."

"Huh." I was thirty-five then; I'd been with whores. It never occurred to me to doubt Arethusa's last statement. Interpret that however you want.

Suddenly I giggled. "S'cuse me: I just pictured us forty years from now, and you said, 'You never *talk* to me any more.' "

She giggled too. "Vee haff vays uff making you talk," she said.

"You do indeed," I admitted. "Say, I just thought: is that 'you' singular or plural? I mean . . . that is—" Was I asking a rude question?

She twinkled. "How many of my bodies have you been in, you mean?"

"Well . . . Yeah. Yeah, I guess that's what I mean." The question didn't seem to offend her.

"One, so far."

"Oh. Uh . . . was it good for you both?"

Her twinkle became a full-scale pulsar, a brilliant smile that seemed to strobe just too fast to see. "*Oh* yes," she assured me.

Huh. "Huh. Interesting. Not the first time I've made love with two women at once—"

"I know," she said.

"—but on such occasions, they were both in the room at the time. Does it ever present any problem for you?"

"How do you mean?"

"Well . . . I picture myself in your shoes: one of me is down in the Parlor, chatting with that priest I saw, say—"

"Father Newman. I chat with him a lot."

"Okay, so you're discussing theology, let's say, and suddenly your other body has an orgasm. Do you ever lose the thread of the conversation?"

She giggled. "Well, no. Not usually. But it's funny you should ask that. Father Newman can always tell when that happens. Most people don't notice at all . . . but he always blushes. I think it's sweet."

So did I. "So Father Newman doesn't . . . uh . . ."

She shrugged. "I couldn't say. *I've* never performed for him. He hasn't asked me."

"Then he doesn't," I said positively. "Look, Arethusa . . . tell me if this is a snoopy question, okay?"

"I will, Joe," she said. "Always. The worst misunderstandings are the unspoken ones."

"Okay, then. I was just wondering . . . is there any special reason *why* . . . I mean, I guess it stands to reason . . ."

She knew where I was heading, and took me off the hook. "When it stands," she said, tweaking it, "it isn't interested in reason. I think I understand your question. See how close I come: you're wondering if one of my bodies is better than the other one at performing the art, and that's why I haven't swapped in the night, the way you think twins would . . . and somewhere in there is a subtext about, does the other one ever subconsciously resent the one that's better? Am I close?"

"It does sound silly," I admitted. "There'd be no point in swapping, would there? And how could either one be better?"

"As a matter of fact," she said, "you're partly right. This body *is* better at sex: that's why it's here. The other one's never had any complaints, but this one is special."

"I don't get it. How can that be?"

"Because artistic talent lies not just in the mind, or even the brain. In large part it's found in the upper spinal column."

"Really?"

"Skills, not 'talent,' excuse me. Skills are the flowers you get if you water your talent bush well enough. Like, if I took you and Oscar Peterson, and transplanted your brains, Mr. Peterson would find that he couldn't play a damn with your fingers. And if you sat down at the piano in his body, you'd find that you knew his whole repertoire—as long as you didn't think about it. You'd never be able to play those pieces with the same *feeling* he does—but you could impress a nonprofessional, because you'd have the spinal column where Mr. Peterson keeps his skills."

"Huh, I saw a guy once in a veterans' hospital. They said he didn't have enough forebrain left to take a decent tissue sample . . . but he could play any early Rolling Stones song you named on the guitar, note for note, and he was pretty good. Couldn't learn a new lick, though, no matter how simple."

"Maybe that was Keith Richards," she said. "Whoever he was, he learned guitar before his injury. Anyway, it's kind of the same with me. This body started out with the most talent for the art, and it's spent the most time developing the skills, so it's better. Not *so* much better that a lot of clients notice it . . . but *I* notice. Nothing but the best for my Joe."

What do you say to something like that?

"And no, of course my other body doesn't resent this one. Does your left hand resent your right because it has better penmanship? And if such a thing were possible, I think this body would envy the other one. *That* one can play the piano—not as good as Mr. Peterson, but damned well—and that is about the only thing a person can do that I'm willing to admit might sometimes be even better than making love. I play here at least a couple of hours, most nights."

"I'd love to hear you play sometime," I said.

"That's not all you'd love. If we rate this body as a ten, at the art, I mean, the other one is about a nine point five. And it has certain digital skills this one lacks. If you're ever in the mood for something manual . . ."

"Most of what I enjoy is in the manual, yes," I tried to say, but she started tickling me before I got the fourth word out. And there was nothing wrong with her fingers. She could have made her own holes in a bowling ball.

Then they were gentle again, and shortly she was showing me an interesting new way to play "Chopsticks." Admittedly it's not a very demanding piece, but she played the hell out of it. Call it a nine point five. And after a while she went back to what her body did best.

It was indeed an *Arethusa bulbosa*: a solitary rose-purple flower, fringed with yellow . . . and I was a busy little bee.

Like I said, one of the favorite mornings in my memory.

FROM there the day got less wonderful, in gradual increments.

Well, it could hardly have helped it, now, could it? That's one of the sweetest parts of a morning like that. Knowing it will end, eventually, and never come back in just the same way again.

But the first increments were so small I scarcely noticed them.

I'd just asked her if she'd been *born* telepathic, and she'd said, "No more than most twins. I have dim half-memories of being two people." So I was going to ask what first brought the change on . . . and there was a knock at the door.

All things considered, it could have been worse timed. "Come in," I said, suppressing a momentary impulse to pull a sheet over us first.

It was Doctor Kate, but it took me a second to recognize her. In her off hours she wore a sweatshirt and baggy comfortable slacks, and her hair loose around her shoulders instead of up in a doctor's bun. But the black bag and stethoscope were a dead giveaway. She approached me briskly, shaking a thermometer.

"Hi, Kate," I said. "I'm feeling much *glorp*." I won't reproduce the rest of the sentence because it sounded like a man trying to talk with a thermometer in his mouth. I raised my hand to adjust it like a cigar and she intercepted the hand to take my pulse, readying her stethoscope and getting out the blood-pressure gizmo with her other hand.

It's funny: right up until then my head hadn't hurt a bit.

By the time I had been pronounced fit to put my pants on, I had a reason to: Lady Sally arrived, looking indecently radiant for that hour of the morning in a soft cranberry silk kimono. She waited politely while Arethusa and I dressed.

I could see the sheaf of printouts in her hand, and the expression on her face, but I did not say, "I told you so." I even managed somehow to wipe the smug look off my face. Not an easy trick for a man who has just passed a night and a splendid morning with Arethusa. Doctor Kate reported that I was "all right," and I decided not to quibble.

Arethusa finished dressing, gave me a brief but emphatic kiss, said, "To be continued . . ." and started to leave with Kate. I took her arm, and she stopped.

"There's something I've been meaning to say to you since I woke up," I said, "and I keep getting sidetracked. I love you too."

"You said it," she told me. "I heard you plainly." She turned and left. I watched until the door closed behind her. God gave women buttocks because sooner or later they have to walk away from us, and at least this way there's some consolation.

"I've listened to some of the tapes—and scanned the MacDonald book," Lady Sally said formally then. "I owe you an apology, Mr. Quigley."

"It'll be in my bill," I said. "But I'll double it if you don't stop calling me 'Mister.' It sounds like an insult on the firing range."

"I must ask you to take my word for it, Joe, that it is unusual for me to be required to apologize to a new employee twice within the first twelve hours of his employment."

"Well," I said, "I can't fault you for doubting the judgment of a guy who's just been laid out with his sap."

She relaxed. "Thank you for taking it that way."

"I'll let you off the hook," I said, "wipe that apology off the bill, if you'll answer one question."

"Ask away," she said.

"Why *didn't* you believe me?"

It's funny. She didn't move a muscle, flicker an eyelid . . . and somehow the temperature in the room went down a couple of degrees. After two seconds, she said, "Are you joking? The idea is so *prima facie* absurd that I can scarcely believe it even after it's been proven to me."

I shook my head. "That's not it."

By now it was cool enough in here that I was glad I was dressed. "It's not?"

"No way in hell. Anybody else I know, okay—the idea *is* so whacky it makes my own head hurt. But the menagerie you run here, with talking dogs and cigar-smoke sculptors and a setup out of the Arabian Nights— Christ, if Donald Duck walked in here and asked for service, you'd just take his hat and tell him to look for somebody that felt like getting down. A simple time machine shouldn't even have made you blink."

She shook her head. "If Donald Duck showed up, I should assume I was hallucinating. I'm willing to accept the fantastic-but-possible and take it in stride—especially once I've had my nose rubbed in it—but up until today I accepted the general consensus that altering the flow of time is simply an impossibility. Provincial of me, I admit, in light of subsequent evidence . . . but if a ghost should suddenly start haunting the place, or a perpetual motion machine be offered me for sale, I would react with the identical skepticism."

I nodded slowly. "I know what you mean. It's hard to strike a balance between keeping an open mind and being a sucker."

"You do it quite well."

I shrugged. "I have this curse. If good logic takes me to a place, and it happens to be in the Twilight Zone, I stay there anyway. I can't seem to reject an answer just because it's ridiculous. I'll give you an example. They had a weird one at a state pen upstate a few years ago. There was a break-in one morning. Three guys set off alarms cutting through a chain-link fence, ran like hell through the garden, and were seen running into the yard. Then the big sirens went off, and all the cons in the yard went into a huddle. They always do that when the horn goes off: the idea is, the guys on the edges of the huddle will stop most of the slugs.

"So the screws sealed the joint tight, got the local cops in to help, and locked down the population one by one. Slow and easy, alert every second. And when they were done counting heads, the three guys were just . . . gone. All they found were their coats. The screws positively identified every human in the joint, and there was nobody that didn't belong there. The general suspicion was that the screws who said they saw the guys run into the yard were drunk or crazy. But there was that hole in the fence, and three sets of footprints through the corn."

"Let me see if I can guess this," Lady Sally said. "Three men broke *out* of the prison by running backwards to a pre-arranged hole. The witnesses all persuaded themselves they'd seen men running forwards, since what they actually saw seemed unreasonable."

I shook my head. "Nobody was missing. They checked ten times; they actually fingerprinted every con and every screw. So they left the place locked down and tore it apart, brick by brick. They got out the architect's plans and accounted for every cubic inch in the complex, one at a time. They used dogs, and X-ray machines, and after a week they finally turned up exactly one possibility: a tunnel from the supplies shop to the outside, an old forgotten maintenance tunnel that dated back to before the place was a prison. It was supposed to be sealed off and it wasn't any more. So now they know how the three guys got out—except the warden's gotta ask himself three questions."

Lady Sally ticked them off. "Why would three men break into a prison and sneak right out again? How did they know of the tunnel's existence when the prisoners themselves didn't? And how did they get from the yard to the tunnel while the whole prison was crawling with triggerhappy guards?"

"Well, four questions, then," I said. "The other one was, how did they manage to get through the fresh cave-in at the far end of the tunnel? Experts dated it to the night *before* the break-in."

Lady Sally looked dubious. "Here we seem to be entering the realm of ghosts and perpetual motion machines again."

"Exactly. So after a week or two of waiting for the other shoe to drop—for a time bomb to go off or somebody to yell 'April Fool!'—the warden did the sensible thing. He put it out of his mind. As often as necessary. There were no prisoners missing; his ass was covered. He had the tunnel quietly resealed, made sure the cons didn't find out about it, and forgot the whole thing."

"And you became involved in this somehow?"

"About six months later I was hanging out at the One-Seven with a gold shield I know named Murphy. He had a good set of prints on a liquor-sticker, a guy that knocks over liquor stores. But when he ran 'em through the computer it came out you got the wrong guy, that guy's doing life upstate, been there thirty years. Shit, Murph says, I thought those prints were good. So I say, maybe they got the wrong guy up there in the joint. Murph says no way, it happens they just printed every guy in that can fresh a few months ago. And he tells me the funny break-in story. And before he gets to the end, *I* tell *him* that the tunnel was blocked at the end."

Lady Sally held up a hand. "This is the point at which I'm supposed to try and solve it myself. Give me a minute." She went into what is called a brown study, for the life of me I don't know why, and played with the puzzle for maybe twenty seconds. Then she looked up and said, "I surrender. I can work out unlikely scenarios for how some of the individual phenomena were produced, but the overall motivation baffles me."

I smiled. "I usually charge a beer to finish the story. You'll love it: even Donald Westlake could never have made up something so brilliantly bent:

"The three guys that broke into the can were inmates."

Her jaw dropped satisfactorily. In less than three seconds I saw the tumblers start to click into place. Suddenly she began to laugh. She had a great laugh onto her. Stuff jiggled.

"The way I reconstruct it, a lifer stumbled across that tunnel and managed to unseal it. It must have taken him weeks, with no guarantee it was worth the trouble—but one night he found himself on the outside, in a ravine. So he walked through the forest, and stole some clothes off a clothesline, which they still have up there, and went into town. I'll bet he had him a good night. But a little before dawn he was trying to hitch out of town, and all of a sudden it came to him that he was cold and broke and scared stiff. So he turned around and sneaked back into the joint, and went to bed.

"From then on, whenever he got restless, he'd sneak out and have himself a night on the town, with money he had some friend wire him care of General Delivery. Then he'd sneak back in before morning headcount. Left a dummy in his bed, just like in the movies. He had the comfort and security of the joint, no bills, no taxes, easy work, and he could step out whenever he wanted. It must have taken a lot of the sting out of a life sentence."

"I imagine so," Lady Sally said, still laughing.

"Sooner or later he just had to tell somebody. Somebody he trusted not to screw things up, not to get himself caught on the outside, or stay out and miss head-check, or brag on the inside. Then one day there were three of them. A secret club, like.

"And one day they all came back at dawn and found the tunnel collapsed . . .

"What could they do? They broke into jail, with civilian coats over their greys. When the cons went into a huddle, they dumped the coats."

A fresh wave of laughter shook the Lady. "And they had the sheer unadulterated crust to unseal the tunnel again and clear the cave-in, and go right back to business? My God, you must have done yourself a bit of good solving that one, Joe!"

My smile went away, and I sighed. About one time in three they say something like that. "Well, no." My head was hurting a *lot* now.

Her laughter tapered off. "Why on earth not?"

"Well, you see," I said, "it's like I told somebody recently: I'm a genius . . . but I've got the worst luck in the world."

"What went wrong?" she asked, looking sympathetic.

"Well, I told Murph my idea, and he got excited, and we took it to the Warden. He's very impressed, very excited. So he asks, how do I figure out *which* three cons, and how do I prove it on them? So I say, no problem: the one thing we *know* is that Murph's booze-bandit perp is one of them; just confront him about the tunnel and sweat him and the job is done. He's in his sixties, how hard could it be?"

"He wouldn't break?" Sally said.

"Worse. He was able to prove that at the time of the robbery, and for twelve hours in either direction, he was under constant observation in the prison hospital. Coronary. So they checked, and the goddam tunnel was still blocked. Murph *did* get a bad set of prints. But there was no way to shut the old guy's mouth after they told him about the tunnel, and about forty seconds after they sent him back to his cell, the whole joint knew about it. They never did nail the three guys, and the Warden decided it was all *my* fault."

Lady Sally looked stricken. "Oh, how ghastly for you."

Now my head hurt *and* I was getting depressed. "It just keeps turning out like that. Over and over. Ninety-five percent of my work is the most boring shit in the world, rent-paying stuff . . . and when the other five percent comes along, the interesting stuff, I wince. Because I know I'll solve it, and I won't make a dime. Once in a while, something really special like the Favila business comes along, and I get to be a laughingstock. A laughingstock, broker. It's like I was a TV private eye, and the scriptwriters have to keep me broke enough to stay in the stupid job without making me an idiot."

"That sounds maddening," Lady Sally said. "To have your life run by scriptwriters—ugh!" She shuddered.

I got up and paced the room. "And the damn thing is, it isn't *necessary*. I love the good parts of my job so much I'd stay in it if I was rich." I lit a smoke. "I'd just cut down on the part that involves Polaroids. And the insurance work. And the skip tracing. Well, most of it, actually."

Lady Sally's voice was soft. "To enjoy as much as five percent of your work makes you an unusually fortunate man for this time and place."

"I know," I said, pacing and smoking.

She nodded. "But the figure, however much above average, is unacceptably low, I know. That's why I opened this menagerie, as you called it." She stroked her chin meditatively. "Well, if things work out, perhaps you could work here part-time. Ninety-five percent of the time."

I snorted. "A PI working out of a whorehouse? Give me a break. They'd pull it after three episodes and replace it with a sitcom. Besides, if Arethusa is a fair sample, I'm not sure I could qualify to fold the towels around here."

"In terms of mechanical skills, on a scale of ten, Arethusa rates about an eight," she said. "On her best day, with her best body."

I stopped pacing.

"But I employ ones and twos here, too, Joe. Mechanical skills aren't all that important. In terms of attitude, Arethusa is at least a nine, and nobody here is below seven."

"Jesus Christ," I said. "If you've got a ten-ten in the House, I hope you require a preliminary physical for all his or her clients."

"Regardless, I'm sure we could find a place for you here. Possibly even some work involving the skills you already have. Never mind; give it time. We'll talk again after . . . after the events of this evening."

I nodded sourly. "After the terrific buildup I just gave you, you must be really looking forward to having me around tonight. Just what you need on a caper like this: a jinx."

"Stop that!" Lady Sally snapped.

"Stop what?"

"Belittling yourself. If it truly needs doing, let someone else do it. I could call Cynthia if you like; she's quite good at it."

My shoulders slumped. I went back to the bed and sat down to stub out my cigarette. When I had mashed it dead, I said, more to myself than to her, "I just get so tired of giving people five pounds of coffee . . ."

"Beg pardon?"

"Sorry. My expression for, 'a gift that turns out to be a pain in the ass.' Somebody gave me five pounds of coffee once. Terrific coffee; that was the worst part. You can't drink more than a pound before it goes stale, but four pounds isn't enough to be worth selling. I figured out later, the time I spent giving it away, half a pound or so at a time, I could have bought myself two pounds of great coffee. But I just couldn't make myself throw it away . . ." I lit another Lucky and started pacing again. "Look, Lady, I want to give you a gift. You gave me a gift, you gave me a chance to meet Arethusa, and I want to give you back a closed case, you see? But the thing is, I keep going over it in my head, and I can't come up with any way my jinx could possibly screw this up *where I'm the only one who gets screwed*. Do you understand?"

"No," she said.

"On the Favila case, the only one who ended up suffering was me. With that prison-break thing, the Warden got shafted too. Not to mention the three guys who lost a perfectly good tunnel—don't think I don't feel guilty sometimes about what I did to them, just so I could try to look clever. But you see, if this goes sour tonight, we're *all* screwed: me, you, Arethusa . . . both Arethusas . . . Pris, Tim, everybody. Once he knows we're on to him, I don't see any way he can let us live. We'll know his name, what he looks like, and what he can do. He couldn't even be sure how many of us know—his smart move would be to torch the whole place, clients and all."

"You're not scaring me," she said. "You're impressing me, but I've handled dangerous snakes before."

"Not with my luck around," I said sourly, spraying smoke.

She snatched the cigarette from my hand and made it go away somehow. I was so startled I let her get away with it. "Is it something about the muscles themselves that does it?" she wondered. "Some side effect of all that tugging at the base of the brain?"

"What do you mean?"

"Why are so many large, muscular men superstitious? You'd think a strong man wouldn't need to be. In many cases, of course, stupidity is a reasonable theory . . . but you're not stupid."

"Thank you," I said stiffly.

"Joe, listen to me. I have been forced to believe in a watch that makes time stop when you twist the stem. If you'll produce one and let me test it, I shall undertake to believe in a ghost or a flying saucer. I am even willing to imagine, for purposes of theoretical discussion, a presidential candidate suited for the job—but the day I concede the existence of such a thing as a 'jinx,' a scarlet chap with a beard, a tail and a pitchfork will place an order for twenty billion pairs of ice skates! If you are feeble-minded enough to want to believe in good and bad joss, the Constitution so entitles you—but have the decency not to try and spread the virus. I'd rather go into this fight with one foot in a bucket than with a hoodoo on my back . . . and if you really do think that Bad Luck has nothing better to do than follow you around, perhaps you *should* just leave this to the rest of us."

I flinched as if she had hit me. No, actually: if she had hit me, I wouldn't have flinched. I flinched as if she had wounded me.

Which she had. Instead of shooting back, I did something unusual for me. I sat down, and rubbed at the back of my aching head . . . and tried to think. She gave me as long as I needed.

Did I believe in Bad Luck?

I certainly had a lot of evidence. My career history to date was an unbroken succession of spectacular failures. Time and again, I had managed to snatch defeat from the jaws of victory, often by only a hair's breadth. Everybody agreed it wasn't my fault: just consistently bad breaks. Lately it had been getting to the point where if somebody mentioned my name, they were as likely as not to add, " . . . poor bastard," after it. There goes Joke Wiggly, the impotent dick.

Well, was I going to accept that?

How many times had I heard other guys, other PIs especially, complain about their bad luck . . . and known what they really meant by that was their stupidity or poor preparedness?

I remembered my friend Murph telling me about a squeal he caught one time on the West Side. Neighbors had complained about an apartment that literally smelled like shit, so of course he arrived expecting to find one or more stiffs. Instead he found an old retired guy who was in the habit of keeping a couple of open buckets of his own shit around the house. "The guy spent forty years of his life workin' in the sewer," Murph explained to me, "and it got good to him."

Had I reached the point where I was making my own bad luck, because being in the shit had gotten good to me?

All at once I remembered what I had just told Lady Sally about invisible scriptwriters plotting my life for me. Could it be that I was manufacturing bad luck for the same reason TV detectives did: so I wouldn't become too successful to remain in the third-rate low-rent job I loved so much?

Had I fallen in love with the romantic image of myself as a loser, a perennial fall-guy, because it gave me an excuse to be as fatalistic and weary and cynical as Sam Spade or Philip Marlowe?

I don't usually dig that deep into myself. I think I might not have, the night before. Before I made love with Arethu-sa . . .

I stopped rubbing at my head, and looked Lady Sally square in the eye.

"You are looking at a walking disaster," I said.

She waited.

"And tonight, it is going to fall, like an express train from a great height, onto the testicles of . . . what *is* his name, anyway? I can't keep calling him 'that scumbag.' "

She smiled, and the room became prettier. "Yes, you may. But his name is Christian Raffalli. And I have just come as close as I ever shall to feeling sorry for him."

"Don't commit yourself," I advised. "You haven't seen what I'm going to do to him yet."

"Whatever it is, I shall not pity him," she said positively. "I'm not keen on rapists in general—but to rape, *here*, calls for a specially twisted mind. By my lights, creatures who hurt my friends are not human beings."

"Uh . . . listen," I said. "Just how tight are you wired with the man across the river? I mean, do we have to give this Raffalli to the cops? And does he have to be healthy at the time?"

"What guy?" she asked.

I smiled. She smiled, We smiled together.

"Impotent dick," my ass! Just ask Arethusa; she'd tell you . . .

From there on, the day improved again for a while.

8. Black Spot

. . . and if ye mingle your affairs with theirs, then
they are your brethren (and sistren) . . .

—the Quran (parentheses added)

WHILE I was heading for the employees' cafeteria in the basement, I suddenly heard an odd sound. Series of sounds. My first wild thought was that I had been transplanted into a Warner Brothers cartoon. I spun on my heel and saw a client coming toward me, from a Studio whose door was just closing. The bearded longhair with the carpenter's tool belt I had seen the night before. No crutch this time. Now he was on a pogo stick . . .

He *boinged* past, flashing me a quick wide smile, and took the spiral staircase without hesitating. The way he looked as he disappeared down and around the stairs made me think of a kangaroo melting as it circled Little Black Sambo.

After a few seconds I started breathing again.

I'm like Lady Sally too, I guess. There are some things I won't believe even if I see them with my own eyes. No *way* could he have really had a faint shimmering glow around his head. It must have been a trick of the light.

That reminded me that I'd been meaning to investigate how they managed to conceal the light sources in this place so cleverly. It was a neat trick. I looked around the hallway, windowless and bright as day.

After five full minutes I had failed to locate a single bulb, except for the tiny red peanut bulbs. I gave up and continued on my way to breakfast.

Breakfast, lunch and dinner were all available on demand, as the staff worked three—not two—shifts,· providing round-the-clock art. The House coffee wasn't Mike Callahan's, but it was damned good for normal coffee. Tanzania Peaberry, a blend very high in caffeine without being sour: fresh ground and dripped. Over *huevos rancheros* I met more of the staff. A stacked short-haired blonde babe called Cat, stunning in a mauve bodysuit that fit her like a sheen of psychedelic perspiration. A quiet, darkly handsome guy in his twenties named Tony, who wore dark slacks, a net shirt and a single earring, and looked like the young De Niro. A sweet Chinese girl named Mei-ling, unselfconsciously naked and built like a three-quarter-scale model of Marilyn Monroe. A happy-go-lucky gal in a jogging suit whom everybody called Juicy Lucy, who never stopped telling jokes, good ones. (I recalled that she was one of Raffalli's victims.) A tall greying gent named Phillip, with the best body I ever saw on a guy in his fifties. He was dressed in only brief denim shorts and slippers, and most of the other artists, male and female, seemed to find reason to touch him a lot as the afternoon wore on. A pleasantly dignified bald old coot named Reggie, a good forty years older than Phillip, wearing a splendid silk robe; he spoke (seldom) with a British accent, even more refined than Lady Sally's, and had an odd knack of seeming to walk without moving his feet, sort of shimmering along as if he were on greased wheels despite his advanced years. I kind of wondered how much use he could be in a whorehouse, but I guess it's like they say: if you can't stir it, you can always lick it. And experience must count for something . . .

And most memorable of all, the ubiquitous but seldom seen Mary. From her voice I had pictured her as young, blonde and athletic. She was in her late thirties, dark-haired, and had to run well over two hundred pounds. I think she was the sexiest woman in the room. Can you picture a sexy *sumo*? If not, there's no point in my trying to describe her to you—and if you can, I just did. Her voice was so powerful, without being strident, that I wondered if she could get a man off with it alone. Even more than anyone else there, she made me feel included, at home, working me into conversations and explaining insider references and so on. At the same time she flirted with Phillip and gently jollied Cat out of a mild depression and demolished Juicy Lucy in a puntest and played mental chess with Reggie (losing valiantly and blasphemously, which latter he ignored) and demolished a six-egg omelet she rustled up herself. Figure out a way to rig a power takeoff on her and you could shut down the Big Allis plant over in Ravenswood. I noticed a wedding band on her hand and hoped for his sake that her old man was at least half machine.

The American Indian whom Tim had introduced as "Many Hands" yesterday came in at a trot, grabbed a cup of coffee, and headed for the door again. For the life of me I couldn't remember his real name. As he went by me I caught his eye and asked him. "What's your name again, friend?"

"I'm Running Behind," he said, and was gone.

Half a dozen whole and partially eaten biscuits hit the door in a cluster as it closed behind him. One of them was mine. Robin, the client who apparently never went home, came scurrying out of the kitchen and cleaned them up almost before they hit the floor. I don't think he was in view for more than three seconds. He was still wearing his Tarzan in Bondage outfit, in which he looked like a short potbellied accountant.

The food was good, the conversation better, and nobody seemed to be in any kind of hurry. I felt strength and contentment flow into me. I didn't even mind much that both Arethusas were elsewhere.

At some point I mentioned to Mary how surprised I'd been the night before to see Priscilla eighty-six a cop with two other buttons standing right there. She smiled and nodded. "Sally can even afford to offend cops." She paused, and did something subtly satanic with her eyebrows. "Lady zings the blues."

A piece of toast bounced off the side of her head. She ignored it magnificently.

"Yeah," Juicy Lucy said, "and sometimes when Cynthia's sick or on vacation, Lady stings the bruised . . ." Mary stirred her coffee sharply, and a spoonful departed in Lucy's direction.

"And whenever she uses that damned iron bobsled . . ." Phillip began, and waited until we'd all turned to look at him before finishing, " . . . Lady dings the slews."

About a meal's worth of various foods accumulated on him. I got him in the chest hair with the eggs and salsa myself.

"And every Monday, after the clients go home," Mary said, over a growing murmur of protest and warning, "Lady springs for brews." Before anyone could react, she turned to me and explained, "Sally figures after spending a whole week with a bunch of do-ers, we're entitled to relax with a few be-ers."

She might as well have stepped under a running shower. Of grapefruit and orange and apple juice, mostly, but there seemed to be a bit of skimmed milk in there. It converged from all sides like a water-balloon explosion filmed in reverse, and I would swear she never flinched.

The softest, most gentle, motherly, fondly indulgent voice I ever heard in my life said, "All right, children, that'll do," and everyone but me froze. I turned to look—

My first impression was that Robin had a small child in black leather with him. Then I changed it to an elf in leather. A wise old mother elf. Finally I realized she was the midget I'd seen briefly in the Parlor the night before. Her body was in perfect proportion for its size, and quite attractive in that leather outfit. Her face was kindly and compassionate at first glance; then you saw the flashing eyes. She was not holding Robin's elbow like an obedient child, she was steering him like a puppeteer with a hand on the back of his gee string. He carried what looked like a large fire extinguisher. In her free hand she had a green plastic trash bag, opened out, and a couple of towels.

Lucy, Phillip and Mary stood up and began undressing. All three looked mildly abashed. Everyone else backed away, so I did too. The leather midget collected all the food-spattered clothing in her bag, and stood back herself. Robin triggered the big canister he held, and hosed the three naked people down with a jet of water. They turned around to assist him. "Damn, that's *cold*," Lucy protested.

" Yes, dear," the little woman said firmly. "A cold shower seems indicated. Things were getting a bit out of hand."

When Robin had them clean, he hosed off the splattered parts of the table as well. I saw that the room floor was tile, with slightly sunken drains at frequent intervals. Robin chased the last swirls of debris into the drains, shut down the spray, and waited for orders.

" Don't just stand there, lovewipe," she told him gently. " You've hardly started your dishes."

" YesMistressI'msorryMistressI'm*such*afoolIdon'tknowwhaton earthiswrongwithmerightawayMistressthankyouma'am," he said, tucked her bag of soiled clothes under his armpit, and sprinted back into the kitchen. I saw that thin vivid pink stripes had been laid across his buttocks so carefully that someone had been able to play four games of tic-tac-toe, to four draws, with a Magic Marker or felt-tip pen.

I think it took that long for it to dawn on me that this maternal pygmy with the soft voice was the dreaded Mistress Cynthia.

"Carry on, children," she said, and followed Robin. All of us sat down except the three who were still toweling their hair. The moment the door swung shut behind her, Mary said, "—and now that they've got those cute male flight attendants, once in a while—"

Three people, one of them me, chorused, "—Lady bangs the stews," and you know, it's a lot of fun to laugh like hell with a whole bunch of people at once, all of you trying to keep the noise down.

It went on being fun like that for maybe another half hour. People drifted in and out, some to eat breakfast, some lunch and some dinner, and some just for coffee or juice. I met a stunning mature brunette named Sherry with a classic model's body. She, I recalled, had been the first person in the House to suffer from Raffalli's sense of humor. She gave Phillip a greeting hug and kiss that gave him an erection—then twinkled at me and did the same for me. I was glad I had not had to undress earlier. If I was going to hang around these people for very long, I'd have to either get over being shy or have my blushing-nerves cut. She welcomed me to the zoo, and told me a funny story about a fellow artist named Colt which I will not repeat as even I don't believe it. And I've met him.

A few minutes later a man came in, about Phillip's age, whom Sherry introduced to me as her husband Willard. I shook his hand politely and told him my name was Ken and congratulated him on his catch. When he went to the coffee machine I wandered along behind him as if I wanted another cup myself. We stood by the machine with our backs to the others, and in a prison-yard whisper I said, "Hello, Professor. Long time no see."

His cup did not tremble. He finished pouring, smiled over his shoulder at me, and said, equally softly, "I thought that was you, Joe. Don't worry, you can't blow my cover—I'm among friends. I haven't actively Professed since I married Sherry almost fifteen years ago . . . but everyone here knows who the Professor *was*."

"So do a lot of guys," I agreed. "Lots of people wondered where the hell you went. I figured you were down. Glad I was wrong. So you finally found something better than the con."

"Well, not really," he said. "In a sense, I always was an artist—but I dealt exclusively in the foreplay. One day I simply decided to switch to customers I *liked*, and start following through. And charging less per head. The results have been gratifying."

I shook my head in wonder. "You know, if anybody could talk me into trying gay, it'd be you."

He inclined his head graciously at the compliment, and knew me well enough not to take it literally. "It has always been a pleasure to work with you in the past, Joseph. Or should I say 'Ken'?"

"Unless it's just the Lady or her old man around, yeah, Prof. Uh, Willard, I mean."

"Whichever you prefer, Ken."

"It's kind of a long story, you know?"

"So long as you're not attempting to run a game on the Lady or her Household, it's none of my business," he said carefully. "Many of us here use House names for one reason or another. My wife, for instance, is 'Maureen' to her intimates."

"If I had been planning to clip the Lady, I'd fold the store right now," I promised him. "But I got out of the game about the same time you did, or a little after. I've been a PI for years now."

He nodded. "Say no more. Let your I be P. 'Client privilege' has many meanings here, all of them sacred."

A memory surfaced. " 'Maureen' . . . Prof, didn't you used to have a skinny little kid roping for you named Maureen?"

"The very same," he said. "She also told the tale, and, on a few memorable occasions, even ran the store. At a profit."

"Well I'll be damned. I'd never have recognized her."

"She has filled out considerably since she was fourteen," he agreed.

"That's not it. Well, it's part of it. But the Maureen I remember had a bad case of self-hate. It stuck out a yard. And Sherry doesn't, it's just as obvious. You've been good for her, Prof."

He smiled, but shook his head. "Lady Sally has been good for her. I've concentrated on not undoing her good work. But thank you, Ken." Despite his words, I could tell I had succeeded in flattering him.

We rejoined the others. More than ever I felt a kinship with this place. The Professor may have been the greatest con man that ever worked the tristate area. Certainly he was the best I ever worked with or heard of. A player's player, one of the immortals. If this life suited him better, perhaps I had better reexamine my primary article of faith, that Private Investigator was the best job on Earth. Eat where the big trucks are parked and you can't go far wrong.

What I had *not* told him was that his own, much better hidden undercurrent of self-contempt was also gone now. He had always accepted himself, squarely, and tried to live up to his own self-imposed standards. But now he *liked* himself too. It stuck out a yard . . .

AFTER brunchner, the Raffalli Eradication Society held its war council in Mary's Snoop Room up on the fourth floor. This was necessary as we all needed to hear the taped records of Raffalli's previous assaults and batteries, and the room was, I was told, designed to erase any tape or floppy disk that left (or entered) it. Regardless of whether one used the door, or cut his own entrance through wall, floor or ceiling. Only one line between that room and the rest of the House was two-way, Mary's intercom, and there was no physical way to patch tape output into that line. It was quite a remarkable room.

It had to be. Lady Sally's House, and her insistence on maximum client privacy, presented unusual surveillance problems. There were a lot of inputs to handle. Ten mikes on the first floor alone. Forty-five on the second or main working floor. Three hallway mikes and two panning cameras on the residential third floor. And four cameras out on the street. (I was professionally annoyed with myself for having failed to spot the one at the entrance I'd used.) Thanks to a clever switching system, hyperactive Mary with her multitasking brain was somehow able to time-share among all currently live inputs fast enough to keep track of everything happening in the House in realtime. A computer helped by constantly monitoring all inputs for certain key signatures, such as the word "Help," or the staff code word that meant the same thing.

But Lady Sally wanted all records maintained for one week, and then automatically erased. Physical handling of that much tape was what a physicist friend of mine calls a nontrivial problem.

So the room held fifty-eight custom-built tape decks. They were neither reel-to-reel nor cassette machines. In a sense they were both, and in a sense neither. They used Maxell XL-1 reel-to-reel tape, but packed into plastic cases exactly the way inked ribbon is packed into a printer-ribbon cassette—except that these "cassettes" were about the size of pizza boxes in the two dimensions not defined by tape-width. Each held a week's worth of tape in an infinite loop, in a jillion little interlocking loops and whorls, just like printer-ribbon—except there was no Möbius twist in the loop because only one side of magnetic recording tape is coated. Instead, the heads moved, each time the end of the tape came past, for a total of four mono tracks per tape. One cassette, a week of recording at 1⅞ ips, took 25,200 feet—the equivalent of fourteen ordinary 7½-inch reels, but without all those plastic hubs.

The decks themselves were stripped down: little more than heads and motorized spindles for the cassettes' two transport wheels (two because, unlike printer-ribbon, recording tape must sometimes go backwards), fixed to bare-bones frames which were not especially cosmetic but must have been convenient when maintenance or repairs were needed. Each could be swung out from its rack on a hinge. In case of disaster, you could just physically remove all the tape from a cassette, feed it through a conventional tape deck onto an 11½-inch reel, and switch to a new empty reel every thirty-two hours' worth.

All amplification and processing of the information recorded was done at a master console that looked like it might have baffled Lieutenant Uhura. (That's one thing about that show that always sourly amused me: they combined their token female and their token black into a single character—and then made her a telephone operator!) The tape decks themselves were racked along three walls like pies waiting for delivery at the world's busiest pizza place, twenty per wall. The wall that was two decks short compensated with six VCRs, feeding a pair of monitors above the master console. One flipflopped between the two residential camera views; the four exterior views rotated on the other screen.

It was a big room. Despite all the hardware, there was ample room for seven bodies and folding chairs. The seven were Lady Sally McGee, Mike Callahan, Mary, Priscilla, Arethusa, and me. Arethusa was two members of the Inner Circle because she had bullied her way in the night before. From her points of view, she and I had been on our way to make love at her place. Then I had dumped her on her floor, run like a madman around the entire third floor, and fallen on my face. Then she had discovered a lump on the back of my head that she knew had not been there moments before. Then Lady Sally herself had shown up on Priscilla's heels, looking unsurprised and upset with herself. So Arethusa had simply pestered her until Sally told her the whole story.

This struck me as good news on several levels. "I think Arethusa could be extremely useful tonight," I said when everyone but me was seated. "In two crucial roles." I put my back against the door and addressed her. "Hon, am I correct in believing that not many of the clients know you come in stereo?"

"Pun intended," one of her agreed. "All the artists know, of course. But they don't talk about it with clients. Like any freak, I get so tired of being gawked at that I've let fewer than half a dozen clients in on my secret since I started working here."

"Thank you for the compliment," I said. "But you're not a freak, Arethusa."

"Yes I am, Joe," she corrected soberly. "That's the truth, and I see no reason to duck it. In a world like this, a freak is no bad thing to be. They proved that back in the Sixties."

"Hear, hear!" Mike said. "Joe, I think I see where you're going—"

I nodded. "We spring both Arethusas on him, to startle him for that one full second of inattention we need—and while he's busy staring at hers, we take him."

"—but I think you're overlooking something," Mike went on.

"I know," I said. "He's had free run of the place, several times: he could have stumbled across both of her. If so, simply seeing both hers together isn't going to tip him off that we're on to him. At worst we have a couple of superfluous bodies in the room." I checked myself and said to her, "Not that either of your bodies could ever be superfluous, babe." Then, to Mike again: "She needn't get in the way much, and she might help a lot. If nothing else she may hold his attention because . . ." I trailed off, unable to phrase it.

"Because he raped me last night, and he'll be wondering what I'd think and say if I knew," Arethusa finished quietly for me. "Or trying to guess which of me it was, so he can try the other one tonight and compare."

Probably not more than half a dozen of them heard my jaw muscles pop. I rubbed my back against the door, thought briefly of how little protection it really afforded. "Right," I said briskly. "So our first step is to play all the tapes we have of Raffalli, concentrating on the sections where he goes into high gear. Know your enemy. Once we do, we can pick the best place to take him."

"I already know the best place," Lady Sally said. "As far as I'm concerned, it's the only place, no matter what we learn about the bastard from those tapes."

"Yes?" was all I said.

But she must have caught the undertone I tried to cover. "Pardon me, Joe," she said. "I know this is your area of expertise, and I don't mean to backseat-drive. May I tell you my reasoning and let you decide?"

"By all means. You've survived a dangerous world a lot longer than I have."

She ignored the dig. "Much longer. I propose that we take him in Reception, just inside the main entrance. For several reasons. For one thing, it is a small space, easily controlled, and soundproof as long as its two doors are closed. For another, it has two priest's holes—concealed doors with stairs to the basement, so that it is possible for two people to appear suddenly and without warning just behind an entrant. But most important, *I don't want that son of a bitch walking into my House ever again.* I will not place my clients at risk again if I can help it."

"There's sense in that," Mike said. "If something goes sour inside the House, we're all cooked. If it goes wrong in Reception, and he gets a chance to twist that watchstem, he might just turn on his heel and take off. The further in he is, the more people are around him, and the more time he's had to build up his . . . anticipation, the worse off we are if we fuck up."

"And there's another advantage," Mary pointed out. "Take him in Reception, and we don't have to explain to the other clients why we just blindsided one of them and laid him out. Or to the staff either. Nobody ever has to know what he was or what he did. The only other way to do it that quietly is to let him go upstairs first—and there's too good a chance he'll wind his watch before he does."

I gave up resenting the idea because it wasn't mine. "There's one final good reason for using Reception," I said, "which I would now like to discuss, to make sure we have our ducks in a row." I waited a few seconds, to make sure I had everyone's attention. "We must agree on our ultimate goal here," I went on then, meeting each person's eyes in turn as I spoke. "There are few things on earth as silly as a liberal vigilante. I say the law cannot help us in this. I say that we are the law. 'I, the jury,' as Mr. Spillane once put it. And you too. I say we are going to listen to these tapes—give him a nice, fair trial—and then we are going to sentence him to death. So a private place, before anyone else knows he's arrived, is best." I looked around at sober faces. "If no one else claims privilege, I will execute him myself. And undertake to dispose of the body, while Arethusa destroys his watch. Then I'll toss his apartment and any other address I can connect him with and burn every piece of paper or floppy disk I don't understand. If I run across anyone who meets the definition of 'accessory before or after the fact,' I will inform Lady Sally and then execute them too, cleaning up after the same way. If anybody has any problem with any of this, now is the time to say so, and defend your position."

The silence lasted perhaps fifteen seconds. Then Lady Sally said, "I waive privilege. Reluctantly—but you are younger, stronger and faster. And you've earned the right."

"Should we not interrogate him before we kill him?" Priscilla asked.

"Not if you ask me," I said. "First, I might accidentally learn how he accomplished the trick—and I don't want to. I don't want anybody to. Second, I might learn something that made me pity him. That would be a shame. Third, and most important, I can kill a man, but I don't think I'm willing to torture him first . . . and nothing less would provide information I could trust. If he has accomplices, I'll find them."

Mike said, "Why Arethusa? To bust up the watch, I mean."

"Because she is the only person in this room, including me, that I'm absolutely certain cannot be tempted by absolute power," I said. "She already has it."

He nodded agreement so quickly that I felt a brief pang of irrational jealousy. More irrational than jealousy always is, I mean. "Good thinking. How 'bout it, Arethusa? You know what the Ring can do to a person . . . are you willing to be our Frodo?"

"Thank you both," said the one of her that happened to be closest to the center of his field of vision. "Yes, I will, if you wish." "I should be safe enough," her other mouth said to me. "I'm already corrupted absolutely."

"Hell," I said, "was I *that* good?"

"Better," she said.

"We've avoided Joe's central question," Lady Sally said. "Does anyone here object to the cold-blooded murder of Christian Raffalli?"

She insisted on conducting a voice vote. When it was done we met all the legal requirements for a conspiracy to commit murder.

"Can I ask what you've got in mind for the *corpus derelicti?*" Mike asked. "Layman's interest."

"There are only two good ways to get rid of a body in the city," I said, "and I don't think the cafeteria has two bottles of relish. Can I assume that somewhere in that basement, near the secret stairs, there is a bathroom? By which I mean, a private room with both a bathtub and a toilet in it?"

"Yes," Lady Sally said. "A large bath. Quite near the stairs."

"And you've got carving knives and a hacksaw in the House?"

Mike and Arethusa paled slightly. Lady Sally just nodded. "Doctor Kate has just about everything a hospital OR would have. Bone saws and such. And there chances to be a heavy-duty grinding wheel in the basement."

"That'll save time," I said. "Still, it'll be about a six-hour job all told. I want people to notice me in the Parlor about every fifteen minutes or so throughout the night. And we do *not* want that toilet backing up on us."

Arethusa surprised me. "I can help you, Joe. And still be visible to everyone in the Parlor all night long, playing the piano."

So I surprised me. "Will you marry me, Arethusa?"

Her eyes widened, but she answered steadily and at once. "No, Joe. Not at this point. But I will live in sin with you indefinitely. And you can keep asking."

You can't ask for a better offer than that, can you? Can you?

Well, I could. But I wasn't going to get one now. And it was certainly a *good* offer. No: a great one, better than most men ever get. The distance between one and a hundred is nothing compared to the distance between zero and one. "Done," I said without hesitation, went and sat in the empty chair between her and kissed her both.

There was a brief smattering of applause.

Twenty-four hours earlier I'd have bet the rent that I would say "Please, God, could I have brain cancer?" long before I ever said the words "Will you marry me?" All I can say is, it had been a long twenty-four hours.

And how many of the girls *you've* known do you think would have volunteered—after one date!—to help you reduce a warm corpse to pieces small enough to flush down a toilet? You find one like that, you fire your grappling hooks and pray.

She hadn't said no . . .

MIKE cleared his throat. "All right, folks," he said, his voice as commanding as Mary's and an octave deeper. "We're engaged in conspiracy to commit assault, murder one from ambush, mutilation, desecration of a corpse, petty larceny, B&E, vandalism, unlicensed burial and public health violations regarding sewage disposal. Shouldn't we give some thought to raping the guy? Just to round things out, like?"

"In more ways than one," both Arethusas chorused. "But aren't the sewers *intended* for human waste?"

"Not if it's known to be diseased," Mary said. "I think we should get serious and listen to these tapes, like Joe suggested in the first place."

"Quite right," Lady Sally agreed. " 'Know your enemy,' I believe you said, Joe. Sorry I sidetracked us."

"I've cued up the relevant sections," Mary said, swiveling her chair to face her console. "I had to splice a dimmer into the power supply to get the tape to run slowly enough. I'll start at half speed."

Ordinarily there were no speakers in the room, only head-phones. I guess so you couldn't play back tape aloud and thus into the intercom mike. But Mary had fetched in a little sugar-shaker-sized speaker for this meeting, and handwired an adaptor so it could run off the headphone jack. *Kloss Experimental* was stenciled on its side, and I later learned it was a superb speaker for its size and weight. But the quality of the sound we first heard wasn't much better than a clock radio. It took a few seconds to identify it as the sounds of Sherry exercising, alone in her Studio, at half speed. The loudest single component was her breathing.

"Sorry about the quality," Mary said apologetically. "It's recorded at real low speed to start with, and I don't demagnetize my heads as often as I really ought to. That constant surf sound you hear is tape hiss at half the normal frequency." Sherry's voice on the tape made what must have been a momentary grunt of effort in realtime, but sounded like a comical belch in slow motion. "Wait, it's coming up now—" She spun a dial on her board, and the tape slowed drastically, like a comedy effect. Just as everything reached the range where the bass capacity of that speaker really started to shine, all sound ceased except the rumbling grey-noise of tape hiss. Mary turned the dial to the limit of its travel and raised a hand for stillness.

Nothing but rumble for perhaps five seconds. Then we heard an opening door. And then there was a long, lingering chuckle that made my hair stand on end. The fidelity was worse than an answering machine, with no high end at all; the hiss noise was as loud as the signal, or louder. But the menace, the *confidence*, came through clearly. It was a happy chuckle. A jolly chuckle.

" ' . . . and finished her off in mid-air . . . ' " he said jovially, quoting an old limerick. He had a pronounced Brooklyn accent. "But maybe not literally. That's a perfectly nice bed . . . and there's no reason to tire my legs out. Come—*unh!*—with me, sweetheart . . ." There were further sounds of effort. "Why pretend to resist," he asked rhetorically, "when you still have your legs open? Ah, that's better . . . flip you—*oof!*—over . . . in for a landing . . . there! My, you look charming . . . nice the way they still stick out even though you're on your back . . . charming expression . . . eyes . . . mouth . . ." There were sounds of hasty undressing. Then there were other sounds. Apparently penetration required considerable effort. Which he seemed to enjoy.

He talked to her as he raped her. Jocularly, if a bit breathlessly. He spoke for instance of the comparative advantages, as exercise, of the jumping jack and of jumping dick. A funny guy. He chided her good-naturedly for her lack of response. Happily his patter didn't last long. As I had deduced from the start, he was a premature ejaculator.

He said things as he climaxed that I don't think I could repeat under hypnosis. I erased them from my mind as I heard them. Then there were only the sounds of him manhandling her back into her original location in mid-air, the barely audible sounds of clothing being collected, and the sound of the door closing behind him. He had left it open throughout. He said nothing after orgasm, as though Sherry had ceased to exist for him as even a make-believe person at that instant.

Mary stopped the tape.

After perhaps five seconds of blessed silence, Lady Sally said formally, "I *identify* that voice as Christian Raffalli. And I am very glad I committed myself to his murder *before* hearing that tape."

"It's an emotional button-pusher," Mary agreed savagely. "But I don't think that makes it unfair evidence."

"No, it isn't," Mike said. "But it doesn't make me want to kill him any more than I already did. Which is just barely enough. Once a man makes the decision to rape, having a good time doing it does not compound his guilt a whole lot."

"But he was so *cheerful*," Mary said. "So fucking *smug*."

"Given what he can do, he has a right to be smug," Mike said. "I don't think many men, given Raffalli's watch, could resist trying a spot of rape, at least once anyway. Not forever."

Mary clouded up. I wished I was armed with something more substantial than a blackjack. "You sound like you approve!"

His voice was a match for even hers. "Which you know perfectly well I don't. Darlin', *all* men think about rape, at least once in their lives. Women have an inexhaustible supply of something we've *got* to have, more precious to us than heroin . . . and most of you rank the business as pleasant enough, but significantly less important than food, shopping or talking about feelings. Or you go to great lengths to seem like you do—because that's *your* correct biological strategy. But some of you charge all the market will bear, in one coin or another, and all of you award the prize, when you do, for what seem to us like arbitrary and baffling reasons. Our single most urgent need—and the best we can hope for is to get lucky. We're all descended from two million years of rapists, every race and tribe of us, and we wouldn't be human if we didn't sometimes fantasize about just knocking you down and taking it. The truly astonishin' thing is how seldom we do. I can only speculate that most of us must love you a lot, for some reason. Peculiar, considering how often you insist we only see you as objects placed here for our gratification. Rape is always a brutal and uncondonable crime—but so is any act of terror. I didn't condemn Christian Raffalli to death because he's a rapist, and I won't do it because he's a happy one with a rotten sense of humor."

"Then why have you condemned him?" Lady Sally asked.

"Several reasons. Because he knows how to stop Time, and that power should not exist. Because there's no other way to be reasonably sure that power will stop existing. Because he rapes *here*—where he not only could have enthusiastic cooperation from just about anyone he wants, but has already paid for it. Because he's a *repeat* rapist, who's found nothing better to do with his magic power for several nights running now. And because his pattern shows he's degrading, rather than getting it out of his system. He does more each time, his jokes get progressively nastier, and he's taken to adding gratuitous attempted murder. If Joe hadn't been Irish, we might all be somewhere else right now, saying how natural he looks. Any of those reasons would do it for me. But not the simple fact of rape."

"What *would* you do to a rapist?" Priscilla asked seriously. "A one-time rapist, say, who doesn't kill."

"If I ruled the world, you mean? Rape him," Mike said flatly. "Like I suggested earlier—I wasn't joking. With just as much violence and/or terror as he'd used. But I'd want to be *certain* of the facts first—and if I wasn't, I'd turn him loose. I'd like to see the same punishment for false accusation of rape, by the way. Rapists who murdered their victims—them I'd execute, after they'd been raped the correct number of times, selecting a method

so as to give them at least ten painful minutes' dying per victim
I'd read their names to him as he died. And I suppose for chroni
non-murdering rapists I'd go as far as, say, breaking kneecaps."

"Not castration?" Priscilla asked. "Surgical or chemical?"

"Hell, no!" he said. "I'd a lot sooner kill him, or put him i
a wheelchair. And I think *that's* too drastic as a general rule
Besides, I'm not sure rape has a lot to do with testosterone c
seminal pressure. And despite that crack about two million year
of rapists, I don't really think the tendency to yield to the basi
instinct is hereditary. Though I'm sure a boy can learn it from hi
father. No, I'm for the Law of Talion in most things. Now, if
rape caused the victim to need a hysterectomy—"

"Gee, Mike," Mary said sarcastically. "It's a damn shame yo
don't rule the world."

"Well," he said, "I do have a terrific idea for women who'v
been raped in the real world."

Lady Sally had just put a hand up to interrupt him and g
us back on track—but at this she checked herself. "I rule thi
digression intriguing enough to allow it," she said. "If you mak
it short."

"You'll love it," he promised. "I read it in a letter a lifer wro
to the *Co-Ev Quarterly* a few years ago. The key to vengeance i
simple and elegant. Don't charge the bastard with rape. Charg
him with indecent exposure."

"I don't get you," Mary said. "How does that help?"

He grinned wolfishly. "Let me count the ways. It is *much* easie
to get a conviction for that charge than for rape. The defense i
not allowed to ask *anything* about your sexual history or how yo
were dressed at the time. Forensic evidence is unnecessary. Th
total public embarrassment to you is cut more than in half. I
many states, a man convicted of indecent exposure will actuall
draw more prison time than a rapist. And whereas rapists ar
sort of prison folk-heroes, weenie-waggers do harder time tha
anybody but a short-eyes. In fact, the plan sort of incorporate
my own suggested punishment."

Mary's grin now looked so much like his that I almost won
dered if they could be related somehow. "Oh, I *like* it, Mike! An
the best part is, you don't have to make a single false statemen
You just don't volunteer extraneous information. What's the gu
going to do, leap up in court and say, 'It's a filthy lie, Your Honor
I raped that bitch!'?"

"It is elegant," Lady Sally interrupted, grinning in a very simila way herself. "But let's discuss it another time. There are other tapes to hear, and plans to finalize. I don't imagine it makes a great deal of difference *why* we kill him as long as we're all agreed."

"It makes a difference to me," Mike insisted.

"Table it. Mary, next tape."

I agreed with Mike. I don't like to kill a man without walking around it a little and kicking the tires. But women are more practical than men.

9. Dick Sees Spots

... t'were best done quickly ...

—SHAKESPEARE, *Macbeth*

WE listened to more tapes. To all the tapes of Raffalli during his interludes as The Flash—or as he signed himself on Ellen, The Phantom. I won't reproduce any of it. We learned a few more things about Raffalli, but nothing relevant and more than you probably need to know about the infinite possibilities of the human spirit.

I lost the last of my hesitation about killing him, if that's any help. I don't think I'm as merciful a man as Mike Callahan.

I managed to keep my cool during the replay of Arethusa's rape. She held my hands tightly throughout that segment, and for as long after as it took me to relax my grip.

Then we listened to a total of about half an hour of Raffalli in the Parlor, in normal conversation with other clients and artists, and watched him approach the front door five times. Enough to give a sketchy picture of him as a human being. His heavy Brooklynese accent bespoke lower-class origins, but he dressed and spoke and carried himself with urbane grace and a high degree of apparent self-confidence. If you had to describe him in a single word, you might pick "dapper." He bounced a little when he walked. He had a tendency to start arguments and win them, to issue small challenges and then back them up, so smoothly that he never provoked any open confrontation or lasting animosity. The one time I'd seen him, I recalled, he'd been arm-wrestling a biker—and winning.

I had Mary play the Parlor tape for that time, cuing from
the song "Huggin' and A-Chalkin'." The playback indicated
strongly that he'd won by cheating. He used his watch to stop
time, got up, and pitted his whole weight against his opponent
until he had him past the point of recovery. Then he resumed
the match with it already won. In other words, during that one
flash glimpse I had of him, I probably actually saw—or rather,
failed to see—him work his trick, in plain sight and in good light.
The two hardest parts must have been getting his wrestling hand
untangled from the biker's frozen grip, and resuming his original
position near-perfectly afterward. What a cocky bastard! With pun
intended.

Lady Sally informed us that during his interview with her at the
time he'd joined the House, Raffalli had given his occupation as
"mathematical physicist." That sounds redundant to me, but what
do I know? He had stated that he taught part-time at Long Island
University. He had politely declined her standard suggestion that
he could choose a House name to give to artists and other clients,
saying he had nothing to hide—doubtless chuckling inside as he
said it. She confessed to us that she had rather liked him. "I have
an unfortunate attraction to cocky men," she added, carefully not
looking at her husband.

"Really, darlin'?" he said. "You've never introduced any of
them to *me*."

"I try not to introduce them to anyone," she said. "They last
longer that way. My point is that I find it odd a man so personable
should need to rape."

"Ted Bundy," Priscilla said briefly.

"*Touché*. Shall we consider the details of Mr. Raffalli's murder? I suggest that the key to the whole matter is to instantly
immobilize his free hand. The right one, assuming he continues
to wear that damnable watch on his left wrist . . ."

NOTHING else of significance happened before the balloon went
up. Unless you want to count me and Arethusa—both of her—
celebrating the new plateau our relationship had reached, as
soon as we could be alone. I certainly do. And the event had
aspects so interesting I could go on at length. But it has no real
bearing on the story. Except to indicate that Arethusa and I all
went into combat exercised, rested, sexually satisfied and freshly
bathed. For all I know, so did all our teammates. That's the way
I'd bet, anyway.

I do recall some of the conversation afterward. I had just had very convincing empirical proof that Arethusa was a single person with two bodies at her control. So I finally got around to asking her, had she been telepathic as far back as the womb, or what? "No," she told me. "I have a few—very few—vague memories of life as two separate children. My parents were . . . well, pretty eccentric. Wonderful parents, but strange. They belonged to a religious sect you've never heard of. You've heard of sects that don't believe in medicine? Well, my folks didn't believe in twins."

I couldn't help it; I giggled. But it was all right: she smiled with me. "I know, it sounds funny. But religion often makes people refuse to believe in things that are right in front of their face. My folks refused to believe that God could allow a soul to be bisected or copied, and they just couldn't see any other way a single act of procreation could produce two people. So it hadn't happened. They insisted on giving me a single name, and treating me as a single person. The observable fact that there were two of me they just . . . ignored. Pretty soon I did too. I think I was six or seven before I really got it through my head that other people could only do one thing at a time, and that other kids *all* went to school *every* day."

During all this her voice kept switching from one side of me to the other, apparently at random. I found myself tending to look at whichever one of her was not speaking at the moment. How often in life do you get to watch someone actually listen to themself? Once in a while they would look at each other, and I would get slightly dizzy thinking about that. "God, it's a good thing you weren't quints," I said. "You'd starve on one paycheck. What a fascinating life you must have had. Be having. To be in two places at once . . ."

"It has its ups and downs," she said.

"Is it hard to run two bodies at once?"

"Is it hard running only one?"

"Well, I've nothing to compare . . . oh. I see what you mean. Silly question. I'm beginning to understand something, I think."

"What's that?" she asked.

"Well, from the moment I met you, you came across as . . . what's the word? Assured? Confident? The first thing I knew about you—" I paused. "No: the *first* thing I knew about you was that you look very good naked. But the next thing was . . . what's that stupid phrase they keep using on talk shows? You feel good about yourself. That's rare in anybody, and especially in women. But it makes sense. Most of us keep constantly doing reality checks. We study how other people react to us, to reassure us that our senses aren't lying to us. We send out little sonar pulses all the time, and study the echoes that come back to see if we're all right. If enough people tell us we're drunk, we lie down. You don't do that. You've *got* your sensory reality check, all the time. It makes you just a little healthier, a little saner, than most people."

"And a little more prone to *folie à deux*, maybe," she said seriously. "That's part of why I decided to let myself fall in love with you, I think."

"How do you mean?"

"I *am* very self-confident. And sometimes both of me are dead wrong. I believe you are smart enough to know when, tough enough to make me believe it, and sweet enough to make me like it."

I blinked. "That's a tall order."

She smiled. "You're a tall man. And I'm worth the trouble."

I did not argue either point.

"And besides," she said, "you didn't flinch when you found out I have two bodies. Most of the people I've told did. One client got depressed at the thought that he was only getting half my attention."

"The man's a fool," I said. "The evidence is clear: you've got twice as much attention to give as a solo. It only makes sense. You've got two brains to use."

"See what I mean? If I let myself love anyone less percep- tive than you, I'd be in terrible danger of developing a split personality."

I made a pun which on reflection I will not repeat, and one thing led to another, and then we took a nap. I don't care what the Raging Bull thought: this is the way to prepare for a fight.

WE conspirators all got together again at six P.M. to have half an hour of final choreography and dress rehearsal while traffic through Reception was at its lightest. Then there was a long period during which Time insisted on tailgating instead of passing, no matter how far I pulled over to let it by. Backstage jitters. Arethusa tried to get me to eat at least a little, but I prefer to go into combat on an empty stomach. It makes you mean and quick, and improves your chances in case of a belly wound. We seven held one last brief meeting at eight P.M., exchanged last-minute thoughts and good wishes, and took our positions.

Then there was nothing but waiting and worrying. After a while I realized I'd discovered a way to make time run slow myself, without a magic watch.

Despite my war talk, I had never killed a man in cold blood before. I had killed an indeterminate number in combat, in Viet Nam, somewhere between six and a hundred thousand or so. You let off a whole lot of rounds in a hopeful spirit, and seldom get to reel the target in and inspect it afterward. But I'd seen many men in pajamas fall at the same time I fired, and had confirmed six kills, one of them by knife. I could live with them, and any others I might have caused there. (Whether we "belonged in" Nam being quite irrelevant.) In peacetime I had killed twice, both times in self-defense, taking a couple of slugs myself on the latter occasion. I could live with both of them, too. But with more difficulty. I'd killed one of them with my hands. It takes a hundred years longer than it does on TV, and lends itself well to nightmares.

But this would be my first planned and paid assassination. From private eye to hooker to hit-man, in under twenty-four hours.

Well, at least I'd found love . . .

Which, I admitted to myself in those last nervous minutes, was the real reason *I* had voted for Christian Raffalli's death. The world was better off without him or his magic watch, sure. But if he had not raped my newfound love, in my helpless presence, I might have settled for, say, breaking his elbows and muting him. Or even simply taking his watch from him and arranging for him to be committed as a dangerous psychotic to someplace very secure. I was sure Lady Sally could arrange something like that with a phone call. Collect.

Instead, I wanted him dead.

I decided I would whack him on the head with my blackjack *after* I killed him. That way it would be just as gratuitous, as pointless, as sapping me had been—

Which started me thinking about that for the first time. How perfectly unnecessary it had been to sap me. A private eye isn't surprised much to be hit on the head; it kind of goes with the territory. But Raffalli had never hit any of his other victims before, male or female, as far as the tapes showed. The emotional logic suddenly seemed skewed to me. If he was going to hit a guy, I thought, you'd think he'd do it at the *start* of his run of fun and games, to prove to himself that he was invulnerable. Not *after* he'd established that . . .

I reran the sequence in my mind, and a horrid suspicion dawned on me. I'd had a momentary sense impression of ghostly fingers touching my wallet and then the sap beside it in my back pocket. What if he had taken out the wallet and examined its contents? *My fucking PI license was in there*. If he found that, his logical move was to pat me down for weapons, find the sap—

—and give me a good clip, to keep me from thinking about the wallet!

I was in the darkened stairwell of one of the two "priest's holes." I broke a thumbnail lighting up my watch. It said 8:45. Raffalli didn't usually show up until at least nine. There should be time to go out into Reception, establish through Mary that the coast outside was clear, and slide outside to warn Arethusa, waiting together in Mike's van. Despite my sudden sense of terrifying urgency, I loosened my .45 in its holster, made sure the safety was off, checked my other weapons, took a quick glance through the peephole in the door at the top of the stairs, and started to ease the door open—

As I did, the front door opened and Arethusa Number One came in, looking bright-eyed but confident and plausible.

Show time . . .

MIKE Callahan was sitting behind the Reception desk, his cigar in his teeth and his big hands out of sight. He saw me crack my door, but pretended he hadn't. He and Arethusa began improvising conversation, as per plan. Time slowed, as if by Raffalli's watch, while I hesitated, balancing the risk of warning him against the need to warn *them* that he might be on to us. As I decided to chance it, I heard the front doorknob start to turn again, and time went from zero to sixty in no time at all. I eased my door shut, fitted my eye to the peephole, and addressed a long and complicated prayer to a God I hadn't believed in since the day I found Uncle Louie. In essence, I asked Him to retroactively order the Universe so that Raffalli had been too cocky to bother checking my wallet, and had simply disturbed it in removing and replacing the blackjack. I added a detailed memo reminding Him of the kind of luck I'd been having for the last twenty years, and broadly hinting that consistency was the something-or-other of small Minds. And I believe I concluded with a promise that if He just let me have this one small murder, I'd never ask for a favor again. It seemed a reasonable request at the time.

All this in the interval it took Raffalli to get the front door open and step inside. Mike and Arethusa Òne were still chattering. To save my life I couldn't tell you what about. My darling turned and looked at Raffalli as she talked, giving him a good clear look at her face, smiling at him with just enough english on it to be sure she had his attention. Then Arethusa Two came in the door behind him, her timing perfect. She made enough of a noisy production out of it to make Raffalli turn and glance at her. As he saw her face, he froze in momentary surprise, just as I'd planned. Then he turned around again to confirm that the same woman was on two sides of him, just as I'd planned.

As he did, I came through that secret door fast and silently behind him. To my right, I caught a flicker in my peripheral vision of Priscilla doing the same on his other flank, as planned. Arethusa One had by now ducked silently behind the desk, according to plan. Mike was holding down on Raffalli with the sawed-off shotgun, just as I'd planned. Raffalli was doing what almost anyone will do if you draw down on them with a twelve gauge: flinging up both hands in a futile but uncontrollable attempt to ward off buckshot.

Everything was going splendidly. By this point nearly all of the potential disasters I'd envisioned had conclusively failed to occur. All that remained was the purely nominal chance that Priscilla and/or I would fuck up what we both did best, and had rehearsed perfectly fifteen times that afternoon. I'm a fairly cocky guy myself, when it comes to physical violence, and Priscilla was as good a partner as I've ever had. In my mind I was dealing with the problem of dissecting him before I ever reached him.

Priscilla reached him a toasted pubic hair before I did. I'm better at quick than I am at fast. She took him perfectly, at right wrist and elbow simultaneously, and locked down. I was expecting him to turn involuntarily in her direction, allowing for that. Even so I took him higher up on the arm than she had, bracketing his left elbow with my hands. I didn't want there to be the slightest chance that I'd brush a sleeve past that watchstem and cause it to twist. I had no sure way to know which direction would be fatal. I felt my grip firm up, knew that come hell or high water I could hold him for the second it would take Arethusa Two to put her .38 into his short ribs, and began to exult.

Nonetheless I kept my eyes firmly fixed to that infernal watch. Time was again passing in great long slow microseconds; I had time to study the thing. I observed for the first time that it had the usual three hands, *and* a three-place digital readout in the center that I had taken for a manufacturer's logo. I deduced that he needed to keep track of elapsed time while in time-stop mode, for some reason. I noted the subtle geometric pattern of the chasing on the casing. I saw that the stanchions for the wristband were an integral part of the casing, not welded-on afterthoughts. It was not a real antique pocket watch, but a modern product made to look a little like one—probably because it needed to be larger than any conventional watch without drawing attention to itself. By the time I realized, looking down his arm at it, seeing it from an angle, that the stem was a single solid integral piece, incapable of twisting, he had already gotten his palm folded and his ring finger more than halfway to the stem. It had to be there for something. If it wasn't a twistable dial, *then it was a pushbutton* . . .

I threw everything I had into shaking his arm, trying to snap it like a whip. But you cannot move something the size and mass of an arm faster than a nerve impulse can travel down it. With sick certainty I knew I would fail. I was sorry I'd never found the time to ask how Lady Sally managed to light her House without visible bulbs. It was a good trick, and now I'd never know the answer. I thought of that, rather than think about the fact that I had probably killed my beloved, killed us all. I was still in hyperdrive. I even had time to realize for the first time that when he had cheated in his arm-wrestling match, he could not possibly have used his right hand to twist a watchstem. The crucial detail I've overlooked always turns out to have been right under my nose, big as life. Jinx my ass—I was a jerk!

And then his fingertip reached the stem and the room changed.

EVERYTHING changed. Everything but me. *Instantly*. The room, the lighting, the smell, the ambient sound, the temperature—even my body itself, with no perceptible transition, was at a different height from the floor, in a different position.

It was not a good position. I could not comprehend it fully right away, but it was uncomfortable to the point of pain, and that told me all I really needed to know for now. I stopped thinking about it, and the surroundings, and concentrated on Raffalli for the moment.

As a general rule, I like my opponents confident. It inclines them toward carelessness. But he had the kind of confidence that is earned. That shook me more than I like to admit. I might have been in more danger, more immediate danger, if he'd been hysterical with fear. But I also might have managed to turn that instability to my advantage. This man was not afraid of me at all . . . and the one thing I knew was that he was smarter than I was. I'd proved that.

And that was my own knife he had in his hand. A very good knife. Very sharp. I'd honed it myself less than an hour ago . . .

So what sustained me? Nothing but the awareness that my whole life had been a preparation for a confrontation like this.

"I've always liked this scene, Raffalli," I told him cheerfully.

He was amused. " 'This scene'?"

"I've read it or seen it a million times. Everybody has. It means, don't go to the bathroom, the climax is coming. The villain gets the hero in his clutches. Then he lectures. He explains how he committed the crime, so he gets to brag and the audience doesn't get cheated of the solution. He tells the story of his life, justifies himself just enough so the viewer gets the point that this is his own dark side we're talking about here. He slaps the hero around just enough to lose audience sympathy for good. And then the hero kills him."

He was smiling broadly. "Too bad life ain't a bad movie."

"No, it's not. But they have that scene in good movies, too."

"Tonight we do the punk version. Where the hero dies. The modern audience likes a cruel twist. It's called realism."

"Tell it to Darth Vader, asshole."

"I must admit that a few of the plot twists have been reminiscent of a bad movie," he said, still smiling. "I couldn't believe it when I checked you out today. Sure enough, you were *that* Joe Quigley. The Favila case. I knew you'd be waiting for me tonight. That one of the few minds on earth capable of both deducing and believing what I've accomplished should chance to be a customer here is . . . well, if this were a movie I'd be demanding my money back. Instead, I'm going to play Editor." The smile became a grin. "You're an implausible character, Quigley. I'm going to cut you. Pun intentional."

"You're history," I said. "By dawn you'll be marine biology. I'm going to flush you down a toilet. For hours."

While I talked tough to try and cheer myself up, my surroundings were soaking in. As I spoke, I was inventorying the environment for liabilities and potential assets. Well before I invoked Darth Vader, I'd finished the job. The results were not encouraging.

He and I were alone. In a room I recognized. Master Henry's Dungeon. No, I was mistaken, the swing set and the Stairway to Hell were nowhere to be seen: it must be Cynthia's Dungeon. I was secured firmly by wrists and ankles to some kind of bondage cross, in an X shape. I strained against the bonds, first covertly and then overtly, and satisfied myself that I could not break them. It wouldn't have helped a lot if I had. I was completely unarmed. Even my best-hidden weapons will not stand up to a skin search, and he had made one. Leaving me in my skin.

Can you think of a worse nightmare than being naked and helpless in a fully equipped S&M dungeon with a guy who's raped your lover, wants you dead and has your own knife in his hand? Even a beleaguered movie hero usually has at least a nailfile or something. I didn't have a place to keep one.

As far as I could see, I had a single item on the asset side of the ledger. We were running in realtime. Somewhere outside this room, my friends were even now observing that Raffalli and I were gone, and taking steps to find us.

Slim comfort. Their first guess would probably be that he had taken me somewhere *outside* the House. We all knew he was cocky, but this was almost unreasonably audacious. Brilliantly so—

Wait—*he didn't know about Mary!*

Did he? Electronic surveillance was surely not something a sane madam would advertise to her customers, however necessary it was for their own protection. Surely he had searched the House at least once, during Stop-Time—but would he have had any plausible reason to search the fourth floor, once he saw it was not used for business? The Snoop Room was several boring doors from the stairs.

We'd already killed a good sixty seconds in conversation since he'd restarted time. Priscilla was quick as a fly and fast as a cheetah. It was possible that she was just outside that door right now—

—getting ready to do what?

Was there any chance that even she could get that door open in utter silence, and sneak up on him so carefully that he never got even a split second's warning?

In the movies, maybe.

I couldn't even cue her accurately. The Dungeon was sound-proof.

"Well, I hope you won't be too disappointed," he went on while my mind raced, "but I have no intention of playing out the scene in the conventional manner. I decline to die. I won't explain my watch even to a dead man breathing—especially not one who looks so much like a reporter. And I haven't met anybody since my mother died to whom I felt any impulse to justify myself."

That I could believe. His vocabulary and diction were excellent, only the single word "ain't" earlier hinting at lower-class origins—but he had never troubled to scrub off the heavy Brooklyn accent that was a much broader hint. He'd learned good speech simply to make himself understood better. He didn't give a damn what anybody thought of him.

"No," I agreed. "You're good at difficult things, but I don't see you as a man to attempt the impossible."

If there had been the slightest chance it'd work, I would have tried bargaining, or even begging, for my life. But he was simply not that stupid. My only hope was to go in the other direction. If I could lead him into a quarrel, we might make enough noise together to cover an approach, for long enough to let Mary pass the word. I was uncomfortably aware that it's hard to piss off a man who knows he holds all the cards. But what choice did I have?

"Oh, everything I've done *can* be justified," he said confidently. "I simply don't like you well enough to try. Or anyone else I know but myself."

"I'm fascinated," I said. "Indulge me, just for the sake of argument. Justify rape for me."

As I hoped, the word "argument" pushed his button. "It would be entertaining," he said, "especially since the longer we chat, the worse it will be for you when I finally get to business. But the question doesn't arise. I've never raped anyone. Well, not in years."

"I know of at least three, and two possibles," I said hotly, trying to raise the volume.

He didn't rise to the bait. "Ask any one of them whether I've ever touched them," he said smugly.

Interesting philosophical point. If the victim herself honestly denies the crime ever took place . . . did it? If a tree falls in the forest, and bounces back upright before it has a chance to realize it . . .

"Well, *one* of them apparently knows, whichever one of those twins I bagged. But only because you told her. Up until then she'd have passed a lie detector test swearing I'd never been within five feet of her. Looked at a certain way, *you* raped her, Hump."

That name made my adrenal glands, already on overtime, go crazy. It is *not* the name on my license, or anywhere else in my wallet, nor on file in any place in the greater New York area. He had to have checked me out *very* thoroughly today: he knew much more about me than I knew about him. Not good. And the name itself has *always* made me crazy. It's not my fault my old man named me Humphrey Bogart Quigley. Now there were three people in New York who knew. More than ever it was necessary that Christian Raffalli die tonight. Now if I could only live to see it . . .

Wait, now: could Priscilla—or Mike or Lady Sally or whoever—manage to find some way to pump sleepy-gas or some other immobilizing agent under the crack of the door? Assuming I could keep him talking long enough for them to fetch it?

I had to reject that one too. Even assuming Sally had a reason to keep such things handy, and even if there was a crack under the door of a soundproof room big enough to pass a nozzle, I knew of no gas that would drop a man in his tracks *instantly*. If Raffalli felt himself getting dizzy, he could tap his watch, take as long as he wanted to recover from the effects, and then discipline whoever had tried to annoy him. I could think of no way to render a man in a locked room instantly unconscious without warning him.

It was up to me to get some noise going here—fast!

"Even if I stipulated that the crimes took place," he continued, "and even if all of them eventually learned what had happened, what's the difference? They were all *whores*."

"You think prostitutes don't mind being raped, you scumbag?" I barked.

"They certainly have no right to claim serious trauma," he said reasonably. "It's analogous to throwing a stuntman off a high place. To you or me it would be terrifying; to him it's another day."

"Let me get this straight: you believe that if a man sells his paintings, it's all right for jerkoffs like you to steal a few?" I was raising my volume with each sentence, trying to lead him into escalation.

But he was simply too smug. "I never stole a thing," he said calmly. "I pay good money to come here, I paid for the right to use those women."

"With their consent! Lady Sally's artists have the right to choose their clients, you must know that, you freak son of a bitch."

"Not one of them said no," he said, smiling. "Not even with body language. Or cried afterward. At the very worst, what I did to them was no worse than a pelvic exam that was over before they knew it. A little residual soreness, perhaps."

"You smirking jackass!"

"It's pointless to shout," he said with his best smirk. "This room is quite soundproof."

Dammit, he was right. Even if I could make him yell back at me once, no one in the hall would *know*. The word could be relayed through Mary—but that meant I needed a *sustained* diversion. He just wasn't irritable enough . . .

"Try looking at it from my point of view," he continued. "I could just as easily have violated virgins in church, brides on their honeymoon bed, nuns in broad daylight. Yet I chose to come here, where even a little chafing wouldn't be that unusual a problem. Would you have been so thoughtful if *you* had discovered what I have?"

The arrogance of him astonished me even more than it infuriated me. He actually wanted to be admired for his discretion. So it was true: no man thought of himself as a villain. Not even this rotten, smarmy little—

The specific epithet that happened to come to mind suggested one last angle of attack that might get him angry enough to raise his voice. If you can't attack a man's morals, try his sexual preference . . .

"So," I said, glancing down at my nudity just long enough to make my point, "now you've finally decided to stop protesting and come out of the closet, huh? Tired of living in denial, faggot?"

In all honesty I was somewhat worried that the charge was not libelous. Now that I thought about it, several of his japes so far had involved nude male clients as well as females. Audiotape does not tell the gender of the person being raped, if there are no victim's cries or even exhalations to be heard. And most men would not report an inexplicable discharge to *anyone* . . . or, probably, recognize the taste. But even self-assured gays or bisexuals frequently flare up at being called faggot by a straight, so I had high hopes for this line of attack.

I might as well have accused him of having green hair. It did more than roll off his back: it seemed to actually please him. "Not at all," he said. "I can see why you might think so—but in fact I'm quite old-fashioned in that regard. I'm very fond of women as a species. Not to the point of fanaticism, no . . . but they'll always be my preferred receptacles. That's why I chose women consistently for the last four days' experiments in what you call 'rape,' and I call 'painless gratification.' The men were just bystanders."

"I see," I said. "You checked me out, and heard all the stories, so you took off all my clothes just to see if it could be true. Pure intellectual curiosity, huh? Nice try, fairy." What the hell else did you call a gay guy to insult him? I'd never gone in for it. "You premature ejaculators usually turn out to be closet cases."

I think I finally winged his ego with that last wild shot. But not enough. "Now, Humphrey," he said, "even a stud like you would be in a hurry too, if you were as excited as I was, and absolutely *had* to be done in ten minutes' time."

So the watch would only work for ten minutes' subjective time per use. We'd never thought to time Mary's tapes. That might be useful information. Suppose Lady Sally and my other friends could build him a trap that took more than ten minutes to get out of? Or did he have as many ten-minuteses as he needed? Did the damned watch need time to recharge, or whatever? If so, how much?

But his next words drove the subject from my mind. "And surely you can think of a reason other than sex why a man might want to take off another man's clothes. Can't you?"

I wished I couldn't. But I could. For the first time there was a gleam of genuine madness in his eyes.

"I'm done with women for a while now," he went on, enjoying himself. "I'm ready to move into Phase Two. It's time to experiment at the opposite end of the spectrum. For the next few days, I intend to explore another old interest of mine: what you would call 'torture,' and I would call 'painful gratification.' For that I prefer men."

I looked around me. At whips, chains, clamps, paddles, flails, cat-o'-nine-tails, electrodes, a cattle prod, for Christ's sake. All perfectly safe, in the hands of any competent professional. Who was interested in repeat business . . .

In the back of every man's mind, until the day he learns the answer, is the question, could I successfully imitate a tough guy under *real* pressure? Until now I'd thought I knew the answer, thought I'd learned it in Nam. But being shot at in a strange land by someone you can't see—with a gun of your own, and the use of your limbs, and your clothes on—that's not real pressure.

So maybe a lifetime of pretending to be cool and unflappable came to my rescue. Or maybe I didn't want to add to the grief of Arethusa and my new friends, who almost had to be waiting helplessly out in the hall by now, hearing all this second-hand and praying for him to make a mistake. I don't know, maybe the ghost of my namesake helped sustain me in my time of trial. Whatever, my voice came out without a quaver, let alone the shuddering I was doing inside my brain. "And you were too cheap to buy your own goddam tools. You pile of pus."

"These toys?" he said happily, waving a hand at the arrayed utensils. "Tourist garbage. For fetishists only. No serious student needs anything that can't be found in any home in the land. A sewing needle or two. Pliers. A candle. String and rubber bands. Perhaps some iodine or Merthiolate. Or simple soap—ever get soap in a cut? Or your eyes? Any kind of stove is good. And I'm particularly fond of those hangers meant for trousers. The ones with the two little sliding jaw-clamps? Once you've found somewhere to affix those, the hook seems almost designed to attach weights to, don't you think? And if there's a garage, radiator clamps and vises and sanding-wheels are all fun. Old enough cars frequently have the old-fashioned kind of jack in the trunk. As Cleve says, anyone who needs whips and other incriminating specialty items in his possession suffers from lack of imagination. The meanest home affords unlimited possibilities. Consider the average silverware drawer."

I had finally found a conversational subject he was interested in. Lucky me. I had terribly underrated this man. Christian Raffalli had been a true monster long before he stumbled across absolute power. I made myself keep looking him in those mad eyes, but it cost me a lot.

"But even if one dabbles in homeless derelicts, one finds that they generally can be relied on to possess a knife of *some* kind," he went on jovially, and brandished my knife theatrically. The area in which he brandished it was intended to make me soil myself, and damned near succeeded. "And now that I've field-tested the watch, there's a little refinement I've invented that I'm *dying* to try." He simpered. "I'm afraid you won't like it at all, Humphrey. But it will be an honor to be its first victim, if that's any consolation." He glanced past me. "Hmm. One of these silly items might prove useful after all."

He had to reach past me to get it. He was not self-conscious about letting his body touch a naked man. Trying to get my teeth on his throat as it came near was worse than futile: not only did I miss by a mile, I ended up with my mouth open for another try that I wasn't going to get. I have since learned that the thing is called a ball-gag. A ball much like a tennis ball, with a strap through it that buckles behind the head. It tasted like rubber and hurt my jaws.

My very last weapon, my mouth, was gone. I'd blown my chance for a wisecracking exit line. I really hated that.

"Ordinarily," he said, as he finished buckling the thing, "I enjoy vocalization. But hypersonics are so much like chalk on a blackboard, don't you agree? What's the matter—cat got your tongue? Don't worry, you'll have a ball. Not for long, of course . . ."

Mary was right. For his sense of humor alone, this man deserved to die.

"We'll have all the time in the world," he crooned in my ear. "I checked before I brought you here. The dominatrix is off shift tonight, sound asleep. And no one else would dare come in here. We've got all night, Hump baby."

He stood back and looked me over proprietarily. Fixing the "Before" in his mind, no doubt. One day soon it would occur to him that now that he had the watch, he could finally afford to keep a photo scrapbook. Or a video library. He enjoyed the sight of me fighting the gag so much I stopped. And then he did something that genuinely astonished me.

He unbuckled his watch, and took it off . . .

AND I couldn't *tell* anybody! I didn't care why he was doing it; it didn't matter in the least why he was doing it; all I wanted in the world was to tell Mary that he had. I tried to bite through that damned gag so hard my vision clouded and my ears roared. Doubtless a thousand others had tried the same thing, under extreme stimulus, and there wasn't a mark on the ball. I probably made enough noise to tell Mary I was gagged, but I don't think a computer could have guessed what I was trying to say, even if she'd had one programmed for the purpose on standby. Absurdly, I wished I had asked for the traditional final cigarette while I still could.

Within seconds, I knew that I was wrong. It *did* matter why he was taking the watch off. It mattered terribly.

Because he reached up, humming softly and cheerfully, and strapped it on my left arm.

He buckled it at the first notch, so that it rode too low on my forearm for me to reach the stud with my fingers, and could be quickly removed if anyone should disturb us. I felt a sharp prick at my arm as he settled the watch in place. I had plenty of time to deduce that the watch must for some reason need to be physically connected to its wearer's bloodstream to function. I had time to guess exactly and specifically what he planned to do next—and believe me, the possibilities were endless! I had lots of time. Time was passing as slowly for me now as it ever had.

But nowhere near as slow as it was about to . . .

Gloat about it, motherfucker. Out loud, please . . .

"It's a variation on Poe, really," he said. " 'The Pit and the Pendulum.' You'll catch on quickly, I'm sure. I've already told you the duration." He put his left hand on the watch, and drew my knife back all the way with his right. My knife is so impressive even that Australian guy in the movie would approve of it, because I hate to use a knife if I can help it, and displaying a large one often ends the argument right there. It was obvious where the thrust would end. The medical term is double orchidectomy. The primal fear.

And I would have ten minutes to watch it coming . . .

10. The Wrath of Jane

Context is everything. Breastfeeding is beneficial for all newborns—but for elderly male cardiac patients it can be fatal.

—NEIL O'HERET BRAIN, *Tits for Tots*

RAFFALLI paused. "You might think it an artistic error, starting big like this. Like a playwright putting his best song in Act One. But I find that if I demoralize you *completely* at the start, everything thereafter has a delicious sense of despair to it, even the comparatively minor indignities. Perhaps I'll ask you if you agree, when it's time to work on your tongue." Suddenly he giggled like a little girl, a sound much more shocking than his usual jovial chuckles and chortles. "Poor man. You've spent your life as a private dick. And you're going to die with no privates, and no dick." He laughed until the tears came.

I had long since set my face in cement, too angry to give him any satisfaction it was still within my power to withhold. But to my dismay tears leaked silently and unbidden from my own eyes. I did not cry or sob, but my eyes ran. And the sick son of a bitch drank my tears like fine wine with his eyes.

"Enjoy your thoughts," he said, and started his knife arm forward, and pushed the watchstem, and turned to smiling stone.

THE first thing that struck me was the change in the light. The fact that it had a strong reddish color didn't surprise me. That had been in the MacDonald book, which I had so stupidly allowed to mislead me about the way a time-slowing watchstem is used. Something about light red-shifting, the visual equivalent of the roar on Mary's tapes that turned out to be hiss at half speed, I guess. What I hadn't been expecting was that the light would have *texture* to it. It was as though the air were full of some shimmering translucent red gas, which could just be seen to boil and swirl, much faster than dust dances on air currents. Like a space-filling swarm of almost invisibly tiny red gnats. It was hard to focus on any particular chunk of it, but in the aggregate it glowed in a shifting random pattern. It reminded me of a special effect meant to indicate an energy creature on *Star Trek*. It seemed to me that even in a drastically slowed world, this did not make sense. If Raffalli's watch slowed time enough to make photons visible, we should not have been able to capture him on tape. And photons as I understood it did not behave like gnats.

But what did I know about physics? Screw the swarming red light; what else was there to see, to occupy my thoughts for the next ten dreadful minutes?

Except for the light, not much. Everything was utterly still. If I tried I could see, at least nearby, the motionless dust motes the gnats were slipping between. A leather sling dangling from the ceiling, which Raffalli had brushed a few moments ago, was frozen about five degrees from vertical. I managed to kill a good thirty seconds thinking about interesting and amusing optical effects you could produce with a watch like this.

Nine minutes and twenty-five seconds to go.

I remembered, and burned for, my boast to Lady Sally earlier today that I would land like a great express train on the testicles of Christian Raffalli this night. *Just backwards, Hump old boy. As usual.*

Nine minutes and twenty seconds, I reckoned.

I mentally photographed everything within my field of vision, using several different focuses and lens stops, applied fixative, and filed all the pix carefully in a folder that was scheduled to be burned before sunrise.

Nine minutes and ten seconds, at a guess.

I remembered for the first time that *I* could move, as much as my bonds allowed. It was harder than usual to move my head or fingers, but not onerously so. Like being in molasses. So I rotated my head through its full traverse and did a further photo study of the entire room from as many angles as I could, and added it all to the file. I would have loved to do a video series, but unfortunately nothing in the room would *move* . . .

No, that wasn't quite true. One thing was moving.

Raffalli's right arm. In ultraslow motion. I noticed it when the blade moved far enough for a swarm of glowing red gnats to take up temporary residence on it as a reflected highlight. It visibly moved along the blade as I watched.

I had discovered during my photo shoot that it was possible to torque my head out far enough forward to get a look at the three-digit readout on the damned watch on my forearm. He'd known it would be. Eight minutes and forty-five seconds.

Was it time yet to think of Arethusa, and how achingly close I had come to having it all? Or save that for near the end? Better perhaps to total up all my life's other regrets first. That ought to fill four minutes handily, even in this hypercharged state. Then another four minutes on what I'd do to Raffalli if I could. Try to avoid the subject of what he was going to do after I was dead: it wasn't my problem any more. Let's see: start with Uncle Louie?

A very small group of red gnats winked at me softly, like a distant firefly. The knife was *not* the only thing moving in the room. There was one other thing.

The doorknob. It was turning . . .

A kind of sick joy swept over me. My friends were risking everything to attempt a desperate last-minute rescue. Either they had pieced together enough clues to guess it was a good shot, or they were placing their trust in God and getting partly lucky. They weren't going to be in time—I knew my gonads were history, waiting only for publishing delay lag—but just maybe Raffalli would find mutilating me engrossing enough to distract his attention for just long enough for Priscilla to tear his spine out. I might even live to bleed on his corpse. The choice between live eunuch and dead stud is a hard but simple one. These days, maybe a man could even live long enough to see testicle regeneration put on the Medicare. I was in the mood for any sort of consolation prize at all.

So it was crucial to gauge just how good Priscilla's timing was going to be, how good her odds of taking him successfully. I tried to cross my eyes, put one on the blade and the other on the doorknob, and estimate relative speeds and distances.

That doorknob was turning awfully damned slow. But so was the knife moving toward me slowly. The doorknob had much less distance to cover than the knife. But the knife only had to reach me. The doorknob had to turn, then get out of the way, and then Pris had to cover a distance much greater than the knife did. But suppose Pris were holding? Say she had a knife herself: could she throw it across a room faster than a man could stab, with accuracy? If she had a gun, could she get a vital spot faster than he could retrieve his watch? So many variables. I spread the fingers of my left hand as far apart as I could, in the hope of preventing him from simply slipping the loosely bound watch off over my hand for faster retrieval. A watchband fastening can be awfully recalcitrant for a man in a hurry. On the other hand he could always duck behind me and use me for cover while he worked on it.

My hopes kept rising and falling like a kangaroo on a trampoline. Minutes ticked slowly by while I oscillated between elation and despair. With every minute my data got better. By the time I had good long baselines for knife and doorknob, the doorknob had stopped turning and was coming toward me. I started to hope that Raffalli's aim was good. It would be a shame if he missed slightly, got my femoral artery, and I never got to learn how it turned out. I couldn't be sure, but my best guesstimate was that Priscilla was going to lose the race by a hair's breadth. And all the rest of us, too—

All at once my heart turned to stone as hard and unmoving as the room.

All I could see by that point through the slowly widening crack at the door was a female fist, clenched and moving, oddly further away from the doorway than seemed right. But almost the instant I recognized it as a fist, I recognized whose it was. I can't tell you how, but I was utterly certain. It was, of course, the last person on Earth I wanted to see come through that door first.

Arethusa . . .

I had a real bad twenty or thirty seconds of subjective time there—especially when her face began to come visible.

And then it began to dawn on me just how unbelievably *fast* she was coming.

Don't get me wrong: it was a snail's pace. But a snail's pace was a *hell* of a lot faster than the door was moving. Or the knife. As I watched and marveled, she hit the door with her shoulder, and within only seconds had convinced it to start getting the fuck out of her way.

I had lots of time for mental calculations. I did the math in my head three times, using varying assumptions. It seemed to me that she was moving just a little more than twice as fast as humanly possible. That gave me a broad enough hint to figure it out.

For all of her life, Arethusa had been, as far as she was concerned, using one mind to run two bodies and two brains simultaneously. Both bodies were her, and she had plenty of energy and attention for both. But *suppose she abandoned one*?

If she poured all her mental energy into a single body, could she not turbocharge it into prodigious feats of strength and speed?

She had backed off to the far side of the hallway, signaled the *second*-quickest person in the building, Pris, to open the door, and gone into warp drive. At this point she was a cannonball in flight.

I tried not to wonder whether her other body could survive, even briefly, as a derelict. Was medulla alone enough to keep its machinery going for the extent of a firefight? And could the supercharged body take that kind of load without burning out? There was all too much time to consider both questions. And no way to answer them . . .

She was running flat out, head down, in great slow leaping strides. She probably could not have interpreted very well what her eyes were seeing at that speed, so she wasn't trying. She had planned her move in detail before the door ever opened, and was now utterly committed to whatever it was.

With infinite slowness, I became ever more certain that she would succeed. She might actually even reach him before he gelded me!

Damn: ten minutes of boring suspense, and then a photo finish! I hoped she'd planned wisely. There was no visible margin for error. The knife was no more than a foot or two away—and the ten minutes had to be nearly up . . .

Halfway to him she gathered herself and left the floor. Her body began rotating slowly, her head and upper body falling behind and her feet coming up.

Her plan became apparent. She had long since reached the highest possible speed any amount of running could give her. Now she planned to send all that awesome kinetic energy down those strong legs and deliver it with both feet to his kidneys. It is the kind of blow that will cause any man to pull his elbows back sharply, instantly, and quite involuntarily. She knew the layout of the room well, and knew his height, and had made an excellent guess as to where he would probably be standing.

The only part she had gotten wrong was the one that only a lot of prior rehearsal could have helped. She fractionally misjudged how long it would take her to get her feet up high enough.

Even then it might have been all right. Her piledriving feet might just have caught him behind the knees, making his torso jerk backwards violently enough to make the knife miss me. Or at least fall short of its intent.

But somehow she sensed her problem in midflight—faster than she should have been able to, and by pure acrobat's intuition—and used the last ten seconds of her trajectory to tuck her feet. It was her knees that caught him in the kidneys, just as no-time ran out on the watch, and flung him into me like a body-checking hockey player.

Suddenly everything was happening at once.

I had a tiny increment of time—how long it was, on what scale, I cannot say—in which to exult. Then I looked down and saw the knife. Or rather the hilt of the knife, sunk flush into the meat between ribs and hip, on my left side. Oh hell, I thought, *that's* not a problem. It'll be at least five great long seconds before it even starts to hurt. But as I thought that, I was simultaneously interpreting a loud dull noise I'd heard at the instant of Time-Start as the front of Arethusa's head impacting against the back of Raffalli's. I recalled that the chances of producing unconsciousness are slightly higher for an impact from the front than one from behind. Sure enough, there was Arethusa coming to rest on the floor, bouncing slightly, out cold—and there was Raffalli, still on his feet, ignoring his shock and the agony he must have been in, and snatching the watch from my forearm with damnably nimble fingers. I could not prevent him.

I saw Priscilla crouched in the open doorway, pointing a gun at him. But the fucking door itself was just bouncing closed again from that initial titanic shove. I saw her decide to hold fire rather than fire wild. Mike or someone would surely kick the door out of her way again for her—but Raffalli had the watch now. He slapped it against his wrist to set the connection, held it there, and reached with one finger for the stud. The door rebounded open and Pris came into view again, but I understood with terrifying certainty that he could reach and press that stud before even a high-velocity slug could reach him.

I still think I was right. But the question never came up. Priscilla's gun did not throw slugs. A red wire, incredibly vivid and bright, suddenly ran arrowstraight from her fist to his head, through it, and past my ear. His head exploded, spraying boiling meat and juice, and the incandescent red wire vanished. A second one grew between Pris and the watch, which was in mid-air, spinning end over end, and it exploded too.

I don't care who else is in the race, or what their stats are. The laser wins, every time. Lightspeed, you know.

My God, I thought, *I've shit myself. And I don't even care. Glad I skipped dinner, I suppose, but I wouldn't mind if I needed a ladder to climb down off the pile. What a tough guy. Wait'll the boys find out.*

I blinked down at Arethusa. And silently said to a God I didn't believe in even then, *Lord, if you've only got enough blessing for two bodies, give it to her*. Doctor Kate was at her side, that was nice. And good ol' Mike was just finishing the unstrapping of my wrists. *It's about time*, I thought, and giggled at the pun. I tried dopily to remove that annoying knife, for cosmetic reasons. He did not have to stop me: my hands were useless. I gave up, and collapsed into Lady Sally's strong, comforting arms.

"You done good, Joe," Mike's booming voice said in my ear. I wasn't sure I believed him, but it was a pleasant thought to take with me into darkness . . .

11. Dick and Jane Are Friends

With thee conversing I forget all time,
All seasons and their change; all please alike.

—JOHN MILTON, *Paradise Lost*

"WHAT the *hell* kind of gun was that?"

It wasn't the first thing I asked. The first was, *"How is Arethusa?"* and I couldn't get a really good breath into my chest until I heard the answer, "She'll be just fine, I promise." But it *was* the second question.

We were alone in Doctor Kate's surgery at the time. Nonetheless Lady Sally McGee took time answering. "A hand laser," she admitted finally.

"Bullshit," I snarled, knowing it was not. My side was hurting a great deal, and it was my own fault for refusing the painkiller she had offered me when I woke, and I was giving consideration to becoming as violently pissed off as a post-op patient can be. I had a lot of anger built up, and what seemed like a perfectly good reason to take some of it out on her. She had been instrumental in risking and then saving my life; I wasn't sure just then which was more unforgivable. "I know a lot more about weapons than some mercs, especially esoteric weapons. Call it a hobby. And I am absolutely certain not even the Joint Chiefs or the Politburo could build a laser powerful enough to boil a man's brain in under a second, that would fit in anything smaller than a van."

"But you saw it with your own eyes, did you not? Didn't I promise to believe in a damned ghost on the same evidence? If it wasn't a laser pistol, what was it?"

"I never said it wasn't," I told her. "What I said was 'Bullshit,' and maybe I did get that wrong. Maybe what I meant to say was 'Chickenshit.' "

Did you ever see somebody who wanted to frown but wasn't sure she should? It's an expression only a Raffalli could really enjoy. But I didn't hate it, as I should have. I was steamed. "Speak plainly, Joe."

"I will if you will," I taunted. "After what I've been through in your service, don't you think maybe you owe me the truth?"

Maybe it had been a long time since anybody had caught her on a spot that raw. I started to lose steam when I saw her expression. But I couldn't quite make myself take the question back.

Finally she reached her decision. "It is not a kind of truth that can be 'owed' to someone—in the way that I can now give you my solemn oath that I will never tell another living soul your birth name. It is not a kind of truth that is mine, to give as a gift to anyone, no matter how great a favor they do me. In the military sense, you do not have adequate Need To Know." She sighed. "But I find I have adequate need, and justification, to *tell* you—and now is as good a time as any, I suppose." She got up from her chair and began to pace. "But I do owe you this much: I will warn you first. If I tell you the truth you want, I will be recruiting you—irrevocably—into a war that will make this last skirmish with Raffalli seem as insignificant as any other knife fight."

"Why does this not surprise me?" I said bitterly. "Come on, spit it out!"

"You sure you won't wait until you're more than a few hours out of abdominal surgery? Your judgment is legally impaired."

"Who says I'm going to pull through?"

"Doctor Kate, who is rarely wrong—but I take your point," she agreed. "All right. If worse comes to worst, I . . . well, we'll leave it at 'all right.' Joe, I am—"

"—a time traveler," I said before she could.

She stopped pacing. For the second time in twenty-four hours I had succeeded in making her gape like an accident witness. It may be a record; I'd have to ask Mike.

"You *knew*?" she finally managed to say.

"Oh Christ, Lady, I've suspected ever since the mention of the words 'time machine' made all your circuits short out. It seemed a little whacky even for *me*, I'll grant you: for once in my life I refused to believe what my intuition told me. But that fucking laser pistol was like a neon sign. In more ways than one. There's only one time in history when they made laser hand weapons—and it hasn't happened yet. Do I look stupid?"

"Yes, actually, a little. It's one of your greatest professional assets. People underrate you easily. I did myself for a short while."

I was beginning to be mollified. "Thank you."

"You're welcome."

"Well? Do I get to hear what you're doing here? I mean 'now'? And Mike too?"

She looked embarrassed. "I'm through lying to you, Joe. We don't know *why* Mike is here/now . . . exactly. Only that it will soon turn out to be terribly necessary that he is, and has been. But I'll tell you what he *does* here, while he waits for the Call, if you like. And more important, I'll tell you why *I'm* here, and what I am doing—and how you can help, if you're willing."

"Attagirl," I said.

"But Joe, listen to me. You *are* only hours out of OR. I would like you to pull through. If you have the bad grace to die on me now, Doctor Kate will have my hide for a skirt, and it will take me the better part of a year to put Arethusa back together again. What I'm asking you is: do you truly need to hear all of this *right now*?"

I thought about it. Hell, I hadn't even gotten past number two on my original list of questions, and now there was a newer and longer list.

So I listened to my body. Now that my bubble of anger was belched, there was no question at all that I was in absolutely last-class shape. My wound hurt brightly. Maybe what a certified superdick like me should do was take a nice nap, and *then* tackle the idea of something that made Christian Raffalli look like a cheap shiv artist.

"Fair enough," I said. "Your gird is solid wold, and I think I stopped being in a hurry permanently sometime back there while I was hanging on the cross, waiting for that clown to butt my calls off." Something about that didn't sound right. "And I am just a tittle bit liared. Tell Arethusa I said—"

"Tell her yourself," Lady Sally said, smiling. "At this moment she is right outside that door on matching gurneys, waiting with immense patience for me to shut the hell up and let Kate and Priscilla wheel her in so you two can start recovering together."

Halfway through her sentence my vision started to grey out, but I managed a smile of my own. Doctors recommend them for postsurgical patients. "The family that heals together—" I began . . . and could not think of a rhyme for "heal." Oh, I was in good shape.

"I do not believe," Lady Sally murmured, putting a tablet on my tongue, "that you will often encounter Arethusa with her heels together." She headed for the door.

"Wait," I called feebly. "Look, I don't know, maybe I talk in my sleep. *Does Arethusa know about you?*"

"She's the one who first advised me to recruit you," Lady Sally said. "She can start filling you in when you both wake, if you like."

"I'd rather year it from who," I told her.

"As you wish."

I held on long enough to feel Arethusa take both of my hands in one of hers from either side. Hey, I'm a tough guy.

I wanted to thank her for saving my life. But there's only one good way to do that—and I simply wasn't strong enough. No hurry. We didn't exchange a single word, as a matter of fact. There was no need.

To this day, we don't need many.

I hadn't had narcotics for years.

No one who's had medically administered morphine—or any of its derivatives or substitutes—can ever again truly despise junkies. Or marvel quite as much at the incredible prodigies of creativity junk can sometimes induce in a Ray Charles or a James Taylor. Someone, that is, who was *already* that talented before they ever got high. The average human in the best of circumstances spends a hell of a lot of attention and energy on monitoring the body's thousand and one aches and pains and twinges and other sudden small alarms. At least as much energy and time goes into constantly combing the environment for immediate dangers or enemies. And as much again is spent on worry about impending or chronic problems, the struggle to stay afloat, the need to be loved, and the underlying awareness of mortality.

A man on a morphine high has *none* of these worries. All he has to do is grin, and bask, and think. If he happens to be predisposed to thinking, he can do a hell of a lot of it, very well, very fast, with better concentration than a Zen archer.

(I'm not *recommending* this, understand. For one thing, you'd waste at least half your thinking on the question *where will I get my next fix?* For another, you'd probably die young. I'm very glad both the celebrity ex-junkies I mentioned have opted to spread their sharp observation and creative insights over a long and healthy life. There's no such thing as a free lunch.)

Under *normal* conditions, logical deductions appear on my mental computer screen in largish chunks, paragraphs at a time. But shoot me full of enough dope to submerge the memory of recent abdominal surgery, and I can grasp pages at a time, skip ahead whole chapters with a sureness that may be intuitive or may just be hyperrational. If there's a difference. It's fun to experience.

Thank God there's just enough masochist in me that all four times I've been on morphine, or one of its analogs like Demerol or Percodan, I got to *missing* pain and aggravation, just about the time the doctors wanted to wean me off the drug. I guess that retired sewer worker Murph told me about would say life has "gotten good to me." Or maybe I'm just too square to enjoy life unless I pay for it as I go. I understand junkies better now—but I don't think I'll ever become one voluntarily.

Having had it forced on me temporarily again, I took advantage.

ONE other thing junk does, it plays tricks with time . . . the exact opposite of the kind Raffalli had enjoyed. Hours sprinted by like greyhounds, too fast to leave tracks.

The next time I saw Lady Sally come in, resplendent in lime-colored evening dress and pearl necklace, I was feeling so mellow that I chose to break her chops in a friendly rather than a wounded tone. "Liable to give a fellow a complex," I said, keeping my voice down so we wouldn't wake Arethusa, who was sleeping. (Both of her, breathing in unison.) It wasn't really necessary. I had learned that Arethusa slept like she did everything else: wholeheartedly. But I kept my voice low anyway.

"I beg your pardon?" Lady Sally said, matching her volume to mine. She came from darkness into the small pool of soft light that spilled around my upper body, and sat by my bedside, on my right.

"Kate tells me I've been out of surgery three days now. About time you came by for a visit."

She stared at me—and got that funny strained expression you get when you're trying not to crack up. She got it under control before I could begin to resent it. "Joe, now you know why they call it dope."

"Huh?"

"I have been here every day. For hours at a time."

"Huh?"

"At least two hours each day. As many as four. In between keeping this Bedlam running, or more accurately, lurching."

I really hate saying "Huh?" "Where was *I*?"

"Right there. Wide awake. Large as life and twice as natural. Witty, charming, and personable. We have had scintillating conversations on several topics. You narrated the plots of each of Donald Westlake's Dortmunder novels—brilliantly, in some cases. Your comparison of the book and film versions of THE HOT ROCK was particularly trenchant, although I'm not certain you've entirely persuaded me that Goldman was right to cut the train-to-the-nuthouse sequence from the screenplay."

"He had no choice," I insisted automatically. "Well, this is really something else. I wonder where *I* was while all this was going on. I wonder who that was minding the store for me. I wonder where *he* is *now*."

"Oh, he was you," Lady Sally said positively. "Ask Arethusa when she wakes up if you don't believe me: she'd know you from your own twin brother."

"How is Arethusa?" I asked suddenly, trying to glance to both sides at once. "I must have been told, but I can't *remember*."

"Calm yourself, Joe—she's perfectly all right. Doctor Kate discharged her this morning: she's still sleeping here in Recovery only because you are. Her second body came out of coma shortly after the first one left overdrive, just as she'd hoped. As a matter of fact, knocking herself unconscious against Raffalli's skull actually helped: from force of habit her consciousness jumped bodies again. Her worst problem was total exhaustion, and she's recovered most of her strength now."

"No matter how loopy I was the last few days, I should have heard *that*," I said, angry at myself.

"You did. But there were no capstans turning up in your Snoop Room. You were making memories, you simply weren't saving any. Like a RAM disk in a computer: every time you cut power by going to sleep, all the data vanished."

"I never heard a better reason to get off narcotics," I said. "Memories are the only real treasures a man has."

"Do you know the story about Steve Wosniak's plane crash?" she asked.

"The guy that invented the Apple computer?"

"And the disk drive. The Great Woz was practicing touch-and-go landings in his plane. He and his passenger walked away from the wreckage, so it wasn't a *bad* landing, but it shook him up a good deal. When he got a phone call from Apple, asking when he would be returning to work, he said, in essence, 'For God's sake, I just crashed my damn plane yesterday, give me a break, will you?' After a pause, they told him the crash had occurred nearly a month before. Like you, he had somehow severed the link between short-term and long-term memory. Armed with this information, the Woz *rebuilt the link*, in a matter of days, from the inside. He was quoted as saying that he 'consciously thought my brain from the zero to the one state.' If you like, I could call him and ask if he has any further technical advice."

"I'd be honored to speak with him. But I'd never understand his advice. I think 'cut back on the narcotics' is a good basic strategy to start with. If that doesn't work, we'll see."

"Sound," she agreed.

"Is Mary recording what we say?"

She shook her head. "This room's bugs are switched off—since I couldn't be sure what you might say while drugged. You can speak freely."

(A shame, that was: if Mary had heard that conversation, she'd have been spared a lot of heartache down the line. But that's another story . . . one I didn't learn myself for months.)*

"Uh, while I was off with the fairies, did we . . ." I cleared my throat. "Did we discuss Topic A? Why you're here? Or rather, why you're *now*?"

"Not at all," she said. "I tried to introduce it into the conversation from time to time, but you kept wanting to analyze John Dortmunder's fatalism in the face of disaster in terms of Buddhist acceptance of suffering, instead."

"I don't know anything about Buddhism!" I said.

"I know," she said drily. "You did, however, raise some interesting points concerning Christian imagery in GOOD BEHAVIOR."

"Christian imagery in what?"

---

*Editor's note: see CALLAHAN'S SECRET (Ace Books, 1986).

"GOOD BEHAVIOR. The new Dortmunder novel."

"I haven't read it."

She pointed silently. On the bedside table was the new Donald Westlake hardcover. I'd never seen it before in my life, hadn't known there was a new Westlake out, let alone a Dortmunder. I picked it up. There was a bookmark. I opened to page 181, read the first sentence of Chapter 35. "*Wilbur Howey came out of the men's room with* Scandinavian Marriage Secrets *under his arm and deep gray circles under his eyes.*" I knew who Wilbur Howey was, and why it was funny that he was carrying the magazine *Scandinavian Marriage Secrets*, and every detail of the complicated caper in which he and Dortmunder and Kelp and Murch and Tiny Bulcher were trying to rob an entire building, and the whole goofy subplot about Dortmunder being forced to steal a nun.

I was quite sure I'd never read a word of this book. I just *knew* things about it, as if I'd always known them.

"Holy shit," I breathed.

"Not a bad alternate title," she agreed. "But somewhat impractical from a sales point of view."

I found that I was dying to know how the Westlake came out. Dortmunder had just stumbled into a meeting of bloodthirsty mercenaries, and they were becoming suspicious of him. But I forced it from my mind. "Obviously Kate has reduced my dosage of Demerol or whatever. I can tell because my side hurts. So there's a good chance I'll remember this conversation in half an hour. Would you be willing to discuss Topic A now, on that assumption? Or would you rather wait until tomorrow and be sure you're not wasting your time?"

She handed me a hat. I recognized it as my own fedora. "Hit the floor with that," she directed.

I did so. Successfully.

"Glib as you've been the last few days," she said, "that would have given you trouble, I think. You resembled in manner and coordination a man with ten stiff drinks in him. Now, on the other hand, you look like a man who could use ten stiff drinks. You have proven you can hit the floor with your hat. I therefore pronounce you competent to manage your affairs, subject to outbreaks of Spoonerism. Do you wish to take on or discharge fluids before I tell you why I'm here/now?"

I made myself as comfortable as I could, moving slowly and carefully. Did you know that every single muscle, tendon, and

ligament in your body is directly connected to your left side?
"No, and no, and since I've had a little time to think, why don't
I tell *you* why you're here/now?"

She raised her eyebrows slightly and then smiled. "You know,
I wish I knew someone foolish enough to bet me that you can't.
All right, Joe: why am I here?"

"To save the world."

"Right in one," she said, immensely pleased.

"MAY I ask how you figured it out?" she went on.

"You're ethical, and you're a time traveler," I said. "So there's
no other possibility. I'm no sci-fi fan, but I've seen enough movies
to know how dangerous it is to monkey with history: only that
motive could justify the risk of making the universe collapse and
disappear."

"Correct again. And thank you. Keep going. What am I trying
to save the world from?"

"This part is just a hunch. But it's a strong one."

"A hunch is often a conclusion based on data you don't know
you possess," she said, seeming to be quoting someone. "Go
on."

"I think you're trying to prevent the Last World War."

Her eyes were sparkling. "Joe Quigley, with a head full of
Demerol you are the equal of Holmes himself. Mycroft Holmes,
Sherlock's smarter brother. Have you considered that intuition
like yours might actually be a genuine paranormal ability, on
a par with Arethusa's telepathy or Amos Garrett's guitar solos?
Never mind; can I ask what led you to that hunch?"

"Well, I've noticed a high percentage of foreigners in your
Parlor and even on your staff. And it occurs to me that out of
all the planet, you chose to locate about as close as you can get
to United Nations headquarters without actually having to be in
Manhattan. It's just across the Bridge. Damned if I can think of
any other reason you'd pick Brooklyn."

"Providence has surely sent you to me, Joe," she said. "Because
until you joined my team, you were probably the most significant
threat to me alive." Suddenly she looked troubled. "I'm compelled
to wonder if there are any more of you out there."

"Me too."

"You present me with a problem. I had intended to exact from
you, as the price of revealing my mission, something like a
formal oath of loyalty and obedience. Now I cannot do that.

According to doctrine, I should perform major memory deletion on you at once, for security's sake." Could *that* be where my memories of the last three days had gone? No, as she went on to explain: "But deletion sufficient to prevent you from simply reaching the same conclusions a second time would have the side effect of using you up. You're far too potentially valuable to me. A waste is a terrible thing to mind, and vice versa. Will you take me off the hook by giving me such an oath voluntarily?"

"No," I said at once. Before I could chicken out and say yes. "I give my loyalty and obedience to one person—me! And I made *that* oath a long time ago, irrevocably—the day I got out of the service. I have no reason to suppose that your interests and mine will always coincide." I waited to see if she would kill me, or mindwipe me, almost wishing I had the kind of faith (or is it courage?) it takes to surrender command to another. It's so much simpler to just be one of the grunts. But look how that had turned out the last time . . .

"Understood," she said reluctantly. "You make it as hard as possible for me to accept you into my army, Joe."

"I can't help that."

"No, you can't. And you are uniquely valuable to me. All right, I accept you formally into my conspiracy without requiring either loyalty or obedience. You're a loose cannon—but a helluva cannon. Still, you must accept in turn that I might some day find it essential to kill you. Or worse."

"You're welcome to try," I said.

"That seems fair enough," she agreed. We both relaxed the barest trifle. "Onward. Do you have any questions before we get to the question of your specific work assignment?"

"Yeah. What I can't understand is, why do you need me? I can't see that you need anybody at all. If you're crazy enough to try and tamper with history, I don't see what's to stop you. Given time travel, and technology including laser pistols, you ought to be able to deal with just about any problem I can imagine. You weren't even tempted to appropriate Raffalli's watch for your own use. What could give you trouble?"

"Ignorance," she said. "And the cussedness of nature, human and otherwise. You see, Joe, we're not trying to *change* history. We're trying to make it *have happened, just the way it did*. And we don't know quite how to do that."

I waited.

She sighed. "This will take some background. If you notice any holes in the background, you may assume I left them there."

"Fire away," I told her.

"When I come from, Joe, it is possible to do something like a detailed systems analysis of history. James Burke does a primitive version of it today, if you've seen his TV series *Connections*. A simple example might be: if someone invents the plough, the invention of trade and thus of arithmetic must soon follow. The plough allows production of more food than the tribe can eat: it becomes necessary to dispose of the excess, and keep track of the resulting commerce."

"I follow," I said.

"The process is capable of nearly infinite refinement," she went on, "given enough accurate data, sufficiently advanced mathematics of chaos and adequate computer power. The more modern the era one examines, the better the data, and the more accurately one can explain precisely why things turned out as they did. Of course, it makes weather prediction look easy. Many experts maintain this sort of analysis will never be useful for predicting *future* events, as some factors can only be identified as 'significant' in retrospect— and personally, I hope that's true. Still, we try, in the hope of lessening human misery by our efforts.

"We kept refining our techniques until we could retroactively 'predict' any portion of existing history from its preceding events—*almost*. But we kept finding anomalies, places where historical events had failed to come about as theory said they should have. Not many, but fairly major disjunctions. It was like Einstein finding a single small village within which E equals mc. Attempts to revise the theory failed utterly. One day one of our greatest geniuses made the intuitive leap to the idea that *something must be perturbing history at such cusps*.

"One classic example thereof is the mysterious failure of human civilization to end by thermonuclear suicide in the late twentieth century. All indications say it should have . . . yet it didn't. The genius historian I spoke of hypothesized that some outside agency must have prevented it from happening. He then realized that said agency must necessarily turn out to have been either him, or else someone he trusted less than himself . . . there being no third category. So he assigned himself—and me—the job."

"*Mike?*" I said.

"The same. The celebrated Mick of Time—me darlin' spouse Michael Callahan."

"Sure an' Gomorrah—the saints add preservatives to us! Do you seriously mean to tell me that the fate of the human race lies in the hands of a couple of historical micks?"

"Yes," she said. "But don't worry: we Irish have been a lot easier to live with since we annexed Great Britain back in the early twenty-first century."

Huh. I should imagine so. "All right: so tell about why you two can't just solve all your problems with a time machine and a brace of laser pistols."

She sighed. "Because we're fighting with a blindfold on and one foot in a bucket. Whatever steps we're supposed to take, the one thing we know for certain is that history didn't . . . won't . . . record them."

"Surely history offers clues. Hints. Your systems analysis—"

"—says that nuclear war should occur, anytime now. In fact, without me and my husband it would have happened by now. As you surmised, I have for several decades been facilitating informal diplomacy between UN delegates and staff here, of a kind which by all the rules should not occur—and that has had a subtle but salutary effect. But according to our 'systems analysis,' it should not be enough to forestall holocaust indefinitely. There is something else that needs to be done if we are all to survive the Eighties. Urgently."

"What's that?"

She looked very unhappy. "I wish to Christ I knew. And the clock is ticking."

I was surprised. "Can that matter to *you*?"

"It certainly can. Joe, there are few 'Laws of Nature' that my contemporaries and I have not learned to rewrite to suit our convenience—but one of them is this: as far as we know, no one can inhabit the same space/time twice. My time-travel gear will take me only to loci in which I do not already exist. If I miss my window of opportunity this time, someone else must hit it for me . . . and there are no other candidates known to me."

"Doesn't mean no one will come along after you and get it right," I pointed out.

"No—but as I mentioned earlier, any such person would be someone I trust less than I do myself. So I'm still working on it."

"Mike too, I assume."

"No, actually," she said. "Mike's specific project is different."

"Can you tell me what it is?"

She hesitated, debating with herself. "Well, in for a penny, in for another penny. It could conceivably become relevant. Do I have your word that you will not divulge this information to anyone else—*including* members of my own task force?"

I thought about it. Curiosity won. "Okay."

"Mike is here to forestall alien invasion."

I could *feel* the blood leaving my head. I clutched at a straw. "By whom, the Chinese?"

She shook her head. "No, I'm afraid. I mean the science-fiction sort of aliens. Creatures from another star. Powerful and paranoid."

"I was pretty sure that was what you meant," I said sadly. Only a few days ago, I had thought sassing a public official was exciting . . .

"They should have arrived here by this decade and exterminated the human race without effort . . . but history doesn't record any such contact for several centuries yet. Mike intends to find out why, and make sure things turn out that way."

"What kind of operation does he have out there on the Island?" I pictured something like the stupendous Wardenclyffe power tower that Nikola Tesla—the discoverer of alternating current—built out at Shoreham back in 1901, ready to hurl fire at the heavens. They'd torn Wardenclyffe down before it was finished. But maybe Mike Callahan had hopped in his time machine and gotten the demolition-and-salvage contract . . .

"A tavern," she said.

"A . . ."

"A bar, out in Suffolk County. Callahan's Place, it's called."

Jesus Christ. I'd heard about that joint all the way in Manhattan. A guy told me once if you couldn't have a good time at Callahan's Place it was your own damned fault. But I couldn't recall him mentioning anything about power towers or banks of laser cannon.

I swallowed with some difficulty. Was I *sure* this was not all a Demerol dream?

Yes. My side hurt. And my head was starting to. "How's he doing?"

"Rather well," she said. "He managed to place himself in the kharmic path of the first scout to reach us—a slave of the creatures we're worried about—and has manumitted him. Meanwhile he's been training combat troops. Things look promising on that front* . . . but only provided we humans don't blow ourselves up before the aliens arrive."

"Look," I said, "if you don't mind, let's just put this whole space monster subplot on the back burner for now, okay?"

"You asked," she pointed out.

"My mistake. Let's return to the comparatively trivial problem of World War Three. Here's what I want to know: given your level of technology . . . why can't you just whomp up a magic thingamajig that keeps us dumb primitives from lobbing ICBMs at each other? A planet-wide Star Wars, that doesn't answer to the Pentagon?"

"If by 'Star Wars' you ignorantly refer to the Strategic Defense Initiative," she said without quite sniffing, "I could design, build, and install such a shield without difficulty. But it would solve nothing."

"I see what you mean—" I began.

"Perhaps not," Lady Sally said. "If you're thinking that such a shield would be noticed, that's not true. I could easily put one in place without anyone else on Earth being the wiser. And I could turn it off on a moment's notice if Mike turns out to need assistance from NORAD. But don't you see: if, as we believe they must, the forces of history will shortly cause a general or a politician to push his figurative red button, *he is bound to notice when nothing happens.* And the consequences of that could scarcely help but leave their mark on history—perhaps in the form of an all-out conventional war almost as destructive as a nuclear exchange. What we must do is so manipulate the forces of history that the politician I've postulated never triggers his missiles. And that is an infinitely more complex task than simply disarming the world. I'm having difficulty at the moment defusing Russian paranoia fast enough. Through off-the-record diplomacy, I've managed to keep the United States propping up the Soviet Union for a long time now, but very shortly the USSR is simply going to collapse of terminal rot, and then there'll be a—what's the matter, Joe, are you in pain?"

I was slow in answering. When I did, my voice sounded funny. The whole Universe had just clicked into place, a degree to the left of where it had been, and I was reeling from the dislocation. "No. That was the expression of a man having the revelation

---

*Editor's note: see CALLAHAN'S SECRET.

of his life." I took a deep breath. "God damn. That was like a five-second acid trip."

Lady Sally sat up straight. Straighter, I mean. She looked alarmed. "Jesus Christ on a bicycle," she breathed. "*You* have just had the revelation of your life? Yes, I see you have. Wait just one moment, please." She got up from her chair, opened one of Kate's cabinets, took out a flask labeled *Disinfectant*, and removed the stopper. At once I could smell the whiskey the flask contained. She took a long pull, replaced the stopper, and put the flask away. "All right," she said, sitting down again. "In the words of a dear departed friend of mine, Dick Buckley, 'Straighten me— 'cause I'm ready.' "

SO she'd known Lord Buckley, eh? It figured. "I think I may have just figured out what's perturbing history. And why history doesn't record it. And why a secret Star W . . . a secret SDI shield would be worse than useless. And I've even got a couple of ideas about what you might be able to do about all of this. It all depends on how much technological magic you have up your sleeve."

She looked as awed as I felt. "Joe, if you can answer those questions, you can have anything that is within my power to grant. As to the limits of my technology . . . well, perhaps it will help to say that I could with some strain turn off the nearest dozen stars, or create a few new ones. Not that I would—but I have the capability, and more."

"Then we may be okay," I said. I shook my head slightly. "Christ, for a while there I thought we had a problem."

"I will not throttle information out of a convalescent," Lady Sally said. "I will *not*. Arethusa would be annoyed with me."

"Like many flashes of insight, it began in a misunderstanding," I said. "You said an SDI shield would solve nothing, and I started to say I understood your reasoning, and you interrupted and explained your reasoning. But it wasn't the reason I'd been thinking about. I was thinking about something else. Something that's been on my mind since I was about fifteen years old, something I've never told anyone about before. The gods have such a twisted sense of humor I didn't want to give them any ideas."

"But you *do* want to give *me* your idea, because you don't want me to forget myself and throttle you," she suggested softly.

"Sorry. Okay, simple question and answer. Question: what's the basic flaw in even a perfect SDI shield? Answer: it only works on missiles."

She blinked.

"And other satellites, I guess."

She thought. As I saw her starting to get it, I went on:

"Question: so what's wrong with that? Answer: *missiles and satellites are not the only way to deliver nuclear weapons.*"

"You mean nuclear cannon? But they—"

"Not cannon either. Why does everybody always think hi tech? What's wrong with air freight? Or a cigarette boat?"

It was as if her puppeteer had cut all the strings. She slumped all over, went as limp as she could get without falling out of her chair. Her eyes were wide and staring at nothing. She murmured something in a language unknown to me. I had no trouble at all translating it as, "Holy *shit!*"

"MISSILES are a *lousy* delivery system, when you think about it," I went on. "There are only three good things about building ICBMs to place your warheads. It can be done quickly, it makes jobs for a lot of voters, and it's gaudy as hell. But if you're not in a hurry, and you're not in a race, and you don't *want* to spend money like water, and you don't care whether the results are phallic and photogenic or not, there's a much better way."

"Nuclear mines," she whispered. "Triggered by radio."

I nodded. "I've been waiting for that other shoe to drop for years now," I agreed. "It just seemed to make too much sense not to happen, sooner or later. Every year millions of pounds of illegal drugs enter this country with no trouble at all: what's so hard about a few hundred pounds of plutonium? Even in lead boxes?"

"So you think the USSR has mined the United States?" Her eyes got even wider. "Or the other way 'round?" Her shoulders twitched. "Oh my God—or both of them! Oh, Joe, things are even worse than I'd imagined—"

"Whoa," I said. "You're thinking like a cheap thriller writer. I don't think either country has placed a single mine. I just told you why not, a couple of seconds ago."

"Why not?"

" 'It makes too much sense,' I said. Can you recall a time since Hiroshima when either the US or the Soviet Union has acted sensibly?"

She frowned. "Now that you mention it, no."

"Think it through. The United States can't undertake such a scheme for one simple reason: the Constitution. Specifically the First Amendment. There's just too much openness in this country, and much too much freedom of the press, for something as elephantine as the US government to keep a scheme like that under wraps. Hell, if the government couldn't get away with U-2 overflights, or even a simple thing like invading Cambodia, how long do you think they'd last sowing nukes around the world? Some clown would smear it across the front page of the *Times* in 72-point type, long before you had enough mines planted in the USSR to do more than enrage them."

"The Soviet Union does not share that weakness," Lady Sally said. "This is exactly the sort of scheme that would appeal to them."

"And how do we know that?" I riposted. "Because they've screwed up so many of them! Secrecy they have plenty of. What they are crucially short of are competence and reliability. If a Soviet Premier were to order a nuclear mine built, he'd be delivered something the size of a Sherman tank, that worked one time out of four . . . and sure as God made little green horseflies, somebody on the very first penetration team would defect. That's the problem they'll never crack: if a man is intelligent enough to be worth sending abroad, they don't dare let him out of the country."

"They build very good missiles," she argued. "That suggests they can produce good technology if they want to badly enough."

"Says who? How often do they ever fire one at a target anyone else can monitor? I told you: esoteric weapons are one of my hobbies."

"Well, very good spaceships—that's the same thing."

"They build *shitty* spaceships. Ever seen the inside of one? They look like something out of Flash Gordon, or the cab of a steam locomotive. Big knife-switches and levers and dials that'd look natural in a Nikola Tesla exhibit. No computers worth mentioning. After the *Apollo-Soyuz* linkup, our guys came back raving at the courage of anyone who would ride a piece of junk like that into space."

"The Soviet space program is much more substantial than America's! It has been since long before *Apollo*."

"With shitty spaceships. It's just that *they don't stop building them*, the way this stupid country has. Did you ever hear the story about the first Soviet space station crew?"

"Died on reentry, didn't they? Something about an air leak?"

"Leonov, the first man ever to walk in space, has been in the identical model reentry vehicle many times. He's been quoted as saying that the crew of that mission *had* to have heard the air whistling out, and that any of the three of them could easily have reached out and plugged the leak with a finger. They died of a combination of bad technology and lousy education. You wait and see: if the Soviets ever open the books and let us compare duds and destructs, you'll find out they had a failure rate *much* higher than ours. You know those rockets they've got now, that everybody admires so much, the 'big dumb boosters'? They could have beat us to the Moon with those. But of the first eight to leave the launch pad, the *most successful* survived for seventeen seconds. So they used a different booster for the Moon project, and it didn't make the nut."

Arethusa woke just then. Don't ask me how I knew. She didn't move, open any of her four eyes, or alter the rhythm of her breathing. But one minute she was asleep, and the next minute she was lying there with her eyes closed, listening to us, and I knew it when it happened. I didn't say anything, because she liked to take her time waking up—and don't ask me how I knew that either. She knew I knew she was awake; she'd join the conversation when she was ready.

For decades I had wondered what it would feel like to fall in love. Some indeterminate time back, without discussing it with myself, I had given up waiting. Now I knew. Even if they didn't open an eye or make a sound, everything was different when they were awake.

Better . . .

Lady Sally was looking confused. "If I'm not mistaken, we've returned to Go, and I don't see my two hundred dollars anywhere. You seem to have proven that there *are* no nuclear mines after all. Oh my stars and garters, wait a half! China—"

I shook my head. "I don't think so. It's just barely possible. China's got the secrecy, and it's got good technology when it decides to spend the money, and like Russia it's got a history of mass murder of innocent civilians. Even more recently. Ask any one of a million Tibetans—and don't hold your breath waiting for an answer. But China's crucially short of one essential resource for a scam like this."

Lady Sally was nodding. "Caucasian agents they can trust absolutely. I see the problem. Chinese tend to stand out in both countries—especially in the Soviet Union, which is the first place they'd want to mine. China's own xenophobia keeps it from getting friendly enough with barbarians to have any great number of barbarian friends. They can't mine us because not enough of us love them. God's teeth. Joe, is your head starting to hurt, or is it just me?"

"Your Ladyship," I said, "barring a few intervals of unconsciousness, orgasm, or drugged stupor, my head has hurt since an hour after I first walked into your House. I'm not complaining . . . but you asked."

"I'm not much surprised, considering the outlandish things that seem to go on inside there." She held up a hand. "All right—take a break for a moment and let me see if I can work this out for myself. Without consulting my computer, or Mike. There's a certain amount of pride involved. This is after all my life-work." She stared down at her pearl necklace, and toyed with it as she thought aloud. I marveled as I watched her. She was old enough to be my mom, and she could make fingering a couple of pearls look lewd without even trying. "Let me see, now: significant nuclear capability dating back at least a decade . . . access to fissionable material . . . not saddled with either too much openness or too much tyranny . . . lots of Caucasian natives . . . major espionage skills . . . *and* an ability to hide fairly large expenditures somewhere in the national budget without attracting notice—that lets out Israel, they're already pushing their limits in that direction . . ." Her fingers stopped moving. She was silent, still, frowning fiercely to herself, for nearly half a minute. I passed the time by watching Arethusa's chest rise and fall. At last Lady Sally looked up at me, still frowning. "Damn it!" she said. "I can't make it work. Joe, there is no nation that answers that description."

There aren't many things a man can do as noble as passing up a chance to show how smart he is. "No," I agreed, and shut up.

"Israelis would have major difficulty getting into, and especially out of, the USSR. India comes closest after Israel . . . and I just don't buy them for it. Their fanatics tend to be the wrong kind of fanatics."

"Me either. And I hope it doesn't turn out to be diehard Nazis trying for a Fourth Reich. I can just hear it now: 'Throw another Ken on Klaus Barbe!' "

A triple pun—this place was getting to me. She ignored me magnificently. "It can't be time travelers from the future," she mused. "Time travel *was* discovered and abandoned three separate times before my people perfected it . . . but those primitive methods all leave unmistakable tracks in the matrix, I'd have *seen* them. And none of the three was ever used by anyone stupid enough to meddle with history on a planetary scale—as conclusively proven by the fact that reality still exists. I am utterly certain that no one from my era could be capable of such a plan—just as I knew Raffalli could not be a contemporary of mine. I could be wrong, but I'm certain. So it *has* to be someone from this space/time . . . and I just can't make myself believe in an extranational conspiracy of private individuals out to conquer the world. For one thing it's difficult for me to imagine competent nuclear physicists being sufficiently tempted by power or money—and they aren't prone to religious fanaticism as a rule. It would require patriotism . . . or something like it . . ."

I waited, and let her worry at it. Arethusa looked edible. Watching her was better for my aching side than narcotics. And I saw her whichever direction I looked in. Did you ever have a woman who was so beautiful, it made you sad you could only see one side of her at a time? Arethusa solved that problem better than any mirror. I could tell somehow that she was nearly ready to admit she was awake.

All at once Lady Sally managed to look happy and dismayed at the same time. "God's golden gonads! Could it really *be*? Oh, even for the Universe this is excessive irony!"

I knew she'd get it. "As Mycroft's brother once said, 'When you have eliminated the impossible, whatever remains . . . ' "

"Do you mean to stand there—lie there—with your bare face hanging out and tell me that all of reality has been placed in mortal jeopardy by—"

"Pacifists," I agreed. "Peace terrorists. That's the way I'd bet, anyway. It can't be anarchists—they'd never get organized enough."

THE better she absorbed the idea, the less she liked it. "You've hit it, I think. It makes psychological sense, at least. There are still a lot of physicists alive from the Manhattan Project days—on both sides of the Iron Curtain—and some of them may well repent. But what rotten luck. Cowards make the deadliest opponents—and pacifists never fight fair: they *can't*. I was hoping for some sort of warriors."

"That's the worst thing about any kind of terrorist," I said. "They're so weak, they have to be monstrous to accomplish anything. And who could be weaker than a pacifist?"

"Hey," Arethusa said from my right, just past Sally. "What's wrong with pacifists? Look at Buddhists: they're nice people."

I gave her my best smile, and got a much better one in trade. Arethusa can smile like a long-distance kiss. I poured her two plastic cups of peach juice from the flask on my bedside table. Lady Sally started to adjust her chair so she could see us both . . . then left it as it was and spoke past me, to Arethusa's other body, which opened its eyes politely.

"They're different," Lady Sally conceded. "They're *honest* pacifists. You don't have to worry about them fighting dirty, because they never fight: they don't have Jihads or Crusades. The strongest weapon they use is reason; the strongest protest they allow themselves is suicide, and they're always careful not to let the flames spread. Pacifism of that sort is no more objectionable than belief in astrology or membership in the Flat Earth Society. I was speaking of the kind of pacifists we grew like hothouse flowers in this country fifteen or twenty years ago, and still have all too many of. Pacifist *terrorists*. The kind who want all wars everywhere to cease and everyone to live in peace . . . and are prepared to keep blowing up wealthier and less enlightened fellow citizens until that day comes. There's nothing wrong with wanting wars to stop—but the moment a pacifist uses *any* weapon but calm speech, he's a hypocrite. If he's willing to kill, he's a psychotic. The only good thing about them as opponents is that it isn't murder to kill one."

She hadn't said it like a joke or hyperbole. "In this country it is," Arethusa replied seriously, and reached to take the peach juice I gave her, one of her after the other. She smiled at me.

"I don't see why," Lady Sally said. "Pacifists—and anarchists, and libertarians—specifically repudiate the right of the state to employ armed agents—to protect them from murder, for instance. So shooting one ought to be no worse than a misdemeanor. 'Disturbing the peace,' say, or 'frivolous discharge of a firearm.' "

" 'Unlicensed hunting,' maybe," I suggested.

"They're not restricted," she pointed out. "As long as you eat the meat, and clean up after . . ."

"I'm particular about what I eat," I said. "But I will kill this bunch. If you can help me track 'em."

"Joseph," Arethusa said plaintively, "when I decided to love you, I had no idea you were so bloodthirsty. Do you realize we've never gone an entire day without you announcing your intention to murder someone?"

"People who plant nuclear mines in major population centers?" I said. "You bet I'll kill them if I get a chance."

"No allowances for good intentions?"

"None," I said firmly. "Even if I stipulate that a world of enforced peace run by something like Weathermen with nukes is a good intention—and I don't—nobody elected these clowns to do the job. They don't have the right. Even a tyrant rules by consent of his people, no matter how difficult he makes it for them to withhold it. He rules openly, a fair target for any assassin. But *these* vermin are worse than a well-poisoner."

She bit her lip. Then she shrugged. "You're right," she said, "but I want you to *promise* me that you'll give up murdering people once we're married."

I forgot all about thermonuclear mines and alien invasion and the collapse of space and time through failure of the logic of history. My side stopped hurting. Everything in the Universe stopped hurting for a moment. You must have noticed it.

"You'll marry me, Arethusa?"

She cocked her head and smiled at me. "What else do you give a man who saves the world?"

Lady Sally obligingly got up and moved out of the way, stepping back out of the pool of light until all I could see of her was Cheshire grin and sparkling eyes. "Don't mind me, children," she murmured.

I sighed. "Darling? Have you ever heard about the mule who was placed equidistant between two piles of hay—and starved? I'm too sore to get up off this bed more than once—"

Bedsprings creaked on either side of me, "Brace yourself, my love," she said in stereo. "You're about to become a hero sandwich."

ONE disadvantage of having a stereo lover: morning breath from two directions is more than doubled, more like squared. A small thing . . . but I cherished that small imperfection.

12. The Wonderful Wizard

"Thunder is good, thunder is impressive, but it's lightning that does the work."

—MARK TWAIN to Nikola Tesla

"THE only part I still don't understand," Arethusa said fifteen minutes later, when order had been restored and we'd agreed to postpone our engagement celebration and Lady Sally and I had filled her in on the parts she'd slept through, "is how come the existence of secret atom bombs scattered around the US and Russia is supposed to alter history—so as to *prevent* nuclear holocaust from happening—when nobody is ever going to find out about them. I mean, if they get discovered, they surely go into history in a big way . . . and if they just sit there and never go off, they have no effect at all on history . . . and if they go off, there *is* no history. I don't see how any of those three alternatives prevents the US and Russia from lobbing missiles at each other on schedule. Or how we can make it come out that way."

I looked toward Lady Sally as if I didn't know the answer myself. She had just put the phone down after checking in with Mary, this room's surveillance from the Snoop Room being presently disconnected.

"The details will have to be worked out," she told us, "but the broad outlines are clear to me. We are going to locate each and every one of those devices, learn how they are triggered and protected, and disarm them—leaving them just where they are. At the same time we will hunt down every one of the lice who built and planted them, and kill them—preserving one of them long enough to talk into a tape recorder if feasible. Then we need only see that two copies of that tape, two maps of *all* the mines in *both* countries, and a short, anonymous letter, go to just the right addresses in Washington and Moscow."

I nodded. "We'll scare the living shit out of the people who control the big red buttons. It's demoralizing to wake up and find you just walked a tightrope over the abyss in your sleep. And they'll *have* to compare notes, to make sure each side got the same information. It'll be a long time before they're quite so ready to push their buttons again."

"Long enough for the Soviet Union to collapse of its own weight," Lady Sally agreed, "ending the Cold War. And demonstrating conclusively, thereafter, that the United States never did want to conquer the world, which eventually will . . . well, there's no point going off into second- and third-order resultants at this juncture."

"For God's sake, let's make sure we've really got the *right* addresses in both countries, though," I said. "If the President and Premier ever find out about this, they're liable to get in the way and make things worse than ever."

"No responsible person would trust *them* with information of this caliber," Lady Sally assured me.

"The Soviet Union is truly on the verge of collapse?" Arethusa asked.

Lady Sally nodded firmly. "I know it must be hard to believe now, halfway through the Eighties . . . but just wait a few years. The cancer is inoperable. If it hadn't been for the US and Canada, they'd all have starved long ago. That's precisely why they're so dangerous at the moment: they're paranoids, and they depend on their enemy to live, and they *know* that, and it's driving them crazy."

"Huh!" I said, struck by an idea. "How about this? Suppose it was someone in the CIA—not the Director, of course, but someone known to the Soviets as sane and reliable—who quietly slipped that tape and map to his opposite number in Moscow?"

Lady Sally smiled. "Lovely. I can think of no better way to win a Russian's trust than to bring him the head of an enemy he didn't know he had."

"You have CIA contacts?"

"CIA is wrong for this job, I think—even if the Director did not have a brain tumor. Their mandate is extranational. The *D*IA would be better: the Defense Intelligence Agency. Much larger, much quieter, less well known—and I have better contacts there. Excellent ones. And the FBI would have an interest; I have friends there, too. You know, you show a talent for this sort of work, Joe."

"Thank you, Your Ladyship," I said soberly, "but I wish I could do as well with the real problem: how to *find* the goddam bombs and terrorists. If we find either one we can get the other . . . but where do we *start*? I don't mind admitting it's got me stumped so far. And I seem to hear the sound of a clock ticking."

"Loudly," she agreed. "The moment the very last mine is installed according to their plan, the bastards will break cover and try to blackmail the world into disarmament. It would be irrational—even by the standards of a pacifist terrorist—to hesitate a single day. And if that day comes, history will have been radically, fatally altered . . . even if no bomb ever actually goes off."

"And all we know about them," I said gloomily, "is that they're so good neither CIA nor KGB has gotten even a whiff of them."

"We have certain advantages in counterespionage over both those agencies," Lady Sally said.

"I don't see it," I persisted. "Even if I credit you with all the sci-fi gizmos I can think of, this is the kind of problem they don't work on very well. I mean, what's the plan? Deep-radar the entire continent—both continents—and personally inspect everything that reads like it might be a lead box? A man could get old doing that. A battalion could. It night take years to stumble across the first bomb . . . and how much good would that do us? I'm sure you could find the damn things, Lady. But can you do it *fast*?"

"Fortunately, I don't think I'll need to. I have a friend who should be able to deal with that aspect of the matter. He should be here any minute; I just called Mary a few moments ago, and asked her to send him up from his shop in the basement."

"Your maintenance man is going to find the nukes," I said, trying for a little comic relief.

"I think so," she agreed. "Ah, here he is now—come in, Nikky!"

Into the room stepped a tall thin handsome man in his thirties with a mane of dark hair, a proud nose and a sanitary-looking mustache. I could see these things clearly because the room lights brightened all by themselves as he came in. I recognized him instantly from photos. And all at once I understood why in Sally McGee's clean, extremely well-lit place I had not been able to find a single light source, nor a single appliance with a power cord.

By this point perhaps you can imagine what it means to say that he was the most astonishing thing I had yet seen in Lady Sally's extraordinary House.

I turned to look at her, and sure enough, she had removed the pearl necklace she'd been wearing. That tore it. I was looking at the one man in all history who might be able to help us.

"Holy—" I began, and remembered that he disliked both obscenity and blasphemy. "—cow," I finished, keeping my voice down to spare his hyperacute hearing.

"Nikola Tesla," Lady Sally said, "allow me to present my very dear friend Kenneth Taggart."

"Honored to meet you, my dear sir," Tesla said, and bowed.

NIKOLA Tesla was born in Smiljan, Croatia in 1856, precisely on the stroke of midnight between the ninth and tenth of July, and came to America during the Panic of 1884. He had invented the bladeless turbine at the start of the American Civil War, when he was five years old—by which time he could speak five languages fluently. Then he'd discovered the love of his life.

The Fire of the Gods . . .

He could do anything that can be done with electricity. *Anything.*

In fact, he *did* just about all the things that can be done with electricity, often decades before others "discovered" them. He conceived alternating current, and damned near ruined himself proving it was superior to Edison's direct current. He made the first induction motor, and had to sign away the rights. He built the first robot, and the first Remote Piloted Vehicle—the first remote-controlled *anything*—in the 1890s, and couldn't interest any government. His trusted aristocrat assistant Guglielmo Marconi stole the idea for radio from him, and got all the credit, even though the US Supreme Court later ruled that Tesla had patented the basic technology in 1897. He invented and patented the "AND gate"—a logic circuit crucial to all computers—in 1903, along with the principles of the transistor; neither could be built at that era's state of the art. He could make lightning— real sky-filling, tree-shattering lightning—do any damn thing he wanted it to, including climb up on the palm of his hand for the amusement of friends of his, like Mark Twain and Paderewski. At one point he conceived a scheme that would have turned the entire planet Earth into something like a stupendous storage battery, so that anywhere on its surface you could draw all the power you wanted just by sinking a rod into the soil—and was forced to abandon it when he admitted to his backer, J. P. Morgan, that there would be no conceivable way to charge customers for the power.

I'd gotten interested in him in the first place because you can't study esoteric weapons for very long without hearing about the Wardenclyffe death-ray he said could score the surface of Mars . . . which of course he never got to build. Trying to read a little about Tesla is like trying to eat one peanut.

I had always felt a terrible affinity with him. Like me, he was an intuitive genius . . . with the worst luck in the history of the world.

But I had never expected to meet him. He died alone and broke in the Hotel New Yorker in Manhattan, at the age of eighty-six, in 1943. I'd seen a photo once of his death mask, commissioned by some guy named Hugo Gernsback the day after his body was discovered.

SO it was disorienting, even to a man who had spent days in Lady Sally's House, to find Nikola Tesla standing before me, alive and healthy-looking and in his late twenties . . . let alone to hear him say he was honored to meet me. Never had a conversational politeness been more absurd. You could make an excellent case for the proposition that he was the greatest man in history.

Even before returning from the dead.

I was glad I had read about him. I had sense enough not to offer him my hand.

You see, Tesla was also probably the most *eccentric* man that ever lived. Wouldn't shake hands with *anyone*—not even J. P. Morgan, from whom he was trying to borrow a million dollars when they met. He was terrified of spherical objects, like oranges or Lady Sally's pearls. When he sat down to a meal, he had to polish all the silverware and china with eighteen linen napkins first (he had an inexplicable preference for numbers divisible by three). Then he had to calculate the cubic contents of the food on his plate before he could eat a bite. He never ordered anything that was on the menu, and the specially prepared meal had to be served by the maitre d' and no one else. He could not bear to touch human hair, and in consequence is believed by all of his biographers to have died a virgin.

No, I'll tell you how weird he was: he *liked pigeons*. Fed the little feathered rats lavishly even when he was broke (often); cared for sick ones with his own hands even when he was a millionaire (equally often). If he walked through a park, they swarmed him like he was St. Francis of Assisi, perching on his shoulders.

I suppose in retrospect I should have at least briefly doubted the evidence of my own eyes. But it never occurred to me to think he was a hallucination. I've got a pretty good imagination—but even on drugs, it isn't *that* good.

So you tell me: what do you say to Nikola Tesla?

What I said was, "Mr. Tesla, I."

HE was neither surprised nor disturbed by someone gawping at him like that. The self-assurance looked out of place on features so young. Then again, I didn't know for sure if he was really as young as he looked. Maybe Lady Sally had edited out a portion of the real youth of the real, historical Tesla, and I was meeting a man who had not yet experienced world fame. But it seemed just as likely that she had picked him up at the instant of his death, and simply revived and rejuvenated him. For all I knew, she'd cloned this Tesla from a tissue sample of the old one. These didn't seem like polite questions to ask.

In any case, he graciously ignored my awe, and responded conversationally. "I see that you are Irish, Mr. Taggart. Would I be correct in guessing that you are some sort of policeman?"

Just what I needed: a tough question to start. "Well, Mr. Tesla . . . with all due respect, sir, suppose I didn't know who *you* were, and I hazarded the guess that you were an inventor."

He blinked, cocked his head like a bird, and then nodded. "I think I see. As I pride myself on being a discoverer, and not a mere inventor like Edison—" That settled that: this Tesla was older than he looked. "—so too you practice a profession which the common man often confuses with that of policeman. A distinction which he considers trivial and which to you is paramount. Might you then be a private inquiries agent, like Mr. Sherlock Holmes?"

Impressive guess. Put me in the company of a mind like that and I get a little giddy. That's the only way I can explain it. What was meant to be a simple agreement came out, "Be he never so humble, there's no police like Holmes."

Lady Sally turned pale and shuddered visibly. Arethusa grimaced and hugged herself. Nikola Tesla merely smiled broadly. "Oh, splendid! I must tell that one to my good friend Sam."

Has anyone ever intimated that one of *your* puns was worthy to be told to Mark Twain? "It's not mine," I said hastily. "Mystery writer named Tony Boucher."

"Your honesty does you credit, Mr. Taggart," he said. "You are indeed no Edison." How weird, to be praised for my honesty under an assumed name! "But I am fascinated to know of your occupation. I have always imagined it to be somewhat similar to my own, in its essentials. As with my work, it consists mainly in collecting information and then phrasing the proper questions: the answers themselves, as I understand it from my reading, then appear in a burst of white light. Is it thus with you?"

"Well . . ." I started to say that detective work in real life was nothing like that. Then I thought about it. "More or less, yeah. The tricky part is, when that light starts to shine . . . don't squint."

He nodded vigorously. "That is indeed the trick. May I ask you to tell me some tales of your work?"

I glanced at Lady Sally. Shouldn't we maybe be getting on with averting thermonuclear holocaust? But she was settling back in her chair and finishing off the last of my peach juice. I could see both Arethusas: one of them moved her chin up slightly, the other down. She was nodding, about as discreetly as it can be done. Okay, I would tell Nikola Tesla war stories until it was time to take my narcotics.

(Which reminded me: I was in next to no pain at all from my wound now. Distraction is almost as good an analgesic as laughter. Next time you're in pain, try to get a famous dead guy to drop by, and see for yourself.)

"If you will trade me for some of your own, sir," I said.

"I do have one anecdote you may enjoy, concerning a policeman . . ."

It seems that one day back in 1898, Tesla was experimenting with electromechanical vibration. He attached an oscillator he'd built to an iron pillar that ran down the center of a loft building he owned on East Houston Street, and sat down in an armchair to play. As he varied the frequency, different objects in his lab began to shimmy around. He became engrossed in trying to determine what he called the "dancing frequency" for every object in the room.

Meanwhile, all around the neighborhood, for blocks around, windows shattered, buildings shook, and terrified people began pouring into the street, screaming in Chinese and Italian . . .

"I had forgotten a basic principle of seismology," he admitted. "Earthquakes are most severe at a distance from their epicenter."

The cops down at Mulberry Street Station had long been darkly suspicious of the notorious wizard in the neighborhood: the sergeant sent two buttons over to Tesla's place to see if it was his earthquake. They got there about ten seconds after Tesla, belatedly realizing something was wrong, had destroyed the oscillator with a sledge hammer. The buttons became impolite in discussing this with him. One of them went so far as to suggest that Tesla had no business playing around with things he didn't understand.

This much of the story had appeared in a couple of Tesla's biographies, but I pretended not to know it out of politeness. It was worth it to hear the part that *hadn't* made it into his memoirs.

"I told him that on the contrary, I understood what I was doing so well that, if he would care to return later that evening, I would treat him to an experience which Mr. Mark Twain had once pronounced to be the most fun in the world."

The cop fell for it. When he returned that night, Tesla had rigged a smaller oscillator, fixed to a free-standing platform. The cop climbed up onto the platform, and when Tesla threw power to the oscillator, the cop did indeed have the experience Sam Clemens had once called the most fun in the world. The platform vibrated so strongly the cop's whole body blurred. He enjoyed it even more than Twain had, hopping around and yelling obscene suggestions for potential uses of the gadget.

"But exhilaration was only the first effect," Tesla went on. "As I had with Sam, I exhorted him to come down after a short time; just as Sam had, he refused. And within less than a minute, the policeman experienced the second effect." And there he paused, like a good storyteller.

I already sensed where this was going, but I was not about to spoil an anecdote for Nikola Tesla. "And what was that, sir?"

"Acute diarrhea," he said gravely.

Laughter is even better analgesic than distraction.

"Regrettably, when I attempted to shut down the oscillator so he could race to the toilet, I accidentally dialed it as far as it would go in the opposite direction, where it jammed. The vibration reached such an intensity that even the policeman could sense it would be dangerous to try to jump clear. By the time I could repair the control, I'm afraid the poor man had become one of New York's Foulest . . ."

Maybe analgesic is the wrong word. If you laugh that hard when you're post-op, you hurt like hell. You just don't give a damn. Hard to understand how a painful experience can leave you feeling better, but there it is.

Sharing the laughter made it even better. It was the first time I had ever seen Arethusa laugh out loud, flat out, and the sight confirmed my already firm intention to marry her. You can learn as much about someone from watching them belly-laugh as you can from making love with them.

"Your turn, Mr. Taggart," Tesla said when our laughter had wound down.

So I told him a few stories. Not disasters, like the Favila Affair or the Prison Break-in. Ones from which I had emerged relatively unscathed. The Robin Hood Bomber, for instance.

There was this mall going up out on the Island back in the Sixties, a year after I got back from Nam. Nobody wanted one there, experts testified it would ruin the community, but the developer had the fix in.

One night at three A.M. the site blew up. Six separate explosions within half a minute, five of them scattered around the central part of the site, where the buildings were. Had been. There were no casualties among the watchmen, which cost their agency that contract and a fat lawsuit: the head of the agency asked me to look into it. Enough money was involved that the cops were pushing it, but what do Long Island cops know about bombers? I was an exotic-weapons buff.

What little evidence they had was baffling. The blasts were clearly high-quality high explosive—but how had it been planted in sufficient quantity without detection? During the day the site crawled with construction workers, and once they left, you had to cross acres of open, lighted asphalt to approach the place. And how had it been set off? No traces of timing devices or radio triggers were found in the ruins. Most confusing of all, why had one of the six bombs been planted uselessly in an open parking lot, three hundred yards from the rest? Even with that anomaly, the job was just too sophisticated for the local community-action leaders the cops were leaning on—librarians and small business types. So I looked at the site, and thought a lot. The five contiguous bombs seemed to have been almost randomly placed. But something about the distribution was familiar . . . and then I had it.

I consulted a computer. The search parameters I specified gave me twelve possibles; I pulled their files and eliminated seven. The moment I parked in front of the third address on my list, where two of my suspects lived together, I knew I had found my men.

The mailbox was not just knocked down, but flattened, with tire marks on it. The front lawn contained abundant crabgrass, beer cans, dog turds, three Harley-Davidson 650 motorcycles, and a pair of dirty red panties. The house itself shook with R&B bass, was very close to being a two-story woofer. The first thing I saw as I went in the wide-open door was a fourth Harley. Or rather, half a Harley, protruding from the living room floor. The back half was in the basement. I later learned that one of the inhabitants had recently tried to ride his bike upstairs while drunk, and blown it. Drying filthy socks hung from the handlebars. Clearly this was the home of serious social architects.

Sure enough, four Hell's Angels lived there, trying to save enough to get the hell back to the West Coast. Two of them had just been discharged after a tour in Viet Nam, like me. Their names were Larry and Teeth. (Apparently he liked to extract them for sport.) It turned out we knew some of the same people. They told me the story.

Many GIs bring souvenirs home. I'd smuggled out my service .45, myself. Larry had brought home a mortar . . . and just before his own discharge, Teeth had shipped him six rounds.

AT this point in the story, Tesla, Lady Sally and Arethusa began to giggle, sensing where I was going.

"One night a few months later," I went on, "a little old widow knocked at their door with a petition against the contested mall. She must have had guts to follow through when she realized what she was dealing with, and they were impressed."

Louder giggles as everyone visualized her situation.

"They were also colossally stoned, and bored. So they signed her petition—'Larry' and 'Teeth'—and let her go, and then got out a good map and a pair of dividers. Later that night Larry went out in the backyard and obliterated the mall."

Whoops of laughter.

"I'd figured out the spacing of the rounds," I told them. "Teeth was spotting for Larry from a pay phone near the site. The first one missed; Teeth fed Larry the correction, and the next five were a textbook example of how much scatter you can get with 'identically' aimed mortar fire. It was the Veterans' Administration computers that helped me track down recent dischargees in that area."

Tesla had a pretty good laugh on him for a skinny guy. "What did you do?" he said when he could manage it.

I shrugged. "What could I do? There was no evidence: you can't do a ballistics match on an expended mortar round. They still had the mortar, but there was no way to prove they'd ever had ammo for it. And however plausible the story sounded in that living room, with the sweatsocks hanging from the handlebars, I knew it'd be a hard sell in a courtroom with Larry and Teeth cleaned up and shaved, in suits. Besides, who wants a couple of Hell's Angels pissed off at you?"

"You left those lunatics loose with a mortar?" Arethusa asked.

"Hell, no. I bought it from them. For two airfares to the Coast. Even without any ammo, it was enough to get the security firm off the hook." I didn't mention that the ungrateful sons of bitches had stiffed me on my expenses: I'd *eaten* those plane tickets, and they'd cost more than the two hundred I got paid for one day's work. But why spoil a good story? "And it got the two Angels out of my neighborhood." Tesla had that eager that-reminds-me expression. "Professor Tesla, you've got a story?"

He nodded. "One of my favorite stories," he said, "It also involves a man who did something novel with a bomb."

Lady Sally and the Arethusas and I exchanged a glance. It was pretty ragged by the time we were through with it.

"This is a true story," Tesla said, "about a man named Theodore Taylor, and a Pall Mall cigarette. Taylor designed atom bombs—"

Another glance was passed around like a basketball.

"—for the United States government after the Second World War. Among other distinctions, he designed both the physically smallest and the most powerful fission bombs ever fired."

My eye muscles were tired; I just kept looking at him.

"Taylor had what I would call a unique mind. One day, as he was waiting with his colleagues for a bomb known as Scorpion to be detonated, he noticed a discarded parabolic reflector lying on the ground. An idea came to him. He set it up facing Ground Zero, and used some stiff wire to hold a Pall Mall cigarette at its focal point. A few minutes later, Scorpion exploded. The Sun came down to Earth; there was a blast of searing heat; the air split with thunder; the terrible toadstool climbed to the heavens; scientists drew in their breath in awe. And Ted Taylor reached down, plucked the Pall Mall from the reflector, and took a puff.

"He had become the first man in history to light a cigarette with an atom bomb."

I couldn't help howling with laughter. What breathtaking audacity! But as I roared, I wondered if this Taylor could be one of the peace terrorists Lady Sally and I were stalking.

It seemed too improbable a coincidence. We consult Nikola Tesla to help us pick a handful of men out of billions—and it turns out he knows a funny story about one of them, and tells it without prompting? Even for Lady Sally's House, this was stretching plausibility. Yet Taylor was on the very short list of men who can make atom bombs, and he certainly seemed to have a loose rivet or two. An atom bomb designer, afflicted with late-life remorse, might make a fine candidate for a nuclear peace terrorist.

So ask him, "Mr. Taggart." You'll never get a better segué . . .

"Dr. Tesla," I said, when the laughter had tapered off, "do you know this Taylor fellow personally?"

"I have met him once or twice," he said. "A most special man." He smiled. "He commented on my resemblance to Nikola Tesla. When I professed not to know the name, he told me some flattering things about myself. Why do you ask?"

I looked to Lady Sally. "Your Ladyship? I may safely assume that Professor Tesla knows at least as much about . . . you and your work as I do?"

She nodded. "Of course."

"Ah," Tesla said. "You are a member of the Inner Circle, Mr. Taggart. In that case, you must call me Nikola." (Accent on the first syllable.)

"If you'll call me Ken," I agreed, a little dizzily. "Then you know why Lady Sally is here—or rather, 'is now'?"

"To learn why World War Three has not happened."

I nodded. "Well, now we think we know, Nikola. Because we're going to stop it."

His turn to nod. "A worthwhile project. Where does Dr. Taylor come in?"

So I told him my theory.

As Lady Sally had, he grasped it at once . . . and liked it. "A most remarkable hypothesis, Ken. Its logical structure is somewhat fragile, but intuitively it is most compelling. May I ask: did you arrive at it logically, or intuitively?"

I had to think. "Both. No, wait, I'm wrong. First intuitively. Then the logic happened to it, and kind of patted it into shape."

He nodded vigorously, his eyes shining. "Yes, yes! It is the same with me! An astonishing sensation, is it not?"

"Well . . . kind of like being hit between the eyes with a hammer. Except it doesn't hurt."

"Exactly!"

Tesla was famous for rarely using drawings or models or notes or experiments. A device would appear in his imagination, complete. He would build it. It would work. The Mark I was the finished product. To have my mental processes compared to his—by him!—was . . . well, a unique experience. Arethusa was looking at me. What wound? I was ready to kick-box a kangaroo . . .

"And you wish Dr. Taylor's advice on the precise nature of the nuclear mines?" he went on.

"Well, I'll tell you, Nikola," I said, "I was more wondering whether he might be . . . uh, one of the major miners."

He broke up. "I laugh at the idea, more than at the pun, Ken. Dr. Taylor would be the last man on earth to belong to such a terrorist group. He gave up building bombs when he saw that even hydrogen bombs could not scare the world into peace, as he had first hoped. His personal nightmare is nuclear weapons in private hands. In recent years he has campaigned vigorously for stricter controls on weapons-grade material, specifically to prevent terrorist groups from building their own nuclear weapons. The great John McPhee wrote an entire book, THE CURVE OF BINDING ENERGY, about Taylor's efforts. That is where I learned the story of the Pall Mall. Believe me, Ken: Taylor cannot possibly be involved with your terrorists."

Lady Sally said, "Nikky is an excellent judge of character, Ken. Especially with regard to scientists."

"Okay," I said, "Taylor isn't one of the terrorists."

Tesla looked thoughtful. "But he might be the best possible source of advice on how to deal with them."

Lady Sally held up a hand. "Nikky, I'm sorry. I must issue a *nolle prosequi*. This conspiracy is too large as it is, and I don't know this Taylor bird. If we can possibly do without his advice, we will. If we can't, we'll try anyway."

Tesla chewed briefly at his mustache. "Your point is well taken, Your Ladyship. Let us see how far we can go on our own. Let me see, I remember McPhee's book fairly well." I'd heard that Nikola

Tesla never read anything twice. Polaroid eyes. "Taylor spoke at length on the practical considerations of building a nuclear mine, such as you envision, in order to refute the common belief that a Manhattan Project would be required. He demonstrated that one would need only public domain documents, a small machine shop, and access to weapons-grade radioactives. He even designed such a mine, hypothetically. As I recall, his design criterion was to produce the physically smallest and lightest bomb which would still be capable of knocking down the World Trade Center."

"What did it *look* like?" I asked. "How much did it weigh? I'm trying to get a mental picture of the damned things, and I keep picturing big evil eggs."

He shook his head. "I do not think an implosion bomb is likely. It would be very hard for a terrorist to get usable plutonium. The current 'street price' is on the order of a hundred dollars a gram: each bomb would cost millions of dollars just for the plutonium. Any that he could steal from the nuclear fuel cycle or from medical sources would be 'hot,' poisoned with enough plutonium-240 to make a bomb go supercritical too soon. I envision rather a uranium bomb, most likely a gun-type. A cylinder lying on its side. It could theoretically be as small as a bazooka. It's difficult to say with any certainty: it depends on what you want the bomb to do, and what design choices you make along the way."

"For instance?"

"Oh, many things . . . your choice of damping material, for instance."

"Damping material?" Arethusa asked.

"Neutron reflector. A nuclear explosion occurs when you bring two barely subcritical masses of fissionable material together, *very* rapidly. If you are to make your bomb as small and inconspicuous as possible, the two masses of fissionable material must be quite close to each other—so close that there is danger their combined radioactivity will cause them to go critical before you wish them to."

"What happens then?"

"It is called a 'fizzle yield.' Heat; much radioactivity; but no explosion. To prevent this, you encase both masses in a damping material, to inhibit their radioactivity. When the masses are slapped together, the damping material then helps contain their neutrons long enough for supercriticality to occur. The better a damping substance you use, the more powerful a bomb you can tuck into a small space. The problem is, the best damping agents are often heavy. This is why the 'suitcase nukes' one finds in fiction are rather improbable. You could build an atom bomb that would fit into a suitcase—but you could not lift the suitcase."

I was hanging on by my fingernails. But I really wanted to try and get as good an image as I could of what I was looking for. I had a dim but intimidating grasp of the size of the haystack; I could only hope it might be useful to know what a needle looked like. "What are good damping materials?" I asked.

"Lithium is one of the classic choices. But there are many others. Natural uranium, steel, copper, lead, aluminum. Solder will do nicely, and can be purchased in large quantities without notice. Even water will serve, actually—ordinary tap water. Damp damping, if you will. Or a few inches of wax. Whatever you select will affect the physical shape and dimensions of the bomb. So will other factors: where it is to be placed, and its desired effect. It is possible, for instance, to shape or direct a nuclear explosion. Taylor created the Orion Project, which tried to build a spaceship propelled by shaped hydrogen bombs."

Orion! My God—I had read about that mad scheme. Freeman Dyson had been involved in it. They'd actually built a model, with conventional high explosive, that worked like a charm: dropped bombs out its anus and goosed itself gently into the sky on a series of bangs. It must have sounded a little like an old one-lung gasoline motor. Then, as they were gearing up to build a real one—a spaceship powerful enough to lift a small town into orbit!—the US and USSR signed a treaty banning nuclear explosions in the atmosphere, and the project died. So Taylor had been behind that . . .

I opened my mouth to say something . . . and somehow as I saw Tesla I found myself thinking of his mechanical oscillator story, and the Hell's Angels with their mortar, and what he had just said about bomb design and the problem of selecting a damper substance—where in New York would you get a lot of copper, lead, solder, even water, without attracting attention?—and the practical placement problem facing a terrorist who wanted to produce maximum destruction with the least detectible bomb . . . and all of a sudden, a hammer hit me, painlessly but quite hard, between the eyes.

Lady Sally sat bolt upright. "Mark his face, Nikky!" she said. "That's the look you get when you have one of your white light visions. Ken's got something; I've seen him do this before." Tesla looked at me with great interest.

My voice came from far away. "I think I know where the mines are," I said.

"What'd I tell you?" she said, and then her jaw dropped.

"In general terms, anyway," I went on. "I can't pinpoint them, but I can tell you where we'll find them. If we do. When we do." I could actually feel blood draining out of my head. "Oh dear Jesus, we *better* find them."

Arethusa took my hand in both of hers and squeezed it tightly. "Where, Ken?"

"Water pipes. They're inside municipal water pipes."

FIVE seconds of horrid silence. Then everyone's eyes widened at once as they began to understand.

"What you said earlier, Nikola," I went on, "about seismic shock being worst further from the epicenter. A terrorist wants the gaudiest effect he can get. Sure, you could knock down the World Trade Center. But that only impresses the people who live in sight of the World Trade Center. *Everybody* in a city lives near a water pipe. Neutron reflector provided for you, free: all the water and lead and tin and solder you want. And all cities keep their water pipes underground—so when it goes boom you get seismic shock and hydrostatic shock at the same time. Maximum bang for your buck. As a bonus you poison the city water supply—for decades to come." I was beginning to babble, from sheer horror. "Not to mention the comedy value! Faucets and hoses spraying live steam, hot both ways; fire hydrants flying like champagne corks, geysers of neutrons; water coolers going off like flashbulbs; thousands of bare asses instantly steam-cooked by boiling toilets—" Arethusa's fingernails were trying to meet through my hand. I shut up and pulled her up to sit beside me on the bed, freed my hand, and put my arm around her. As we clutched at each other, she sat down on my other side and I put my other arm around her. All three of us rocked together. It helped.

Tesla was pale, but nodding vigorously. "I think you are right, Ken. That is where I would put nuclear mines. The pipes would be fairly similar from city to city. Here in New York, I would probably choose a site somewhere in Tunnel One or Tunnel Two, which convey all the city's water from upstate. Possibly both."

"That narrows the search area," Lady Sally said grimly.

"Not enough," I said. "Those are two damn big damn long tunnels. You could fit a submarine into either one of them with no trouble, and they go on for miles. Not to mention any of several dozen tributaries that'd serve almost as well. And that's just this city. We still need another conceptual breakthrough."

"I do not think so," Tesla said quietly. "I believe I can locate them."

We all stared at him.

"Nikola," I said, "I yield to no one in my respect for you. But how the he . . ." He hated profanity. "Excuse me. How on earth can you do it? The da . . . the things *have* to be shielded. Sure, they've got water outside them and maybe damping water inside, but the two won't mix: there'll be no radioactivity to trace. Wait a minute: they'll be warm, won't they? Heat-warm, I mean. Lady Sally, have you got infrared gear good enough to pick up small hot spots in the city water system?"

"Yes," she said. "But Ken—there are millions of them."

"True."

Tesla spoke. "You overlook the obvious, friend Ken."

"A specialty of mine," I agreed bitterly. "It's only the obscure I see at once. Okay, what did I miss?"

"Assume you are one of these terrorists. You have nuclear mines set up all over the country. What do you plan to do with them?"

"Threaten to set them off."

"And for this threat to be credible, you must in fact be able to set them off. How will you do so?"

"Why, by—"

If I hadn't had both arms around Arethusas, I'd have smacked myself in the forehead.

"—by radio," he finished. "You will perhaps recall that, a little less than ninety years ago—"

"—you *invented* radio, of course. Stupid of me. You mean you . . . what do you mean?"

"It would be a simple matter, for me at any rate, to build a device which would register the existence and location of every radio receiver in the metropolitan New York area, whether they happen to be functioning at the time or not."

I did *not* point out that this would yield quite a few more targets than the total population of the city. I just said, "And?"

"And I would be able to distinguish those which are located underwater."

Had I been holding my breath? There seemed to be a lot of air in my chest to exhale. I felt myself smiling. Arethusa was hugging me tightly on both sides. "Could you tell what frequency they're tuned to receive?"

"Or pattern of frequencies, yes, I believe so." He frowned. "Given enough time, I could even learn the precise code which, transmitted over that frequency, would arm and trigger the mines. Unfortunately, the only way I could do that would be to stumble across it—triggering the mines."

"Never mind that, Nikola," I assured him. "You find me a mine, even one of them, and I'll get the code."

"Attaboy!" Arethusa said, in stereo.

"Your Ladyship?" I said.

"Yes, Ken?"

"I need to put together a task force. I want the names of everyone cleared to be on it."

She didn't hesitate. "All of us in this room. Michael. Priscilla. Willard and Sherry. Tim, Doctor Kate, Father Newman. Ralph Von Wau Wau. Robin. And Mistress Cynthia, of course: Robin has no secrets at all from her. Mary, if you really need her. I have taken one or two others into my confidence who are not presently in this area; I could probably round most of them up if you need them. And there are others in my employ who may have figured out things about me, and kept it to themselves. I can provide perhaps another twenty effectives who will fight for me without asking questions."

"My Lady," Arethusa said, "any artist in this House will fight for you without asking questions. And at least half the clients."

"Thank you, dear. How big a task force do you envision, Ken?"

"I don't know," I admitted. "I'm making this up as I go along. I just wanted to know how many troops I could call on. Let me make sure I've got it right. Fifteen who can be told everything, and twenty or more who can be given limited objectives, but not the whole picture?"

"If you find it necessary," she said, "you may tell anything you wish to any member of my staff. I don't employ anyone I don't trust that much. I've done my best not to burden *any* of them with my secrets . . . but over the years, one thing and another have forced me to break cover to some fifteen of them, yes."

"And you say you've got good contacts in the DIA and FBI?"

She looked briefly nostalgic; her nipples came up. "And in the Komitet Gosudarstvenno Bezopasnosti as well."

"Not for more troops; we hand them a *fait accompli* or nothing. I just mean, you can get information to the right people once we have it?"

"You may always leave the little things to me," she said. "As the bishop said to the actress."

"Well, hell," I said dizzily, "these guys are candy!"

"You think so, Ken?" Lady Sally asked.

I quoted her friend Lord Buckley. " 'Take it off your mind, Nazz: it's covered.' We're gonna tangle these murkies, make it from tea."

Lady Sally blinked. "Beg pardon?"

"We'll nick 'em in the cuts."

Arethusa stood up on my right. "I'll get Kate," she said.

"It was bound to happen Spooner or later," Lady Sally agreed.

Things got fuzzy after that. Doctor Kate arrived, and did something wonderful; after that everyone melted away like the Wicked Witch. Except for Arethusa.

You know how, when you're sleeping with someone you love, and making a spoon, it's hard sometimes to decide whether you'd rather be on the inside or the outside of the spoon? Boy, is it nice not to have to make a choice . . .

13. Radio Drama

Wives are not property.   —LAZARUS LONG

HALFWAY through shaving, whistling Louis Jordan's "Blue Light Boogie," I looked at myself in the mirror and asked, *What's wrong with this picture?*

Well, I replied, nothing much that I can see. Or no more than usual. Naked white male in pretty good shape, happy, loved, and recently laid. Not so much as a pimple, or a—

—or a scar! Smooth, unblemished skin, from my scalp down as far as the mirror showed, about hip height. No sign of the two bullet scars in my arm and shoulder, no trace of the old razor scar across my right pec or the shrapnel tracks on the left one . . . and especially, no sign of a recent puncture wound in my side . . .

It dawned on me for the first time that the vigorous and glorious sex I had woken in the middle of, some ten minutes ago, should not have been possible for a post-op patient—dope or no dope.

I pawed at my side, as though I might pull aside some flap of meat and locate the missing wound. I prodded the area, gently at first, and then harder. Soon I was punching at it with the side of my fist.

I was so pissed I stormed out of the bathroom and barked at Arethusa. "Where the hell is Lady Sally? I'm gonna kill her!"

"What's wrong, Joe?" she said, wide-eyed. There was only one of her present, dressed in perspiration and glory.

"What's *wrong*? God damn it, *nothing*. That's what's wrong! Oh, Kate probably actually did it—but the orders came from Sally. The rotten bitch went and healed me . . . without so much as a 'By

185

your leave'! I'm not going to stand for this—"

She burst out laughing, strove at once to stop.

"Dammit to hell, I *earned* those scars. She had no right—"

She had it under control now. Way under control. "Joe Quigley, did you or did you not verbally acknowledge recruitment into an army, just yesterday?"

"Well, yeah, but—"

"Did you or did you not verbally acknowledge, just yesterday, that the crisis in your war could come at any moment?"

"Yes, but—"

"Soldier, shut up and soldier. The Lady did what she had to."

Oof. "But you don't—"

"The world is supposed to balance on a knife edge, while you take R&R in a cathouse, just so you can preserve the record of your mistakes, to impress the new meat? It was necessary to heal you quickly."

Every prostitute in America knows grunt talk. "Dammit, Arethusa, those scars were my combat ribbons—"

"Are you the kind of soldier who *needs* his ribbons? More than he needs to get his job done?"

Well, if you put it that way . . .

After a time, I stopped frowning and sat down beside her. "Thanks for straightening me out, baby," I said, and put my arm around her.

"I understand, Joe," she said, snuggling into me. "I'd have been mad too. But it was necessary. Now that you know Lady Sally's secret, there was no longer any reason for you to waste time recuperating normally."

I glanced down at myself. "I'll miss them. Most expensive ornaments I ever bought."

"You can always have them tattooed back on, after all this is over," she suggested.

"No," I said. "It's done."

She looked hesitant. "Well, if you really have accepted it, I guess I should tell you the rest of it."

I gritted my teeth. "Out with it."

"Uh . . . I'm afraid you're never going to get sick again, darling."

You can't grit your teeth and gape at the same time. "*Never?* Ever?"

She shook her head sadly. "I'm afraid not. Your DNA has been optimized. It was an unavoidable side effect of healing you quickly. If it makes you feel any better, it's been done to me too. If we're going to die, my love, it'll have to be accident, murder, or suicide—and even that will have to be a kind that kills instantly."

That redheaded bitch, *making me immortal without asking me first, why, I oughta . . .*

"Let me finish shaving, and we'll go down for some breakfast," I said. My voice sounded odd to me.

"Sit there," she directed, and went into the bathroom. She came back with the electric razor. It harmonized with the buzzing in my ears. I sat passively as she completed my shave.

How do you wrap your mind around the knowledge that you could safely kiss a leper, or dance naked in snow, or share a needle with a promiscuous Haitian male prostitute? As far as I could get was to wonder if I could somehow get a refund on my Blue Cross and life insurance without blowing Lady Sally's cover . . .

No, maybe I shouldn't do that. It had only been a few days since the last attempt on my life. And I had new enemies . . .

"Darling," my Arethusa said as she ran the razor across my face, "there's a conversation I think we ought to have before we go down to eat."

I raised an eyebrow or two. "Really? How could we possibly be in any hurry about anything? Except saving space and time, I mean."

"Maybe we should have had it long before now. Things have been rushed since we met." Understatement of the century. "I barely found time to propose to you—"

"I know. I'd been waiting for a chance myself for hours."

"—and I'm very glad you've agreed to marry me. But perhaps it's past time we defined what that means. The worst misunderstandings are the unspoken ones. What do you and I expect of each other?"

I honestly didn't know what she meant. "A square deal."

"Then let's negotiate the deal. Not necessarily in writing—but explicitly."

"That's easy. You can have anything I've got, and I'll take anything you feel like giving me."

She chased down the last bit of stubble, shut off the razor, and smiled. "I'd love to have that reciprocal agreement with you. But have you thought it through?"

I blinked. "I hadn't thought of it as something that needed thinking through."

She acquired a look of tender exasperation. "I guess I'll have to spell it out. You know what I do for a living. I have no plans to quit working. Do you anticipate that being a problem for you?"

At last I got it. By God, she was right. This was certainly something a man ought to think through before climbing into his tux. How could I have failed to wonder about it myself?

So I thought about it.

I probed within my heart for jealousy, possessiveness.

No echo came back.

Why not? I'd always had the normal male human complement of both vices.

Think it through, Joe. What are the reasons that make a man unhappy if his love starts having sex with other people?

Maybe she'll find a better lover than me, and leave me . . .

She'd already had hundreds, perhaps thousands, of lovers, male, female, and otherwise . . . and found me good enough to propose to, took the very first chance she got, not even waiting for privacy. And who says women choose mates by athletic criteria? No possible marriage partner could be *less* likely to abandon a good relationship with me for mere hot sex. If it wasn't a good relationship, that was my fault, not somebody else's.

How will I know whose the children are? . . .

In the first place, she was professionally competent at managing contraception, proven so over time. In the second place, what the hell did I care? Any child that came out of that beautiful belly would be lovable, worth cherishing and raising, whether it happened to carry my personal congenital deficiencies or not.

Maybe she'll bring home some jerk I don't like. Or some germ that doesn't like me . . .

In the first place, none of her clients would be staying that long. In the second place, they'd all have been prescreened by Lady Sally, who didn't seem to tolerate jerks in her House. As to health, they'd all be monitored by Doctor Kate. Arethusa was *less* likely to give me an infection than the average secretary I'd meet in a bar.

Maybe I'll have to compete for her attention . . .

This argument might possibly have applied . . . to any of Lady Sally's artists *except* Arethusa. There were *two* of her. And one of her rarely entertained clients, except on the piano.

All this intellectualizing was fine. What did my ape glands think? I looked at my beloved, and visualized handsome men touching her, making love to her, making her throw back her head and clench her eyes shut and cry out with joy the way she did . . . come to think of it, it might just as well be beautiful *women*, who knew more about pleasing another woman than I ever would, driving her wild . . . Or both . . .

I found I was getting an erection.

"No problem at all," I assured her. "But it raises an interesting corollary question. I've been offered a permanent job here—assuming that the world and I both continue to exist—and I'm thinking seriously of taking it. The trouble with being a private eye is all that goddam *privacy*. Do you anticipate that being a problem for *you*?"

She blinked. "*Touché*. I never thought about it."

"Think about it. There are two of you, and only one of me. And even if there were only one of you, the supply and demand equations are different for men and women. You can make love to a thousand men, and still bring me all you've got. My equipment takes a lot longer to reload."

"So what? Erections are certainly useful in pleasing a woman, but I've never understood why so many people seem to think they're essential. Sure, they're flattering—but a man who *doesn't* have an erection and still wants to make love to me: now, that's *flattering*. Joseph my darling fiancé, if you were a paraplegic, I think you could send me through the roof with your eyelids."

As I envisioned that, my erection, too dumb to know it had been insulted, intensified and began to climb. "But are you the jealous type? It's not a silly question. I've known jealous prostitutes. What if you smell some other woman on those eyelids?"

She grinned. "Ah, but I'm twice the woman she is—no matter who she is. No, really, Joe: the jealous type I am not. I was when I came here, a little, but this place cured me. My first hour in the Bower cured me. I'd love to see you making love with someone else."

Up to half mast now.

"I'll prove it to you, a little later today. Doctor Kate has this unusual billing policy, you see. She believes in reaping what she sews—and she did quite a lot of sewing on you, even if the evidence is gone. You won't mind if I watch, will you? I *know* she won't. But I promise I won't be disappointed if you'd rather I didn't. Well, not too disappointed. I really don't need to own you, my darling. Just to share my life with you."

Something bumped me just below the navel.

"I'm more concerned about *you*, love," she went on. "You've only been here a few days—and you come from a macho kind of background—"

"I come from a background that almost guaranteed I was gonna drink myself to death all alone in the Old Dicks' Home one day," I told her. "That sounded romantic to me when I was a kid starting out, but as I get older it sounds less and less attractive. I'm ready for a change." The words surprised me as they came out, but I knew they were true.

"Yes, but are your emotions?"

I started to answer, and hesitated, frowning. "I know what you mean. I rummage around in my head looking for jealousy, and I don't seem to find any—but it may be different in practice. All I can tell you is, I'm being honest when I say I don't anticipate a problem. But I admit I could be wrong. I'm willing to gamble if you are."

Her eyes were bright. "Joe . . . shall we test it?"

"Now, you mean? How? Invite somebody in?"

"It's not necessary."

"I don't get you—oh!"

She nodded. "My other body went on-shift a few hours ago. I've been out of rotation for days now, and my clients were starting to miss me. As an experiment, why don't we lie back down here, while I tell you just what I'm doing . . . and what is being done to me . . . at this moment, a few doors away? A sort of blow-by-blow description . . ."

AS she meshed her two body-awarenesses, there came a time when she no longer needed to tell me, verbally, what was happening down the hall. I could tell, to a large extent, by her local body's responses.

It was a transcendentally strange sensation. Four bodies were having sex . . . but all the action was being directed by one of us. The one that I had never met. What jealousy? How could he possess my woman?—he didn't even know that I was in her too as he plunged away; he was sublimely unaware of my existence.

And as I paid more and closer attention to Arethusa's body and facial expressions—*without* the distraction of having to think about what she might like me to do to her next, or how I was "performing"—I knew her ever better, grew ever closer to her, understood her ever more deeply. She had previously displayed a limited ability to read my thoughts during lovemaking; somewhere in there a switch was thrown and *I* was inside *her* head. The one down the hall.

I was—at least in part, like an overlay—a beautiful, highly aroused woman, and an acceptable male was making more than acceptable love to me . . .

Like most heterosexual men, I had sometimes wondered what a homosexual experience might be like. Like most heterosexual men, I had occasionally wished to find out. Like most heterosexual men, I had never been able to figure out a way to do so without risking loss of dignity. Now that I found myself, as it were, in the middle of things, I felt the same impulse most heterosexual men would feel. Panic . . .

But it faded almost as I felt it. How could I possibly doubt my masculinity? Even as I felt my vagina joyously plundered, my clitoris electrified, my breasts squeezed, a man's tongue in my mouth, I could feel Arethusa's vagina embracing my penis, her strong fingers clutching my back, her sweet mouth opening under mine, the lush scent of her in my nostrils. I might not have known how to enjoy being penetrated, being invaded . . . but she was right there with me, teaching me how, *showing* me how. For the first time in my life I began to dimly understand just how *lucky* women are . . .

As he spilled into me, Arethusa spilled into me, and I into her, and I knew that jealousy was not going to be a problem in our marriage.

Sometime in there, the last of my annoyance at Lady Sally leaked out of me. It *was* nice having my strength back again . . .

WE saw Tesla in the cafeteria, eating dinner at a table in the far corner and reading. The eighteen crumpled but snow-white linen napkins he had used to polish his knife and fork before beginning to eat were piled on the table beside him. It was a good thing I'd read about Nikky, or I might have tried to join him at his table, and upset him. He hated company at meals, because it distracted him while he was busy trying to compute the cubic contents of each bite. You don't give indigestion to the man who's going to help you save reality. Not when you've just acquired such a compelling reason to love reality as Arethusa . . .

But the moment he was done eating, he put his book down and called us over to join him. I glanced at the open book as we reached his table; it seemed to be poetry by somebody named Kranjcevic.

"Ken, my friend," he said as he seated Arethusa, "I was talking to Arethusa's avatar a few hours ago, and she informed me that you and she are affianced. May I offer you my sincere congratulations? You probably believe you know how fortunate you are . . . but I suspect you are wrong by at least an order of magnitude. You have accomplished something very much like reaching into a chest of splendid jewels and plucking out the Koh-i-noor."

"You don't know the half of it, Nikky," Arethusa told him. "I was the first eligible woman he laid eyes on in the House."

His bushy eyebrows rose. "Remarkable!"

"The first, and the last," I added in reflex gallantry.

She pinched me. "Ken, that lie is not just outrageous, it's unnecessary. Didn't we just settle that a while ago?"

I grinned at her. "You were the first, and you're going to be the last if I have my way. I didn't say anything about in between."

She twinkled. "That's better. I like my flattery plausible."

"I did have a pulse, last time I checked."

"Oh my, yes. Nikky, you'll come to our wedding, won't you?"

"I would not miss it for the world, dear lady," Tesla said gravely.

"That would be the one acceptable excuse," I said. "But we've got it tentatively scheduled for the day *after* we save the world. Whenever that is."

"That is the second reason I asked you both to join me," Tesla said. He glanced around and lowered his voice slightly. "That day approaches."

For no reason at all I thought: it's not "adrenaline," like everybody thinks it is, it's "adrenalin," a pharmaceutical trade name for norepinephrine that passed into the language like jello or kleenex. You can even catch doctors with that one. "You've got results *already*, Nikola? Overnight?"

Again his gaze flicked from side to side. "Yes, but I am reluctant to discuss them here."

Just then there was a mild disturbance at a nearby table. Reggie, the aged Brit I'd met on my previous visit to the cafeteria, was being braced by an agitated client. He was also a Brit, and nearly as aged, dressed expensively but in appalling taste; he might as well have been wearing a sign saying RICH QUEER. He had allowed his voice to rise in pitch and volume, and was close to hysteria.

"But I mean, dash it all! I've lost Bingo and Tuppy and Sippy and Corky and Rocky and Biffy, all the Drones are gone, Aunt Dahlia—even Aunt Agatha, impossible as it seems, turned out to be mortal—I mean to say, old man, you're simply the only thing left on Earth that I understand."

Reggie didn't seem at all embarrassed; if anything there was compassion in his ancient eyes. "I'm very sorry, sir," he said gravely. "You know you are welcome to visit me regularly . . . but you must make your own way in the world now."

"But *why?*"

"Because, sir, I do not play that scene any more. As the poet Wordsworth said, 'A Briton, even in love, should be a subject, not a slave!' I have come to agree."

Reggie's client stood up. "Blast the poet Wordsworth! In fact, damn the man, and his heirs and assigns! No, hang on a minute—wasn't he the cove who worked that wheeze about a thousand pine tables?"

" 'And homeless near a thousand homes I stood, and near a thousand tables pined and wanted food,' yes, sir," Reggie agreed.

"Well, there you have the thing in a nutshell!"

Reggie looked pained. He took a deep breath, and said patiently, "I can only repeat my suggestion that you form a liaison with Master Henry or Mistress Cynthia."

The man's shoulders slumped. "Not the same," he said. "You only made me surrender one garment at a time. And they won't let me *talk*. Oh, very well, I suppose there's nothing left to say." He spun on his heel and headed for the door, face contorted with grief.

Reggie's face was still impassive . . . but a single tear was trying to solve the maze of wrinkles that led to his chin. "Goodbye, Bertie," he said, so softly that I'm sure the guy never heard him.

No one had been exactly staring, but suddenly the conversations in the room were more animated. "You're right, Nikola," I said. "Let's find someplace more private to talk. I'm open to suggestions."

"Let us go to my laboratory," Tesla said.

I'd been hoping he'd ask . . .

IT was an honor to be in Nikola Tesla's laboratory. That was about all it was.

One thing most PIs are notoriously good at: if we've spent more than a few seconds in a place, we can give you a fairly detailed description of it, maybe not as poetic as John D. MacDonald could make it, but accurate enough to reconstruct a crime scene for a jury. It's the part of the job we share with a Zen monk: trying to be aware of *everything*. They do it to transcend the illusion of consciousness; we do it to not get killed. I'm a little better at it than most PIs.

Nikola Tesla's laboratory was a rectangular solid with stuff in it.

The only thing I recognized was an electric typewriter keyboard, without a typewriter under it. I'd have taken it for a computer terminal, but it wasn't attached to *anything*, and it didn't seem to have any of those funny extra keys they have. And I didn't see anything around that looked like the brain part of a computer (or anything else I could name). There was a cylinder along its top end that looked like some kind of hinge; I decided maybe that was where the typewriter part attached. On a soft grey pad next to the keyboard was a little widget that looked like an electric guitarist's foot-switch. It, too, wasn't attached or wired to anything. The two objects were sitting on . . . well, it looked sort of like a piece of window glass, blued with age, suspended in mid-air.

Everything else in the room was *much* weirder.

Tesla (I could *call* him Nikola, but I couldn't seem to make myself *think* of him as Nikola) took some small objects off some larger objects that had flat surfaces on top, and bade us sit. They weren't chairs, but they agreed to hold our weight. Tesla sat on . . . climbed into . . . achieved comfortable equilibrium with something else. "There," he said, "now we can talk."

Confuse a PI and you get a wisecrack. Spenser says it's in the oath. "Testing," I said. "By God, you're right: I can." It went over like a lead balloon, so I gave it up. "Okay, Nikola—*how many and where?*"

He didn't try to drag it out. "Four each in the United States and the Soviet Union. One in each country that would be in a position to effectively employ a nuclear weapon of its own if it knew the two chief combatants were disarmed. A total of thirty."

I blinked a bit at the total—the last I'd heard, there were only supposed to be about a dozen members in The Club—but I let it pass. Catch me questioning Nikola Tesla's figures. "And you have them all located?"

He . . . well, sort of swiveled, both in and on his object, so that the keyboard was convenient to his hands. He did something to the hinge-like gizmo, and it opened up vertically like an upside-down home movie screen, widening somehow at the same time, to a size just a little larger than an open *Time* magazine and no thicker. As it finished growing it started glowing, blue-white. "Welcome to Macintosh" was written on it in black type. *Thanks, I prefer Granny Smiths*, I thought, but kept my mouth shut. In a few seconds, the thing changed color and little pictures appeared on it along the right side. He touched the fuzztone foot-switch with his hand, and everything changed again, much faster this time. Now it was a map of the world, two polar projections on black background that looked like live high-resolution video from some spacecraft, except that there were a total of thirty "hot spots" marked with tiny bright red crosses, almost all of them in the Northern Hemisphere. The four U.S. sites appeared to be Los Angeles, Chicago (or possibly Detroit; I'm vague on middle America), Washington, and New York. The only Soviet site I could name with any confidence was Moscow; another might have been Kiev. But Tesla must know them all.

"That's terrific," I said, feeling real confidence for the first time since I'd understood what we were up against. "That's a lot more than we knew yesterday. Is there any chance you'll be able to narrow one of them down closer? That one that seems to be in New York, say? And how soon?"

Tesla looked startled, then smiled. "Forgive me, Ken. I oscillate between a tendency to treat everyone around me as ignorant children, and a tendency to assume they know everything I do. Observe." He took hold of the little widget. A small arrow appeared on the screen. He used the widget to nurse it up against one of the tiny red crucifixes, the one in New York, and pushed the switch on the widget. At once the polar projections were gone, replaced by a highly detailed map of Manhattan Island. The tiny red cross was now roughly at Madison Square Garden. I opened my mouth to say something, and Tesla moved the pointer to a little cartoon of a magnifying glass and worked the switch again. Suddenly we were looking down on Penn Station from about fifteen stories above the roof, as if we were in a blimp. Again it looked like live color video—I could see traffic crawling down Seventh and along Thirty-third, and swarms of ants moving like people—but a long thin red hollow rectangle shimmered in and out of existence, running north and south (well, uptown and downtown). A major tributary of Water Tunnel One, by the width of it. Where it crossed Penn Station, it contained a very small solid red rectangular object, which also shimmered. As Tesla had prophesied, a cylindrical gun-type device. A tiny green hollow rectangle nearby on the left was connected to it by a series of thin green lines that doglegged several times on the way.

"What the hell . . . excuse me, Nikola. What on earth *is* that thing?"

Tesla looked surprised. "An atom bomb," he explained.

I said nothing at all for five seconds. Then, very quietly, I said, "I meant, 'What is that thing there that's showing me the atom bomb?' "

I'm the kind of guy, when I catch myself being dumb, I get mad at myself and my voice gets very very soft. Tesla was the kind of guy, he chuckled. I envied him that gift; it was healthier. (Then suddenly remembered that I didn't have to worry about staying healthy any more. I was free to be as stupid as I wanted to be.) "I have done it again, Ken. Please pardon me. This will one day be marketed under the name 'Macintosh Five' . . . but I am told that its designers will privately call it 'Son of Jobs.' It is about minus twenty-five years old. It has a giggle bite of rum, three and a half tear a bites of ram, bubble mammary, super-seedy worm drive, and can perform some preposterously high number of trips."

I'm pretty sure that's what he said.

"Thank you," I said very very softly. "But what is that thing there that's showing me the atomb bomb?"

This time he laughed out loud. Since I knew perfectly well it was himself he was laughing at, I let him live. After a very few *ha*'s, he saw the veins in my forehead and tapered off. "Again I beg your pardon, my friend. It is a computer, which will be produced in the year 2010. Her Ladyship provided it for me. Its earliest ancestor has only been on sale for a few months at this time." He waited to see if *that* was simple enough.

It didn't look like a computer. It didn't even look like one of those toy Apple computers they gave schoolkids in those days. And I thought computers were supposed to be the *fathers* of jobs. But what did I know? "Ah. I see. Like, some kind of super-IBM."

He said, "That's correct: a kind of super-IBM," with such an absolutely straight face that I knew I'd said something funny again. (I later learned that in 2007, IBM would save itself from receivership by subcontracting to supply the on-off switches for this model's predecessor—but that this one, which didn't need such a switch, would eventually finish them off. Why that's funny, maybe a computer person could tell you.)

To hell with it. Keep on asking questions and don't stop, and sooner or later you'll be asking intelligent ones. If you live long enough. "And it can pinpoint the other thirty-three toadstools that accurately?"

"In combination with certain equipment of my own, with which it is interfaced—excuse me, 'connected'—it has already done so. It contains the information in incorruptible form, in a series of Ultracard stacks that . . . in a conveniently manipulable format. The computer subsumes every existing human computer network or database, in much the same way that a Ferrari Testarossa usually includes a good FM radio. By that I mean that you can obtain literally any specific relevant datum that is presently known to mankind, and some which are not, in under a second, with a simple touch of the mouse."

I sighed, and straightened a kink out of my neck. "I was hanging on pretty good, right up until that last word," I said sadly.

"Oh!" he said. He pointed to the widget. "That input device is called a mouse."

"Why?"

He said, "Because . . ." and stopped. Then he said, "It's because . . ." and stopped. Then he said, "I think it's . . ." and stopped again. Finally he frowned and said, "There is no reason."

"Got it. Go on." I felt like Rocky Balboa. I was *not* going down . . .

"I connected the computer with the equipment of mine I told you about yesterday, which detects functional radio receivers. First I made a list of every receiver on the planet. That took under five minutes . . . although to display the data, at the fastest rate a human could even theoretically comprehend, would have taken hours. Fortunately this was not necessary. I pruned the basic list to those receivers whose characteristic signature indicated that they were underwater, and stationary. That took less than two minutes. Then I summoned up a list of all licensed, legitimate underwater receivers from the FCC and its planetary analogs, and assorted military databases, and subtracted that from my own list. Another five seconds. The remainder I investigated in some detail by diverse means. Altogether it was another hour before I had the last of the mines pinpointed as closely as that one on the screen."

"You're sure you've got them all."

"I am prepared to state authoritatively that there are no others *with radio triggers*, underwater or otherwise. Once I knew the characteristics of the enemy's radio triggers, I searched my original list for any of that type that were not underwater, and found none. But bear in mind that they may have one or more, either underwater or otherwise, that are not radio-triggered. If so, I can presently think of no way to find them."

"I can," I said grimly.

"Joe," Arethusa said softly, "isn't there something in the Geneva Conventions about torturing prisoners?"

"What if there is? I never signed it," I said. "And if I had, it seems to me jokers who plant nuclear mines are in a poor position to invoke it."

"Perhaps not," she agreed. "But one day you and I must sit down and work out the moral equation in detail. To save how many lives is it moral to torture one person? Do we double that for two people, and so on? Does it matter if the lives we're saving are those of people we dislike? Or if the person we're torturing did not consciously *intend* harm? This is not a simple question."

"In this special case it is. More than six billion lives are at stake."

"Far more than that, Ken," Tesla put in. "The terrorists *intend* to place six billions at risk. But if they succeed—if they merely succeed in letting the world know that those mines ever existed— they will destroy all those now living, *and all those who ever would have lived*. I cannot give an upper limit, but from things Lady Sally has let slip in conversation, I believe that exceeds a quadrillion lives . . . virtually all of them centuries in length."

Ever wake up in the morning wondering if there was any purpose to going on? Since that day, I never have again. "If there are any more mines, I'll find them. Whatever it takes."

"Yes, Ken," Arethusa said. "Uh . . . now, by the way."

"Beg pardon?"

She glanced at Tesla and colored slightly. "You asked me earlier to let you know whenever . . ."

"Oh. Oh! Right. Thanks." I felt a silly grin on my face.

There was one on hers too. "It is nice. Sharing it with a third party."

"Yes, it is." Somewhere else in the building, Arethusa had just had an orgasm. I put out telepathic feelers—or tried to—but detected nothing. Well, the circumstances weren't ideal. And it was still nice sharing the knowledge . . .

Tesla cleared his throat gently.

"Sorry, Nikola. Private matter." Back to business. "Well, say, this is all good cheese. You've done as splendidly as I knew you would: a full quarter of our job is done. I always say, if you're going to tackle a tough one, try to get the smartest man that ever lived to help."

"Thank you, Ken," Tesla said gravely. Maybe I was among the first ten thousand people to call him that, and maybe I wasn't. "But why do you say only 'a quarter'?"

"Well, the job breaks down into four parts. Find the mines, disarm the mines, find the miners, inform the proper people."

"In that case," he said, "we are half done."

I could actually recall a time—less than a week ago!—when surprises were surprising. "Go on."

"Once I had located the receivers, it was a simple matter to determine what frequency they were all set to receive—"

"Hold on a half. There have to be thirty different transmitters, one within radio range of each receiver, right?"

Tesla shook his head. "They have the capacity to piggy-back on satellite transmission and conventional land lines. One transmitter covers the globe. It is located in Switzerland."

"Naturally. Okay, go on."

"I identified the pertinent frequency. A good choice, an obscure one."

"But you can't know what the trigger code is."

"Unfortunately, no. If their triggering software were a little more sophisticated, I could ask it questions on the order of, 'What would you do if I were to do thus-and-so?' As things are, I dare not. But I do not really need to know the trigger code."

"Why not?"

He looked slightly sheepish. "Here I may have overstepped my authority."

"Is that possible?"

"Lady Sally has told me that you are in overall charge—"

Surprises could still be surprising. "*Me?* Hell, no! It's her show; I'm just a consultant. Per diem and expense account. A merc."

"She was quite explicit," he said. "You are in command."

Jesus Christ on a bicycle! When I let Lady Sally recruit me, I assumed it was at the rank of buck private. In my wildest dreams, corporal. Commanding officer was one helluva field promotion . . .

Well, no time to admire my eagles: the battle was in progress. "I see," I said, and took three long deep breaths. "Tell me how you overstepped your authority, Nikola."

"I could not wake you while you were being rejuvenated. But it did not seem wise to allow things to remain as they were. So I took action. I apologize if I was imprudent. It was a very agonizing decision for me. I hope you will not be angry with me."

"Not if you tell me what you did within the next five seconds," I said carefully.

"I initiated a broadcast. Perhaps you slept through the brownout last night? Yes. I call your attention to the particular mine there on the screen, the one beneath Pennsylvania Station. Where once there was a radio receiver, now is melted plastic, melted copper, new glass, iron filings, and minor contaminants. The mine is disabled. I can disable the other twenty-nine anytime you wish. So you see, the job is nearly *half* done."

14. Gathering Shadows

What shall it profit a man if he gaineth the whole
world, yet he hath no deductions?

—EDISON RIPSBORN

"NEARLY?" I said weakly, trying to get a deep breath.

Tesla looked troubled. "That mine is disabled . . . not disarmed.
Only the radio trigger is destroyed. Its owners could yet hand-
trigger it, by physically going to the site. It would be a suicide
mission, of course, but I don't think that rules it out."

"But they have no reason to do so," I pointed out. "As far as
they know, all their mines are safe and ready to go. We're safe
for at least as long as it takes them to push that button and notice
how quiet everything is in New York."

It was a good thing Tesla didn't wear glasses; when he frowned
like that, those eyebrows would have brushed them right off his
face. "Ken, I am forced to assume that the master terrorist—we
may as well call him The Miner—is as intelligent as myself. I do
not consider this likely, but I must assume it."

"I'll buy that."

"I put myself in his place. I propose to blackmail the world into
disarmament. One fine day, I announce my threat to the world, as
publicly as possible. Of course the world's governments do not
capitulate . . . so I set off *one* of my mines, telling them in advance
when and in what city I will do so, to prove my control. Then I
set off one every forty-eight hours until I get what I want."

"I'll buy that too."

"In that case, I wish to be utterly certain that each mine is
functioning correctly, will detonate when I tell it to. Malfunction

201

would be embarrassing, and embarrassment is fatal to a bluff."

"*What* bluff? The Miner's got thirty nukes!"

"Ken, imagine you are the Chief of the Joint Chiefs of Staff. I tell you that to retain your job, you must sacrifice four American cities. And a few dozen foreign ones, four of them Soviet. How will you decide? Remember that one of the cities is Los Angeles."

The answer was obscene, but undeniable. "I get you. The Miner's bluff depends on making everyone think he has an unlimited number of nukes, that he can keep on taking out cities until he gets his way. And he's gambling that neither of the major players will go higher than four cities before folding. Okay, how does that affect our problem?"

"If I were The Miner, I would have a means of *testing* my radio receivers at frequent intervals. Some test that would not trigger the bomb, but would give assurance that the trigger was still operational."

Trade name for norepinephrine. Common side effects: elevated pulse and temp, buzzing in ears, dry mouth . . .

"Nikola," I said gently, "I'm aware of your feelings on strong language. But if we're going to keep having conversations like this, sooner or later I'm going to have to say, 'JESUS CHRIST!' " I shouted the last two words. "Suppose the guy has some kind of continuous failsafe light on every bomb: he may already know something's wrong!"

"Since his trigger is radio, his failure warning would be so as well. A hardwired monitor would be a trail to him. None of the thirty mines has broadcast anything since I began observing them."

"But they could be set to do so at regular intervals."

"I'm sorry, Ken. I said it was a difficult decision. I feared that our enemy might trigger his bombs at any moment. We have no way of being sure he has not already begun blackmailing governments as we speak. Or he could begin with an explosion, to get their attention—and he might well select New York. I reasoned that at a minimum I must preserve the only living humans who know where the mines are."

"No, no! I'm not second-guessing the decision: you did what you had to do. But now there's a clock ticking: we've got to move *fast*."

"That is correct," he agreed.

"What I don't understand," Arethusa said, "is why we have any time at all. You say there's a bomb planted in every country that's nuclear-capable. Why hasn't he acted already?"

"Damn good question," I said.

"Yes it is," Tesla said. "I can offer two hypotheses. Either there are one or two more marginally nuclear-capable nations left on his list, and he is now busy mining them . . . or he is waiting for some specific, psychologically appropriate date."

That hammer of light hit me between the eyes. I tried not to squint. "August sixth," I heard myself say.

Tesla said something in Croatian. Somehow I knew it was the equivalent of "JESUS CHRIST!" "Of course," he added in English. "How stupid of me."

"What's August sixth?" Arethusa asked.

"Hiroshima Day. But that's not important now." For an instant I had the wild feeling I was Leslie Nielsen in *Airplane*. "And don't call me Shirley. The important thing is, how often does The Miner test his receivers?"

"He has to strike a balance," Tesla said. "Too frequent broadcasts from a water pipe, even brief ones, might be noticed somewhere, and commented upon. And each test lowers the mean time until failure; if one tests a system too often one risks wearing it out. Assuming a target date no more than months away, I should guess something on the order of once a week would strike him as prudent."

I relaxed a trifle; I'd been thinking in terms of daily, or even hourly.

Come to think of it, I had no assurance at all that he *ever* tested his receivers. *I* hadn't thought of it, and maybe the Miner *wasn't* as intelligent as Nikola Tesla.

I had to assume he was, with stakes like these. But at least I didn't have to mount a military assault within the next hour.

Oh, hell—maybe I did have to. His next weekly check could be as much as six days away . . . but it could be in the next ten minutes.

Time to start acting like a commanding officer.

"Does Mary have ears in this room?" I asked.

Tesla looked puzzled. Arethusa said, "No, Ken. Nowhere on this floor."

"Nikola, is there a telephone in here?"

"What number do you wish?" he asked.

"Lady Sally! As quickly as possible."

He touched his computer. The keyboard stuck out its tongue, to the right. A smaller keypad. A calculator. He pushed numeral one and one other key.

"Coming, Nikky!" Lady Sally said, sounding as though she were sitting in front of me. A second later, she was.

I'D half expected it. And still I was startled. Whatever device she'd used to get here, she was not carrying it on her. We had caught her in the shower; she wore only fragrant suds.

I wasted seconds staring.

No, I take that back. I wasted nothing. I spent seconds staring. Clothed, Lady Sally McGee was a very striking woman. Dressed in foam, she was the second most beautiful thing I had ever seen.

"What is it, Ken?" she said.

"Red alert!" I blurted, forcing my attention back to the war. "I want Pris and . . . who's the next best fighter in the House?"

"Me."

"Then I want you," I said, suppressing my pun generator.

"And after me, Father Newman. He was Special Forces."

"Him too, then. And the Professor and Ralph Von Wau Wau and Cynthia and Tim . . . and Mike, if he's available."

She closed her eyes briefly. "He is."

"Can I have Mary too?"

"Sorry: she's out of town on personal business. What equipment do you want?"

Shoot for the Moon. I gave her my Christmas list. "Walkie-talkies, bulletproof vests, handguns and knives for everybody—laser pistols for anyone checked out on them. I've got my own handgun and knife. Ammo. Tear gas grenades would be nice. Binoculars. Enough field rations to last three people at least a week. We'll be working in teams of three on eight-hour shifts around the clock. And for God's sake make sure Ralph has a license tag good for Manhattan."

"No problem so far," she said. "But for the pistols, lasers, and tear gas, may I substitute one of these?" There was a weapon in her hand. Don't ask me where it came from; I don't want to think about it. And don't ask me how I knew it was a weapon: it looked like a midget trumpet, with less than normal flaring to the bell and with the three keys placed inside the loop part instead of on the shaft. She didn't hold it like a firearm or a trumpet: she held it down at her side by the loop part, seemingly upside down, the bell facing in my general direction but not pointed at any one of us. Maybe that was why I was sure that if her fingers were to press upward on those keys in the right way, nastiness would come out the bell.

"It's better than the laser pistol that got Raffalli?"

"Much better."

"What does it do?" I asked.

"Stun, blind, or drill holes through *anything*, from a millimeter to two meters in diameter, in well under a nanosecond. Range is line of sight. Ammo effectively infinite. Battlefield failure rate, zero, over the course of a busy century. A mirror won't deflect it like a laser beam."

I liked it. It was like those silly guns Buster Crabbe used to use when he was Flash Gordon, only upside down it wasn't silly any more. It was the ultimate quick-draw weapon: you could fire from the hip without so much as torquing your wrist upward to bring a barrel to bear. It would be more awkward than a pistol to bring up to eye level for a dead bead—but that firehose cone-of-effectiveness made precise aim less important. Best of all, it didn't look much like a weapon, even in firing position. At least, not to anyone who didn't know you were a time traveler. "Issue one to everyone that's ever fired one before. The rest of us will drill on it as time allows, and stick to weapons we know until then—with the proviso that no one packs less than thirty-eight caliber. You've got something equally good in body armor?"

"Yes. It'll stop small arms fire. A direct hit to the head from a heavy enough gun might knock you out. Well, not *you*, but someone with a normal skull."

"That we'll all use right away."

"How soon do you want us to assemble?"

"As soon as possible."

"Give me an hour," she said, and was gone.

"What about me?" Arethusa said dangerously.

I blinked, and nearly said, "What *about* you?" But it was not possible to say those words to Arethusa, so I said, "You are the most beautiful, intelligent, and captivating woman in the world and I love you with all my heart. What *else* about you?"

"I'm in, aren't I?"

"Good God, yes! You doubted it?"

She was mollified. "Well . . . you're an unusual private eye, my love. I was a little afraid you might get all macho about not exposing your wife to danger."

"I am. I wouldn't want you to accidentally suffer any harm while beating the shit out of me for trying to keep you out of the party. You could forget and hit me on the head, and hurt your knuckles."

"I wouldn't have hit you on the head," she assured me.

"Something else to worry about," I agreed. "But the issue doesn't arise. You're in. On my shift. And I'm afraid your clients are going to have to be understanding again. I'm only bringing one of you—but I want the other to be lying down alone in a quiet dark room, undistracted. I need your full attention."

"The clients will survive if we do," she said. "About ten minutes ago, by the way."

"Eh?"

" 'Now!' " she explained. "Well, 'then,' I mean. When it happened, the conversation here was at a point where I might have started a panic if I'd said, 'Now!' "

"Oh. Sorry I missed it."

"How much of the next hour do you need?" she asked. "I could give you a sort of instant replay . . ."

Well, we *were* going to be on short rations for as much as a week. A practical woman, my wife.

"Uh, Nikola?" I said. "Would you excuse us?"

He stood, beaming, and placed a hand on top of each of our heads. "Go in peace, my children."

ON our way from basement level up to the second floor, we passed through the Parlor. It had been too long since I'd been in that splendid room; I tried to absorb everything I could as I went through.

It wasn't easy. It was a little after nine o'clock: the place was packed. There was a contingent of Japanese at the bar, grinning and photographing everything in sight. Willard's wife Sherry was apparently leading a pun contest over by the fireplace; I heard her raise an appreciative groan with something about a junkies' hamburger stand, where every order comes with the works. The two smoke-artists were working at the other end of the room. She blew a naked woman with streaming hair; her partner studied it a moment, blew a naked man that approached the smoke-woman, grew an erection, moved forward to mingle with her—and a dozen flashbulbs went off at once. Near the room was a short blonde in a gold sari, leading an ocelot on a leash. Male of course. A paper airplane sailed past me and landed where I could see it: it was a traffic ticket. Near the spiral staircase, a slender gent with a goatee and the look of a kindly faun seemed to be giving hugging lessons to a group of attentive ladies. Seated near him was one of the indoor ice-skaters, only he wasn't skating tonight: he was talking sternly to a cat.

The same old guy was playing piano tonight. He still looked like Hoagy Carmichael, and he was playing "New Orleans." But all the singing was being done by his accompanist: a tall skinny galoot with long brown hair and a beard, playing an acoustic guitar. And he had changed the lyrics, so strikingly that Arethusa and I actually stopped to listen. Hoagy had written that song something like fifty years ago; this guy was updating it:

> *If you've ever seen a shithole Southern city,*
> *One-time pretty,*
> *That's New Orleans . . .*

> *And if you have to live there, that's a pity:*
> *Man, it's shitty*
> *In New Orleans . . .*

> *It will remind you   Of old tarnished slums*
> *For a glass of wine   They'll eat it till it comes*

> *See that little Creole whore? She is nine years old . . .*
> *Goin' down, in New Orleans*

> *So if you're passin' through, I think you oughta*
> *Stay in the Quarter:*
> *Bag New Orleans.*

> *And don't you wander far away from Bourbon;*
> *Man, it's disturbin',*
> *The real Orleans . . .*

> *It will depress you,   Like your mother's grave;*
> *If you stay long,   You're either dumb or brave.*

> *See that Old Man River there? He is tryin' and tryin'*
> *To get out*
> *Of New Orleans . . .*

Some people made approving sounds when he was done, and some were silent. Whoever that was at the ivories clapped his hands harder than a piano player ought to. "There y'are, Jake," he said happily.

Maybe you're from New Orleans, and think a guy from New York had no business criticizing *any* city. I won't argue. I'd made my first visit to the Big Easy a year before. I'd gone to pay my respects to the famous statue of Satchelmouth in Armstrong Park. What is it, four blocks from Bourbon Street? An abandoned area, filthy and unkempt, the pond a cesspool of stagnant water. A New York crackhead wouldn't have gone there to cop. I got mugged in broad daylight. Lost two hundred bucks, my watch, and a gun I was fond of. Louie smiled down at me sheepishly. At least New York doesn't claim to be quaint and charming.

I shook off my stasis—what a fine, melancholy voice that Jake had!—dropped a twenty into the ten-gallon hat he had upright on the floor, and led Arethusa to the staircase.

An attractive brunette in her fifties was just coming down; she paused as she passed us, said to me, with the most infectious smile I ever saw, "Keep that one," and was gone.

"I will," I said to her back. Arethusa smiled at me. "Do you know her?" I asked.

"No, but here's to her."

As we were ascending, we heard a man say, "Aw come on, Sherry . . . you know I can do it like a bunny."

"That's the problem," she told him. "I just washed my thing, and I can't do a hare with it."

Arethusa folded up with the giggles.

"A more appropriate note to leave on," I said, chuckling myself.

"I don't know what's gotten into Sherry tonight," she said. "She *hates* puns."

"I'm more interested in what's gotten into you tonight."

"I could get into that," she agreed. "Let's go join me and we'll tell you all about it."

One of these days I was going to have to walk up that staircase with Arethusa *slowly* . . .

THERE'S nothing like the prospect of impending combat to et cetera. And so forth. You know what two people do when they're in love—don't you?—so I'll say only that once again I felt a taste of that telepathic union that had startled me on our last encounter. Not as strong, maybe, but unmistakable. God, it's so *different* for women! I began dimly to grasp why they put up with us.

I could not decide whether the phenomenon was specific to Arethusa, related to her own peculiar self-telepathy . . . or whether perhaps this was simply the first time in my life I'd ever really been in love. Others suffering from that condition have reported similar symptoms . . .

What I finally decided was, *what the hell difference does it make?*

We barely made it on time to the war council I had called.

WE'D left enough time—but on our way back down through the Parlor, we had to pull up short to avoid a collision. That hippie again. The one with the carpenter's tool belt. Riding a bicycle, this time.

"Easy, Nazz," Arethusa said, smiling across the handlebars at him. He smiled back at her.

"Forgive me," he said. "I knew not what I did."

While I groped for a reply, he took a jug from the bike's basket, gave it to me, and pedaled away, weaving in and out of Parlor traffic with easy grace. As he passed by the brunette with the infectious grin, I heard him say, "I love you more than you'll know, Ev." She smiled.

I blinked down at the jug, pulled the stopper, sniffed. No one who's ever been in the Orient will ever forget the smell. Rice liquor.

"What's the jug for?" Arethusa said.

The answer hit me like a blow to the solar plexus. "It's . . . it's for Christ's sâke," I said weakly . . . and fell down laughing.

The funniest part was that I wouldn't have bet five cents he wasn't . . . who he seemed to be.

But eventually I pulled myself together. "Well," I said, "I've got this jug, and thou beside me—now all I need is a loaf of bread."

"Yippee, I owe Khayyam," she sang.

So I had to tickle her, and we were nearly late for the meeting.

It was just as I was entering Tesla's lab that the penny dropped. When we'd left him an hour ago, he had touched us both on the head. On the head! His violent aversion to touching human hair seemed to finally be gone.

Which implied—given his address and his smouldering good looks—that Nikola Tesla was no longer a virgin any more . . .

That cheered me up even more . . . and I needed it.

Everyone I'd asked for was present, including Mike Callahan. He lived more than an hour's travel time away . . . but only if you were restricted to conventional transport. I introduced myself as "Ken Taggart" to Cynthia and Father Newman (there was no longer any need for that masquerade, but this seemed the wrong time to start confusing everyone), winked at the Professor, winked in a different way at Tim, scratched Ralph behind the ear, nodded to Pris, and shook hands with Mike, who was kind enough to return my hand afterward. If you still need any clues as to just what an extraordinary assemblage of people that was, try this: it took less than fifteen minutes by my watch to bring everybody there up to speed.

Nikola's Raincoat Five computer helped a lot: there's nothing like visual aids to get a presentation over. But that was only part of it. Not one dumb question or extraneous issue was raised. Nobody wasted time on shock or disbelief or oratorical posturing. And nobody needed to be told anything twice. It reminded me a little of the Army, with one guy up front saying impossible and unspeakable things, and all the rest waiting in patient silence for their cue to salute. (Except that it was impossible to look at that motley crew and be reminded much of the Army. Mike was the only one who wasn't hopelessly miscast: he'd have made a great DI or platoon sergeant. But Tim? Nikola Tesla? Father Newman? Mistress Cynthia? Ralph Von Wau Wau? Even during Nam they took few recruits that wonky.) The longer that briefing went on— no, the longer it *didn't* go on—the better I felt about my squad.

Nobody objected, as I had thought someone might, that we had made an awful lot of stew from one oyster—our sole fact being that civilization had inexplicably not yet been consumed in thermonuclear fire. They all found the circumstantial evidence for the existence of The Miner as compelling as Lady Sally had, and nobody knocked any holes in the logic structure, and when Nikola showed them some of the radio-equipped cylinders in municipal water pipes with his computer screen, nobody thought of anything they could be but private enterprise nuclear weapons.

"Nikola," I finished at last, "has persuaded me that the terrorist mastermind we've been calling The Miner either does regular systems checks on his mines, or is an idiot. We're guessing that he checks about once a week, and we know the New York mine will fail. So we're going to stake it out for a week or two, and try to tail whoever shows up to see what's wrong. If he spots the tail, we capture him, or kill him, in that order of preference. If nothing happens by the second week, we'll fall back and revise our plans on the assumption that we're dealing with an idiot. I *think* this should be safe enough. If I'm wrong and the world comes to an end, I'll accept any criticisms you have. We have no *proof* that his final target date is six August . . . but both Nikola and I have had strong intuitions about it."

"That's good enough for me," Lady Sally and Mike said together.

"We'll work three-man shifts," I said, "so even when somebody has to pee we'll have at least two in position at all times. We may well get ample warning: Nikola's got widgets running that will sound an alarm the instant anyone broadcasts or narrowcasts anything on that frequency, worldwide, and locate the source. If the systems check should be initiated by The Miner from his end, we'll know exactly when he gets his out-of-order message. Even so, we will fucking well stay alert at all times. The device may have been preset to report at regular or irregular intervals—which it no longer will—or, if The Miner has the manpower, he might even do his systems checks by eyeball, in corpus, and there's no telling when.

"Fortunately, Penn Station lends itself well to this kind of operation—we could probably all *sleep* there for a month without causing much talk. But do please try your best not to draw the attention of the local heat, hookers, hustlers, or heroin addicts. We can't afford the distraction of being jugged, hugged, mugged or plugged just now."

Mike Callahan put up a hand the size of a first baseman's mitt.

"Yes, Mike?"

"When we spot him . . . are you sure you want to fall back and go for a tail? He could always be a kamikaze, there to *set off* that particular bomb and radio-trigger the others from there. I know that's stupid—but do you know that old one about, 'Never attribute to evil what can be satisfactorily explained by stupidity'?"

"True enough," I admitted. "That's why on every shift, one of us will be stationed within sight of the bomb at all times. I think it's reasonable to assume that even if he walks in there intending to light the candle, he'll pause to find out why his radio trigger has melted. That gives us time. If he then reaches for any other component of the bomb, the inside man drops him in his tracks with one of those magic trumpets, and we take him back here for an interview.

"But for me the ideal outcome would be: he inspects the bomb, curses at the spoiled trigger, scratches his head, and makes a beeline for Bad Guy HQ to report, wagging his tails behind him. That way we're sure of getting some information. One thing I learned in Nam about interrogating fanatics: they have this frustrating tendency to die too soon on you. Poison tooth, special ring, chew open an artery . . . I saw a guy do it by sheer willpower, once. Restrained so well all he could move were his eyes and his asshole, and he just plain made up his mind to die.

"Please bear in mind at all times our ultimate objective, and make sure you've got it straight. It's not simply to prevent any bombs going off. If someone were to wave a magic wand right now and make all thirty nukes disappear, *we would have failed*. What we must do, if we are to safeguard the present and the future, is to disable those nukes, leave them in place, and then very quietly tell the DIA and KGB about them. That is what it will take to shock both sides into fixing that annoying rattle they have in their sabers these days, to nurse history through the next five critical years. Remember how the Cuban Missile Crisis sobered 'em all up for a while? The difference here will be that this one *must not* make the news. Ever—even after it's over.

"But this strategic situation presents us with a tactical problem. Lady Sally has appropriate contacts in both agencies—but we can't simply give them the mines. *We must also give them The Miner*, and as many minor Miners as we can identify, and as much information on them and their operations as we can get. As a great man once said to Mary Astor, 'Shumbody's got to take the fall.' If we don't supply a whole lot of convincing fanatics, the spooks will take *us*—and even Lady Sally's many years of goodwill won't help us. She and Mike wouldn't even be able to use future-magic to get us all clear and underground. They'd risk blowing their cover as time travelers—which would be precisely as bad as one or more of those atom bombs going off."

"Surely not to the people near to the bomb," Father Newman said mildly. He was in his fifties, grizzled and grey but very fit, with that indefinable air of being ready to run up the side of a five-story building that Special Forces guys seldom seem to lose, even in retirement.

"I'm afraid so, Father. And don't call me Shirley. At least I think so. Mike, Your Ladyship, Nikola, check me out: there's a point at the beginning of a nuclear explosion past which nothing could conceivably stop it, yes?"

"Sure," Mike said.

"A *very* tiny slice of a second after the two subcritical masses meet, right?"

"Take a right at the decimal point, and bring your hiking boots," he agreed.

"So at that instant, a historical paradox exists . . . and the universe goes away. A man standing next to the bomb wouldn't have time to die before he ceased to ever have been."

He frowned. "You're right," he said, and worked his jaws. I could tell he wanted to chew on his cigar. But if he took it out, he'd have to light it; . . . and this was Nikola Tesla's laboratory.

"What an extraordinary situation!" Tesla said. "Thirty armed atom bombs, and none of them can possibly hurt anybody. Yet we must prevent one going off at all costs."

When someone starts to talk about the amazing philosophical aspects of a combat situation, it's time to move the briefing along. "Okay: if we do get a miner, small *m* or large, and he does inspect the damage and go to report back, the person nearest the bomb stays there while the others tail the bastard. We do not leave that bomb alone. On each shift, one of the two backups is going to be playing a blind beggar, tin cup and all. That's our excuse for having Ralph around. Ralph, you're going to be there around the clock, but you don't have to stay awake all the time. You're going to do the actual tailing—by smell. The others will follow *you*. There's no way the miner can spot that tail."

"If I get too close," Ralph said, "he may zee it vagging."

"Ken," the Professor said urgently, "I see a problem. A blind man can't just walk into Penn Station and set up a pitch, any more than a girl can just pick out a street corner and start hooking. You can get cut that way. It's a turf situation."

I frowned. "You're right. Damn. Excuse me, Nikola. I wanted the kind of person most people would look away from."

"I don't sink it vill be a problem," Ralph said. "If anyvun giffs us trouble, I vill tell him to go avay. Humans haff a tendency to obey ven I tell zem ziss. If he duss not, I shall urinate upon him vile speaking disparagingly uff hiss muzzer. Ziss neffer fails."

"Well, hold it to a minimum," I said. "If The Miner happens to hear a German shepherd talking, he's liable to start thinking in terms of James Bond, which is just what we don't want. All right, let's issue ordnance and materiel. Quartermistress!"

Lady Sally began passing out party favors. First the little trumpets, to those checked out on them: Mike, Pris, Father Newman (to my mild surprise) and Tim (to my stronger surprise). Then 9mm Smith & Wesson 559s for the others, with dum-dum ammo. She brought out a box of assorted throwing and carving knives and invited everyone to take their pick. (Pris and the Professor turned out to have their own.) Each of us was issued a powerful flashlight and two pairs of handcuffs: good cop handcuffs, not bondage toys. Then things got more exotic.

The binoculars I'd asked for came in the form of little contact lenses. The Lady had to put mine in for me. I was acutely conscious of them for a few seconds, and then I never noticed them again unless I was using them. "Don't worry about them falling out," she told me, "they can't. When you want far-sight, just squint and hold it."

I did—and after about three seconds, there was a zoom lens effect. I relaxed my eyes, and it went away at once. I stepped out into the hallway and experimented while she outfitted the others. The max effect approximated a pair of 7X35 binoculars, although it hurt to squint that hard for very long. "Slick," I told Lady Sally when I reentered the lab. "I can't wait to see the walkie-talkies."

"You'll only see them twice," she said, and held out her hand. On it was the Arnold Schwarzenegger of caraway seeds. "Pay attention, darlings," she said merrily to the group. "Observe this small device. It is not alive, in any technical sense, but it does excellent impressions. I shall place one of these in each of your mouths. There will be a short pause while it realizes I have done so, at which point it will begin to move of its own accord. Please do not be alarmed. It will seek out a convenient crevice somewhere on the inside of your teeth, and nest there. It will then buzz gently for some ten seconds to enable you to locate it with your tongue. If you are dissatisfied with its placement, hold your tongue against it for five seconds, and it will try again. Once it's found a place you like, say the vowel *e* and hold it until the seed stops buzzing. From that point on, if you touch your tongue to it firmly and then speak, you will be heard clearly by everyone else within a mile who is similarly equipped. Be aware that the picophone is voice-activated: if you stop talking for one full second, you are no longer sending; you'll have to tongue it back on again. It is quite discreet: civilians around your listeners will hear nothing, as the sound is carried by bone conduction. When the job is done, hold your tongue against the seed for more than ten seconds. It will head for your tongue and wait there to be expectorated."

"My God," I said. "The inventor of that thing must have died rich. I mean, 'must be going to die rich.' If for some reason he decides to die."

"Actually," Tesla said, "I died penniless. Fortunately, it did not stop me."

I stared at him. I should have guessed. It was a radio, wasn't it? "Nikola," I said slowly, "I know this is irrelevant—but I haven't had a chance to ask before now, and I might never get another. Do you mind if I ask what you're working on these days? When you're not saving space and time, I mean?"

"Not at all, Ken. I'm investigating electrical aspects of nanotechnology."

I knew it was hopeless, but asked, "*What* kind of technology?"

"Nano," he said. "Nano."

I blinked at him. "You're telling me with a straight face that you work with Mork from Ork?"

He blinked at me. "Who?"

I gave it up. "Never mind, Nikola. I knew I wouldn't understand the answer. Your Ladyship, let me have one of those seeds."

It wasn't half as bad as it sounds. It didn't taste like anything at all, and it wasn't moving for that long, and once it settled in place it was not obtrusive, and when tested it worked as advertised.

"Okay, let's see your body armor," I told her.

I was expecting something odd, and she didn't let me down. "Certainly, Ken. Please take off all your clothes."

"Yes, ma'am." Even for a PI, there are times not to make a wisecrack. I set down my weapons on . . . one of those somethings Tesla filled his lab with, and began to strip.

"All the rest of you save Nikky too, please, darlings," she said.

Dammit, there were so *many* wonderful wisecracks to suppress. I thought of at least a dozen . . . and knew that to make them, here, in this House, to this crew, at this time, would be to mark myself a jerk. A garment or two later, it dawned on me that to have made them anywhere, to anyone, would have made me just as much of a jerk—even if nobody else had noticed. God, if I was going to start growing up, it was a good thing I was getting out of the detective business.

Finally we were all bare except Tesla. It was by no means the first time I'd been in a room with a bunch of naked people. But it was unquestionably the best-looking group of naked people I'd ever been part of. Arethusa had the advantage, of course: she was in stereo.

"Tastes like peanut butter to me," Tim murmured near me.

"Beg pardon?" I said.

"Oh, you don't know that one? I thought everybody did. Back in the Sixties a guy I knew was ordered to report for his induction physical. That morning he gave himself a thorough antiseptic enema—and then inserted about half a pint of peanut butter where the sun don't shine. Creamy, of course. He got to about this point here in the physical, and the doctor with the rubber glove recoiled and said, 'Jesus, what the hell is *that*?' So the guy reaches behind himself for a sample, takes a lick, and says, 'Tastes like peanut butter to me.' They threw him out on the sidewalk, threw his clothes after him."

If I was the only one present who hadn't heard that one, then I guess everybody else collapsed into weeping hysterics just to be polite. Despite the prevailing climate of gung-ho, there had been a lot of free-floating tension in the room, waiting to be released. Tim's story did the trick. I thought Tesla was going to pee in his pants.

I'll say one thing for that group, though: nobody tried to keep it going, come up with a topper. Everyone laughed long and thoroughly . . . and then they stopped, and Lady Sally gave us our body armor.

It was preposterous, naturally. She produced a gizmo that was the spitting image of a roll-on deodorant . . . and used it to draw on me. From head to toe in two long continuous strokes, down the front and up the back, not excluding the soles of the feet. Three times around the torso. From one armpit down and up that arm, across the shoulder girdle and up the neck, right into the hair, then down the other side to the other armpit. The roller left a thick purple line, which spread slowly, growing paler as it did so, until it met itself everywhere and I was just a little pinker than a new sunburn victim. She walked around me, studying me carefully, and touched up one or two places. They tickled.

"Be sure and get the heels this time, Ma," I said.

"You have a tendon-cy to say things like that," she growled. "Would you open the door and go stand in the hall, please? I want to shoot you." Agreeably I went out into the hall and turned to look back through the open doorway, and she shot me. With one of the Smith & Wessons. A hollowpoint 9mm slug pancakes to the size of a .70-caliber shell when it hits something, and the 559 will throw one hard enough to pierce the engine block on a Jaguar.

She had told me she was going to make me invulnerable, and then she had told me she was going to shoot me; nonetheless I was startled. I flinched backwards—

—and that was all the backward motion I achieved. All straight back, too: I didn't spin, even though I was certain the slug had taken me on the left side just above the hipbone. I could feel a stinging sensation there, as if a small child had punched me as hard as he could. I looked down, and of course the spot was unmarked. I remembered that less than twenty-four hours ago, there had been stitches and a drain there . . .

I touched the spot with my hand. It felt like me, Humphrey Bogart Quigley. Even my bogus sunburn was gone now.

I glanced down the hall to my left. Minutes ago I had been looking at that wall with binoculars; there hadn't been a bullet hole in it *then*. I smelled cordite. I took a firm hold on my temper. The reason you don't like people pointing guns at you is they could hurt you.

"Very nice," I said. Everything sounded the way it does when a powerful handgun has gone off near you. If you know, I don't have to explain, and if you don't, I can't. "How long does this stuff last?"

"Until I remove it," she said. "You can go a month without risk of skin trouble. It's not perfect. If someone were to lean a knife against you and push slowly, the shield would let it in—and it won't stop chemical weapons or laser fire or a few other things. But at what it does do, it is failsafe. Money-back warrantee. Cynthia, I'll do you next."

"My Lady," Cynthia said carefully, "no one appreciates your sense of humor more than I . . . but if you point that gun at me, Doctor Kate will have to return it to you, and by then you might not want it any more."

"Well," I said a few minutes later, "we're immortal, just this side of invulnerable, we have the eyes of an eagle, we're wired better than a federal narc, and each team is armed with stun guns and death rays, with which for all I know we can also produce a few bars of Dixieland. All the enemy has is atom bombs, and he doesn't know we exist. Anybody want to quit?"

"It does sound like a boat-race," the Professor agreed.

"Well," I said, "theoretically I suppose we're vulnerable to betrayal. But that's the best thing about this group: we're all X-rated."

"Huh?" Tim said obligingly.

"Not for sale to miners."

Three people shot me at once, two in the belly and one lower. It stung, but I had no kick coming. (Or is that another pun?) The ricochets whined around the lab for a while and finally all found homes. Tesla made no objection; he seemed to feel it had been something that had to be done.

"Okay, people," I said at last, when we'd all finished getting dressed again. "The teams are: me, Arethusa and Pris, midnight to eight. Second team, Mike, Cynthia and the Professor. From four to midnight, Father Newman, Lady Sally and Tim. Ralph Von Wau Wau, triple shifts, a dog's life. Any questions?"

Amazingly, there were none.

"Okay, I've got some. I ought to ask some of these privately, but there just isn't time. Cynthia?"

"Yes, Ken?"

"This is probably a rude question, don't mean it that way, okay? I understand the difference between a *persona* and a personality . . . but I know absolutely nothing about you except your scene. Will you have a problem taking orders?"

She looked me square in the eye and took her time answering. I looked her square in the eye and waited. I'll play poker with God if I have to, but I was privately glad to be invulnerable.

But when she spoke, her voice was gentle and calm. "I concede that I have a problem in that direction. Everyone else here knows that. But I am also my *own* Mistress . . . and I understand the stakes. In this cause I would take orders from Robin."

"Okay, you'll take orders. Will you obey them?"

Her dark eyes flashed, and Tim stepped back a pace. But all she said was, "Yes, sir." Tim stared at her. And then stared at me, the way twelve-year-old boys stare at me when they find out I'm a real live detective.

"Thank you," I said.

"You had to ask," she said.

"You'll command your team," I told her.

She looked at Mike and the Professor. "Yes," she said. "I will."

Neither of them had any comment.

"Your Ladyship, you'll command your team. Father Newman, a question for you. Did you get that collar before or after you were Special Forces?"

He had the kind of warm avuncular Pat O'Brien smile that can calm a PCP zombie or charm a head nurse. I hoped I'd have a chance to become his friend. "You're asking me if I will kill in combat."

"Yes."

"If necessary, yes. But only on my own initiative, or that of an authority I've personally selected. That's why I had to swap uniforms. Here and now, you are my general, and Lady Sally is my captain." His smile faltered. "I have one reservation you'd better know. I will not be part of an interrogation that includes torture."

"*I* will," the Professor said quietly. "For these stakes."

"Shut up, Willard," I said. "If I want volunteers, I'll appoint 'em. Father, as your commanding officer I order you to pray that things don't go that sour."

"I'll take that seriously," he said.

"That's how I meant it," I agreed. "You look competent to me, so we can table that question for good. Back to my original question. Tim . . . no, let's speed this up. I want a show of hands. How many here have never taken a life?"

As I had expected, Arethusa raised two hands. Lady Sally raised a hand too, to my mild surprise. Just as surprisingly, Tim did not.

"If any of you think you might hesitate, say so now. Please be honest: you can't flunk out, but I need to know."

This time Tim's was the only hand.

"Thank you, Tim. Next question: would everyone please hold up one finger for each language you speak well enough to get by? Enough to conduct an interrogation, say."

The lowest number of fingers I saw was six. Lady Sally and Mike held up ten fingers each, but I figured them for double that. "Russian?" I asked, and nobody lowered any fingers. Well, it figured the staff of a bordello across the river from the UN would run to polyglots. That could prove very useful if The Miner was not American. But I was glad the commanding officer doesn't have to answer his own questions. The only languages I could speak fluently were American and English . . . although I could get along in Canadian, in a pinch.

"Okay, one last question." I glanced at my watch. "Father, how short can you make a wedding?"

Arethusa began to glow. There was a general murmur of surprise and approval. Cynthia's face lost all its sternness for the first time since I'd known her; Mike's face was split in a broad pirate's grin; Nikola Tesla was practically purring; Ralph's tail wagged.

Father Newman didn't so much as crack a smile. "You want to be married?"

"Yes!" I said.

Arethusa came to me and looked up at me. You could swim in those eyes . . . if you could take the undertow. Either pair. She took both my hands and faced the priest. "Yes," "Yes," she said, spacing it so that each sounded clearly.

"Anybody here got a beef?" he asked, looking around.

No one spoke.

"You're married," he said. And *then* he cracked a smile, half as big as his head.

"Is that legal?" Arethusa asked.

"Yes," he said, "but what the hell does that matter? It's morally binding."

"Yes," she said. "Yes, it is." The one of her on my right turned me to face her, took me by the ears, and kissed the living hell out of me.

The applause was loud and enthusiastic.

There was a tap on my shoulder, and she cut in on herself.

The applause redoubled in volume and took on a ribald undertone.

Just for a second there, and not for the first time, I envied my darling. I kind of wished I could see myself being that happy.

"Thank you, my general," she said when we came up for air. "For fitting that into the agenda."

"It was a pleasure," I said. "And a privilege."

"You don't know the half of it," she promised. "And right back at you. But we've got work to do first."

"Right you are," I agreed. "Let's go shadow us a terrorist or two."

There was a rumble of agreement and high morale.

"It's going to be a real switch for some of us," Lady Sally said thoughtfully.

"How do you mean?" I asked foolishly.

"Being a tail of peace, for a change."

"Don't shoot her!" I cried quickly. "It'd be a shame to spoil that dress."

I was barely in time.

"OKAY, people," I said shortly. "That's all I have on my agenda. One last chance to ask questions or raise objections." Silence. "Okay, Teams Two and Three, you're dismissed. Priscilla, Arethusa, wait here, please. Lady Sally, may I speak with you privately a moment?"

"Step into my office, dear boy," she said, and led me down the hall to that very place.

The most extraordinary thing about it was that I could see nothing extraordinary about it. An office. Desk. Typewriter. Bric-a-brac. Bookshelves. Couch, chairs, assorted flat surfaces. This, the inner sanctum of the strangest woman I had ever met, could have been the office of any madam. Or for that matter, a stockbroker.

I wouldn't have cared if it made Tesla's lab look ordinary. As I took a chair, my head was spinning. Too much had happened to me in too few days. In too few hours! I was on a huge emotional roller coaster . . . and the moment I'd dismissed my troops, I'd felt it start the downhill ride.

"WHAT is it, Joe?"

I bit my lip and stared at the floor.

She gave me a minute. Maybe two. When she did speak, her voice had softened, lost its whiskey rasp and a good deal of its British accent. "What's wrong?"

"Lady," I said slowly, "I couldn't say anything in front of the others. But I'm telling you now, officially, that I think you should assume command of this show. Or Mike, if you don't want the job."

"Good Lord, why?" she asked, genuinely startled. "You've already done most of the work. Except for the worrying—and I'll be doing that too, if it's any comfort to you. We all will."

"I know that," I said irritably. "I'm not trying to duck the worry. I don't care about the worry. It's the responsibility. Just that, the nominal responsibility."

"I'm not sure I grasp the distinction," she said slowly.

"Remember a few minutes back, when I was describing our assets in morale-building detail for the troops? We're just this side of immortal and invulnerable, we've got the greatest genius in the history of the world spotting for us, we're packing death rays and magic specs, and we've got a talking dog. A 'boat-race,' the Professor called it. What could possibly go wrong?"

"You tell me."

"Do you by any chance recall the last boat-race you and I bet on together? Just a few days ago, in the Reception area? Did we or did we not have Christian Raffalli nailed down just as tight as this? No, tighter, by God: we knew what he looked like, and which door he'd come in, and it went down on our own turf." I heard my own voice rising in pitch and volume.

"What is it you're afraid of, Joe?" she asked.

"God damn it, you've seen it in operation! The famous Quigley Jinx! It came within a highly fractionated second of getting us all killed—and turning me into a soprano."

"Oh, for Christ's sake!" Lady Sally barked.

"The hero you've selected had to have the heroine and a muscular ingenue literally save his nuts for him the last time out."

"You don't want *me*," she said witheringly. "I'll give you a chit to see Father Newman."

"Will you listen to me? This isn't a male pride thing, it's not a question of my morale. I can deal with women saving my bacon; that's been permissible in detective stories for years now. I can live with the absolute certainty that I'm going to come out of this looking like a fool; I got used to that a long time ago—"

"Joe, for God's sake, the dice have no memory—"

"You haven't got the right to say that to a man who's been rolling sevens for thirty years straight! I'll withdraw my request if you can answer one question. Take your time: can you conceive of any way this operation could go a *little bit* wrong?"

She started to answer . . . and stopped with her mouth open.

"The way I see it, it's total success or total failure. I haven't had all that many *total* failures in my life. But I've *never* had a total success."

"Oh."

Those binocular lenses were making my eyes sting. "Lady, I'm not a wimp. I can live with failure. The proof is that I'm not dead yet." Bullshit, lenses, I was crying. "But I can't live with *this* failure! Not on my wedding night! Even if there's no history to go down in for it, I don't want to be the guy who literally fucked up *everything*!" I remembered the last time I had cried, the night my mother died, and lost it completely.

Lady Sally gathered me into her arms and onto her lap as if I weighed no more than a child, and let me cry it out against her throat. She stroked my hair and said soothing things, not to make me stop crying but to make the flow emerge easier.

After a long time I became aware that she was speaking to me. "Can you hear me, Humphrey?"

"Snuff."

"You survived Raffalli. Didn't you?"

"Yeah. But—"

"Here: blow. In fact, that whole caper was a *success* for you. Things went wrong . . . but for the first time, nothing went *irrevocably* wrong, did it?"

"Huh," I said. My breathing was under control now. "Actually, you're right. I wonder why not."

"Humphrey Joseph Kenneth," she said fondly, "I love you—but sometimes you are an awful chump."

I frowned. "What are you talking about?"

"Let's overlook the fact that *whoever* leads this expedition is going to have to cope with your alleged jinx, and you have the most experience. Apropos of nothing, how many children do you think could have survived being brought up by people as crazy as Arethusa's parents?"

It was a curious digression—but I'd been thinking about those two birds a *lot* the past few days, in between the cracks, trying to figure out whether I was angry at them or not. "That's right," I agreed, "she was very lu . . ."

Pause.

"Ah, you're beginning to see it at last," Lady Sally said. "How many whorehouses would you say feature really good piano in the parlor any more these days? How many places are there *where Arethusa could practice both her arts, within the same building?* And how many of those would you estimate are run by madams broadminded enough to deal with a single broad who has two telepathic bodies—on her terms?"

I sat up and knuckled my eyes. "Jesus—"

"That she stumbled across this place, the perfect home for her, is a miracle. That she should find her True Love here, the week before Armageddon, is good fortune beggaring the imagination. Face it, Joe: Arethusa is Luck on four lovely legs."

"Holy *shit*—" The world tilted on its axis.

"And now she is your luck. And the evidence suggests it's just enough to keep your balls out of trouble. As with all good marriages: between you, you seem to make up a more or less normal human being."

I could barely believe what I was about to say, but the words came out in spite of me. "Do you mean to stand there with your bare face hanging out and tell me that the reason a nice girl like her is working in a place like this—"

And she grinned broadly and gave the classic punchline:

"Just lucky, I guess . . ."

15. Miner Disturbance

" . . . hanging by my fingertips from the rim of my
own anus, to keep from falling out . . ."

—DAVID SPIWACK, in conversation

"PRIS, this is the first chance I've had to thank you for coring
Raffalli's head. You saved my testicles, not to mention my life."

"Yeah, I know, that's been bothering me," she said soberly.
"I'm sorry, Ken: I did try to come take you off the hook a couple
of times since then. But whenever you were awake, I was on duty.
You're welcome, okay? You can save my life some day if you
want."

I stared at her. She had been concerned that in saving my life,
she had placed me under onerous obligation. "I'll do that. If it
ever needs saving. I don't think I'll hold my breath, though. You
know, all this aside . . . I *like* you, Priscilla."

"I like you too," she said. "You risked everything to help the
Lady. And you're going to do it again. If we live through this,
what do you say we get drunk together some night?"

"That'll be fun," I said, and meant it. I don't know, maybe
I'd learned something from Arethusa about relating to someone
physically stronger than me. Pris didn't intimidate me any more.

We were in Lady Sally's office, preparing to ship out—
although just exactly how, I didn't have a clue. Me, Priscilla,
one Arethusa—the other was upstairs, under mild sedation, so I
could have her full attention—and Ralph Von Wau Wau. We were
all gathered around the Lady's desk, staring at the best map we
had of the route from the bowels of Penn Station to the manhole
that gave access to a maintenance chamber surrounding the water
main. (I do not intend to be more specific than that. If you want

to look for it yourself, feel free. But remember that there are a *lot* of people prowling around Penn Station . . . and the attrition rate is high.)

It was actually a damn good map. I'd be surprised if the City Engineer had one as good. Tesla said it was a printout from his computer, but I think he was pulling my leg: it looked like real printing to me. He claimed it was done with a laser beam, which is ridiculous. However he got it, it showed the salient features of the terrain we were headed for.

"I think you should arrive here," Lady Sally said, pointing to a spot on the map.

"Why there?" I asked.

"For all we know, The Miner—or minor Miner, but let's call him that until we know better—The Miner may very well be looking over that bomb *right now*, as we speak. This spot is midway between said bomb and the point at which one leaves Penn Station proper to approach it. A person standing right *here* cannot be seen either from the bomb chamber or from the Station. If he's passing that spot as you arrive, you have him; if he's approaching it, you have time to hide and jump him; if he's already at the bomb, he has to come to you, like it or not. We can't lose."

"The hell we can't," I said. "We've agreed to assume that this guy isn't a moron, right? So if he's even as smart as me, he'll have the whole approach wired some way. Electric eye, heat sensor, motion sensor, something. *Especially* along that corridor."

"Ah," she said, "but he shan't be as smart as I, who have procured from Nikola Tesla this magic talisman." She handed me a little widget that looked like a transistor radio someone left on a stove. "All three of the devices of which you speak, and cameras and acoustic listening devices as well, will cause this light here to glow—even if they're on the other side of several inches of steel or cement. Push this button, and the Talisman ruins them."

I frowned at it. Combat is a lousy place to test new technology. "Does Tesla guarantee it'll do it faster than they can get off a signal?"

Her turn to frown. "Well, Nikky says he *thinks* so."

I shook my head. "That tears it. If there's going to be even a momentary alarm, I want it to come from the bomb chamber, where The Miner already knows there's some sort of electrical malfunction. I don't want him thinking about anybody coming along that approach. We arrive in the bomb chamber, and use Tesla's Talisman on the approach corridor *from there*, through the manhole cover. Then Pris, Arethusa and Ralph work their way back out from there, very cautiously, waving the Talisman before them as they go."

Do you have any idea how few people stop arguing instantly just because they realize they're wrong? "Right you are: the bomb room it is." She squinted at the map, reached into a desk drawer, and twiddled something out of sight. "You'll arrive on the far side of the pipe, facing across it at the bomb access area and the exit ladder to the manhole. It's a bloody big pipe, but there should be plenty of clearance above and below it. Whenever you say."

I looked around at my companions. Alert intelligent faces looked back at me, every commanding officer's dream, far more precious than invulnerable armor or handheld death rays. Arethusa's face actually seemed to hold twice as much personality as usual, although that was probably just power of suggestion. "I guess we're as ready as we'll ever be. About this 'arriving' stuff . . . just how is that done, exactly?"

She closed the drawer, locked it, and stood up. "Ken Taggart, my new friend and champion, do you trust me?" she asked.

"Yes," I said without hesitation.

She went to a big floor-to-ceiling bookcase that covered an entire wall. She selected a big reference book, pulled it halfway from the shelf. The whole bookcase slid smoothly down into the floor, with just the faintest whisper of sound, exposing the bare wall.

"Walk through that wall," Lady Sally said. "And step to the left on the far side."

I counted to five, sighed, and walked through the wall.

IT was the eeriest thing I've ever done. It looked exactly like a solid wall, right down to the dust highlighting the painter's brushmarks—even as my nose was entering it, my eyes were trying to tell me that it was a solid wall. I tried to keep my eyes open, but I couldn't manage it; the flinch was quite involuntary. There was absolutely no sensation of penetration or transition; that wall was as substantial as a campaign promise.

On the other side of it was pitch-blackness that smelled like a bathtub drain.

Of *course* I should have been expecting darkness. You don't leave a night light on by your clandestine nuclear weapon. In fact, dammit, I *was* expecting it, that was why I had a flashlight clipped to my belt. I just hadn't *remembered* that I was expecting it . . .

I stopped short, and as I was groping for the flashlight I recalled that Lady Sally had said to step to the left. I've always hated imbeciles who stop just inside a door myself. I stepped to the left, got the flashlight loose, tripped over something low and angular and stubborn. I went down heavily, felt the flashlight go ballistic, whanged my head painlessly against something that felt remarkably like a crowbar, and landed in a heap, smacking my head again on clammy concrete floor.

The flashlight snapped on when it landed. It bounced crazily, came down upright, spun like a top for a while like a little emergency light, and came to rest, pointing at the floor. Try and do that. It didn't even break. But the total illumination approximated that of a fading match at five yards. I closed my eyes and took a deep breath. Perversely, I was quite irritated that the double impact had not hurt my head at all. I deserved a headache . . .

Much too close to me, something made a sound, and I knew that sound. I smelled the faintest trace of something, and I knew that smell. I remained perfectly still, holding my breath, until I was nearly out of air, and then I opened my eyes again.

If the ghostly circle of glow from the flashlight was a distant match, then these were no more than the ember at the tip of a match that has just gone out. Two of them. Side by side.

I did not scream, because I knew that Arethusa would be the second one through that wall, any second now. But I really hate rats.

Sure, everybody hates rats. But I got a rat story I'm not even going to tell you. Let it stand that I *really* hate rats.

Especially rats out of whom I have just literally scared the living shit. One minute he was alone, and then this. I could discern just enough of his silhouette to see that he was paralyzed with fear. At least he wasn't cornered. But he was frozen between fight and flight, and he had to decide soon. My stomach suggested a good trick, a very old reflex, but I did not want The Miner to know something was wrong the instant he cracked the lid to this chamber.

Instead I growled. Loud, and as evil as I was scared, a horrid sound distilled from two million years of successful primate bluff.

Ralph Von Wau Wau couldn't have done better. Templeton remembered a previous engagement and bugged out. I found it oddly hard to stop growling, but I managed just as Arethusa arrived. She had her flashlight on, of course.

"Is everything okay, Joe?"

"Ginger peachy," I said tightly. "I'm just having a bit of a lie-down. And dammit, I'm 'Ken' while we're on this caper, okay? Most of the troops know me by that name, and there's no sense confusing things any more than they already are."

"Yes, Ken."

"Sorry," I said. "It wasn't your head I meant to bite off." I was still trembling slightly with reaction, and I wished she'd aim her flashlight somewhere else.

I got to my feet, reclaimed my own flash, noted that I had tripped over a large plumber's toolbox and that the "crowbar" was a bracing bar for one of the big cement trusses that supported the huge water main. Logical things to expect and be looking out for if you were going to wander around a place like this in the dark.

Arethusa reached a hand back through the solid concrete wall of the chamber and pulled Priscilla through. I wished I'd been bright enough to do that for her. They stepped to the right together and Ralph emerged into the pool of light from their flashlights. His eyes were slits, his ears up, his nostrils wide. "Ratzhit!" he growled at once.

"What's the matter?" Pris asked.

"Ratzhit, I set. Fresh."

"He's gone," I said wearily. "I chased him away."

Ralph's slit eyes opened to as wide as they could go. "You chased avay a Manhattan tunnel vrat?" he said slowly. His nostrils wrinkled. "You mate him zhit himzelf?"

"I growled at him," I said.

Ralph stared. "You . . . gwowled at him. Ant he zhit himzelf." He dropped his eyes, his ears flattened, and he stepped back a pace.

Well, I had succeeded in winning Ralph's respect, anyway. And the rat's too, come to think of it. I started to feel better. Time to get this show on the road.

"Okay, who's got Tesla's bug-hunter?"

"You do, Ken," Arethusa said.

IT was in my shirt pocket, where I had stashed it without thinking. Fortunately, when I took it out it was not glowing. "Right," I said. "Pris, Arethusa, stay here and douse your lights. Ralph, come with me."

The pipe was about six feet in diameter, and there were about three feet of clearance above and below it. The rectangular chamber ended in a featureless bulkhead in either direction, and enclosed perhaps fifty feet of pipe, supported by two massive trusses. I picked a spot on the far side of one of the trusses. I was glad that it was dusty in that chamber, it meant that there was air circulation, but I got even dirtier than I was already by the time I came out from under that pipe on the other side. It reminded me that I had fetched a drop cloth for this purpose. Ralph, of course, had no trouble. Dogs usually excel in Limbo contests.

In a cavern, in a canyon, excavating for a mine . . .

On the far side of the pipe were two steel ladders. One was bolted onto the side of the pipe itself; the other was secured to the far wall and led up to the access hatch and Penn Station. I approached that one carefully, brandishing the Talisman with my finger poised over the "ruin-it" button, watching for the first flicker. When I got as far as the top of the ladder without a reading, I went back down again, and shone my flashlight back at the other ladder, up its length.

There was an inspection plate up at the top of that pipe.

I slid the circle of light back down the side of the pipe, centered it.

Death was in there. Death, and worse than death. All this was real. The intuitive certainty I had braced with so much guesswork had been as reliable as my intuitions always were.

Did that mean my jinx was still reliable too?

All at once I wondered why I was so sure I was not being irradiated as I stood there. Sure, it made sense that The Miner would want his mines indetectible—but just how much radiation was going to escape from this crypt, to what detector? Consolidated Edison maintenance men wouldn't carry Geiger counters. (I had the vague idea Con Ed handled city water system maintenance; I later learned that's wrong.) I remembered someone who was provably smarter than Edison, and I started to tell Arethusa to stick her head back into Brooklyn and ask Tesla for a Geiger counter. Then I remembered that The Miner had had to bring the bomb down here and install it himself. It would not be hot. Calm down, Joe! I mean, Ken.

Oh, a CO's life is not a happy one. How had I ended up holding the sack? I had gone to Nam a corporal, come back a private, albeit a private with a Silver Star. My genre was mysteries, not spy stories. Damn Lady Sally for needing a genius gumshoe to solve her puzzles for her. Damn The Miner for existing.

I got out my drop cloth and unfolded it. It seemed to be made of cobwebs, but Lady Sally had sworn that nothing I was liable to encounter could tear or abrade it. From a tiny bundle it unfolded out so big I was able to refold it with two layers on the bottom and a third to slide under. I placed it on the spot I'd already dusted with my own body. "Be careful coming under, Arethusa," I said. "Don't get dirty if you can help it."

She was careful. Pris, on the other hand, pointedly ignored the drop cloth and picked a nice dirty spot to wriggle under. She was costumed and made up as the blind beggar with the Seeing Eye dog; the fresh grime added color to the effect. Also odor. People would tend to leave the blind beggar alone.

"Okay, the corridor just above the manhole checks out clean," I said. "Let Ralph go first. He's got the best nose, and will be the least upsetting to anyone coming the other way. When you get to the Station proper, fan out and pick spots where you can keep an eye on the approach without being seen. If you see a live one, do nothing. Just jungle up, wait for my transmission, and get ready to tail him when he comes back out. Arethusa, look me in the eye."

She did so. In the weak light she was so beautiful my heart hurt.

"Tell me what you will do if I have trouble—if The Miner spots me and kills me, or captures me."

She kept looking me in the eye. "I will stay where I am, and mourn quietly, and tail him when he emerges. He will not spot me. He will not lose me. And I will not kill him until Lady Sally says I may."

I kissed her. Thoroughly. As if it was the last time. Then I gave her the Talisman, so that Pris would have both hands free. "Pris," I said then, "you get the manhole cover. Ralph, you go through first and sniff for trouble—but don't advance until Arethusa gives you the green light, got it?"

The manhole cover did not want to yield; for a moment I was afraid it was dogged down from above. But Pris reasoned with it. It let go with a sound like a dinosaur being killed. Before I thought the opening large enough, Ralph Von Wau Wau was through it. Pris slid the heavy cover aside and followed him. In a moment she reached down and hauled Arethusa up bodily after her. "See you in a little under eight hours, Ken," she called back down softly.

"Don't get spotted coming back here," I cautioned pointlessly.

The cover groaned back into place and seated with another baritone squeal.

I touched my tongue to the crevice between two teeth. "Testing," I said. "All units, report!"

"Unit one," Pris's voice said clearly from everywhere at once.

"Unit two," Arethusa's lyrical voice sang.

I waited for "Unit sree," and nothing happened. "Ralph, God damn it—"

"Sorry, boss," Pris said. "He says the damn thing must not like dog spit. Ralph's deaf and dumb as far as you're concerned."

I fretted about that, but there was no solution. "Well, keep him in sight. *Especially* when the tail starts."

"He says not to worry, he'll leave a trail."

I was too keyed up to be amused. "Let's keep radio silence for the rest of the shift. If you do spot an incoming bogie, report *after* you're sure he can't hear you. I'll still have plenty of warning."

They took me literally; I didn't even get a roger-wilco. Silence descended like a damp fog. I couldn't even hear their departing footsteps through the small holes in the manhole cover.

Then it got even quieter than that.

I was alone, in something very like a tomb or catacomb, with a live nuclear weapon of uncertain megatonnage. There was nothing for me to do but wait. If I was lucky, I had eight hours to kill . . .

I moved the toolbox over behind the truss where it would not be seen by anyone approaching the bomb, glanced incuriously at its contents, and sat down on it. I switched my flashlight off and waited for my pulse to stop racing. I tried to anticipate contingencies, I tried not to be sleepy. I tried hard not to wonder if Arethusa's luck was really as strong as my jinx. I tried very hard not to think about Manhattan tunnel rats.

After about five minutes I sighed, switched the light back on, propped it on the toolbox, made sure I had several spare batteries, and got out GOOD BEHAVIOR, by Donald Westlake. There was no chance I would fall asleep before I finished it. I was determined to find out how Dortmunder got away from those mercenaries before I died.

After a while my eyelids got heavy, so I closed them and lay down.

WHEN I opened them again, the light was slightly better. I saw Arethusa sleeping beside me. For some reason, that did not please me. Beyond her I could hear Pris snoring. Someone else was moving around nearby, very near, and it didn't sound like Ralph Von Wau Wau. I tried to lift my head and investigate, and found that I could not. I tried to worry about that, and could not do that either.

Damn, I thought, Dortmunder was still in deep shit, and now I'll never find out how he escaped . . .

16. Half Life

Shared despair is squared; shared hope is cubed
(or better).

—Lady Sally McGee

DISTANTLY I listened to the sounds he made, and deciphered
them. He was handcuffing people to things. Shortly he got to me.
He cuffed my wrists behind me, and my ankles to the bracing
rod of the pipe truss. That was funny. How come he happened
to have six pairs of handcuffs? Oh, of course. He was using ours.
Thoughtful of us to have fetched them for him. That implied
that he had taken my weapons too. A pity. I'm always losing
guns I like.

He rolled me over with his foot, and I got my first glimpse of
him. Not a very good one; the light was poor and he was not in the
center of my field of vision, which I could not move. He appeared
to be in his fifties, balding and thin to the point of gauntness, with
a beak that would have made a good head for a splitting wedge. I
wished vaguely that I could see it used so. Arethusa and Pris were
both cuffed by the ankles to the other truss, on their sides so they
wouldn't be lying on their cuffed wrists. Damn civil of him.

He slid the needle in slowly, and so my magic skin accepted
it.

An antidote to whatever hypnotic gas he had piped through the
holes in the manhole cover. We had forgotten that we were not
the only ones in this game who played with hi-tech toys . . .

Goody: now I could be terrified again.

I sat up stiffly, and used that stiffness as excuse to move around
enough to take inventory. Sure enough, my gun was gone, and my
knife and brass knuckles and sap and belt and the contents of all

235

my pockets. If I had fetched wallet or ID he'd have had that too. I didn't even see the book. He squatted near me, carefully out of my reach, and when he saw that my eyes were tracking, he said, " 'Allo."

Oh Christ, I thought, a Frenchman.

Look, I apologize, okay? I try to be as little bigoted as a New York private eye can be. Stereotypes are an excuse to keep napping. I have known good and bad in all races, colors, creeds and nationalities. Except the French. I know it's just my personal experience; I'm sure there are lots of very nice French people. But every one I ever chanced to meet was crazier than a shithouse rat. I don't know, maybe it has something to do with having had their asses consistently kicked by their neighbors for something like two centuries straight. They tended to come in two flavors: invincibly ignorant and right wing, or intellectual and more Marxist than Stalin. Both kinds were, even by New York standards, colossally rude. The only thing they seemed to agree on was that France, a place where Jerry Lewis is a genius and the urinals are kept out on the sidewalk, had produced the planet's only true civilization.

Of course, The Miner could be French Canadian. The only two Québecois I'd ever met were both decent guys, no more snobbish toward Americans than any other Canadian.

I remembered my erstwhile employer, only a matter of days ago, asking me if I was related to that Inspector Clazoo. It now seemed a reasonable question.

"Not now, Cato, you fuel," I grunted.

He got the reference and frowned. Swell: I'd annoyed him.

"I nearly 'ad a 'eart attack when I first saw you," he complained. " 'As anyone ever told you that you resemble—"

"Only every third person," I said wearily. Yeah, that must have shaken him up a little, all right . . .

I saw that I was on the other side of the pipe now, on the access side. I wondered how he had handcuffed Ralph. I glanced around, and didn't see Ralph anywhere. Interesting. Did hypno-gas work on a German shepherd? Was Ralph alive and active somewhere above? Or was he dead in the corridor? I knew his tooth-transceiver didn't trans . . . but did it ceive? I touched my tongue to the radio seed. "Okay," I said. "We're cuffed. Now what happens?"

"Now I ask you questions," he said.

"Isn't this the place where the villain has his big speech?" I said. "You're supposed to try to justify yourself now."

One side of his mouth smiled. "I have read the same books, and seen the same films. The primary purpose of this speech is to give the 'ero time to get free and kill the villain. As I am not a villain, I must decline this honor."

"You're sure?" I said. "The way I read you, you've been *dying* to gloat to somebody about this for at least five years now. Think of me as a preview audience."

"I 'ave no interest in the opinions of others," he said. "Certainly not Americans."

"I was only born here," I said. "Actually I'm Irish." Whenever I wasn't speaking, I had my tongue on that seed. It was hard to say why. It didn't seem reasonable that Ralph could still be alive. Looked at one way, Lady Sally's office was only a few yards away—it seemed I ought to be able to raise her with a loud shout. But in fact she was well outside the one-mile range of Tesla's radio seed. I gave myself strict orders not to be seen glancing at my watch, not to let him guess that I was expecting eventual relief—but I sure wished I knew how soon eight A.M. would be here.

He snorted. "You 'ave my sympathy." He turned and went to the toolbox, which had been moved well out of my reach.

The moment his back was turned I snuck a look at my watch, which thank God had a luminous display. Jesus Christ—a little after five! Almost three hours until relief. Five hours since I had kissed Arethusa.

Maybe he *was* Canadian. Even at a dead run, with a military jet, he could not have gotten here from Europe this quickly. Toronto, maybe. No, Ottawa. The Canadian mine would not be in Ottawa, not if one of the terrorists was Québecois.

I took what comfort I could from her gentle snoring.

The Miner straightened up from the toolbox with a blowtorch in his hand. "Now for the questions."

He lit the torch with a clicker. The chamber brightened slightly. He adjusted the flame to a fuel-wasting bright tongue that shivered impressively, making the shadows shimmer.

I had never thought to ask Lady Sally whether her magic body armor was proof against extreme heat, but I had the dismal certainty that I knew the answer. Impact was the only thing specified on the warrantee. As Tom Waits said, the large print giveth, and the small print taketh away.

I had a major problem here. A Miner problem, if you will. Not only were all the lies I could think of wildly implausible . . . so was the truth. I could see myself trying to convince this guy that on the other side of that wall over there was a Brooklyn whorehouse run by a redheaded time traveler with terrific legs.

Rats are less fussy than cats. They'll accept their meat overcooked. Templeton was going to have his revenge.

"If I were you," the Frenchman said, raising his voice slightly to be heard over the hiss, "I would answer candidly. It will 'asten your death, and so we will both be 'appy."

I lied quickly. "I will answer any question you ask fully and responsively and with great honesty if you'll answer me a couple of quick easy ones, first."

He glanced at his own watch. "Ver' quick."

"You've been fairly sophisticated so far. Why not use scopolamine? Nothing else you've done is crude."

By God, the flattery got to him, canceled my Clouseau reference, won me a tiny morsel of goodwill. "I am sorry. One of life's infernal details, a side effect of the gas I used on you. For the next twenty-four 'ours or so, scopolamine would kill you. I regret the crudity, but I *must* know what you know. I promise I will kill you the moment I am sure you 'ave been 'onest and . . . q'est-ce que vous dit? . . . forthcoming."

"Did you kill my dog?"

He nodded sadly. "I believe so. I could find no pulse in 'is t'roat. The dog's metabolism is so small, you see." He gripped the torch, and shadows danced. "To work."

"One more," I begged. "How did you take us?"

"Ah," he said, "of course you would wish to know. Pressure switches under the floor of the corridor trigger the gas. Then an alarm is sent."

Shit! A simple mechanical linkage, too unsophisticated to alarm Tesla's Talisman. By the time it had started to glow, no one was awake to push the button.

"What if a legitimate maintenance man came along?"

"I know the schedule of maintenance, and shut the system down at those times."

"And what if he opened that inspection plate?"

" 'E would find that 'e lacked the proper tools. It is now sealed with European bolts. If I found wrench marks on them at my next inspection, I would prepare an accident for 'im."

With a wave of horror, I realized that my friends had gone down within seconds of assuming radio silence at my command! They had lain there unconscious, yards away from me, for hours—for however long it had taken The Miner to come investigate . . . while I sat in the dark, reading Donald Westlake.

Shrewd work, General Taggart, sir. Armed only with invulnerability, a death ray and a magic talisman, you managed to cobble up a fiasco.

In my mind's ear I seemed to hear Lady Sally say contemptuously, *You don't want me—I'll give you a chit to see the chaplain . . .* and then say lovingly, *Arethusa is your luck . . .*

My luck was out cold. Her other body was not as heavily drugged but still drowsing under a sleeping pill, and the consciousness that might have roused it and raised the alarm was wholly stunned. This Frenchman intended to kill her local body. Would her hypnotized *self* manage to find its way back home to Brooklyn? I had never had time to question her closely about the effects of separation on her telepathy . . .

Don't depend on your luck, said an old Master Sergeant in my mind. (Very old: he'd been in Nam over a year and a half when I met him.)

Okay, what were my assets?

As far as I could see they totaled two, both potential rather than immediately available. If I could con him into reviving Arethusa—say, by claiming that only she possessed certain crucial information—then maybe she could make the mental leap to Brooklyn (if you see what I mean), shake her other body awake, and bring armed reinforcements within minutes. Wouldn't he be surprised when she came through that wall? Which suggested my only other asset: sole possession of the knowledge that a section of wall opened onto Lady Sally's office. If I could only fling something through that wall!

I no longer had any items on me to throw even if I hadn't been cuffed, and the toolbox was out of reach, and with my ankles cuffed too I could not even kick a shoe that far. Even if I could, what were the chances that Lady Sally was in her office at five o'clock in the morning? If she came in and found a shoe on the carpet, would she interpret its significance?

All this went through my head in the few seconds The Miner gave me to absorb the humiliating ease of my defeat. Then he was approaching me with that blowtorch and I stopped thinking about abstract hypothetical situations. "Thank you," I said, and continued quickly, "Well, I won't hold you any longer, uh—" I paused, doing it in the way that triggers someone to insert their name so they won't hold up your sentence.

He didn't bite. "You may call me 'Doc,' " he said.

He set my own flashlight on the truss, to illuminate his working area: me. It was now theoretically possible, if I heaved up and twisted at just the right instant with great luck and skill, to grab my flashlight and shine it in his eyes. Even in fantasy, I couldn't see myself lobbing it over that pipe and into just the right section of wall. With *one* hand tied behind my back, maybe, but . . .

"All right, I didn't expect you to fall for that one. But at least tell me this: are you the Master Maniac, or just a stooge?"

He frowned, offended.

"I have the right to know who kills me," I said.

"True," he conceded. "And I know you are not wired. Very well. Yes, as you 'ave guessed, I am the Chief of Surgery. But now you must tell me 'oo *you* are, and very quigley."

"Certainly, Doc. My name is Ken Taggart. I'm a licensed proctologist. I clean out diseased assholes."

He sighed. "Mr. Taggart, I tell you again that I refuse to follow your movie script. You will not be the smart ass and waste my time. I am reluctant to begin burning you so soon, because you must answer many questions before you die. So the next time I find one of your answers unsatisfactory, I will kill one of your friends." He produced my own gun and held it where I could see it.

Ah. That sounded promising. If he shot one of them, the bullet wouldn't hurt them any, and the ricochet might just hit *him* . . .

Okay, my move was to be the wisecracking detective. Simon Templar. Make him mad enough to blaze away. Perhaps a wild bounce would *thunk* into Lady Sally's desk and bring the Marines.

"I didn't know you did it retail, dear heart," I said cheerily. "Murder, I mean. I thought it took numbers of a million and up to give your little reptile-brain an erection."

His face tightened, and he slapped me hard on the side of the face with my gun. It's a heavy weapon. Thank God I had instinctively tried to roll with it, and so simulated the natural motion he expected from a man slapped that hard. If he figured out the invisible body armor, he would not waste time shooting us. I had the presence of mind to register great pain nearly at once. I could not simulate a bruise, but the light was poor. "My, I must have touched a sore spot. Do you know, I actually believe you might have *thought* about doing that even if I *weren't* helpless."

To my disappointment, he got a grip on himself. "You will tell me what agency all of you work for now," he said tightly.

"I'm sorry to disappoint you, Doc," I said. "But the God's honest truth is, we're freelance. Well, inexpensive lance, but we're doing this on our own time."

"And you carry weapons so arcane that I do not even understand what they do." He closed his eyes and shook his head slightly. "Very well," he said.

He went to where Pris and Arethusa lay side by side, breathing in slow rhythmic swells. He bent and placed the barrel of my gun in Pris's mouth and pulled the trigger.

My heart broke in that instant, and a man with a broken heart is a dangerous opponent.

The sound it made was unique and horrible, a muffled, *wet* bang that took a long time to fade. Her brains and the slug did not erupt from the back of her head, because the useless magic body armor worked just as well from the inside. Instead the slug whanged around in there churning everything into mush until chance sent it down into her body cavity. Things emerged from her ears, nostrils and mouth, and both her eyes bulged from internal pressure. None of this struck him as unusual; he was not familiar with handguns, just A-bombs.

The Miner removed my gun and made a face, wiped the end of it fastidiously in Pris's hair.

"God damn you," I roared, "I told you the fucking truth."

"Ridiculous," he said. "How could you have stumbled onto this?" He climbed over Pris and squatted by Arethusa.

"It started out theoretical," I said desperately. "This could be done. Why hasn't anyone tried it? How do we know no one has? If someone did, how might one find out? We *deduced* you."

"I do not believe it," he said. "How?"

"Neutron reflector," I improvised frantically. "We got to thinking about design and placement as a single problem, and realized that a water main would be an ideal environment for a nuke. Then I studied a city services map and looked for good places to leave one."

"And how do you finance this 'obby?" he snorted.

"I'm rich—" I tried.

He snorted. "You are not and never 'ave been rich. Never mind, I see you will not answer this question until I begin with the torch.

Instead, answer this one: 'ow did you succeed where your friends failed, and enter this chamber without setting off the alarm?"

"I had a gas mask then," I said, knowing it wouldn't stand up.

He shook his head. "I 'ave looked quite carefully. There is no such mask here, and no way it could 'ave been removed. Even if there was, it is not necessary to breathe the gas to be affected by it." He put the gun into Arethusa's sweet slack mouth.

"Wait!" I roared. "For God's sake, Doc, wait! My wife's the only one who can explain that, I swear!"

It was the best I could come up with. I had no plausible lie, and the truth would not serve.

He started, and stared from me to Arethusa. "Neither of you wore a ring."

"We just got married, I swear to God. Wake her up, she'll tell you everything you want to know. She's the brains of the outfit; she's a genius electrical engineer, a disciple of Nikola Tesla. She located your mine with a gadget she built: it detects radio receivers that are located underwater, by the resonance or something. The little trumpet things you thought were weapons. We used them to wreck your radio trigger."

He removed the gun from her mouth. "That is the first thing you've said that is remotely plausible. Very unlikely, but possible."

"She really is a genius, Doc, I swear. She's the one that's rich. Give her some of that stuff you injected me with and she can tell you anything you want to know."

He set the torch down and tapped the gun against his palm. "A student of Nikola Tesla. And she is truly your wife?"

"Do you want to hear me beg? Okay, I'm begging: if you've got to kill us both, *do me first*."

He ran his tongue across the inside of his lower lip, making it pooch out briefly. "I begin to believe for the first time that you may actually be independents," he said slowly. He was thinking aloud, reasoning it out for himself. "Or if you are affiliated with an intelligence agency, you are acting without authorization. They would not send a 'usband and wife. I also believe that you do not know my name or location, or you would not have tried to set a trap for me 'ere. So even if you have other confederates, the maximum risk they represent is the loss of this single bomb. I do not think there is any way it can be traced back to me, and I can always reset the frequencies . . ."

I let my eyes widen in horror. "Oh Jesus Christ, you've got *other* mines? *Where?*"

"Thank you, Monsieur Taggart," he said gently. "That was the last thing I 'ad to know."

He stood up and shot me three times in the torso.

The ricochets were frighteningly loud, but I reacted convincingly, pitching sideways and twisting so he wouldn't notice that the new holes in my clothes were dry. Maybe he didn't *count* the ricochets, or maybe he just assumed the slugs had gone clean through me. Whatever, he bought me as a corpse.

I held my breath and prayed.

And heard the sound I feared most of all to hear.

The rustle of his trouser legs as he squatted back down again.

I knew then, the instant I heard that silken whisper in the darkness, I had gambled, and failed. My heart died, and a man without even a broken heart is a very dangerous antagonist.

Frozen helplessly in my limp sprawl, I heard again that hideous muffled liquid *thud-d-d* as a .45 slug smashed Arethusa's brain to jelly.

17. The Car Chase

Bad luck, bad luck is killin' me:
I just can't stand no more of this third degree.

—Traditional blues lyric

*OH my love, forgive me! I have failed you utterly; I cannot even
cry out at your murder—lest all the world be lost and your death
unavenged . . .*

Cold black despair saturated my heart. My luck was gone now,
gone with my heart. Now The Miner would check my pulse to
make sure I was dead, and when he saw I was not he would put
one into *my* mouth to make sure . . .

There was a brief fumbling sound, and then I heard the safety
catch of my gun snap closed. The gun landed on the floor with a
sound so loud and unexpected I barely suppressed the flinch.

He had no stomach for firing a make-sure shot into the mouth
of someone he knew damn well was dead. He had aimed three
shots at my chest, and was too ignorant to know how astonishing
it was that he had actually hit a target that size with a handgun
from ten feet.

A ladder groaned softly under weight. I hoped it was the one
to the manhole exit. If it was the one to the inspection plate, if he
were going to try and repair his radio trigger now, then he would
probably decide to take my flashlight with him when he left, and
that would be bad.

I heard him grunt hugely with effort, and the manhole cover
came free. Faint light spilled down into the chamber. Excellent.
Either he had done whatever he could with the bomb before
waking me for a chat, or he had written it off in his haste to quit
the scene of his debut murders. He scrambled from the chamber,

and wrestled the manhole cover into place behind him.

I sat up at once and looked around.

With an immense effort, I suppressed all emotion. I considered the tactical situation with icy dispassion, from the kind of Olympian perspective from which the slaughter of my beloved was a trivial sidebar. How badly was our cause damaged?

The Miner was now very likely to advance his plans, go public with his mines in advance of his target date. That was bad. I knew nothing useful about him that I had not known in Lady Sally's office. That was bad. In order to have any hope at all of salvaging the situation, it was imperative that I get free at once and tail him.

Assets within reach: a flashlight. If I didn't mind working in darkness, I could have three D-size batteries. No, wait, here was something really useful, almost within reach: a drop cloth.

That fucking toolbox was probably bulging with things far more precious than rubies. It was more than a body length out of reach.

I inspected the angled bracing bar I was double-cuffed to. At either end it was set into a retaining collar a good inch deep. I strained at it experimentally until spots swam before my eyes, but I knew there was no way I was going to snap off something meant to help support that mammoth pipe.

A bell rang in the back of my mind. John D. MacDonald's Travis McGee had faced a situation like this once. Cuffed to an angled bracing bar in the bow of his houseboat, as I recalled. I had tools analogous to the ones he had used. Maybe even better . . .

I studied the situation. The concrete truss was shaped like what an antique naval cannon sits on. On either side there was a transverse rectangular hole about two inches by four all the way through the concrete. I would guess they were there to accommodate some kind of girder that hadn't been used in that chamber. They were just where I needed them.

Hurry!

I only had to strain my cuffed arms half out of their sockets to get hold of the drop cloth. Working awkwardly behind myself, I got it folded once cattycorner and twisted into a crude rope. With even more difficult contortions I worked an end of it through the hole in the truss, tied a secure knot, led the bigger end over the bracing bar. There was just enough to reach back down to the knot at the truss again. I tied it off as tight and as securely as I could manage. Now for a lever. The only thing within reach was the flashlight. I plucked apart the two strands of taut drop cloth in the middle of their span from truss to bar, tucked the flashlight in between them, and began winding the drop cloth like a rubber band.

In theory, what had worked for Travis McGee should work for an agent of Lady Sally McGee. Something about the screw of Archimedes. Same principle as an automobile jack, I think. Wind the drop cloth/screw tight enough, and the bar, designed to take longitudinal stress, should deform, bend sideways enough to pop out of its collar at one end or the other. At that time it would probably try to break one of my major bones, but I was armored against that.

In practice, it was unbelievably difficult to keep hold of that fucking flashlight, and keep on winding it against increasing tension, with cuffed hands, behind my back, with the desperate awareness that the clock was ticking, that The Miner was getting further and further into the vast anonymity of Penn Station, while moisture that had collected on the drop cloth transferred itself to the flashlight and made it slippery . . .

Finally it got away from me. The drop cloth went into high revs, and the flashlight, unbalanced, worked free and went flying. It broke when it landed, but not before I had time to see for sure that it was hopelessly out of reach.

I wasted no time on curses or tears. I tried to kick off a shoe in such a way that I could reach it, succeeded on the second try. I got it into the drop cloth and tried winding again.

A shoe doesn't work. Not stiff enough.

IN all the world I had one tiny morsel of hope left, one I hated to even consider because it hurt too much to think about. But I no longer had such luxuries.

I went inside my head, where it was even darker and colder and lonelier than the chamber, and where another kind of nuclear device waited. I went way back deep inside, as close as I dared to the hot pulsing place where emotions surged and boiled like captive neutrons behind the lead walls. And I opened up a porthole into Hell.

Arethusa, I screamed into that vortex, *help me! Help us all! Brooklyn is that way! Find your other body, my love, and wake it up!*

I tried desperately to remember every lingering microsecond of those golden moments when Arethusa and I had experienced something like telepathic union. Those memories tore like claws now, but I needed to do anything I could to tune my telepathic transmitter to what I remembered of her receiver frequency, to send her a pattern she would recognize and recall and respond to.

Here I am, love. Remember? This is me, Ken/Joe/Humphrey, your husband, someone back in the land of the living, who still needs you. Hitchhike on my carrier wave if you need to, if you can, but find Brooklyn and wake up!

Not all of my telepathic scream was directed at her. I think some of it went into what I believe is called "praying." Don't ask me Who to; you wouldn't believe me if I told you. Telepathic screams need not pause for breath; mine went on for a long, measureless time.

Light bloomed on the far side of the pipe.

"Here I come, Joe," Arethusa said, and for the second time that night, I bawled like a baby.

HOW long does the soul linger after the brain is destroyed? Or had her soul, whatever that is, flown to Brooklyn at the instant of the shot, and waited there too weak or confused or traumatized to wake until I yelled? I was too busy to ask her.

Mike Callahan was on her heels. As Arethusa and I blubbered, he dealt with the bracing bar, then the handcuff chains. I didn't see how and didn't care. My arms went around Arethusa and clung for dear life. After a timeless time I became vaguely aware that the Professor was picking the locks on the cuffs themselves and removing them.

Figuring that detail out jumpstarted my brain. "We may still catch him," I cried, and leaped to my feet. I didn't fall down again. Those ankle cuffs had been tight, and I'd stressed them fussing with the drop cloth, but my magic skin had protected the circulation within.

Mike had already heaved the manhole cover clear with one hand. "Come on, Ken," he boomed, and held out his big mitt. I took it and was hauled upward as easily as Priscilla—oh God, Priscilla!—had hoisted Arethusa, a hundred years ago. He pressed a Smith & Wesson into my hand.

I set off at a dead run.

As I rounded the corner, I skidded to a halt. There was that fucking raised floor. I tried to spot the gas jets, and failed. Except for the floor, the corridor was utterly featureless except for bare light bulbs. People began to pile up behind me. Nobody said anything.

Damn it, The Miner had walked that floor. If he used some handheld device to do so, I was screwed; we'd have to fall back to Lady Sally's, and have her reset her magic gate to deliver us to some point past the boobytrapped corridor. I hated to take the time to go backwards. Suppose my luck was back: suppose he *didn't* have a handheld trap-suppressor. Then there had to be a short-term cutoff located at each end of the hall. If so, there was only one place for it to be.

I reached under the floor, felt the little switch, and threw it. When I stepped onto the floor, nothing happened.

I sprinted again.

It was very good that that corridor was completely empty. It did not contain the corpse of Ralph Von Wau Wau. That suggested The Miner (the *hell* with the name "Doc," with his conception of himself as a planetary surgeon) had been either sentimental enough, or cautious enough, to take time to dispose of his body. The bastard hadn't bothered to do that with my body, or Arethusa's or Pris's, but he'd taken the trouble for a dog. I didn't care why he'd done it; the point was that it had to have slowed him down some.

As I ran I was trying to recall details of the map. At the end of the fatal corridor I took a right and was relieved to see a door where my memory said it ought to be. I tucked my gun away in my pants and kept on running.

A while later I emerged from a door marked "No Admittance" into an obscure part of Penn Station, with Mike, the Professor, Arethusa, Father Newman, and Tim right behind me. Mistress Cynthia too had managed to keep up somehow on her shorter legs. There were citizens in sight, but no one seemed to notice us despite the obvious bullet holes in my clothes. I looked around wildly, trying to catch my breath.

Lady Sally materialized in mid-air in front of me, squeaked, and dropped two feet to the floor with cat-like grace, dressed in a stunning Kelly-green jumpsuit and sneakers. This event *was* noticed. But we were after all in New York; those who witnessed it ignored it except to note the nearest exit.

"I don't see him," I called.

She spun in a slow circle. "Look!" she cried.

One of the prettiest sights I had ever seen. Over by the base of a stairway leading up to the world: a little pile of dogshit.

Ralph was alive! He must have recovered while The Miner was dealing with me, and even though he'd heard nothing from us, he was following the original plan . . .

I went up those stairs, got off at the landing with the turd, followed my instincts and found myself in the main terminal. I skidded to a halt and spun around like a yokel. "Fan out," I cried, and my friends each picked an exit and headed for it.

I took the nearest one.

Ralph was waiting by the mouth of the exit, peering cautiously around the corner into Seventh Avenue in an obvious agony of indecision.

"Ralph," I called out when I saw him.

He whirled and spotted me. "*Danke schön, lieber Gott,*" he barked. "Qvigley, Ken! He iss in a car, he hass started it. He iss pulling away!"

The nearest car I could see with muscle was a black-and-white, parked by the curb. It was empty; I couldn't see its owners anywhere from where I stood. I didn't like it—I couldn't shadow him in a cop car, I'd be committed to capturing him fast—but there wasn't time to hotwire something else.

"Describe the car," I rapped.

"Red Ferrari Mondiale. Diplomatic platez."

Sure. What else could park outside Penn Station with impunity? Easy to spot. Hard to catch on the highway, maybe, but in midtown, with a black-and-white under me, nothing could lose me.

"Run back inside and howl like a son of a bitch until you draw the others," I said, and sprinted for the black-and-white.

Keys present, thank the Lord for lazy cops. Engine fired right up. After five hundred movies, I was going to have my first real live car chase—in a copmobile, chasing a red Ferrari through midtown Manhattan at dawn. I began to almost enjoy myself.

There he was! I gunned it out into traffic, causing an accident and not giving a damn. There was the red Ferrari, just turning west on Thirty-first with a predator growl. I made a similar growl myself and floored it, cornering like Jim Rockford.

I squinted at him. My trick contact lenses made him zoom closer: I clearly saw him spot me in his rear-view, saw him start visibly as he recognized me behind the wheel. Now the car chase would begin!

He stopped dead, in front of Madison Square Garden.

I stood up on the brakes (which sucked). I was indignant. In the movies, the other half of the car chase never refuses to play. It was a given: you realize someone is on your tail, and you floor it.

I took out the Smith and opened the car door.

He peeled out.

I leaped back into the seat and floored it, letting inertia slam the door.

He stopped.

I stopped, and said a word that should have curdled his brains in his skull even at that distance.

Not once during all those movies had I ever considered what would happen in this situation.

The bastard was damned smart, or near as intuitive as me. I was at the wheel of a cop car, and I certainly was not a uniformed officer, and I was not running lights and siren even in a situation where that would have been appropriate. Therefore I had stolen the cop car, and had some reason for not simply telling its rightful owners to run him down for me. For some reason, I did not want official involvement any more than he did. I was not going to start blasting away at him in front of Madison Square Garden. He was not getting away . . . but sooner or later, someone was going to come peel me out of this squad car and give him the chance to take off.

I saw him staring at me in the rear-view mirror, waiting for my next move.

I sighed, and opened the door again. As he started to shriek away, I took very careful aim and shot out both back tires.

(Fellow movie fans, I'm very sorry, but there is nothing you can do to a car with a gun that will make it blow up. At most, you might start a fire under the trunk. Falling off a cliff won't make a car blow up. Only a dissatisfied business rival or a stunt coordinator can do that. Pity the hundreds of spinal cases pulled every year from wrecks by movie fans afraid of the inevitable explosion.)

He tried to keep going on the rims, but I ran him down easily, and put the gun to the driver's side window. He stopped, and blinked at me through the window. He shut the engine off. I assumed shooter's stance.

"Freeze!" a stentorian voice bellowed from my right.

I took a snap glance. A uniform with a dead bead on me.

"I'm on the job," I snapped. "Gold Shield out of the One-Three, Taggart. Hold down on this skell for me while I call for backup."

It should have worked. Five bits of cop lingo in one breath. "There's no dick named Taggart in the One-Three," he hollered back. "Drop the piece or I swear to God I'll put you away."

I kept one eye on The Miner and put the other on the cop. He was serious, and he was not going to believe the truth. At best he would run us both in, and the shit would hit the media. Being shot was a nuisance I could tolerate, but to get rid of him without giving The Miner time to sprint for it, I would have to shoot. I took another look; no, I'd have to kill. I hate to shoot a good cop; there aren't any spares. But I didn't see any choice.

I shot a wild glance over my shoulder, back toward Seventh Avenue. I saw something, squinted.

Lady Sally's blessed face zoomed at me. She was squinting too. Our eyes met.

I looked back to the cop, ostentatiously raised my piece and made it safe. When it hit the pavement a satisfactory distance away from me, he lifted his own gun a scant few inches and began to approach. I turned to face him, hands high.

Lady Sally McGee appeared on the sidewalk behind him. In her upraised arm was a bottle of champagne I later learned she had commandeered from the liquor store in Penn Station. She pegged it accurately and vigorously at the back of the cop's head. He went down like a felled steer.

I heard the Ferrari door pop open. I had judged the distance nicely. As The Miner made his break, I pivoted, screwed my feet into the pavement, and brought my right hand down in a long looping arc that gathered up all the momentum of the pivot and all the weight of my body and delivered them to the point of that lordly Gallic nose, spreading it flat across his skinny face.

He sat down in the street and said, "*Sacré bleu,*" which I have never in my life understood. Why would anyone under stress say, "Holy blue?"

Lady Sally trotted out to join me. "Topping shot, Ken," she said.

"I can't take you anywhere," I said, caressing my knuckles, which had not broken thanks to her roll-on protection.

She shrugged. "Lady slings the booze," she said.

I gave no reaction at all. I was unarmed.

Many people were staring, and not a few of them were nervously fingering guns of their own. New York is one of those cities where you see signs saying, "Hospital zone: please affix your silencer." I frowned.

"Let's get this clown out of here," I suggested.

"Take his hand and mine," she directed.

I did so, and three seconds later I was sinking, heavily and gratefully, into her cushy desk chair in her glorious House.

SHE left me there with him for a few moments and ducked into the wall again. Reggie held down on him with a big scattergun, one of those Atcheson alley-sweepers, but it was quite unnecessary. The Miner kept both hands on his smashed nose, did not move anything but his eyes. He seemed fascinated by the bullet holes in my clothes.

When Arethusa emerged from the bare wall, he began to whine very much like a dog, and backed up, using only his hams to propel himself, until he banged against the bookcase opposite.

I sprang back up from the chair, and she ran into my arms. I began to shiver as if I were freezing. We clung to each other and sobbed together.

Ralph Von Wau Wau emerged from the wall. "*Vunderbar*," he said when he saw The Miner. "Nice vork, Ken!"

The Miner began to sob.

Shortly Lady Sally arrived with the rest of the crew. They all looked The Miner over with intent, silent interest. For some reason it was the sight of Mistress Cynthia that caused him to finally go into genuine hysterics. The Lady touched him behind one ear, and he slept.

"Leave us now, children," she said musically. "You too, I'm afraid, Arethusa. Ken and I have some private calls to make. He'll come for you when he's done."

"Count on it," I said into her shining eyes.

"I am," she told me.

Was it a trick of light, or was there just about twice as much brightness as usual in those eyes?

Everyone filed out, and Lady Sally punched a number on her speakerphone. It had thirteen digits. I heard one ring. She hung up, pressed redial, let it ring three times, and disconnected again. This time when she redialed it was answered in the middle of the first ring. "Yes," said a robot-like voice.

"The Greeks reckon time by the kalends," she said carefully.

"One moment."

A short pause, and a different, more jocular voice came on the line. "Don't look at me," it said. "I wasn't anywhere near there nine months ago."

"It must be yours, George," Lady Sally said. "I can't get it off the tit."

"So it's not stupid. That doesn't prove it's mine. Hi, Honeybritches. Who are your two friends?"

I was impressed. That phone circuit had existed for less than fifteen seconds. "I'm Ken Taggart," I said. "The other guy's asleep, and I don't know his name."

"What can I do for you, Mr. Taggart?" he asked.

"George," Lady Sally said, "I'm going to initiate scramble."

"If you wish," he agreed. After a few squawks, his voice returned. "Go ahead."

"The sleeping gentleman, name not known to myself either, is a member of the diplomatic community—never mind what nation." (It turned out to be Switzerland, by the way. They speak French there, some of them. I don't know where he'd been when his alarms went off; maybe it had been Canada.) "Acting—to my certain knowledge—purely as a private individual, he assembled a small organization which has planted a radio-triggered nuclear device in midtown Manhattan, and in twenty-nine other cities around the world."

"*Jesus fucking Christ*," he scroaned, "*shut up!*"

"I thought this line was secure," she said irritably.

"It *is*—from enemies!" he said. "But do you want this to *leak*? Give me a moment . . . there. Go on—but for God's sake, quickly!"

"Mr. Taggart, an artist in my employ, has wrecked the New York bomb and placed its master under citizen's arrest. He proposes to meet with you privately and deliver the said terrorist, detailed maps of the other twenty-nine bombs—one in Washington, and several annotated in Cyrillic alphabet—and most important of all, the precise radio frequency which must be jammed to neutralize them."

"My God," he said hoarsely. "I can be there in an hour and a half. Are you still at the same location?"

"George, George," she chided. " 'If it's messy, eat it over the sink.' Let's meet elsewhere."

"Forgive me," he said. "And pardon my language just now. Uh . . . Honeybritches, do you remember where we . . . ?" He trailed off.

"Of course I do," she said, smiling reminiscently.

"An hour and a half?"

"Make it two," she said. "It's been a long night. Our delegation will consist of myself, Mr. Taggart, one other associate, and the alleged perpetrator. He's a pacifist-type terrorist, by the way. And George . . . do come alone."

"Something I do all too often these days," he said mournfully. "Two hours from . . . mark."

The connection was broken.

Lady Sally held up a hand to me for silence. After a short time there was a screech. Another voice said, "I think they both hung up at once. Holy sh—"

Now the line was dead.

"Poppycock," she muttered fondly. "I'd bet my House George hasn't come alone since 1939." She pressed the button that hung up her end. "But he will *arrive* alone. He'll be there an hour from now, of course, but he'll arrive alone and wait alone, and he'll be alone when we get there. George is an honorable man." She smiled. "I, on the contrary, am neither honorable nor a man. Fortunately."

She got another dial tone, punched another complex number, went through a similar routine, and had a substantially similar conversation—in Russian, this time. It sounded a little bawdier in spots, and once he made her laugh deep in her throat.

NO sense dragging this story out any longer. We had a meet with George and Anatoly. You don't need to know anything more about them. They were considerably startled to see and recognize each other, but they got over it; they had always secretly wanted to meet each other. They took everything we were prepared to give them, and they didn't try too hard for too long to take too much more, and after about an hour they left together, with thirty maps and The Miner. I knew that they would not let him leave their sight until they had personally wrung him dry together, and I knew that they would wring him dry. Of course, some of what he would say, they'd have to discount as obvious hallucination . . .

All of us in Lady Sally's inner circle kept a close eye on the papers and TV news for the next while, hoping for blessed silence and holding our collective metaphorical breath. But the single ripple that appeared on the media pond, several months later, nearly made me bust a gut laughing. It seems a certain TV news personality I had always despised was accosted on the sidewalk near his home in the Upper East Eighties by two men with foreign accents, in trench coats, who proceeded to beat the mortal shit out of him . . . while repeating, over and over again, the cryptic words "Kenneth, what is the frequency?" He was never the same after that, and eventually the day came when people stopped commenting to me on the resemblance . . .

MY original client never did get an explanation of what he had paid me to do—and he did pay me, in full—but he did get a Lifetime Comp at Lady Sally's House out of the deal. Then less than a year later the House closed, for reasons too complex to explain here, and shortly he retired a broken man. So everyone in the city made out a little, in a sense. Above and beyond simply not being killed or vanished.

ON a more somber note, I must report that it was her pianist-avatar—the one with the best hand-eye coordination— that Arethusa had elected to send through that wall into combat. I never did get to hear her play the piano . . . and I never will; she will not touch the instrument any more. That is a loss neither of us will ever really stop mourning. But we're learning to live with it.

And Lady Sally, in her capacity as consulting xenogeneticist assures us that our son will combine both of my wife's talents and my own. I hope I can stand the little bastard. (His conception predated our marriage by hours, I'm told.) He'll probably have a life filled with lots of good luck and lots of bad luck, powerful intuition, fine music, and a whole lot of love . . . and what the hell more can you ask of life, anyway?

NIKOLA Tesla is doing . . . what he does. How the hell would I know what? How would I explain it to you if I did? You will hear more of him again one day, I promise you that. His historic bad luck seems to be slowly changing at last, just like mine.

I have a sneaking suspicion Lady Sally may be *his* Luck . . .

AS for Lady Sally, she and Mike were alive and well and happy last time I heard, practicing other professions in a place far from here and now, and that is all you need to know about them at this time. At least I hope so, for if you would know more of those two, you must look elsewhere.

BUT all of what I've described, believe it or not, was *not only* not the last case I ever worked on . . . it wasn't even the weirdest case I ever had.

I haven't got room here to tell you about that last one—a thumbnail sketch of a synopsis of the treatment would take twenty pages—but as long as I live, I'll never forget the day it began, or the remarkable words that began it:

"Was it necessary," asked the judge, "to produce this entire lake in evidence?"